SELECTIONS FROM *Annihilating Distance*

from *Rebels:*

As she came around the car he leaned over to open the door, leaned over again to lock it once she was inside, his arm across her like a safety bar, and stared at her, stared at her face, from that close. He stared at her eyes, into her eyes, at her eyebrows and eyelashes, at her cheeks, her lips, her hair, his face blank, like you would examine a photograph of someone interesting. Was she interesting, this unflinching unblinking let-me-know-when-you're-through teenager, her face smeared so thick her make-up made a mask, her lips made large with red, her eyes with black?

from *Strangers:*

After they had clinked glasses and tested the first sip, he turned away. "I like your friends," he mumbled, "but I barely know them. They're so young."
"They're as old as I am."
"That's what I mean," he said turning back.
She took his glass away and put it and hers on the table. "We're lovers," she whispered, fixing his eyes. "Lovers have no age."

from *Zola, A Fiction:*

Zola sits, suspended in time and place, unaware as yet that he has been struck by flying glass and is bleeding. He feels nothing and sees little, though he will claim to remember an intense alertness. His sole specific memory will be that of the face of one of the assailants…, a face profoundly unconscious of itself, contorted… into a mask, a repulsive version of itself. Though in five minutes Zola would be unable to identify the man in a group, he will later confide to Fasquelle that he will carry the vision of that face to his grave.

from *Toward the Annihilation of Distance:*

Beyond where the plow had stopped, a four-wheel drive had cut neat tracts into the deep snow on the road, just wide enough for the sled. The child climbed on with wordless excitement and they set off alone into an untouched white world. Before them the road rose several feet, shortening the view, so there were no sweeping vistas. The world was intimate, a silent, a white birth world. The trees, empty of all clutter, took only the snow to their undefended arms.

The stranger turned back to the tree to watch the liquid roll off the tap into the bucket. Truly, she felt to her gradually increasing amazement, there was something wonderful about this whole experience. A secret had been discovered. While she had been shivering and cursing at the mud, the earth was silently waking up. Looking at the dripping sap, she suddenly felt the entire woods as something living. For her whole life she could have walked through it or around it and never have... felt part of it. Now here she was, inside looking out, for the first time.

———————————————

Whether from next door or from history, these characters come right at you. In thirteen thrilling stories, circumstance forces them to decide what they most believe in and how they will behave—and to confront the implications. Deeply imaginative and passionate, the stories combine the excitement and pleasure of popular novels with the subtlety and seriousness of literary fiction.

ANNIHILATING
DISTANCE

June 2003

Also by David Vigoda:

NUCLEUS
(a novel)

ANNIHILATING
DISTANCE

Selected Stories

DAVID VIGODA

COLLIOURE BOOKS

ALBANY, NEW YORK

Published by Collioure Books
21 Aviation Road
Albany, NY 12205
www.whyitsgreat.com

colliourebooks@whyitsgreat.com

(800) 720-1170

Library of Congress Control Number (LCCN): 2003101121

ISBN: 0-9728250-5-3

Book design by Martin Lubin, cover design by Liz Vigoda and Martin Lubin.

Cover: Painting, "Home" by Liz Vigoda.

Printed and bound in the United States of America.

1 3 5 7 9 10 8 6 4 2

Special thanks to
The National Endowment for the Arts,
members of PEN American Center
(you know who you are),
and Ann Elmo, my New York agent
oh so many years ago,
who got me started.

PREFACE

If you're reading this, you're not the average reader. In an age when 'literary fiction' is a genre like 'mystery,' it takes a special reader to rediscover the pleasure of reading a book that provokes thought and reflection.

I love mysteries. I'd probably write one if I had the talent. But a mystery by definition is an entertainment. This book seeks to entertain, but it also seeks to express through fiction some of the profound concerns I believe we all share.

We want to feel safe, we want to feel loved and appreciated, we want dignity; yet how often are these threatened one way or another. It's so hard, sometimes, to know what to do; yet, since doing nothing is doing something, we have no choice but to choose.

Life is arguably more dangerous, more threatened, more fragile than at any other time in history. We destroy each other—which means ourselves—with ever more terrifying weapons. We destroy the earth itself. Yet could it not be more clear by now that two propositions must certainly be true, first, that a person is a person is a person is a person, second, that when we've ruined the earth we don't get another one?

At the same time—big irony—being here is pretty wonderful.

Those are big subjects, but they're little ones too, they come into play as soon as the alarm clock goes off. They've inspired our best stories and I hope the ones in this book make some contribution. They're not your typical American fiction, but you're not your typical American reader. They're like sushi: raw and sophisticated, with subtle flavors. (Joke.)

But of course you judge for yourself. Let me know what you think. Really. (There's contact information at the back of the book.) And, if you like them, tell somebody you know, okay?

CONTENTS

PREFACE 9

INTRODUCTION 13

From *Rebels Outlaws Spies Dreamers Prisoners Strangers*
    REBELS 24
    OUTLAWS *(Homage to Dostoevsky)* 42
    PRISONERS 64
    STRANGERS 82

From *Exhalations of the Intellect*
    DOING THE RIGHT THING 98
    THE GODDAMN STUFF OF LIFE 117
    MAKE A WISH, JOAN 144

From *Against Us, Tyranny*
    ZOLA, A FICTION 168
    SAINT CAMUS 187

    Toward the Annihilation of Distance
    PROLOGUE 210
    I   AUTUMN MORNING CHILD TREE 211
    II   WINTER AFTERNOON MAN HOUSE 230
    III   SPRING EVENING STRANGER BIRD 247
    IV   SUMMER NIGHT WOMAN ROCK 265
    EPILOGUE 282

INTRODUCTION

Writers are admonished to write only what they know. My problem has always been that I don't know anything. Somewhere I wrote, "motivation, always and everywhere a dark continent." I'm not a writer because I know what makes people tick, but partly because I'm fascinated by how mysterious they are, how inscrutable, how finally unknowable.

Of course it's easy enough to accumulate details that give a necessary verisimilitude to fiction, but even here the advice is over-rated. Haven't you noticed how it may be the detail whose reality you can't substantiate but whose truth immediately seizes you that gives fiction its power to create insight, that is, its purpose? How else is a reader expected to *understand* a university student in a far-away place a long time ago so delirious with depravation and confused by philosophical theory that he murders an old woman with an axe? How inexplicable is it that, if we had to choose one novel, *Crime and Punishment* is likely to be it? Are we helped by knowing that more recently two American university students, all too real, actually did commit a brutal murder to test that same theory? Am I helped by knowing that Leopold and Loeb not only went to the same university as me and took the same courses, but one of them lived across the street from me, though well before I got there, in what at the time was a luxurious neighborhood?

Yet most of my stories are based on actual events, some might be called 'historical fiction.' While that is partly an artifact of selection, since my novels and plays are not based on actual events, clearly my imagination is not infrequently fired by them. It is no accident that as an undergraduate I majored in history rather than literature or philosophy, both of which I sampled. But I quickly became disillusioned by 'history' as a discipline, preferring 'story,' because only the latter, I believed (and still do), is capable of converting what is real into what is true.

The truth of art is not easily argued in a culture that values 'facts' above all else and, ironically, when it is tired seeks diversion in fantasy. Nonetheless I claim that the leap from an accumulation of detail, bound by its factuality no matter how brilliantly realized, to a 'world' we believe we understand though it seems utterly alien, can be accomplished only with a feat of imagination. It is up to you, the reader, to judge whether what I have imagined is true enough so that for you it becomes real and so true for you too.

My stories range widely in time and place, setting and circumstance, and thus the style also varies considerably. Some may see in this another violation of good advice. I plead innocent, that as a writer I merely follow where my imagination leads. I also claim that what unifies them, unifies all my work, is plain for anyone to see, because expressed through the varying attributes of fiction are a few basic ideas or themes. Some writers have the gift for inventing wonderful plots, and for bringing to their plots the characters and scenery to realize them excitingly, thereby expressing implicit themes; whereas I, lacking this gift, typically start with 'what I want to say' and then grope for a way to say it. For better or worse this does not mean 'what I have to say' is obvious or simple, you have only to read a story to see this.

It would seem helpful to make a few comments on the stories, at least to indicate which events really occurred.

EXHALATIONS OF THE INTELLECT

This is a perfect example of why I write fiction: I go to my old notebooks to see what got me started on genetic engineering and here's what I find: On August 14 (1986) I wrote a fairly bizarre brief story I'm not capable of describing. It contains paragraphs like, "One night I smelled smoke. My kid brother smelled it too and tried following me until he stopped cold, rubbing the place where I had hit him with all my strength. On the other side of the woods was a band of fierce-looking people, not of our kind, who only stared at me with hatred and ill-will, but made no move against me."

That was August 14. The next entry in my notebook begins on August 15 like this: "Microbiology is my field." What follows (not all on that day) is the rest of the story, the first of the series that was to become *Exhalations of the Intellect* four years later. Not a hint as to where it came from, how it could have followed the other without a pause. Motivation, always and everywhere a dark continent.

So I don't remember what first piqued my interest in genetic engineering. Something obviously did and I spent a considerable amount of time doing research, even going through microfilms (or microfiches) in the basement of the Albany library of the State University of New York. I will thus stand by the authenticity of the science story, in other words this is one case where verisimilitude, more, accuracy in reporting, is important. The experiments, the philosophical and scientific controversies, the commercialization, all of it I assert as fact. The rest is fiction, characters, settings, events, dialogue ... though they are not completely divorced from actual people, events, and recorded comments.

Developments in science don't often form the basis for fiction, that is, 'literary' fiction, since they are everywhere in science fiction. Clearly, if you can't muster any interest in this particular development, you may not cherish these stories; but I would urge you to give it a try, because genetic engineering is shaping up to be one of the biggest stories ever. It would be difficult to overstate its impact, not just on how we live, but on how we think and feel, indeed on what we are and conceive ourselves to be. What I describe is its birth thirty years ago.

The science and profession of biology have changed dramatically and fundamentally during those three decades. Today, commercialism has penetrated to the core of the profession as, for example, meaningful distinctions hardly exist between university research to gain knowledge and company 'research and development' to develop products. Patenting of information, parts of living organisms *and even entire organisms*—plants and animals—has become routine, as has the formation of profit-seeking corporations by professors. And the voices calling for a thorough review and understanding of what the science and the business are actually about still tend to be isolated and intimidated. Joan Barrett, my protagonist, would either be as frustrated today as she was then or would have long since set aside any reservations.

Those with a fixed position on the issue of genetic engineering may not be completely pleased with my stories, for they refuse to take a position. They are stories, not essays. I myself am not opposed to genetic engineering per se; I am opposed to the current situation in which science is redefined as business and packaged into corporations, which then in the pursuit of profit, not knowledge, in effect conduct uncontrolled experiments on the world, with consequences unknown. They may turn out to be benign. They may turn out to be catastrophic. No one can say for sure—yet. Eventually we will all know.

One result of what can properly be called a genetic engineering gold rush seems clear to me: When the science of life trivializes life, the prospects for life and all things possessing it don't appear good.

REBELS OUTLAWS SPIES DREAMERS PRISONERS STRANGERS

After completing most of *Exhalations of the Intellect* in 1989, I wrote a series of vignettes based on a novel by Simone de Beauvoir, *The Mandarins*, in which each vignette is based on a sentence from the novel. Out of this came the idea for writing a series with the working title of *Parables*. Parable number one, written at the end of 1989 and later to become *Rebels*, is an expansion of one of the vignettes, whose sentence is this: "He knew neither my country, my language, my friends, nor my worries, only my voice, my eyes, my skin." You could see in that, not just the basis of *Rebels*, but the aesthetic kernel of the other stories in the series as well. The vignette became the conclusion of the story.

Parable number two became *Strangers* and is also an expansion of one of the vignettes. Its sentence reads, "Why, he wondered, was he in this train, opposite that almost total stranger who was breathing heavily in her sleep?" The incident with the policeman's horse rearing up at a street demonstration is true, though I think I may have been a young teenager at the time. The poetry extracts are taken from poems I have written, with the exception of the prisoner's limerick written for the story, which hopefully conveys something of the ordeal of interrogation and solitary confinement.

Prisoners was the fourth story to be written and, like *Spies* that preceded it, has no connection to the vignettes: The *Parables* have now assumed their own existence. Although there is nothing in my notes to suggest it, I believe the character of the old man is inspired by a Sunday school teacher I had, an extraordinary man who developed with me an extraordinary friendship. As a college student I visited his apartment in New York once, though I recall nothing of it except that it was in a large public housing project. I'm pretty sure the last time I saw him was when my father died in 1973. I picked him up at the bus station in New Jersey. As he came off the bus he smiled broadly at me, then took my hand in both of his and just held it, looking into my eyes with sorrow. Actually he had a way of pushing on my hand as he arched his back, it's that gesture I remember. Then he held my hand. We stood that way, saying nothing out loud. Incidentally the strange manuscript his character in the story is said to have written actually exists. I wrote it.

Outlaws came a few weeks later. Apparently almost immediately—though for reasons lost to time—I hit on the idea of writing a version of *Notes from Underground*. The story behind the story, the one about the outlaw's hometown, is true. The town is in Pennsylvania and I read about it in the May/June, 1990 issue of *The Sciences*. Even the incident with the boy is true. It would have to be, it's too strange for fiction. Also unbelievably true is what happened at Pleiku, Vietnam. At least the friend of mine who was there swore that's the way it was.

AGAINST US, TYRANNY

While writing *Outlaws* I began making notes, based on a recently published biography I'd been reading, for a story about the writer Emile Zola's connection with the Dreyfus Affair, and the day I finished the one I began the other. I find Zola an extraordinary person and the Dreyfus Affair an extraordinary historical episode. Those, at least in the US, who have heard of it typically think it had something to do with anti-Semitism, and in fact it did have much to do with it, but the Affair went far beyond it. It would be no exaggeration to claim that, taken in its totality, it constituted a vast re-appraisal of what a nation is or could be and how it should function. Zola represented a critical voice in that vast conversation, both in his actions and his writings, both fiction and non-fiction. The comparison with our contemporary American situation seems stark and significant.

At the time I conceived *Zola, A Fiction* as the next of the parables, though that was to change after writing two more stories in the series, for a total of eight. The first became *Dreamers*, a story inspired by things my father told me about his youth, and the second was based on the life of another French novelist, Céline. Only after writing *Saint Camus* a year later about Albert Camus, having completed *The Innocent Alone Crave Justice*, a nine-story series concerning the Dreyfus Affair, did I decide to break the two prior novelist stories out of the *Parables* series and have them form their own little group, *Against Us, Tyranny* (the title may be recognized as a phrase from *La Marseillaise*). The title *Saint Camus* parallels *Saint Genet*, Jean-Paul Sartre's non-fiction treatment of the writer Jean Genet.

The first three paragraphs that form the introduction of the story are a deliberate paraphrase of the opening of *The Plague*. In stark contrast to Zola, Camus was not prolific and struggled almost his entire working life against writer's block, but they shared a passionate commitment to justice and decency and were both great writers. In those ways, both heroes of mine. In 1998 my wife and I visited the village of Lourmarin in Provence where Camus bought a place to live with some of his Nobel Prize winnings. My notes of the occasion say: "This is where he used to hang out, arguing over local soccer teams. He was far from a completely likable person—he was particularly a stinker to his wife, for example, and he practically ignored the children, much too self-absorbed—but nonetheless he was serious and maybe even a little brave in a way Sartre, for example, never was, and, in any case, nothing can erase the fact that *The Plague* is certainly among the great novels of the century. As I recall, there is no marker on his house, just a street named for him, which isn't necessarily where he lived. It was returning to Paris from here that he died."

Not recorded in my notes is that I pretended for the occasion that he did live in the little Rue Camus and that I imagined him there at the time, struggling inside one of its room to write something worthy. *The Plague* ends with the central character deciding to write down the story the novel recounts, why, because it's interesting, dramatic, entertaining, important? He says he does it—I am translating myself— "so as not to be among those who keep silent, to bear witness for the victims, to leave at least a memory of the injustice and violence that was done to them, and to say simply that what one learns in the middle of such a scourge is that there is in people more to admire than to despise." As Kurt Vonnegut might say, good words.

TOWARD THE ANNIHILATION OF DISTANCE

Camus led directly to what I have always referred to as the "Cold Mountain stories," the series' sub-title until it was dropped in deference to the fact that a Google search on 'Cold Mountain' turned up 44,000 entries if I remember right, including a novel that reportedly sold 1.6 million copies and was made into a movie starring Tom Cruise. But Cold Mountain was the name we gave to the old farmhouse on top of a mountain we lived in for nine years. We named it after a poet. Han Shan, whose name apparently translates as "Cold Mountain," is the name given to an ancient Chinese hermit who lived in the mountains and left the world a most remarkable set of poems, of which there have been several English translations. We loved the spirit of the poems and they seemed to suit our isolated existence. Also, we moved up there in March with a foot or two of snow and a good wind.

I mention this because of the following, written in my notebook a week after completing the stories (in August 1994): "These stories require an explanation. Much of what occurs in them actually occurred, though there has been substantial re-working to adapt them to fictional treatment. The stranger is wholly fictional, as, happily, are the incidents of violence. The idea for the stranger is, however, based on an actual incident."

One chilly summer evening, a woman showed up at our front door. She frightened me a little at first, because it was obvious something was wrong. She hardly spoke, gave no indication of what she was doing standing at our door (which had no lock), was pretty bedraggled, and was under-dressed for the evening chill in a thin cotton dress. But she seemed harmless enough, so we brought her inside and gave her some tea and kept her company, hoping she would say something. As near as we could work it out, she was depressed about something, and though she never said exactly what the something was, we got the feeling it was some family upset, not unlikely connected with a husband or lover. In any case, evening was becoming night and we frankly didn't feel safe letting her stay with us, so I got her to let me drive her home ... which was a good nine miles away, down in the valley. Apparently she had walked all the way up and found herself, for reasons she never indicated, on our doorstep. We never saw her again.

Everything connected with her in the stories is fiction. The incidents of violence, for example, are based on a poem written earlier. I did get a shotgun for self-defense, but against woodchucks, not people. As my character says in the story, our garden, which in the exhausted stony soil required a lot of labor, was either for us or them, and if it was for us, we had no choice but to shoot them. We tried everything else. Everything. No doubt the connection from that experience to the story is clear.

Finally I must plead guilty to having shamelessly dramatized myself.

You may have noticed that, until this series, all of them were in multiples of three. That's not by chance and has its origin in music history. Mozart and Haydn, for example, wrote quartets in groups of six and I took that as a challenge to write stories in groups of six. But four is also a good number in music—quartets and four movement symphonies, for example—and so I decided the time had come to see if I could write to a different specification.

But not just in the number of stories in the series. I wanted everything to be in fours. Bach wrote sublime music within the most restrictive of artistic strictures. The great and famous Chaconne from the Second Partita for Unaccompanied Violin, for example, seems to flow as though it were improvised, and so, perhaps, it was, but in strict eight-measure sections, each of which is further divided into rising and falling four-measure sub-sections. So, as the titles indicate, there are four seasons, four times of day, four characters, and four symbolic objects, and one of each characterizes each of the four stories. Each story is told from the point of view of a different character. Each of the four stories is divided into four parts, in each of which a different character is dominant. While one symbolic object is dominant in each story, all of them figure in each one.

Why did I do it? Just for fun, to see if I could. I was interested in making explicit what is always at least implicit, that the technique of art is the attempt to exceed limitations. But with such restrictions, could the stories possibly breathe? Bach did it. Judge for yourself whether I have had any success.

By the way, the stories were made autonomous as a concession to the publishing limitations of literary journals, otherwise they would have been made a single piece. As they stand, the repetitions of necessary information hopefully won't mar what is after all a single work. That's why, of all the story series, it alone is included in this volume in full.

Rebels

Outlaws

Spies

Dreamers

Prisoners

Strangers

REBELS

As she came around the car he leaned over to open the door, leaned over again to lock it once she was inside, his arm across her like a safety bar, and stared at her, stared at her face, from that close. He stared at her eyes, into her eyes, at her eyebrows and eyelashes, at her cheeks, her lips, her hair, his face blank, like you would examine a photograph of someone interesting. Was she interesting, this unflinching unblinking let-me-know-when-you're-through teenager, her face smeared so thick her make-up made a mask, her lips made large with red, her eyes with black?

He gazed over her shoulder, down the street, methodically.

"You said something about a room," she said finally.

"Shut up," he replied gently, without conviction.

Her hands were in her lap, her lap tiny like her skirt. Her nails were claws, painted the color of her lips. They could slice you neat, they could tear you, they could take out your eyes.

"Those real?"

"What?"

"Those. Your nails."

"What do you mean? No, you buy them."

"Kiss me, Silver Lips," he said, looking into her eyes. For the first time she reacted. "Kissing's extra." He gazed over her shoulder again, looking down the street, into doorways, under shop awnings, between cars. "You're not going to be weird, are you?" she asked. She wasn't worried, just wanted to know.

He sat back, put it in first, gunned it through a red light, making it screech around the corner.

"That how you get your kicks? What is this thing, anyway?" He drove in silence, eventually she began to look out the window, at the city, the traffic, traffic lights, closed up shops, garbage cans, garbage, everywhere people, old women, old men, kids, kids with boom boxes, parked cars, gutters. "What about that room?" she asked, not worried, just asking. "The meter's running, you know."

He pulled over, leaned towards her again, gazing into her face again, while she waited, impatient now, looking off to the side but not seeing anything. He breathed audibly, spoke quietly. "I think that under all that greasepaint you're probably pretty."

"Aw, man, are we going to do it here?"

He didn't smile, just shifted his gaze to her forehead, then to her eyes again. "I want to see your pimp."

Her face broke out in scorn. She pursed her lips, made a sound with them. "Man, what's wrong with you?" He only looked at her. Time went by. "You want to see my pimp?" He nodded minutely, still looking at her. "Stop looking at me," she said suddenly.

Gunning it again, he returned to her neighborhood, pulled up beside a group of toughs all in black fake leather plastic, rolled down the window, called 'hey you' loudly. This guy turned slowly, came over, leaned down, his hands on the windowsill, leaned in to look. Before he could speak the man said, "Where's her pimp?"

The guy's eyes narrowed, enlarged, his head turned just a little. "Where's her pimp? I want to see her pimp."

The girl groaned with impatience, the guy's eyes narrowed again, and he leaned in a little more. "Tell you what, jack, I don't know shit about no pimp. Don't know and don't—"

"Any of them know? I said any of them know? Hey," he shouted, "I'm looking for this girl's pimp. Any of you know where he is?"

"Say," started the guy at the window, reaching in for the door handle, "you looking for some trouble, maybe you want to step out the car."

The man started, but the girl grabbed him. "You crazy, man? What the hell you doing?" She pulled him back.

"I just want to see her pimp," explained the man.

"You just want to get yourself cut," muttered the girl. "He don't mean nothing," she shouted. "He's high."

They drove again, not talking, staring, the city again. "Want some food?" he asked quietly.

"Tell you what I want," she started in a pretend voice, her hand moving suggestively.

"Don't do that," he said quietly, authoritatively, stopping her.

"You're a weird asshole, you know that? If you don't have a room, I know a place."

"Your pimp there?"

"You better pray he ain't."

"Is he?"

"Man, what do you want with my pimp? He'll hurt you."

"Just show him to me."

"Fuck you."

He pulled over again, looked at her again, but from a distance this time, leaning back against his door, smiling at her this time. "My guess is that under all that shit you're a good-looking girl."

"You want to do me?"

He said nothing, looked at her, looked away across the sidewalk behind her, three garbage cans against a brick wall, looked back at her. "What's your name?"

She thought of several responses, some of them mean, some insulting, one or two just noncommittal, finally started to tell him her professional name, but for some reason told him her real one.

"Carla," she whispered, wondering why she was telling him, a little angry at herself, impatient with herself, looking out the window. "Carla," he said, trying it out, repeating it. "Carla." Like he was tasting wine. He nodded.

*   *   *

He put it in gear again, pulled out gently into traffic, drove in silence, even when he pulled onto the bridge she didn't say anything, not a word, maybe she was asleep. He looked over at her. She was staring straight ahead, not a thought inside her, nothing moving, nothing. They headed up the highway on the other side of the river, the signs meant nothing to her, this was another world, as foreign as Tibet, maybe she'd had johns from here, but they went across the river to her world, this was nowhere to her, just a road, late night, head light, driving north with some guy, going nowhere.

You can't see anything from the highway, not even in the daytime, it's just a highway through trees, the whole world is on the other side where you can't see it but you know it's there. The car drove itself, not fast, veering always to the right of the approaching headlights, without will or intention, just gas. It's dark inside the car, it has no existence, it's a point without location, moving through some medium you can't see with just two headlights staring straight ahead into the night. She was patient, pretty sure his credit was good, in any case all she had to do was make a phone call, and it was more comfortable inside than out, better to be invisible gazing into nothingness than be part of nothing itself, always leading with your pelvis towards traffic, never knowing if you're going to be hired and insulted or just insulted. He only looked straight ahead, both hands on the wheel, almost relaxed, not really seeing, not really thinking, not really tired, not really concerned, though he should have been, there must be something he could be concerned about. When he tried, he tried to think about where the car was going. Where would they be when the gas ran out and he had to turn to her and say something that sounded real?

The car drove to a big motel, national chain, next to an exit along the highway. It was just driving when this motel appeared by an exit ramp and it pulled off and came to a stop before the office door. Did they look at each other then, did they notice a fleeting thought or feeling?

"What do you do, anyway? For a living, I mean."

"I make things."

"What kind of things?"

"Money."

The next thing she knew there was a little noise to her right, just outside her window, and she turned, jolted, to see the room key he was jangling, his face just saying 'here's the room key.' They walked down a long corridor, she in front, though she didn't know the room number, maybe she wanted him to see her legs or watch the way her ass wriggled from the spiked heels, maybe she was trying to get this over with, maybe, off her turf, she was embarrassed. He looked only at room numbers, his brain slogging through its marshy minefield of unfocused thought. He called her back, let her enter first, stood in the entryway while she looked the place over. She looked over the whole room, including the closet and the bathroom, noting that the closet was empty except for a few hangers you couldn't take off the bar, that even the bathroom had no odor, that somebody had folded the end of the toilet paper roll, that there wasn't a wrinkle in the bedspreads, that all you could see out the window wall was a parking lot and turned on him suddenly, snapping, "You drove two fucking hours to get here?"

This is an answer he thought of making, but didn't: "I had no idea where to go. We just ended up here. I didn't really know what we were doing. I still don't." This is an answer he almost said: "All I know is we needed to get away. We can be safe here." "It's clean," he suggested.

"Morgues are clean," she spat out. "Hospitals are clean."

He shrugged, hurt, thought of offering to look for another place. She turned her back on him, pulled the curtain behind her, stared down at the parking lot. "Say mister," she called suddenly from the other side of the curtain, "you got any idea what this is going to cost you?" Unsatisfied, she pulled at the curtain till it was away from her and confronted him. "Show me your fucking dough," she hissed.

He smiled. "Kiss me, Silver Lips."

"Show me some jack, jack," she hissed again, approaching him with real hate, now that she was finally afraid.

He let her come on, making no move, he would have let her use her nails on his face, but she stopped short because she saw that in his eyes, and they both stood there, arms dangling, separated by ten feet of fake woolen plastic carpeting, waiting for the scene to end.

"It's a line from an old Humphrey Bogart movie," he explained, trying to appear as harmless as he felt.

"What is?" she replied, pouting.

Surprised, he smiled at last. "That line: 'Kiss me, Silver Lips.'" He chuckled. "Who's Humphrey Bogart, right?"

"Man, I don't know what the fuck you're talking about."

It flickered, but he kept the smile going. "It's at the end of the movie. He's in a pretty tight spot." He started to say more, but suddenly whatever energy he'd had was exhausted, he tasted his lips and they had no taste, and then the carpet was in his sight instead of the girl, and time went on without them.

"What now?" asked the girl, without warning, quietly, truly wondering, even sheepish.

He looked up at her and let her know he didn't know either.

"Why'd you bring us here?"

That was it, he thought, that was the question he'd been avoiding. "Would you do me a favor? I'll pay you," he added quickly. "Would you wash all that crap off your face? And take off those ridiculous shoes. Carla."

"What?"

"No, I was just saying your name."

She went in the bathroom, turned on the light, turned on the strip of lights across the top of the mirror, the ones that show you what you really look like, looked at her face, into her own eyes, didn't see a whole lot there and, for the first time in her life, wondered if that was how it was supposed to be, looked at her painted lips, made them move, looked at her painted eyelashes, painted eyebrows, painted cheeks, her lips still now, until, pulling with her fingers, she distorted them, smearing lipstick along her cheek.

*   *   *

When she came out, opening the door without warning after being in there so long, he jumped to his feet, realized he didn't know what he'd been doing, maybe he hadn't even been awake. She just stood there by the bathroom door across the room from him, waiting to see what he would do, barefoot. "I didn't know if you wanted me to keep my clothes on," she said quietly.

He walked over, slowly. "I hate those clothes. Put my shirt on." When she had buttoned it up he smiled and said, "I was right, Carla. You're pretty."

"Do you really mean it?"

He nodded.

"I like it when you call me by my name," she practically whispered, and he felt a wave of feeling come over him, not a wave of desire, but the desire to shelter her, protect her, comfort her. He gently cradled her head in his hands and kissed her.

Turning to the room he asked her which bed she wanted. Her eyes went to him suddenly, but he had his back to her, she was stung, no, hurt. So, after all, he was just another weirdo. "What you got in mind, jack?"

He turned suddenly, saw how suddenly her eyes had hardened, tried to protest, "No, I … I just thought we were tired, I thought in the morning—"

"You think I got till morning?"

"Why not? I'll pay you."

"I don't show till morning, my pimp will cut my face."

"Call him up."

"What, you think he's got an office or something? Get real, will you?"

"There's got to be a way to call him. What if you were in trouble?"

She stared at him in silence for a long time, then asked quietly, "How much you pay me for the whole night?"

"Whatever you want."

"You got that much?"

He nodded slowly.

She chose the bed farther from the door. He lay awake for what seemed hours, wondered if she was awake too, if she was also thinking about nothing.

She fell asleep almost immediately, but when she awoke couldn't remember why she'd done that, looked across to the other bed and wondered who this guy was, what his game was. For some reason she'd committed the cardinal sin with him, she'd trusted him, and she lay there trying to remember why she'd done that. When the wave of panic came over her she jumped out of bed, but, suddenly dizzy, had to sit on the edge and, facing him, staring at him, watching him sleep, lost the urge to rifle his belongings, no, felt the desire to not know, to keep things as they were, make that fleeting experience of comfort return, happen again.

When he opened his eyes she was lying on her side, looking at him. He blinked, hard, more than once, stared back, not seeing at first, his sight covered by thought, trying to remember why he was being such a fool, then seeing her, remembering, deciding again, turned on his side, rested his head in his palm, watched her, watched her. Several times either she or he almost smiled, the corners of the lips moving up, breaking ranks, acting without orders, then settling back, like leaves after a gust of wind has passed.

"It's your move, jack," she said.

"We need to get you some clothes."

Her eyes didn't move, but the expression changed as thought covered them, then passed like clouds, leaving them clear again.

"He'll come after us, you know."

He said: "Kiss me, Silver Lips." This time she smiled instead of him.

They drove to a shopping center. She'd never been to one before, never having been out of the city. People stared at them, wondered what kind of couple they were, a teenage girl dressed like a prostitute holding hands with a guy too old to be her boyfriend and too young to be her father. The first thing he bought her was sneakers, it was those ridiculous high heels more than anything that marked her, now the painted face was gone, then shirts, pants, socks, underwear, a regular brassiere instead of the push-up kind. He breathed a sigh of relief to see her now, while she giggled at herself in the three-way mirror, as though this was her costume and the other her regular clothes. She waited in the dressing room while he paid, then they strolled through the mall just for the novelty of it, swinging the old clothes in a shopping bag, which he moved to drop in a trash barrel, but she restrained him for reasons unidentified.

While they were eating she asked his name. He told her it was Dennis and she asked him what he did for a living.

"I make things," he said.

"What kind of things?" she asked.

"Money," he replied, and they both smiled, decided to go to the movies, see a cop thriller with back alleys and bars, night shots and gun shots, and he put his arm around her, almost brotherly, while she put her head on his shoulder like he was her boyfriend, they were out on a date, had been intimate, felt secure with each other. But when it was over, when the credits were running and the room was voiding rapidly, leaving them alone in an empty auditorium facing a screen about to go blank, she didn't have to say anything, he turned her face to him and told her not to worry, he was protecting her, she didn't ever have to go back.

"What if he finds me?" she asked, lips trembling, eyes moist, pleading.

He kissed her lips, kissed her eyes. "If you don't go back, he can't find you, and if he finds you, I'll protect you."

"He's strong," she insisted. "He has a gun, a knife, goons to run for him, he can be mean, real mean."

He held her, whispered, "I don't want you ever to be afraid again. Carla."

"What?"

"I was just saying your name."

She looked into his eyes as far as she could, trying to find certainty. "But who are you?" He tried to calm her, but she pulled away, almost angry, insisting he didn't understand. "He'd kill you, you'd have to kill him, can you do that, can you fight, can you kill?"

He grabbed her head with both hands, held her steady, looked almost angrily into her eyes. "If I have to kill him, I'll kill him."

"You don't even have a knife or nothing."

"I'll use his." He nodded to let her know he was serious, and she saw he was, felt he could really do that somehow, maybe he'd been in the army, she didn't ask, it was better to believe. The trembling stopped, she smiled, he kissed away the last tear, but later that evening, back in the motel room, he caught her looking at the door over and over and knew what she'd done.

* * *

The trembling had stopped and she'd smiled, but she didn't want to be in a shopping center anymore, or a restaurant, or any public place with people around, she wanted to be back in the room with just the two of them behind a dead-bolt lock and a chain on the door, so they returned, ate pizza from a box, and he almost made her laugh when he stuffed a piece in his mouth, smearing sauce on his cheeks, which she licked up, and they watched one movie after another on television. One was a gentle tale of an unlikely romance between an illiterate in Dublin who shovels horse manure off the streets and a Connecticut co-ed studying literature at Trinity College. Another was a wacky comedy about New York at night, where some slightly nebbishy straight-arrow who visits a woman he meets in a diner spends the whole night getting bounced from one weird threatening experience to another. It might have been that, he reasoned. When it was over he went to the bathroom and it was during the next movie she started to seem tense again, looking towards the door, even though it would be two hours from the phone call before anyone could be there. He felt especially tender towards her during that time, turning to her during the movie—some stupid sex murder combo about police corruption in New Orleans—to nuzzle her hair, feel the smoothness of her cheek. Every so often she would squeeze his hand, and for a while she nestled her head against his shoulder, but mostly she just let him caress her.

There wasn't a time in his life, he believed, when he'd felt so tender towards someone, so utterly tender, ludicrously so, wanting to be silly or foolhardy, anything that would make her laugh, make her mantle of fear fall away, make her see deeply into his being and know in her bones that no harm could ever come to her, know that she was beautiful, that she was loved. Ludicrous how loving he felt, he even laughed out loud, pretended it was the stupidity of the movie, pretended to fall asleep, having decided that was the best way not to hurt her.

He wondered how she would manage it, but it was simple, when the movie ended she eased herself away, turned off the television, drew a cover over him, and went to the bathroom, detouring to the door on the way back, then lay in her bed under the covers without having undressed. He lost track of time, but it seemed hours before the door began to open slowly, slowly, the girl suddenly jumping up, moving quickly to it, trying to step outside and close it behind her, but the man pushing her away, coming into the room, with increasingly loud whispering until she called out his name loudly to rouse him, before being pushed brutally against a wall.

"It's all right," he replied tenderly as he stepped away from the bed, talking to her past the man coming towards him slowly, hands ready, a knife in one of them. "I didn't think he'd just leave. Are you all right?"

The man smiled in the dark, still approaching, evidently he enjoyed his work or maybe that was just what his face did when he was concentrating, but it ended quickly when his lunge caught nothing and his head and back sustained a few rapid blows that left him on the floor staring blankly. The girl was in the doorway silhouetted against the hallway light, both hands unknowingly at her mouth, a childish silent-film gesture of fear. He shut the door, turned on the light, lowered her hands for her.

She stared at him, at the man on the floor, long stares, until finally she approached the body, moved to where she could see the face and said, in a normal voice, "You must have hit him hard, he looks dead."

"He is dead."

She stared again, back and forth, long looks, with that slowness of wit, that numbness that follows danger. "Did you stab him?" she asked stupidly.

"No, I don't like blood."

Again she stared. The trembling started, then the heaving, the sobs. He went to her, drew her up, led her to the bed, sat beside her, his arms around her, rocking with her. When he could feel she was calm, he began nuzzling her again. All he said was, "It's all right."

She said nothing, let him caress her, looked forward, thought nothing definite. "Dennis," she whispered.

"What?" he whispered back.

"No, I was just saying your name."

*   *   *

"What do we do now, Dennis?"

"What everyone does when they kill somebody, we get rid of the body."

"Don't talk that way, okay?"

He rifled the guy's pockets, collecting the cash, returning everything else except the car keys, counted it carefully. "Not bad," he said.

"That's not him, you know."

"Of course not." He looked at the body. "He wouldn't come himself." He started to add something, caught himself, instead asked her to give him a hand with the body.

They loaded the guy back into his car, he drove it out some back roads he knew to an old shale pit, she followed, waited where he told her, lights off, while he used the guy's shirt as a wick into the gas tank, lit it, and ran back to where she was waiting. As he pulled away, lights still off, the car in the pit exploded into flames and, straining to see out the back, she said, "My God, you're burning him up?"

"Cremation," he said.

She looked at him for a long time, all the way back to the main road, when he finally turned the headlights back on. "He'll come after us, won't he?" she asked, without much fear in her voice, mainly just wanting to know, but when he told her not to worry, the fear surfaced. "Oh God," she whispered, "now you've burned him up, you killed Tony and burned him up."

"And?" he prompted.

"There's no going back."

"Correct," he nodded.

She turned away from him, pressed her face against the window though nothing could be seen through it, not speaking until finally she mumbled, "You're a crazy son of a bitch," and he let her say it, said nothing until they were back at the motel, pulling in with the lights off. "Now what?" she asked as they came to a stop.

"We sleep till check-out time."

"Sleep? You can sleep now?"

"Okay, we won't sleep."

She let him lead her back into the room, he made her watch him lock up the door, made her sit on the edge of the bed, knelt down before her, took her hands, kissed each of them, said, "I said I'd protect you. No harm will come to you, I swear it."

She looked earnestly into his eyes. "You promise? Dennis?"

"I promise, Carla," he whispered. "No one will ever hurt you again."

Still watching his eyes she asked, "Not even you?"

He nodded. "Not even me." He kissed her hands again, moved to embrace her, but she resisted sheepishly. He smiled. "Want to watch a late movie?"

She nodded.

They drove up the highway, up another highway, pulled into a shopping center and bought everything for camping, food, supplies, equipment, everything, and continued up the highway, finally onto a side road, pulled up to a poorly marked trail head, loaded up the packs with the first load, and started hiking. It was only a few easy miles to the lean-to, they made two trips, she never complaining once though it wasn't easy for her, wearing a pack for the first time, then he made a fire on the rise before the lean-to overlooking the pond, showing her how it was done. After eating they sat arm in arm within the circle of pines, watching the water, he pointed out to her at the far end a family of ducks moving in line along the shore, fishing for supper no doubt, she turning to him suddenly kissing him sweetly on his cheek, snuggled a little closer, said, "You're good to me."

He turned his face to her, a playful smile, said, "Kiss me, Silver Lips."

"What's that from?" she purred, cuddling against his shoulder, so he told her about forties gum-shoe novels and Hollywood who-dunits, about the last scene in "The Big Sleep" when Marlowe comes to, finds himself, hands cuffed behind him, in a strange living room, knows he's in a tough spot, but there's a cool dish alone with him, distant, unconcerned, Eddie Mars' wife, Eddie Mars the gangster, the killer. In the novel she has a silver-colored wig, after she lights a cigarette for him he says, "Kiss me, Silver Wig," but they changed it in the movie. "Changed the whole ending, but both are good."

When they could no longer see the pond they watched the fire, the stars. He showed her a shooting star and she laughed like a child. They listened to the crackling of the fire, to the snapping twigs of the woods at night, smelled its freshness, its coolness, its piney scent, smelled the wood smoke, threw more wood on the fire and pushed at it with long sticks.

In the morning he ran back to the car, returned with more sup-plies, prepared a huge breakfast, fried eggs and potatoes, sweet rolls and coffee, told her laughing they had to eat too much. Days passed, only sporadically did she have bouts of fear, usually at night, with the dark and strange noises like footfalls. He would reach for her with both arms, cradle her, caress her, nuzzle his face against her hair, breathing in its odor, wanting her, wanting to protect her, speaking words of comfort, safety, solicitude, and she would be comforted, holding him tightly with both arms, with all her strength, sometimes wanting him then, but he would stop her with kisses, not wanting it that way, in the shadow of a pimp, not that way.

One morning at sunrise they were awakened by the calling of loons. He had to explain it to her, that that fantastic sound was a bird calling across the water in the stillness of dawn, she sitting up in the tent, uncomprehending, still mostly asleep, and they falling back asleep nestled against each other, the calling of the loons gliding smoothly into the circle of their repose, so that later she would ask him if it had really occurred.

Once she asked him, "What did you do when you lived in the world?"

"I made things," he replied, and they both laughed.

A storm came. Lightning and thunder, sheets of rain, they sitting in the lean-to, knees drawn up with their arms around them, side by side, staring out at it, lost in its din and splendor. When it was over she said, "I never knew rain was like that"; he said nothing.

When the meat was gone he hunted deer, she couldn't believe it, he using a bow and arrow like an Indian, he telling her he was an Indian, she not believing it because of the way he said it, besides his name was Dennis, and he said, "Can't an Indian be named Dennis?" He left her before dawn, when it was still mostly dark, she reaching for him still asleep, mumbling through dreams, "So early?", he pulling away gently, the one responsible, protector and provider, separating himself from her, to merge into the dawn wild world where a chipmunk's back can be broken by a weasel before your eyes, a great blue heron stands all but invisible in marshy water, then lifting itself with huge flapping wings slowly into the air, the fish's tail still protruding from its beak.

No bait was needed, they would come to the water, and he could position himself for a clear shot, perched in the crook of a large branch downwind, obscured by leaves, the bowstring fully extended, the bow a crescent moon, silent, its only speech a large triangle of steel poised for release. He had the doe in his sights, all he had to do was gently straighten those two leather-thonged fingers, the deer would lay in reddened water, its eyes wide with incomprehension, a long shaft protruding from its neck, and a fawn would already be gone, merged into its forest, with loping strides, saving itself, understanding nothing, just running, voiceless with bulging eyes and pounding heart. Mercifully those deer left and another one came, he shot that one, pulling it quickly from the water before too much blood oozed from the incision he had made, pulling it from that spot where deer come at dawn to drink, to a place downwind, gutting it quickly with neat strokes of his sharp blade, splashing its insides with cool water, to return to camp with it around his neck.

She stared at him, at it, as, panting, he heaved it off himself, letting it plop to the ground, her eyes wide, flinching at the thud, her nostrils involuntarily flared with vague revulsion, unable to fully comprehend that this had been a live animal, breathing, running, and he had made it dead, then amazed, bewildered by how quickly and mysteriously this deer became venison as he skinned and butchered it.

The first pieces were roasting on a spit when he became suddenly alert to some indefinable subtle change of the air. Call it that sixth sense hunted animals have, and soldiers in battle, and fugitives, or perhaps his brain had simply registered an audible human footfall as danger, moving so quickly from sensation to interpretation that sensation was immediately forgotten, but one moment he was mindlessly watching the fire and the next loping to the lean-to where the girl was sitting with her arms wrapped around drawn-up legs, knowing what had happened, what he had to do. He pressed his mouth against her ear, whispered, "They've come, but don't worry. Only don't cry out and no harm will come to you." His eyes wandered shut involuntarily as he kissed the top of her head, cradling it with his hands, lifting her face so, opening his eyes, he could look into hers.

"Ssh," he whispered, kissed each of them lightly, as if that could make the fear he saw there go away, moved away quickly, soundlessly towards the woods in a direction oblique to the careless footfall, his mind, his body dreadfully calm, as though the world had suddenly stopped and only he were moving, somehow just knowing where he must go, what he must do.

Wisely they had separated, but unwisely had moved to predictable positions. And one of them careless with his feet, no doubt too eager, already tasting blood, involuntarily in the grip of his quickening pulse as he stalked his prey, thinking smugly he would take him by surprise. That one he killed first, didn't even pause to look at the corpse, wondered, already surging towards the next, had he lived long enough to realize he was being killed?

Returning to camp he called out from a distance to let the girl know it was he. "Did you use the bow and arrow?" she asked, looking up at him with large dark eyes. In reply he turned his gaze to the bow and arrow hanging on the wall, then back to her unblinking eyes. "Did you use a knife?"

He mumbled, "I told you I don't like blood. See?" He showed her his hands, cradled her face with them. "How I love thee," he whispered, kissing her on the lips. "No harm shall come to thee."

She moved away a lock that had slipped across one eye, said, "There's something I don't understand," her voice that had become so important to him suddenly foreign, childlike. "Remember you said you can't see the wings of a hummingbird because they're moving so fast? Maybe you never see them because they're always somewhere else. But you should be able to see them because they're moving so fast they're always everywhere." She gazed up at him, fully expecting an answer, as far as she could detect nothing else on her mind but this question. He only shrugged his shoulders. When her lower lip pouted like that with uncertainty, it filled him with desire. She continued, "Could it be the same, being nowhere all the time and being everywhere? It can't, because you can't both see the wings and not see the wings."

He looked away, told her he had to do something with the bodies, walked off, turned before entering the woods to look at her, she still sitting as she'd been the whole time, legs drawn up to her chin, held with her arms. When he returned she was tending the fire. "The meat burned," she said.

He was angry, angry the pimp had only sent two men against him, and one of them careless. The chattery fuss of the grackles and the squirrels disturbed him, he wanted to exhaust himself in some labor or scream, not realizing he was already exhausted. "It's nice here," she said. He picked up fresh pieces of meat and put them on the spit.

After eating they sat in the lean-to arm in arm gazing across the pond, watching the sun go down, each thinking, 'Who is this stranger? What does this stranger know about me?' He cradled her with his arms, kissed her again and again, until it was dark, then they listened to the occasional lapping of the water.

"I want to die here," he whispered.

"Let's never go back to the world," she sighed.

She fell asleep that way, her head against his chest, holding him, held tightly. Once, when he thought she'd already fallen asleep, she murmured, "You're nice," and then she was asleep, while he remained awake, trembling long into the night at the wild yodeling call of the loon.

OUTLAWS

(Homage to Dostoevsky)

You won't like me, I'm not a solid citizen. And I don't believe in your reforms. Reformer! Social reformer! Screw you, buddy.

I picture you sitting in your study, you have one, don't you, you're an intellectual type, don't you people have "studies" with a big leather chair, a carpet, lots of bookcases, where you go to hide from the world and feel important? You're sitting there calmly, all over the professional, eyes vacant but relaxed as you listen to this tape—am I right? I'm calm too, after all we're just two guys chatting across the fence, right? Neighbors batting the breeze. I'm calm all the time, not like you, injustice pisses you off, makes you so angry you write letters to your congressman, you go on protest demonstrations—am I right? What does it get you? Now me, I stay calm, that's the secret of my success.

I do a lot of walking. That's something you want to know about me, because, being a social worker, you like to get to know your patients or whatever the hell you call them, so I'm going to let you get inside my head. I do a lot of walking, like I said, I don't know why, I'll leave the motivation crap to you, I'll let you assign a reason to it so you can feel you understand it, understand me. That way you get to feel superior. You understand, you know. Let me tell you something, buddy, you don't know squat. You don't know diddly. I love those words, squat and diddly.

I was telling you about my walking, wasn't I. Walking, yeah, I don't know, I just like to do it. I always liked to do it. I could walk for hours and not even know time was passing, all over this fucking burg. I don't even know what I'm looking at sometimes, I just walk, even in the winter with the wind blowing like hell, you got the whole damn city to yourself then. Ice storms, they're the best. Nobody goes out in ice storms, not even cops, you can do anything you want in an ice storm, you could blow up city hall. Think I'm exaggerating? Maybe I am, just to keep you on your toes. Maybe I'm trying to impress you.

Not just the good parts, too. You think I walk around the burbs? Suppose I do, just to trample a few flowers, but I'm just as happy on broken beer bottles, it's all the same to me. I even prefer it, it's more real. When you people get pissed off you go out and mow your lawn, they throw bottles. You can't imagine that, can you, being that … messy. Anti-social. Hey, I got an idea, let's you and me get together sometime, we can go to this place I know, knock back a few and then go out and slam beer bottles against the wall. And then piss on it. There's nothing like it, it's … it's a kind of salute. Yes, sir! Fuck you! Really, we'll have to do that sometime. You call that male bonding, right? I figure you hear about that stuff when you do your social work, I figure they tell you, 'Well, sir, I guess me and my buddies had one too many and we just started throwing these bottles,' and you say to yourself, 'Ah, yes, male bonding.' What if a guy does it alone, then what is it? How about inarticulate protest?

The way I figure it, you have to put names on things to pretend you know what's going on, otherwise you're just another dumb shit like me, spends all his time walking and don't even know what the hell he does it for. You got a degree, right? Of course you do, you're a social worker, you got to have a degree, I know because I applied for a social work job once and they turned me down because I didn't have the paper. Got to have that paper. I went to college for a while, but I didn't get the paper.

That was ages ago, I was still living at home, still green—young, dumb, and too dumb to know it. There was this community college not far from my town and I thought maybe I'd take up some kind of engineering. Know what I learned? I learned how to drain construction sites. You know, if it's wetland and they can't build on it, they got to drain it, well that was me. It was really a joke when you think of my town because it wasn't any ordinary town. It wasn't even any ordinary broken down, busted up, burnt out ... Well, that's sort of it, because, you see, my town, the one where my parents still live, where some of my old buddies are, the ones that ain't dead, my town sits right on top of a bunch of old coal mines. And those coal mines have been burning for almost thirty years. You probably don't believe me, but it's true, thirty stinking years of gases seeping into houses and up the streets, land caving in because there's nothing underneath it anymore ... See what I mean about how funny it was, me learning how to drain land? So I left college and I left home and joined up and they sent me you know where and I did you know what.

... I don't want to talk about that. Let's talk about the weather. Beautiful weather, ain't it? I drive a bus. That's my job, driving a bus. It's not bad work if you don't mind being swore at all the time and treated like shit and driving around and around in circles day after day. That's a metaphor, get it? That's what I like about the job, it's a metaphor, that's why I put up with it. It could be the middle of winter, streets sloppy with soot-blackened snow with dog shit on top of it, people climbing on it to get to the bus, mostly old people, and inside the bus it's so hot you can't breathe, and some stinking wino's trying to talk his way past you without paying so he can warm up till you throw him off, and some asshole behind you is sitting on his horn because you're blocking his way ... and you know what I do? I smile to myself and say, 'It's a metaphor, man, ain't it great?'

I don't have a study like you, that bus is my study, that little space around the driver's seat between the window and the metal bar that keeps the people off me. All day long I sit in my study and work out my ideas. You see, I've got a theory. My theory is that all the fat cats and all the people who work for the fat cats—which is just about everybody—and that includes all the politicians—don't know what they're doing. Everybody's just going about their business, getting up and going to work, some of them are running businesses and some of them are making wars and some of them are making speeches and passing laws and there isn't a goddamn one of them who'd know his own ass from a hole in the wall. That's the easy part of the theory. Maybe you're thinking, 'That's a theory? Any half-wit can see we're going down the tubes,' but the real question is, why is that? I mean what kind of people flush themselves down the toilet?

I think I got the answer. I'm serious now, I think it's important for jerk-offs like you to realize how out of it they are. I've been working on this for a long time and I think it's because there's no ideas anymore. There's ideas in the colleges, but, see, they don't matter because nobody pays attention to them. I mean, who runs society, businessmen and politicians, right? Not professors. They're in their corners babbling at each other, they're not in the world. Religion don't mean anything anymore, so that's out. There's only one idea to guide us. Know what it is? Sales! Supply and demand. Marketing. And what kind of idea is that? No idea.

Nobody's got an idea. Think about that. Nobody's got a clue! So I'm driving around in circles getting nowhere and, guess what, so's everybody else, the poor suckers like my old man who chopped coal and the smooth neat guys in fancy suits who make their buck off it, and I'm driving my bus splitting my gut laughing at every god-forsaken one of them, because don't think I give a shit. Because . . . I'm stopping here, that's enough for one session.

*　　*　　*

Hi, asshole, it's me again. I listened to myself. I don't think I explained certain things very well, and I have to if I'm going to make you understand why you're such an asshole and why I'm making this tape. I didn't really say much about the walking, did I?

Like I said, my town was burning up—it's still burning up, by the way, the feds spent about fifty million bucks trying to put out the fire, but it didn't do no good, so all that's left of the feds is the monoxide monitors they put in the houses so folks can tell how much poison they're breathing and every so often I hear they come around with clipboards and check off boxes on their forms. The whole thing's just ripped the town apart, people accusing each other of one thing or another, sniping at each other, slashing each other's tires, egging their houses. So I just decided I wasn't going to live with that shit anymore and I got the hell out. I just left one day and ended up in the army and they sent me over to kill gooks.

I'll bet anything you didn't go. Am I right, Mister Social Reformer? I'll bet you got yourself a draft deferment, you and all your college buddies, and protested the war while we were crawling through the jungle with leeches all over us or getting booby-trapped or ambushed. Shit. When I think of my buddies who ... who didn't make it, I get so goddamned ... Don't worry, I'm not going to tell you my war stories. I'm going to tell you about my walking.

What does this mean to you: Lou-Bea's Pizza. Think about it: Lou-Bea's Pizza. It's like I figured, it don't mean anything to you, and you're supposed to be a social worker. Come on, you dumb shit, think! Lou-Bea's Pizza, well there's Lou and Bea and they make pizza, what's so damn hard about that? Let's try another one: Persico's Hardware. Are you thinking? There's somebody named Persico and he's got a hardware store, right? Not so hard, right? And the city's full of them. Here's a tougher one: Central Plumbing Supply. Not owned by a guy named Central, that's for sure, no, you got to go deeper for something like that, and, like I say, the city's full of these places. Some of them are just names, like Justin's, Laura Taylor, they could be night spots, restaurants, gift shops, you can't tell, but, once you know, it's like the name has a certain ring to it. Laura Taylor, that's women's clothes, kind of formal. Mike's Subs, that's one I really like. Mike's Subs: it really says something, you know?

You don't know what the hell I'm talking about, do you? What the hell, is this guy cracked or what? That's because you're not really part of it, you don't see. You see things through glasses, you're a professional, you keep your distance, even when you try not to, you can't help it, because for you everything is intellectual. That's why you want to improve things. You think it's ideas, but it's not ideas, it's lack of contact. You don't really look, you judge. 'Yes, we can certainly improve things. All it takes is some adjustments. Nip here, tuck there.' You think that makes you a good person, but it doesn't, it makes you a dumb shit.

When I got to Nam, the very first day I'm on a chopper up to Pleiku to join my unit, and we're flying low over this rice paddy and there's this old man standing up in this little flat boat in the middle of the paddy. The chopper swerves down low right for the guy, takes his head right off, and I'm like my jaw's hanging open and there's this strangled gasp trying to come out and my eyes are bugging out and I look around at the other guys, I mean like I'm not sure if I really saw what I saw, and they're all laughing. They're laughing, man.

That's day one, welcome to the Nam. Want me to tell you about day two and three and nineteen and eighty-four and all the other fucked up days? Ever hear of Pleiku, know what happened there? Big base camp, secure perimeter, trip wires, land mines. We had these neat little gizmos, kind of like mines except the shrapnel is directional, we set them around the perimeter, any gook trips one, he and his buddies are one sorry mess. Oh, I forget to mention what went down before I got there. A whole stinking company of VC penetrated our perimeter and took out a bunch of guys sleeping. You got that? In their fucking sleep, man, never knew what happened. There was a lot of hand to hand stuff that night, close range stuff. Guys wouldn't talk about it much, but in the morning, you know, there were pieces all over the place.

So BHQ decides to beef up troop strength and increase patrols. Take the war to the VC. By the time I got there, we'd go out on patrol all right, but we'd be sure to make noise. We posted double watch overnight—one to keep the fire nice and big. You know what I'm saying? It wouldn't have mattered anyway—even the first lieutenant was stoned. But here's the good part: Charlie wanted to let us know that he was digging it, so when we returned to base camp in the morning we had to re-set all those rockets, turn them back out. You get it? Charlie would come every night and turn them in towards camp. Never tripped one, not a goddamn one. So we'd turn them back out, it was a game, like they're saying, 'Hey, fellas, how's it going, just thought we'd let you know we were in the neighborhood.'

Yeah, Nam was something. I learned one thing there: I learned that nobody knows a damn thing about anything. You think you know your best friend? You think you know yourself? You don't know shit till you've faced some doped out VC kid coming at you with a long knife. That's when you learn some interesting things. Yeah, that's when you learn some interesting things. I like to walk around the city, you know. I don't know, I just like it. You know, you think you know what you might do, how you might feel ... You don't. You don't know squat ... It's not you. It's no place you've ever been. And once you've been there ... you don't ever leave.

Life is on the streets. That's the only place where anything's happening, I mean it ain't in school and it ain't in church and it sure ain't in the quote workplace ... and it ain't in the malls or any place like that. I'll tell you one place you can find it: in the ballpark. But, you know, how often can you go, it's the exact same game every time. There's the bars, but that's part of the streets. (Check out the names of bars: Jimmy's, The Washington Tavern, The Chances R—great names!) And if you're not where it's happening, where the hell are you, you may as well just stay in your hole.

I walk all the time, man, hot, cold, dry, wet, it don't matter. Most of the time I just walk, but sometimes I go somewhere, you know, I head for one of my watering holes. Not that I got that many—I'm not really a drinker—and sometimes I like to go some-place I've never been, but you got to be a little careful sometimes. Most places are okay, but sometimes ... It's not like this is the big city or nothing, but you want to look the place over sometimes before you sit down.

It's amazing what you can see if you're looking. Kids playing, that's the best, I never get tired of that. But old people are something too. You just watch them walking their dog or going shopping. Of course there's more people out in the summer time, and then you can go to the park, too. Let me tell you how I met the Jones family. You'll like this part, it's very wholesome.

The Jones family. First there's Papa Jones, mid-twenties, kind of skinny, average height, glasses. Always a slight smile, that's one of the things that got me about him, this slight smile, like you wonder if it's really a smile, maybe that's the way his face is, high cheeks with a crease, who knows, maybe he's an Indian. Then there's Baby Jones, I mention him next because he's sitting on Papa Jones' shoulders, one hand grabbing his face to hold on, the other one pointing right and left, and there's this excited wild look in his eyes, he can hardly sit still—Papa's holding on to both his legs—and he's shouting, "What's that, what's that!" as he points. Real excited, like he's never seen the world before and the dumb little shit thinks it's some sort of big deal. He's, I don't know, maybe two years old. Cute little guy. Real excited, pushing his father's face to make him pay attention and stop talking to Mama Jones. Now Mama, she's pushing the empty what-do-you-call-it, stroller. I mean what is this, the kid never sits in the thing, but they bring it anyway, I don't get it.

I guess it was probably the kid first caught my attention, all those antics, you know, oh and he's got this belly laugh too, if he thinks something's funny. Cute little guy, but it was his dad, that shit-eating grin of his that got me. Like I almost hated the guy just looking at him. All that solid citizen bullshit. Family man, good job, smart ... like he made the world, that's why he's so calm about it, or he trained it, looking at it like you'd look at your dog. 'Here, world, here. Roll over. Go fetch.'

If it wasn't for his wife and kid I might've walked up to him, nice and calm like him, with the same shit-faced grin, and smashed his face. Don't say anything, just walk up and break his face. First time I saw them they were walking in the park. Lots of people, barbecue, throw-and-catch, radios, blankets on the grass, the whole bit, but it was him that caught my eye, him, Mister Jones.

I saw them way on the other side of this big open area, the kid up there so excited he's almost falling off, and, I don't know, there was just something about it, I started walking towards them and they were coming towards me, and pretty soon we're almost passing each other and I want to stare at Mister Jones, just stare at him, look him over, but as we get close I look away and we pass each other like that. I don't know what came over me. It was weird. I felt like shit.

They kept right on going, so I turned and followed, but it was no good looking at their backs. Suddenly I stopped. 'Jesus Christ,' I thought, 'what the hell are you doing?' I'd never done anything like that before. They went off onto the grass and spread out a blanket and I walked on. 'Forget it,' I said to myself, 'just forget it.' But a while later I returned and they were still there.

They seemed so damn ... well adjusted. Smiles. Laughs. The little kid with his toy truck. I know you're thinking it depressed me because I'm all alone, or maybe I was jealous because they seemed to have it all and I don't have a frigging thing, but you're wrong, man, you couldn't be more wrong. You'll see.

*　　*　　*

Sorry I cut that session off so abruptly, I had to take a crap. So where were we? Oh yeah.

I followed them home. Oh, not that day. No, I walked on and forgot all about them, but the next Sunday there they were again, and I figured there's something going on here. I mean, figure the odds on something like that. So I decided I had to get to the bottom of this thing. I wasn't pissed anymore. I mean I was, but not in the same way. I think my anger was getting more refined because it made me laugh. The same half-smile, the same world's my oyster. I figured the guy for a college professor.

By the way, I thought you might like to know that all that stuff about Vietnam was a crock. What I'm saying is, I made it all up. I never saw any action, I spent my whole tour in a motor pool in Subic Bay. Okay, forget it, I'll tell you the truth: I was never in the army at all. I flunked the physical, you believe that? So, you want to know where I got all that bullshit from? From the movies. I got it all from flicks I've seen. That's why I didn't know the name of those do-hickey rocket things, remember, the things the VC used to turn around? You didn't notice, did you, that I didn't know what they're called.

Speaking of movies, I'm writing a screenplay. That's the truth, I really am. I've been working on it for a couple of months now, I figure I'll sell it for a bundle and quit driving this stinking bus. Want to know what it's about? I bet you do, but I'm not that stupid, man. Shit. Okay, I'll tell you this much: a lot of people get messed up and a lot of people get laid. Big hint, right? I got my stars all picked out.

I haven't got that much, you know, actually written down yet, but I will. It takes time. It's hard, writing, you know? Ever try it? You wouldn't think it'd be so hard, once you had the plot and the characters and all, but ... shit! Okay, I'll tell you what it's about, I mean what are you going to do?

This guy's been kicked out of the CIA—it's one of those spy thrillers—because he fucked up real bad, but he can't make it on the outside, you know, it's too tame, and besides he's positive somebody double-crossed him, so he decides to set up on his own and nail the dude, but all kinds of shit starts coming down on him. I still got to work out the details. The original idea was that he figures he's been double-crossed by another agent or 'Control,' but it turns out some heavy-weights are into some serious shit with dope smuggling, you know, that sort of thing, but that's sort of obvious. I'm looking for a twist, but, let me tell you, it ain't easy. Hey, if you think of something, I'll let you have five percent!

Like I was saying, I followed him home, that's how I found out his real name. I wasn't really planning anything, I just sort of did it. And then I didn't know what to do, they went inside and I felt weird hanging around—I'm no peeping tom and I'm not into any kinky stuff, so I left, started walking. I felt ... I don't know, I felt ... don't laugh, okay? I felt like I didn't know anybody—well, I hardly do know anybody—and I was a stranger, like I didn't belong, I shouldn't have been there, like sneaking into a Communist country without a visa. I walked for hours after that, and I just felt weird the whole time. I wondered if anybody was noticing me. Maybe I was invisible.

You know how late it stays light these days, but it was dark by the time I got back to my place. I didn't feel like going in, but I was starving and I didn't want to go out anywhere—I didn't want ... I felt exposed—so I went in and fried up some hotdogs. It was while I was eating I first got the idea of visiting him.

I let it sit there for a while, I didn't, like, pounce on it or try to reject it, I just— I was a sea and it was an oil spill and I just let it spread over me to see how much damage it would do. When I woke up in the morning, I just opened my eyes and I saw, sure enough, the oil had spread during the night. Still I didn't react. Would it foul my beaches or break up in the surf? All that week I drove my bus while the oil did its work. I had to work Saturday. Sunday it rained, but I went to the park anyway. Of course they weren't there; I took it as a sign.

I didn't want to just rush into it. Something like this had to be worked out carefully. I knew I'd never get another chance. But I was too excited to plan. Exactly what would I say, what would I wear, what kind of look would I have on my face, and what would he do, I mean I had to plan for every possibility, think of everything he might say and plan my answers. What a job! I couldn't face it, I started feeling tired all the time, my walks got shorter until I stopped going out entirely. I spent all my time in front of the boob tube. I got depressed.

Finally I gave up the idea. Strangers can't meet. In my town, I mean the town I grew up in, the burning underground and the cave-ins tore up the community, just pulled everyone apart. It was like in a story, families turning against each other, friends breaking up. There was this thing that happened that was like a symbol. This kid—I didn't know him, but I knew his family, it was like six blocks from my house, he was just walking across the backyard and the next thing you knew he was hanging on to some tree roots because the whole backyard just disappeared into a hole a hundred feet deep. Smoke and gas came out of it. It's a miracle for the kid—the gases could have overpowered him, and he just would have disappeared, but he pulled himself out. That's a true story, I'm not bullshitting you, it was in all the papers. Man, I don't want to even know about that kid's dreams, you know what I mean? So how am I going to just knock on some guy's door and say, 'Hey, I'm just trying to figure out what makes you tick'?

So I let it go. I figured the hell with him, I got my walking, I got my screenplay. But I wasn't going out and I wasn't getting any-where, I was thinking about what I would have done if I'd gone through with it, what I would have worn and said, how I would have pulled it off.

First I thought I would have gone as a door-to-door salesman, then I thought of going as one of those religious groups that go door-to-door, you know what I'm talking about. You answer the doorbell and some guy with a briefcase says, "Good morning, sir, do you believe that men can still rule the world?" But then I thought, nah, I like the salesman idea, don't ask me why, and I started looking around for my costume. First of all, everything had to be polyester, jacket, pants, shirt, tie, everything, and it had to look like polyester, otherwise it wouldn't work. It was great because I never realized what a great place thrift shops are. Not only did I find the clothes I needed—including this really great tie, barely an inch wide with some kind of black lightning bolt on silvery white, I think I paid fifty cents for it, but it ought to be worth a million bucks and hang in a museum. Anyway they had all this old kitchen crap, all these contraptions and old dishes, it was like looking at the remains of an earlier civilization, one that was even dumber and uglier than you thought.

The shoes were the hardest part, I didn't know what to get, so I just bought something that fit. What did it really matter, I wasn't going through with it anyway. Besides, who looks at shoes? But what would I sell, that was important. Right off the bat I decided some sort of encyclopedia, and I never gave it another thought, I just knew that was it. Door-to-door encyclopedia salesman with a narrow black and white lightning bolt tie, beige polyester jacket and chocolate brown polyester pants, don't you just love it? I tried it on one night and started laughing so hard I had to fight for breath.

It turned out it wasn't so easy to find the encyclopedia. I mean it was easy to find them, but not in good condition, and not without owner's names written in them. I finally found one volume that looked pretty good. I didn't know how I was going to explain why I had volume OP and not A, but what did it matter if I wasn't really going to do this? But I was, wasn't I? I was playing a game with myself and I knew it, and I also knew that the only way I could deal with it was to pretend I thought it was a game … and to pretend I didn't know I was pretending! Man, when God put psychology in us, he must have been stoned, don't you think so, Mister Idea-man?

The hard part was working out how it was going to go, what I'd say, what he'd say, what I'd say. I took up walking again, it helped me think. A bunch of times I'd start talking out loud and gesturing—you'd know something weird was going on when people started getting out of your way and then you'd realize what it was and you'd want to tell them, 'Hey, it's okay, I'm just rehearsing, I'm an actor,' but they were gone and you knew you weren't really going to say anything anyway. Nobody ever does.

Well, eventually the crisis came, of course: which level of pretense was it going to be, one where I went through with it or one where I didn't? One night I got in costume, looked in the mirror, tried to salute in that incredibly disrespectful way the grunts perfected over there, and said, "Never happen, sir." Later I tossed the clothes on a chair, put on civvies and went out.

If you're thinking I went past his house, you're wrong, I told you I'm no goddamn peeper. I just walked, I don't even know where I went. I decided I needed to find out more about this guy so I'd at least know what I was going up against. The problem was, I didn't know how to do it. I mean here I was, I was writing this spy movie, and I couldn't even figure out how to find out what this guy did for a living. That hurt. Finally I said, fuck it, it may not be pretty but it works, so I parked outside his place one morning and tailed him. He worked downtown in a building filled with social service agencies (I like that name, 'social service,' don't you, it's so positive). I almost lost him going inside—couldn't find a parking spot—but I made it.

He worked with kids, teenagers. I guess he's supposed to tame wild kids, civilize them. Hey, I'm not against it, I just know what he's up against. It's like trying to re-attach a severed head. You can sew up the skin easy enough, but how are you going to reconnect all those nerves? Besides, what's the point trying to reconnect severed heads without doing something about the guy swinging the ax? But why am I talking to you like this, Mister Social Reformer, you're with him. You're mad as hell. "Something must be done about these severed heads!" You just don't get it, do you? You dumb shits.

By the way, I made up all that stuff about my town. No, just kidding, it's really true. Just kidding, man. I said I'm just kidding, all right?

… You're trying to guess whether I did it in the end, well I did. I walked to his house every night for a week—I could have driven, but I walked—and I couldn't do it. I couldn't do it. And I really hated myself for that, I mean really disgusted, like I was really disappointed I was me. Who the hell was this guy, some king? What was I afraid of? But I couldn't do it. I actually got sick, fever and all, I couldn't drive for two days, two stinking days laying in bed hating myself. Finally I made peace, I tried reasoning with myself. Who does something like this? I asked, a reasonable question. Do you know anyone who's ever done this, ever seen it in the movies? Be reasonable, I only meant it as a joke. That's all it was, when I decided to be an encyclopedia salesman and went out looking for clothes—just a game, something to do.

I felt better. I took a shower, went out for a little walk. I still felt a bit nauseous. When I got back, I put on the clothes, just for fun, now I knew for sure it would be absurd to go through with it. It was raining, so I drove over there, and suddenly I realized I was missing two essential props: an attaché case to put my sample volume OP in, and some sales literature. How could you sell without sales literature? (By the way, don't you love that term, 'sales literature'—I'd like to meet the dude who made that up.) But, what the hell, it didn't matter, I wasn't going to really do it. In fact it was better this way, because now there was an objective reason why I couldn't do it, whether I wanted to or not.

I felt better. I started to laugh. I felt so good I got out of the car, ran across the street to keep volume OP dry, and rang his bell.

You don't believe me, do you? No, you know I did it.

I got confidence from the fact that all my preparations had paid off, so I wasn't fazed in the least when it was she came to the door, not he. (I was going to refer to her as Mama Jones, but why use the generic term when I'd known for weeks her actual name was Mrs. Smith?) Was I nervous while I waited for her to bring Mr. Smith to the door? Not in the slightest. In fact I felt nothing, for the simple reason—see if you can understand this—that I had ceased to exist.

I'll admit I had to push a little to get past him into his living room, but aren't door-to-door salesmen supposed to be pushy? He had a funny look on his face, like he couldn't believe he'd allowed me to come into his living room. I didn't have a funny look on my face—mine was prepared. I went right into my sales pitch. "Sir, I know you're busy, I'll only take a minute of your time, if at any time you're not completely satisfied, all your money will be cheerfully refunded," etcetera etcetera. Then: "Sir," I asked, "have you given any thought to the importance of having the world's greatest reference work in the comfort of your own living room? Particularly as I see you have a child"—I pointed to the toys scattered around. "For example, isn't it possible that you're just a bit rusty on your history of the Panama Canal?" Here I threw out a few facts to prove my point. "Or the incredible story of penicillin. Or the marvelous development of the modern opera"—and again I tossed off a few neat facts to let him realize how ignorant he was versus how much I obviously knew. "Now," I continued, "for the incredibly low price of just nineteen ninety-five a month, that's nineteen ninety-five a month, you can receive, volume by beautifully bound volume—"

"I don't think we're interested," he said.

But of course I'd foreseen this. "Not interested in history, in the arts, in the great advances of modern science?"

"Not interested in your encyclopedia."

"But how do you know until you've seen it? For example, did you know that one reason Verdi was so popular was because, writing at the peak of Italian nationalism, his name was an acronym for the popular king of Italy?" I opened volume OP at random on his coffee table and turned pages. "Just look at these illuminating photographs, the easy-to-read text … "

"Thank you," he said, trying to get rid of me.

"Please don't thank me yet," I replied, and tried to continue, but he interrupted me.

"Excuse me, but you don't seem to understand. We're just not interested. We're asking you to please leave."

It was the moment I'd been waiting for, the moment I'd been working towards, planning and scheming for weeks, years, ages, it seemed. I have to admit, I think I outdid myself, first with a look of surprise, then mild defeat, perhaps with a pinch of hurt, then polite resignation. "Certainly, sir," I said, banging shut the open volume between my hands. "Some sales organizations never take no for an answer, but that's not our policy. I'll leave immediately." I stood up, took a few steps towards the exit, then paused briefly as if thinking, turned and said, "If I could just ask you one question to satisfy my curiosity … " Naturally he agreed and that's when I stabbed him.

Just kidding. No, I stabbed him intellectually. I stabbed him and watched him bleed, just as I had planned. What was my question? Very simple. Pointing to the two large bookcases I said, "It's obvious you appreciate learning. With all the educated people in this country, don't you find it amazing that so few ideas penetrate the mainstream?" At first there was this completely blank look on his face, then a quizzical one as he tried to figure out what in blazes was going on. "Think of it," I continued with high seriousness, returning to my place at the couch as though he had invited me back, "there are thousands of colleges but I dare you to find an idea in business, politics, or the arts. We're a nation wedded to pragmatism, which I define as making and fixing things without caring to know how they work."

Guess what happened then? That famous half-smile returned to his face, but I couldn't tell what was going on behind it. "Is this a joke?" he asked.

I pretended to be a little hurt. "A joke, sir? Certainly not. I'm a very serious person."

"But you're not really an encyclopedia salesman."

I relented. "No, sir. Merely a bus driver. I'm trying to improve myself in my spare time." I assumed, being a social worker, that would get him. To clinch it I added: "I haven't sold many encyclopedias yet, but I have met some really nice people. Smart, too. Educated."

I could see he was trying to decide whether to throw me out or offer me a beer. I helped him. "You got a really nice place here. Lots of books. You a teacher?"

"No, actually, a social worker. I work with teen offenders."

I leaned towards him. "Then you especially should know what I'm talking about."

"How so?"

His mouth was over the hook. All I had to do was yank the line. "Because you believe in improvement."

You won't believe this, but, when he heard that, his half-smile turned into a full one. Suddenly I wasn't sure if I had prepared for this. I felt this panic rising in me, and as it rose it was turning into hatred. Hatred, do you hear me? "Why are you laughing?" I asked in a choked voice, trying to restrain myself.

"I'm not laughing," he protested. "It's just that ... I'm not sure I do."

I stared at him until he turned away. "You have to," I said finally, still choked.

"That's the question," he said quietly, still with this smile on his face. It was eerie. I couldn't make it out, like maybe he was crazy. Then—all of a sudden—I figured it out.

"I get it," I blurted out, "you used to, but now you're not so sure." Then I added softly, grinning wickedly, "Has faith been shaken?"

He stared at me then, stared hard, we were really glaring at each other for a moment. Then he said, "I asked you before: who are you? What do you want?"

To cool him out I smiled and leaned back against the sofa. "Just a guy selling encyclopedias on the side, trying to improve himself."

"Seriously?" he asked, looking me over.

I nodded. "Sure, why not? Think I want to be driving a bus all my life?"

The sucker took it. "Sorry about the books. We're just not in the market."

I found my voice again. "Oh, don't worry about that, sir. It's not really the money. To me it's worth it just to have the chance to talk to people like yourself." Believe it, I really said that! I really said 'sir,' too, at least I'm pretty sure I did. "The thing is," I started again, leaning into him, "the thing is, is that ... I mean ... where are the ideas?"

I remember a long silence then, then him saying, "I'm not sure I follow you."

"I have a theory about it. My theory is that people have this need to pretend to have ideas, but the idea of having ideas—to really have ideas and not just bullshit about it—that scares the shit out of them."

He interrupted me—he was getting into it. "I don't know," he said, his face completely serious, "sometimes I think we have too many ideas and they just cancel each other out."

"You're wrong. That's not ideas, that's pretending to have ideas. You get it? It's not really thinking, it's making sales."

"Making sales?" he said, that smile instantly returning.

"Everybody's on the make. Not just salesmen, everybody. Politicians, you name it."

His head went back. "I like that," he announced.

"You do?" I stammered. It had been going well, but suddenly the film had jumped the sprockets. I needed to get it back on track. "Don't you see, it means what you're doing is bullshit." He nodded energetically, a big stupid smile, I felt that panic-into-hatred thing again, and this time I was losing it. "It means"—I hadn't meant to, but I was shouting—"it means you're just hustling like everyone else. You don't really want to change things, you want to make change. You get it? You make a sale, you get paid, and you make change. That's all you're doing."

His wife came in the room then, she must have heard me raise my voice, and I think she freaked when she saw me, I mean I know I was getting worked up, my face was probably twisted around, anyway she had this worried look on her face and I knew she wanted me out of there. Was that what I wanted? It's funny, but, with all that planning I did, I never pictured what it would be like. Now here we were: she figured there was some psychopath in their living room, I don't know what he thought—he was a social worker, after all, he had to try to understand me—and me, I wasn't sure if this was what I'd wanted.

I think we were all trying to catch our breath. "It's all right, Jane," he said in this ... voice, this—I think the word is unctuous, syrupy-like, like a politician, and I saw myself jump up and smash my fist into his face. I didn't do it, I just felt like it, I actually saw myself doing it.

"It's all right, Jane," I mimicked, "I was just leaving. Well, sir, I appreciate the opportunity to show you our encyclopedia. If you change your mind, let me know."

"You know," he said quietly as I headed for the door, that usual half-smile back in place, "who would have the strength to live in such a world?"

*　　*　　*

Tell me the truth: did you realize right from the get-go that I was the encyclopedia salesman? The way I figure it, you had to—it seems so obvious. Did you recognize me from the park when I came to your door? That was the one thing I couldn't get past, that you'd recognize me and think I was weird or something.

So did you? Recognize me, I mean. I really couldn't tell, you got this goddamn look on your face all the time, I can't tell what's going on behind your eyes. It's like looking in the ocean. Couple of times I thought for sure you were going to nail me. I thought, 'This guy's playing me.' Were you?

Don't expect me to tell you what I did after I left your place or what was going on in my head for the next few weeks—I wouldn't give you the satisfaction. I went to work—I drove the stinking bus, day after day, round and round—I walked, I worked on my screenplay. By the way, I got the basic idea worked out. The guy gets kicked out of the CIA for leaving his buddy in the lurch. See, they're always good guys in these movies. Even when they're bad guys they're good guys somehow. So I figure I'll do something different, make him really a bad guy, somebody who really fucked up, but won't admit it and he's looking for revenge. Good, huh? There goes your five percent.

My wife showed up a while ago. I know, you didn't know I was married, now you know. Big deal, we're not really married anymore. I came back from walking and there she was, sitting on the front steps. "Hi," she said. Took me by surprise, I wasn't paying attention. "Howdy," I said and went past her to let her in.

She got up and came into the living room, sort of looked around, and said, "So how have you been, Sally? Oh, so-so, can't complain I guess, how have you been? Okay, so what brings you here?"

Very funny. So I asked her how she was and what was up and she didn't answer either question, which was why I didn't ask them in the first place. I gave us each a beer and plopped down in my chair. I had a pretty good idea what was coming.

Don't worry, I'll spare you the blow-by-blow. Knowing you, you probably want to hear it. I'll spare you anyway.

I think it'd been more than a year since we'd last seen each other, more than two since I split or she threw me out, depending on whose version you take. Tell you the truth, she wasn't looking that good, made me think I'd done the right thing.

I asked how the old hometown was and she told me she'd been shacking up with my old high school buddy, Tom. "Lucky guy," I said. I was going to be patient. I figured she'd tell me what was up when she was ready.

She just sat there in my kitchen, sucking on this bottle of beer until I told her to ease up. "You know you drink that fast, it's going to mess you up." She tried to slow down, but I could see something was getting ready to come out. When it was empty she started playing with the bottle. Finally I asked her if she was hungry and she told me she came to see how I was doing.

"So how am I doing?" I asked.

"I don't know," she said, "how are you doing?"

"You tell me," I said, "how am I doing?"

Or something like that, you get the idea. She kept playing with the beer bottle, she wouldn't look at me, and finally I said, "Hello? You mind telling me what's happening here?"

"I told you," she said, forcing herself to look up at me and smile— I could see she was forcing herself, "I came to see how you were."

"You came all the way out here to see how I am. How'd you get here? Drive by yourself?"

She looked up her sleeves. "Far as I know," she said and made herself smile. She looked terrible, anyway I can't remember if it was then or later she finally got it out. She said she'd been doing a lot of thinking and I said, "Uh-oh," and she said, "Seriously." She said moving back home had kind of opened up her eyes, made her realize that I was right. To do what I'd done, she meant.

"The earth burning up right under you'll kind of do that, I guess."

She nodded. I was surprised, I'd never seen her like this, something was going on. She looked me right in the eye and said, "You were right, I was wrong," and then it was my turn to play with the beer bottle. "You had to do what you did. You had no choice."

"Of course I had a choice. I could've kept my mouth shut like you wanted."

"I was wrong. I had to learn that, but I know it now. When I see what the fire's doing to the town ... "

"Kind of hit home as they say, is that it?"

"I guess that's what it takes sometimes, you know?" She seemed real earnest.

I went: "If it does, there ain't much hope, is there?"

Later she said, "I've been down."

"Happens to the best of us," I said, trying to be breezy, but she was focused on what she had to say.

"What happened, anyway?"

"You mean how could I have blown the whistle?"

"No. To us. Was it because I didn't get it? Was it me?"

I didn't answer. I didn't look at her. When she said that, I felt things way down that I didn't want coming over me, not ever again. I saw it all then. I knew why she'd come, I knew what she'd been through, the only thing I didn't know was what she wanted, but I knew, whatever it was, I couldn't handle it. That's what made me do what I did. I was cruel, I know it, I didn't want to be, it's just ... that's the way it is sometimes. Hey, I didn't make the rules.

... So I said something I regretted. Right then I regretted it, but ... Shit, man. You got to know there's some real history between me and her. She was hurt, I knew it, but right then there wasn't anything anybody could've done about it. Besides, I started thinking, what the hell was this, anyway? Her boyfriend boots her out, so she starts thinking maybe I wasn't so bad, maybe she'll forgive me, maybe what I did wasn't so stupid after all, and—what—I'm supposed to go crawling back? She gives me the nod and I jump? Screw that.

She got up and went in the living room and I let her go. I just sat there. I wasn't thirsty or hungry or anything. I don't know what I was. I realized I hadn't turned any lights on and it was getting dark. I could hear the creaking of the chair she was sitting in. After a while I went to the bathroom and, when I came out, she was gone.

I walked outside and then I ran up to the corner—why, I don't know—why I ran, I mean—but she was gone. My gut was all knotted up. "Stupid bitch," I kept saying. I sat outside for a long time, thinking she'd come back—I figured she'd drive around, cool off, and come back. Where the hell was she going to go, she'd just driven all day. When she didn't show and I was getting tired I went inside, but I felt cooped up and went out walking.

Then I figured she'd spend the night in a cheap motel and show up in the morning, but she didn't. The dumb shit, she left, she actually left. I mean, what'd she expect, she'd just show up out of the blue and we'd play house together? Shit.

I felt pretty bad. I didn't want to hurt her, that stuff's all past now. Anyway, I got to thinking about it and—maybe this is just rationalizing, but, in a way, it's better this way. Really. I mean there's no way we're getting back together.

She'll be okay. You know what I say? Better a big pain than a small happiness. Of course you don't see it that way, Mister Social Worker, but what do you know, you're just a walking textbook. Take it from me, no charge.

I didn't like her seeing the way I live, you know?

Anyway, I've been doing a lot of walking. Somewhere in there I got the idea of making this tape, sending it to you. I don't know if I will. We'll see.

PRISONERS

The principal difference between a great city and an
ordinary one is that in a great
city one can have an adventure. Impossible in an ordinary one, which
has no neighborhoods one could remember with fond enmity as "the
old neighborhood," no great squares or renowned avenues, no world
famous buildings or pre-eminent museums, no sense that what goes
on is not merely event but history, that its citizenry do not so much
simply go about their business as create a texture of urban life ... But
in the great city, what adventures are not possible! Oh yes, there is
the violent, the sordid, the dirty and the impoverished, but, like its
own tall buildings, a great city rises out of that, not so much to
grandeur as to some inchoate sense that what happens has aesthetic
value.

Merely to approach a lunch counter to order some assimilated
ethnic specialty can be sufficient to expose one, to include one even,
in the mundane daily tumult that, now here, now there, in the
creases of a weathered face or the uncanny freshness of an expensive

topcoat, represents the mystery of great cities, which, like all mysteries, seems at once both near and ever distant. Many times in my deliberate wanderings (at first with a street map discreetly pocketed but eventually "flying without instruments") I came upon a face, overheard a conversational fragment, or observed some tiny inconsequential transaction that seemed to me infused with ... with something that made it more than what it was, with that aesthetic value to which I often refer but cannot truly grasp.

Not for want of trying, mind you, have I failed in my attempts—and, note well, there have been attempts. Though a civil servant of modest liberal education, I fancy myself a bit of a writer; one, I might add, who, as a hopeless *inamorato* of earlier times and foreign places, sometimes feels imprisoned by his particular time and place. To this I attribute the desire to discover in the metropolis, not the squalor that is everywhere to be met, but an ineffable human quality capable of participating, if only a little, in the good, the true, and the beautiful. But, as I say, though I have tried to transmute this experience into art, my literary powers are evidently too poor, and I am so condemned—some might say blessed—to be of those who can appreciate the creativity of others, but cannot muster any of their own.

Naturally I did not achieve this realization unaided. No sooner having completed a brief cycle of short stories—graced, as I recall, with some predictably horrific title as *Urban Tales*—I began "sending it out" ... and collecting a growing pile of rejection letters. These, stupidly, I bore as the badge of the aspiring writer, resolving, as each arrived, to persevere. Who knows how deeply I might have sunk in this unfortunate vanity had I not received— mercifully before the pile had grown so large as to launch me into a great novel!—a letter of acceptance. It was hardly, to say the least, from a top literary journal; on the contrary this was apparently a publicly funded effort "to document the regional art" of my locale. To my credit I could not dispel the notion that my work had been damned with faint praise, as the editor had found my stories to have "a charming freshness." Presumably the thing was published; to my knowledge I never received a copy—I probably tossed it with the other junk mail. In any case, after the hurt had sufficiently sub-sided, and pride commensurate recovered, I recognized that, if there was any hope for improving my literary skills, some formal training was in order, something more demanding than the occa-sional office memo. In short I determined to return to the rank of student.

No "continuing education" course for me, which I believed would be little more than a breeding ground for the same literary self-indulgence I had just painfully survived; rather a true college-level course, where I would be required to submit to the tyranny of the masters of literature. Thus, after some weeks as an earnest scholar (among the few in the class, I might add) I happily befriended my professor, a man twenty years my junior, but, unlike myself, married with family.

His field was nineteenth century European literature and he had an infectious enthusiasm for it that well exceeded the required level of professional interest, which, in my line of work, where little beyond the adequate is asked or appreciated, I felt qualified to meas-ure. I found myself peppering him with questions after each class until it became a habit for us to walk off together to a nearby cafete-ria where we could continue our conversation on the topic of the day. It was a dreary place, noisy, over-lit, vacuous, just the sort of life-less functional design one would expect of a public college in a provincial city, far from the wondrous Parisian café of my imagina-tion, but, so absorbing were the subjects of our discussions and so insightful did I find my teacher's reflections, I at least soon ceased to care where we were located.

It was during one of those *tête-à-têtes*, in March I believe, for I remember the weather being more foul than frigid, that he told me of a most extraordinary experience he had recently had. It shouldn't be surprising that such a man with such an interest would enjoy lit-erary bookstores or that he would particularly enjoy those specializ-ing in old and used books—of which none existed in our own city—but at the moment it struck me as extraordinary that we should both be devotees of escaping on a Saturday to the big city where such places were to be found.

He had barely begun to recount his experience when I interrupted him by exclaiming, "de Maupassant. This reminds me of a story by de Maupassant."

"Really, which one?"

"Oh, not any particular one," I said. "Of course the details would have to be changed. Get rid of this awful cafeteria … I'm sorry, go ahead."

As he went on with his tale I couldn't help smiling inwardly. 'But it is so much like a story by de Maupassant! Well, perhaps not … '

"—He was an elderly man, I'll guess seventy-five, not at all frail in appearance, but clearly showing his age. He had a way of picking up a book—I think it was that I found so attractive about him—it was two things at the same time, reverent and familiar—if you can imagine that. I pretended to browse, but I couldn't take my eyes off him. Very gentle. Almost pathetic. I mean, in the confines of an old bookstore, maybe such a person could exist; but outside … he couldn't last a minute.

"I can tell you, I was … riveted, hypnotized. He was a presence from another world, a different time and place."

Suddenly my professor felt the strong desire to know the title of the book the old man was perusing. He knew from where he was standing the subject must be history, political science, possibly sociology; but what subject specifically? Though embarrassed, he felt compelled to return the Steegmuller translation of *Madame Bovary* to the shelf and move closer to where he might espy the title of the book in the man's hand. In this way he found himself in anthropology, a subject not at all to his liking. He withdrew Malinowski's *Crime and Custom in Savage Society* from the shelf and pretended to inspect it. Opening at random he discovered this sentence, which some earlier reader had underlined carefully in red pencil: "Thus the binding force of these rules is due to the natural mental trend of self-interest, ambition and vanity, set into play by a special social mechanism into which the obligatory actions are framed."

Unless he were willing to risk looking suspicious or, worse, having his purpose discovered, he must move closer, for it was clearly impossible to make out the title of a book that was being held at a distance, never at an advantageous angle, and constantly moving; so, after feigning modest interest in a few related texts, he moved closer: sociology. Was there a subject in which he had less interest, he wondered. Frustrated, he reached out and took down the first book that came under his hand. He noticed that the old man was smiling at him and realized he'd been doing the same. He looked down at the book in his hand and opened it randomly. There was an old black and white photograph of poor quality showing a man of indeterminate age standing in the entranceway of a shop. He had on a long worker's apron; his big handlebar mustache marked him as an immigrant of an earlier day. The caption at the bottom of the page read: "Urban di Prato, the shoemaker, in whose shop a bundle of dynamite was found."

Fascinated, he leafed through the book. Pictures of striking workers, marches, confrontations with troops, mounted troops and infantry with bayonets at the ready. The great labor struggles. You could believe you were fighting for human liberation, the dawn of a new age, a new age … The old man was intent upon his book. When he looked up absent-mindedly, perhaps musing on something he'd just read, the professor would look down suddenly, then up again. What was there about this old man? he asked himself. Perhaps it was—yes, that was it, it was his face: old-world intellectual, but also … sad. Yes, sad. He returned the book to the shelf and advanced to political science. He was close enough to the man now, they were neighbors. If he would just turn the book so the cover could be seen … but he was reading; slowly, gracefully, he turned a page—the professor was surprised to note how much grace was in those worn hands.

Daring all, he moved to within a few feet of the old man and was able to confirm that the subject was history after all. He pretended to browse with interest and was about to withdraw a large and battered tome when the old man looked up from his reading to ask, "Have you ever been struck by a phrase?" Startled, almost embarrassed, shy, he turned to look at the man, smiled, but then didn't know what to say. "I think I have, yes," he replied finally.

"The end of American innocence," said the old man, holding up the book in his hands so the professor could see that that was the title. "What a phrase! I didn't know it had ended, did you?" The professor couldn't figure out how to respond. "I didn't know what to say," he told me. "You know how you always feel when you're in a public place and somebody behaves in some way that transgresses social convention. By approaching they threaten your anonymity. At first I thought, 'oh no, a weirdo,' and I felt like getting out of there, but it only lasted an instant until I saw that he was just talking to me, that it wasn't the sort of frightening demented loneliness you sometimes find among old people in the big city. You've seen them. They pretend to be shopping or eating or going somewhere, but one look at them tells you it's nothing of the sort, these are the worn out and broken old parts of the social machine waiting to be carted off to the landfill. What do you do with worn out and broken old parts when it's the machine that needs fixing? Anyway, the initial panic once subsided, I could see he was just making conversation, one bibliophile to another, so I searched for an answer, but couldn't find one."

The old man, seeing the professor appeared interested, or at least receptive—he was, in fact, fascinated, not so much by the topic as the old man—proceeded to relate the author's thesis. "It never ceases to amaze me how historians always manage to find endings and beginnings. From my reading, last year is always judged innocent from the vantagepoint of this year, no matter what it seemed like at the time. But then the book was published in 1959. Maybe the author couldn't know how much innocence remained to be lost." He began searching in it and soon found his page. "I found this in it: 'It is hard today, when the metropolis is a few hours from anywhere and familiar to everybody, at least via television and movies, to recognize what the city meant to the young intellectual from the provinces in, say, 1913.'"

The professor looked at him warmly. "You?"

"My father." He laughed. "I'm old, but not … "

The professor laughed too. "Arithmetic was never … "

"Have you begun searching for your father's world yet, or are you too young?"

The professor looked at the old man's eyes that were looking right at his. "I'm young, but not … " he bantered, then added quietly, "How did you know? Is that why we come to these places?"

"I'm sorry," said the old man, indicating he hadn't heard well, "the ears don't work so good anymore."

The professor repeated himself in a louder but shy voice, not wanting to be overheard and embarrassed to see if he was.

The old man reflected before speaking. "I think we come for many reasons. I love books. All my life I've loved books. Every so often I buy one so they don't throw me out." He considered the book he was holding. "I should buy this," he said, almost to himself, adding, "It's interesting to see how historians treat people you've known."

The professor's eyes widened. "You knew people in there?"

"Oh sure," said the old man.

"Who's in there?"

"Intellectuals. Revolutionaries." There wasn't a hint of guile in his manner.

The professor thought: the old man was wrong; worlds do end and give way to new ones. Those archaic terms… "Which one were you?" he mumbled, then, remembering, repeated it more loudly, only to apologize immediately for having used the past tense.

The old man gestured elaborately. Finally he said, "I'm not sure yet," and chuckled. As if in explanation he added, "All my life I've tried to be both. I'm still not sure that's possible."

The professor stood there in silence for what seemed a long time, feeling more than actually thinking how much he loved these old bookstores. A browser wandered into their space—the history section; both of them looked at him, but he remained oblivious, until, oblivious, he moved on to philosophy. The professor and the old man looked at each other, each apparently waiting for something to be said, sensing somehow that something would be. The professor framed a question, but, stumbling over the issue of tenses, withdrew it for rephrasing. "Are you a retired teacher?" was how he finally put it.

"A teacher, yes. Retired? At my age … To you it probably looks like retirement." He smiled and the professor smiled too.

"You teach history, I presume. Where do you teach?"

The old man laughed as if a joke had been told. "Where do I teach? What do I teach? Such questions!" The professor was discomfited at the *faux pas* he had evidently made, but the old man seemed to enjoy it. "Look at history," he continued, pointing to the bookshelves, "two rows, barely—what—twenty, thirty square feet? What about those rows and those rows—philosophy on one side, social science on the other—there is some law that says I can't teach those? And what about—incredible as it may seem—what about all those books over there, on the other side of this table? If I try to go over there, will some, some … fissure open up in the floor and I'll fall in and disappear? If I read a book of literature, a great giant of a book maybe, like *Crime and Punishment*, or maybe not so big, maybe just— Is it so terrible that I should read such books, and, having read, that I should think they shed light on the human condition, and that, having thought, I should teach? This is terrible? This is against the law?"

The professor laughed and laughed. "It is where I come from," he blabbered, still laughing.

"And I'll tell you something," continued the old man in a voice almost hushed, his eyes twinkling, "if you keep going that way"— he pointed towards philosophy—"you come to psychology, and from there, if you are not careful, if you don't keep your eyes staring at the books in front of you, do you know what books you can see, what forbidden fruit? Science!" He pretended to clutch his head in pain and moan. "Surely it is not right that I should think of going over there. What do you think?"

The professor was startled by the sudden question and fumbled for a reply.

"Forgive me, let me ask you a simpler question: How many square feet do you browse in?"

"Actually I don't belong here at all," he replied gaily. "I'm supposed to be over there, on the other side of the table."

"Literature? Ah, I see, you belong there, but you're here— another lawbreaker. And over there, where you belong, which row is yours—American, European … ?"

"European."

"European," repeated the old man. "And if I may ask, in this row, which shelf—the nineteenth century, the eighteenth century...?"

"The nineteenth century."

"The nineteenth, I see. And—if I might inquire—on this shelf, which part is yours, the English, the French ...?"

"No," said the professor, thoroughly enjoying this, "now you've gone too far. Actually I dare to read the entire shelf."

The old man, his eyes still twinkling, appeared to find that answer fascinating. "You don't say. This I find ... unusual, if you'll forgive me for speaking frankly. The entire shelf. You're not one of those who only allows himself six inches?"

"There are a few of us left."

"I see, I see." He made a face, as though he were impressed. "You teach?" The professor nodded. "In a school."

"Is there any other place to teach?" he commented breezily.

"For a man such as myself, who never taught in a school, who never studied in a school ... Oh, here and there. I mean a great, a university, a fine college. Where do you teach?"

"State school. Upstate."

"Ah, you don't live in the city."

The professor shook his head. "I visit." The two of them stood there looking at each other. The professor didn't find it uncomfortable and the old man didn't appear to either. "If you don't mind my asking—"

"What's that? Sorry, the ears."

"If you don't mind my asking, if you don't teach in a school, where do you teach?"

"You know, in the Jewish faith, you don't need a synagogue to perform the service. All you need is ten men, it could be anywhere, a laundromat even. To teach you only need two: a teacher and a student. Mostly they come to my apartment."

"Do you have many students?"

The old man shook his head. "Here and there a lawbreaker."

"How do—"

"They find me. Who knows how." He shrugged.

At this point in the narrative my professor paused, gazing about the cafeteria as though seeking someone, the way one does sometimes for no apparent reason. Suddenly he was nervous again, he said, that the old man was some sort of crackpot. "I must have taken a step back because the old man suddenly made a gesture as if to stop himself from talking too much." He apologized for keeping the professor from his books, but the latter, to his own surprise, said he had lots of time and expressed interest in knowing what the man's work might be. At this the old man made a face as if he would consider the request, and then appeared to do so. The professor waited, watching him, no longer nervous, simply fascinated like before.

The old man appeared to have made a decision. "Permit me to ask you a question," he said, coming out of his deliberation, and then asked it without waiting for permission. "You're a student of literature. What do you think is the fundamental question in literature?" At first the professor assumed the question was rhetorical, but the old man was looking at him and waiting as though expecting an answer, so he began fumbling for a response. Fortunately the old man continued before he'd had a chance to reply that it would be professional suicide to even pose a fundamental question, let alone try to answer one—perhaps it had been a rhetorical question after all.

"As long as I can remember," resumed the old man, "I've been trying to understand why people are so cruel to each other. In 1933 I was in Flint, Michigan during the great strike against General Motors. Of course you don't know anything about this. The workers had taken over the factory instead of setting up picket lines. Picket lines could be broken by cops and goons and the company could bring in strikebreakers, so we hit on the idea of just staying right where we were. They called it a sit-in." He had a far-away look in his eyes as he paused. The professor, rapt, just watched him, an old man folding back his memory over more than half a century.

I had to interrupt the story to make sure I'd heard correctly: The old man had said "we"—he had been in this strike? The professor nodded and added that the story was true—he'd looked it up later. Vigilante groups were organized and the police mounted machine guns on the hoods of their cars. I shook my head. "This really happened?"

The professor nodded again. "Negotiations bogged down and the situation looked pretty desperate. The workers in the factory sent out a letter. They hoped for a settlement, but, if not, they wanted to say goodbye to their families."

"Wait a minute," I said, incredulous, "this is for real? You're not pulling my leg?"

Again the professor nodded. "And this old man had been there. But to look at him you'd never— Well, what does a person look like who's made history? I take that back, there was something about him."

I urged him to continue the story. At first he seemed to hesitate; a loud noise distracted him momentarily; he seemed to be deciding where to pick up the thread of his narrative. What struck the old man, he said, was that these people—the police and vigilantes—were perfectly willing—eager, even—to gun down as many strikers as they could get at. "'Why?' asked the old man. Fifty years later he's asking a stranger in a bookstore why." He shook his head and appeared to withdraw into silent musing until I prodded him into continuing.

Suddenly, he said, the old man seemed to remember that he'd begun by asking about literature. "The fundamental theme in history is cruelty and the fundamental question in literature is how are we to understand this violence?"

"I couldn't help smiling," said the professor. "I almost burst out laughing. As a professor of literature I should have received a remark like that with condescending amusement if not scornful anger. Instead I found it ... exciting. It was literally outrageous. The guy didn't realize what a gadfly he was—if he was for real ... and if anybody paid any attention to him."

"Was he? Did they?"

"That's what I wanted to find out. If this guy was for real, he was ... I don't know what he was. But I was intrigued—even though I couldn't agree with his proposition in any rigorous way. I asked him sheepishly if he had published."

"Let me guess," I interrupted. "He had a four thousand page manuscript that had been turned down by everyone."

"Wrong. It was only three hundred pages, it wasn't finished yet, and he hadn't shown it to anyone."

"But he wanted to show it to you," I added mischievously.

"Hey," snapped my professor merrily, "whose story is this?"

I made a show of sitting back and folding my hands. "Please continue," I requested demurely.

"Since you insist," replied my professor with poorly hidden pleasure. "Here's the scene," he began.

"I can picture the scene," I interrupted. "Cut to the chase."

"All right. He invited me to see the manuscript at his apartment and I agreed." He looked at me, perhaps wondering if I'd request any details. I gestured for him to continue. "He bought the book he'd been holding and we went out into the cold and windy grayness of a mid-afternoon late winter day in the city. It struck me then how old he was. The wind was going right through me, I wanted to pull him along and run to the subway. He just walked along, holding his coat closed at this throat."

It was a long subway ride, during which they didn't converse at all, because of the screeching of the train. During the entire time the old man looked down at his lap, perhaps having learned from unfortunate experience that in the subway making eye contact with strangers was risky. Once confined by the slamming of the doors inside that crowded lurching car, said my professor, the human mass was reduced to an assemblage of isolated individuals and further reduced back to an undifferentiated mass. "You couldn't look or speak, but you remained alert for danger."

Once again he was seized with a kind of panic. Was he crazy to be going off with some stranger he'd met in a bookstore? What would he say if the manuscript was gibberish or didn't even exist? After all, what did he know about the old man? A stranger! Had he been younger he never would have gone with him, it would have been folly. Clearly he felt safe enough in his frailty, but, still, to go off to his apartment … he didn't even know if he had a wife.

Suddenly the lights went out. The darkness was so complete, the professor found that thought had stopped as though his mind was holding its breath. When the light returned as suddenly as it had disappeared it was almost surprising to find things as they'd been before. The old man hadn't moved; he might have been dozing. The professor scrutinized him. His clothes were decent, certainly not second-hand, clean, tidy, the shirt buttoned at the collar, the shoes not scuffed too badly; nothing distinguishing about them, nothing to give pause, cause one to wonder who this particular old man was, where he'd been, what he'd done.

Suddenly it was surrealistic, the professor said. One was moving at high speed through dark tunnels beneath a huge city, millions of people jammed into a vast edifice of towers and tunnels going where, doing what? This old man across from him clutching a book described himself as a revolutionary and an intellectual—what did such embarrassingly anachronistic terms mean anymore? There were other old people in the car, also staring into their laps, probably praying they weren't noticed—or too used to the routine to pray anymore—who were they, what had they done? "I saw myself in a story. I don't think I would have been shocked to learn that we had wandered onto a set, that the whole thing was being filmed. At the same time, however, I felt like I was the one behind the camera."

They surfaced in a neighborhood my professor had never been in before and walked several blocks to a street lined with four- or five-story apartment houses, neither luxurious nor poor, merely nondescript and inadequately maintained. At one of them the old man fished out his key and they entered a fairly drab lobby with faded wallpaper and large vases of dusty plastic flowers. In a corner a knot of teenagers were making a lot of noise and when the old man and the professor entered one of them shouted, "Hey, grandpa, give me some money."

They looked pretty tough and my professor became concerned when a few of them approached. The old man grumbled, "Don't pay any attention to them," and kept walking to the elevator with his head down. My professor did likewise and took his first breath when the elevator doors had closed on them. "Hooligans," growled the old man in disgust. "When it's warm they hang around the street corners."

There were questions the professor thought of asking, but in the end he kept silent and the old man volunteered no more information. He seemed to have already put them out of his mind. The elevator opened onto a fifth-floor hallway that matched the lobby, except for an indefinable odor that might have been food or some mysterious emanations of old occupants of old buildings that the professor chose not to try to identify. He expected the old man's apartment to be of a piece with the rest—faded, nondescript, and a little smelly—but instead it was nicely if inexpensively furnished, and somehow it seemed bright although little light was coming in through the single living room window.

The old man immediately excused himself for a minute, leaving the professor to look over the shelves of books, which alone added individuality to an otherwise anonymous living room. He'd expected a room full of them, but there were only a few shelves' worth. He approached and looked over the titles and was instantly struck by the diversity of the subject matter (which he might have expected) and the fact that they were not arranged in any apparent order. A slim volume entitled *The Industrial Revolution* was sandwiched between *Huckleberry Finn* and *Translations from the Chinese*, Aristotle's *Nicomachean Ethics* was next to *The Complete Poems of Hart Crane*. Sounds came from the kitchen—the old man's wife? The place was very neat and none of the books were dusty, but perhaps that didn't prove the old man wasn't single.

A book called *Men of Ideas* caught his attention; he took it down and read the jacket cover. "The first part of this study deals with those institutions that have nurtured the intellectual vocation since the eighteenth century. In the book's second part, relations are explored between men of power and men of ideas—the relation of intellectuals to politics." He was still reading when the old man appeared with his wife, a shy and frail woman who walked haltingly and asked, barely daring to look at him, if he would like some graham crackers and tea. The old man had a pile of paper in his hand, which he set down on the coffee table; the professor seated himself in front of it.

There was no title page—"I haven't figured out what to call the damn thing," said the old man with a show of self-reproach—nor a table of contents. It simply began: Chapter One, Introduction, Violence in the Big and the Little. The first sentence was a question (or perhaps not a question): "We all know that war is war; but do we admit how many of our other forms of relationship are also war." It was handwritten in large enough letters to fill an entire page. Browsing, he noticed what appeared to be a continuing melange of poetry, aphorisms, commentaries, and conventional text; his heart sank. "Maybe you could tell me about this," he asked in a voice he hoped covered his emergent desperation.

The old man, apparently unaware of his discomfort, answered as if he were being interviewed. "A student studies; an activist acts; in my life I have tried to put the two together. Because study without action is useless, meaningless; and action without understanding is also useless, because it will fail. So how do you put the two together? You could say, 'These shall think and these shall act,' but that is no solution. I took a problem, violence—not this or that kind of violence, just … violence—and I tried to explain it—what it is, how it comes about. Without that kind of fundamental approach you can't make fundamental changes. Reforms fail, revolutions fail. Look at the table of contents."

"Is there one? I didn't see it."

The old man mumbled something and took back the pile of pages. "Here it is. It got on the bottom somehow. Books are beautiful, aren't they? You realize it when you look at a typescript. This isn't a book. You can't hold it in your hand, pages get misplaced—it just doesn't feel right. But a real book … "

The professor scanned the chapter titles: Attachment, Desire, Pain and Fear, Non-violence and Violence, Exploitation and Oppression, Marxism-Leninism, Power, Persecution and Liberation. 'What is this to me?' he thought, 'I'm a professor of literature.' "It seems like two books," he muttered sheepishly, only to repeat it loudly so the old man could hear.

"You're trying to decide what shelf to put it on."

The professor tried to chuckle. "Knee-jerk reaction. Have you … have you shown it to people? A publisher?"

The old man made a face. "A publisher? Who'd publish this? What shelf would they put it on?"

"I didn't know how to reply," said the professor. "I was aghast. To do all that work ... for nothing?"

"You're assuming it was real, aren't you?" I said.

"It was filled with references. Whether it was rigorous I don't know. How do you evaluate a thesis that refuses to submit to the constraints of any particular field? In the same paper he refers to experiments in cognitive psychology and what he calls the genocide of Native Americans."

"Then you read it."

"I read parts of it. It was three hundred pages. His wife came in with tea and the two of them sat there in silence while I read."

"That must have been something," I said. "I bet she stared at you surreptitiously, trying to learn from your eyes whether you were the one who would redeem her husband's labors and get him the recognition he deserved before it was too late."

My professor wagged his finger at me. "You're writing a story."

"Guilty," I confessed, smiling.

"Then you can finish the tale yourself," he said, rising. "I'm already late for a department meeting and, besides, I can't stand this cafeteria any longer. It's so ... uncomfortable."

I had no choice but to let him go, but I couldn't let him drop the story like that. "Come on," I pleaded, standing, "you can't just walk away in the middle of a story."

He pretended to look at me harshly. "If you've been paying attention in class you know damn well the story's almost over and that the climax and resolution occur at almost the same moment."

"But," I protested, "I want to know what happened."

My professor said nothing while we made our way out of the cafeteria into the rawness of a chilly, windy March day. "Actually it was kind of neat," he said at last.

"You see? You're holding out on me."

"Suspense," he replied didactically. "I have to admit, the work was intriguing. As scholarship I won't begin to judge it, but as a creative work it had a certain attractiveness. He wove quotations through the text from *The Brothers Karamasov* and a history of the American Indians that did some interesting things. They added texture, established different layers of meaning. I've never seen that before."

"And?"

"I was afraid anything I'd say might offend him, so I just kept reading and they just kept sitting there, but then I had the feeling there was some silent communication between them and the old man suddenly asked me if I liked old movies."

"He did what?"

"It took me by surprise too, but there's an explanation. It seems that he and his wife really liked old movies—maybe they used to go out a lot when they were younger—and every Saturday they would watch one on television."

"I don't get it," I pronounced.

"It was time, you see. The movie was starting in a minute and it was obvious they didn't want to miss it."

"And that was more important than discussing the paper?"

"Interesting, no? Work that into your story. He obviously didn't care what I thought. It was enough that I'd seen it, or agreed to read it."

I shook my head emphatically. "No one could be that aloof. He was afraid of your opinion."

"I assure you he wasn't the slightest bit afraid."

"Maybe he was tired."

"He was pulling up the TV and his wife was getting a fresh pot of tea."

"Maybe they like old movies that much. Maybe this was a particular one. What was it?"

"'The Third Man.'"

"I don't know it."

"A real classic, I rented the video last week. Very heavy direction—British. It's about—"

"You're digressing," I interrupted.

My professor shrugged his shoulders. We reached his building and went inside. "I'm really late," he said, heading towards the elevator, "shall I get you the various references?"

"Pardon me?"

"So you'll have the exact quotes in your story."

"Oh, sure. Sure," I repeated, catching the twinkle in his eye, "but did it really end like that?"

The elevator arrived and my professor stepped inside and pressed the button that kept the door open. "The old man invited me to watch the film with them, but I referred to a train schedule. He waved away my excuse and shook my hand warmly, thanking me for my interest in his work."

"That's it?" I pressed, unbelieving. "He just thanked you for your interest?"

He said something like, 'Who knows, maybe some day you'll find it in a used bookstore,' and shrugged his shoulders like he knew it would never happen."

I was shaking my head. "Incredible. To be so ... free."

My professor reflected. "Free? On one level, perhaps. But on another ... He was carrying a lot of weight. Think about it. Anyway, his wife called out that the movie was starting and I assured him I could let myself out. The last I saw of him, he was settling himself on the couch next to his wife while she poured tea as the film came on." Then my professor reminded me that, truth being stranger than fiction, writing truthful fiction was damned hard. He let the elevator door close and I stepped outside into a gust of wind that made me hurry to my car.

STRANGERS

From the time the train left the station he had stared out the window, even when it had become quite dark and little could be seen beyond an occasional light in some building or dwelling in the distance, making him wonder, 'What is that building, is it a barn, a farmhouse, what is life like there, what are the people who live there doing right now, what are they thinking about?' A train leaving its terminal, a great grand palace of a station with beginnings and endings of journeys, reunions and separations, joyful and sad, with huge clocks and passages, hissing of brakes and shouts of recognition, wonder-eyed children tightly handled begging bars of chocolate, and, on the quays, the departing piling into crowded cars, making absurd piles of luggage somehow fit in inadequate spaces, then leaning out the window for a last chat with those not coming, those on the quay to see the travelers off, speaking now only of the unimportant, the silly, or what has already been said, not 'I love you,' not 'I'm worried about you,' but 'Make sure you keep warm,' 'Don't forget to remind Uncle So-and-so ... '

Conductors move through the cars with obscure purposes, pushing by passengers, ignored, until at last there is a jolt, every passenger suddenly looks at someone, absurdly surprised to feel the train moving. The mother or grandmother already cutting salami and hunks of bread may not stir, but every child and many adults not yet at a window will go to one for a final wave or just with some inexplicable interest in watching the station recede, become distant, be left behind, a whole world of schedules and moving masses, a world center, an *axis mundus* of joinings and separations, and now this train packed with passengers, the in transit, those now between, some bearing gifts, some excited, some anxious, lurches forward, and every passenger somehow feels that lurch as more than merely the transition of immobility into motion.

There was no one on the quay for him, no one wiping tears on his behalf or waving, no shy half-comprehending toddler, bundled against mid-winter cold, watching him disappear around the turn, but he watched those there for others, sharing in this mystery of embarkation, undiminished by such trivia as that this one does it every week or that one is just going to a business meeting. He looked back as long as he could, until the train was no longer leaving the station, but moving through working class suburbs in unroofed tunnels of concrete walls and electric wires, gradually accelerating. He pulled open the glass door to the compartment and sat by the window. His travelling companion seated opposite looked at him briefly without expression, then returned to gazing out the window, as he did.

Perhaps she knew to leave him alone or simply had no need for his attention beyond offering a piece of chocolate or asking for a cigarette. After a while she took a novel from her purse and idled the time reading, but he stayed at the window, even when darkness came and little could be seen beyond his own reflection. He didn't know himself what he was looking at, or for, if he was interested or bored, tired or alert, only that he had no will to turn away and become just a man in a moving vehicle. From time to time the train would speed through a village station, not even slowing down, and this utter lack of acknowledgement, even on the part of railway workers who barely glanced up from their labor, seemed rude to him, if not bizarre. Each place, like a person, deserved at least to be noticed, if only because, without it, existence could not be verified.

There are people out there, he would think, great masses of them, each with a life, with tasks and cares, acquaintances, relatives, familiar places, particular habits, a need for aspirin or skin cream, a fondness for raspberry jam.

Forty years earlier his parents had gone with him to a demonstration to oppose the war of that time. It was not a large crowd and riot police were everywhere, with barricades to isolate the demonstrators and vans to carry them off to jail. Many police were mounted on large beautiful horses, chestnut colored, on saddles of rich thick leather. He could still remember the scene, and the policeman not five feet from him, but far above him, absolutely distant, superbly hostile. During a rousing speech, punctuated with frequent applause amid calls for negotiated peace, the horse suddenly reared up and came down right beside him. He, a child, thought little of it beyond the beauty of this majestic creature rising on its hind legs, but his father was suddenly taken with rage. He saw his mother, her face a picture of concern, put a restraining hand on his arm while he hissed at her, "These horses are trained, you think they rear up for no reason? What if one of the hooves had—?" But in the end his father said nothing to the policeman, only glared up at him. Whether the latter glared back or even deigned to look could not be known, being perfectly hidden behind mirrored sunglasses.

How beautiful the world in winter, he thought—no, not thought, merely sensed—how beautiful the snowed-over fields, the evergreen woods, stone boundaries and dwellings, and sometimes smoke rising from a chimney in a brief poem of warmth and family. What are the ideas in there? What concepts? He spent hours at the window, staring outside, pulling on cigarette after cigarette, simply staring, often without thought almost or reaction, sometimes barely noticing the changing country, the hills and fields. Even when it became too dark to see, he sat there staring, practically immobile, like a mental patient or a prisoner.

'What am I?' he thought. 'What is this journey?' He couldn't determine finally what his thoughts were, or even what he was thinking about. Was this a return? A pilgrimage? He would have been the first to admit that the years of imprisonment had sapped him of a certain vitality, of clarity. A train speeding through the night remains one of the most suggestive cliches, alluring images, remaining to a dying breed of romantic intellectual. He hadn't enough cigarettes to last the night. That thought made him tired, exhausted even.

Many years earlier, a young man with a wife and a baby in a time of national belligerence, a young man reeking of ideas, he had written, 'Thus am I returned to the blessed nothingness of which I am composed.'

Later, having gained a certain notoriety, students had flocked to him, swamped him with questions like 'What is the true purpose of art?' and 'What does this poem really mean?' He would smile, seated on the floor with them, so careful never to be above anyone, and try to teach them that profound questions are not posed so that answers can be found, they are posed so that answers may be considered. Then he would preach to them about engagement, about the artist's responsibility to express truth, how that was the first principle of art, from which all else flowed.

"I have another book if you want it," offered his young travelling companion, though she knew what he thought of her popular novels.

He barely turned from the window. "Thank you, no," he said.

"Bored?" she persevered.

He shook his head slightly, though in truth he couldn't say exactly what he felt. 'What is this journey?' he asked himself again. He thought back over the letters, the phone calls, messages delivered by intermediaries, hints, suggestions, words of advice in his own best interest delivered in all candor by true friends. 'What is this journey, so long in the making?' Years in the making, a lifetime. His wife was gone, his child gone, what was this journey?

"I don't know who you are," his wife would say to him, not when they were young and full of energy, but later, later. "They say you are important, some say dangerous, but to me you're just a poet." She would shrug and stand there, expecting an answer, while he turned away. If she were especially angry she might add, "And these co-eds who follow you, who hang on your every word and sigh at your readings—how many of them do you sleep with?" Long after she'd leave his study he would remain where he was, immobile, standing at the window.

Standing at that window, watching the world, waiting for the line of poetry or the critical idea, was among the things he missed most in prison. Well before they released him, his wife was gone.

"Sure you don't want to try it?" his companion persevered. "It sounds pretty good."

Sighing, he turned to look at her, feeling he owed her that courtesy. "No thanks," he said and smiled gently.

"I suppose you're nervous, is that it?"

For some reason he turned suddenly back to the window, then to the other passengers in the compartment, all sleeping, and gestured noncommittally. Suddenly it seemed almost embarrassing to be travelling with this woman half his age. He was relieved everyone was asleep, and wished that she would sleep. Who was she? She seemed like a stranger to him now, yet they had been intimate, had had pleasant times together.

"Do you have anything to eat?"

"Tons," she said with a twinkle, knowing he knew that.

Reaching for the bag of food, she nudged awake the elderly man pressed between her and his portly wife on the inside corner. He opened his eyes wide enough to show he was bothered by the lights they declined to turn off and then willed himself back to sleep with a turning of his body. The young woman made a face of amusement over this, not in the slightest affected by the old man's discomfort, and cut hunks of bread and salami in conscious mimicry of the motherly art.

He took it with a silent nod of thanks and began to eat it without much interest or enjoyment.

"I'd be nervous too," she said suddenly, and like an outburst of anger or criticism that simple comment unseated him mentally. He tried to mislead her with a smile, but she saw through it even before it had faded to a dull flat gaze from eyes grown tired of looking in.

"You don't know a damn thing about it," he muttered, thinking to himself, 'Ah, anger, the flimsy refuge of the guilty,' then, in confession, sighed, then laughed.

"I'd say you're in an odd mood," she pronounced, staring at him.

He was thinking of a poem he'd written once. It began,

the grim texture in which man's toys
in which man's toys so real to him

and ended,

thus the laugh must look both ways
before crossing to its certain shelter

"An odd mood, yes," he agreed. "As usual, no? I keep forgetting to look both ways. Does anyone remember?"

Of course she couldn't understand. "Are you making fun of me?" she asked, losing patience.

He shook his head reassuringly, comfortingly. 'How could she understand?' he thought. 'Not even a more perceptive person...'

"Is your book any good?" he inquired gently.

"You wouldn't like it," she replied, still a bit miffed.

"What's it about?"

"Spies."

He nodded and spoke no more. In response to a question, he had once told his interrogator, "No, I'm not a spy; but I am under deep cover." He had said that, even though he knew the interrogator was disgusted—or pretended to be disgusted—at his penchant for speaking on the same terms as he wrote: hint, imagery, innuendo. Because of that he had been treated harshly, roughed up a few times, insulted, and periodically held, without warning or explanation, in solitary confinement.

The man with the decorated chest would call him a romantic and snigger. "You romantics..." Or he might say, almost gently, "Once again, the romantic," and shake his head pityingly.

But he couldn't help speaking as he did, any more than he could change his way of writing. Neither was something chosen.

And he was helpless to see this experience as something other than the stuff of art. Imprisonment, like a journey by train, was such an arch-metaphor, and interrogation ... They knew how to frighten him, but when he wasn't frightened or in pain or maddened by inactivity he couldn't help but be moved almost by the artfulness of his circumstances.

Once, returned from solitary confinement to interrogation, he recited merrily,

> There once was a prisoner who'd know it
> If someone neglected to show it
> He'd point to his mask
> Saying 'don't even ask
> Because, don't you see, I'm a poet.'

At the time he was so taken with his work, he could scarcely blurt it out before doubling over in laughter.

Suddenly she was handing him a glass of red wine. "What's that?" he asked idiotically.

"Let's drink a whole bottle each and get drunk. It's like a morgue in here. Let's be gay." She was holding his glass towards him, watching his eyes that seemed only to stare at her until she pushed the glass into his hand, then held up hers for clinking.

Shortly before the first rumors began to arrive of his proposed "restoration," as it amused him to call it, they had gone late to a café after having been to the cinema to see a revival of "Gaslight," and had reveled in the parts of Ingrid Bergman and Charles Boyer until evicted by the proprietor with the single word, "closing," muttered half with apology and half resentment. They delighted in swaying their way back to his flat, arm in arm, he repeatedly saying "Paula" in that cloying, infuriating way, and each time they'd launch themselves into a fresh fit of laughter, until somehow she accidentally snapped her necklace of fake pearls, which she insisted on wearing, because, being a working woman, she must always dress up for occasions, never down. Fortunately a policeman came by and, with his flashlight, they were able to retrieve every pearl. They then thanked him and he saluted and went on his way, leaving the poet smiling vaguely to himself in the half-dark.

Upstairs she insisted on starting a fresh bottle of wine. "But," he protested, "it's late. How will you get up for church?"

"But I am not going to church tomorrow," she replied with a wicked and conspiratorial air, "I am going to lay in bed with you."

"But your friends, won't they be expecting you?" he countered, already selecting a bottle.

"But I have told them not to expect me," she said closing on him, her eyes twinkling. "But I have told them to come here instead, afterwards, and bring tons of food and all our friends."

He began to object mildly, with qualms. "But ... "

"But we are going to have a party. But first you are going to find a corkscrew and open that bottle."

After they had clinked glasses and tested the first sip, he turned away. "I like your friends," he mumbled, "but I barely know them. They're so young."

"They're as old as I am."

"That's what I mean," he said turning back.

She took his glass away and put it and hers on the table. "We're lovers," she whispered, fixing his eyes. "Lovers have no age."

He touched his glass to hers and drank mechanically, trying not to look at her, but not fully aware of his trying.

"Does the motion of the train disturb you? Drink," she urged. "You'll feel better."

"I feel fine," he protested half-heartedly. "I'm just tired."

"You're a bit nervous. It's all right," she added quickly, "who wouldn't be? On the other hand, of course I know nothing of such things, but they say it's a great honor. Don't you feel honored?"

He tried to answer. After all she was right, he thought, at least in a sense, in her terms. The problem was that he had always rejected honor—not being honorable, but accepting honors, accolades. Applause, praise had never really touched him because he could never fully accept its premise, that, if honestly bestowed—which he always doubted—it meant his art had succeeded. "Art must always fail," he had taught, "but fail in a certain way, of its own success, if you will. Art that merely succeeds is superficial, pandering." He felt badly: she really was trying to buoy his spirits, and the more she tried the more he resisted. He should have been willing to let her succeed, at least for her sake, but all he could do was remark at how unbearably hot it had become in the compartment and fill the ensuing silence with pretended interest in his wine, going so far as to inquire about the vintage.

She suggested they try to sleep, noting that he'd said he was tired. When he didn't object she urged him to drain his glass—to help him sleep—and took her own advice.

He sat in the dark until he judged she was asleep and then lit up a cigarette. In the flicker of the match he thought fleetingly that she was as wakeful as he, and sitting there resentful of his little deceit, but realized with relief he was alone. For a while he sat there trying to enjoy the cigarette before giving in to his usual practice of smoking without noticing it because he was thinking or writing.

A student once asked how he wrote. "I write the same way I go to the bathroom," he replied, and everyone tittered. "Excuse me for using a crude image, but the analogy is accurate. When I feel like I have a poem to write, I go to my study and write it. All I have before I write is an idea or a feeling—more often a feeling." He shrugged apologetically. "Some prefer the analogy of sex. For me it's not like that."

For a while he thought he might have a poem coming. He hoped not, because he would have to put the light back on and wake people up, so he tried to think about what he might say in his acceptance speech. As before he was unsuccessful. He'd always taught that an artist can't know what he's doing, or how well, unless he knows what he's trying to do, and that was precisely his problem: he couldn't decide what to do with this … occasion. Sometimes he thought he might stand at the microphone just long enough to say, 'Ladies and gentlemen, thank you very much,' and then return to his seat, leaving it to his hosts to resolve the ensuing confusion. Other times he imagined telling the entire biography of his exile, but that quickly fractured into misleading digressions, images that lacked clarity, or sardonic humor. It was that last that frightened him most. He saw it as self-pitying, hence weak, and he would not show weakness, he would not, he would not …

When it had finally dawned on him that his interrogator might have been telling the truth when he'd informed him that his wife was gone, his entire body had begun to tremble, beginning with his hands and then travelling up his arms and down to his legs that buckled beneath him. For hours he sat on the cold floor in the corner, his head against the wall, in a kind of delirium, thinking feverishly without thought, racked by emotions that terrified him. 'Why so bereft,' he kept repeating, 'she's been gone for quite a while, only now it's a confirmed physical fact.' Perhaps that was what was so painful, the objective confirmation. He tried to console himself by noting that she had never accepted his fame, nor his notoriety—of course, neither had he, but in a different sense—but it didn't help. Her abandonment seemed a final indignity. He tried seeking refuge in the possibility that the interrogator was lying—after all, he had lied often, deceit was his stock in trade—but his first idea subverted the second: She'd been gone for quite a while; what did it matter whether or not she was still there?

Eventually his thoughts centered on the realization that he was probably going to be taken for interrogation soon—he became certain of it as he was certain they had told him about his wife (true or false, it didn't matter) in hopes of breaking him down—and he could not bear the sight of himself trembling before his tormentor. He had never accepted the concept of manliness, such as the notion that it was weak to show hurt, but he became possessed of a steely determination not to show pain. He must face him with a steady gaze and discuss the situation without flinching—but why? Why, he kept asking himself, must he behave so, what consequence could it have? For that matter, what was the point of this entire … drama he was playing out, why didn't he simply denounce his own work as they demanded and be done with it? Whether he did or not, the end would be the same; his work had already been denounced by everyone else, at least everyone whose voice was heard. But of course he knew why. Because the interrogator was correct: he belonged to a dying breed of romantic intellectual.

He discovered himself staring out the window. It was easier to see with the lights off, though there was still little to be discerned—lines of trees, buildings, hedgerows. He realized he had finished his cigarette and was wanting another, but he felt in the pack that there were only a few left, so he tried to lose himself in the movement of the train. He knew he was back in his own country: the train had stopped a while back, that would be the border. Passport control officials would be working their way through the compartments. As he had that thought he watched himself for any particular reaction; there was a slight one, not much. He wondered if they would hesitate over his passport, ask him questions in front of the four strangers in the compartment that would start them wondering about this person who wouldn't sleep, but he closed the thought with a shrug. Who was he, anyway, hardly some notable. Just a middle-aged man in an old rumpled suit, staring out the window of a dark train compartment as it sped through the night, thinking this and hoping it wasn't the seed of a new poem: darkness out there, darkness out there, darkness out there, darkness out there ...

These words came to him:

> nobody makes trees—they come from their own land which we
>
> cannot name, thank God, we cannot name it

The glass door slid open without warning and the younger of two officials called for passports as he turned on the light. The poet flinched in surprise and squinted at the sudden brightness as the other passengers tore themselves from sleep. His companion looked at him and he felt she knew he hadn't been sleeping, which made him feel almost ashamed, as though he had deceived her, and so he watched her with an affectionate smile as the older official took his passport.

Almost immediately, it seemed, it was being returned to him, and with a nod of solicitude, if not deference. They'd barely had time to look at it, he thought. 'Is it possible they recognize my name?' Then what to make of their politeness?

They left as suddenly as they came, with the suggestion of a salute, the room returned to dark, and the noisy slide of the heavy glass door. He could do nothing but sit there, trying to dispense with silly conjectures about what significance there might have been in the routine inspection of a passport, instead trying to listen to the grunts of the passengers as they tried to find a comfortable position in which to fall back asleep, when his companion suddenly got up to turn the light back on.

"Ah, no," complained the old man beside her, "but what does this mean?" The others merely watched in silence.

"I can't sleep," she replied. "If you can, I suggest you do so," and, with a grunt of displeasure, the old man did just that, accompanied by the others, leaving the poet and his companion to stare at each other in uncertain silence.

"I couldn't sleep," he said finally with a shrug, defending himself.

"I'll stay up with you," she replied, keeping her eyes on his.

He tried to protest—actually he would have preferred to be left alone—but she insisted, demanding a cigarette, which he lit for her before handing it over without speaking.

"Aren't you having one?"

"There are only a few left."

She made a face. "For God sake, I've got two more packs in my bag." With the slightest of blank nods he reached for another cigarette. She watched him inhale deeply and exhale a great quantity of smoke, then pick off a piece of tobacco from his lip. "You don't find me attractive anymore, do you?" she asked simply.

He waved away the question with his cigarette hand, then turned to the window, unable for the first time to peer beyond his own reflection. "I wonder where we are. Bizarre, isn't it, to not know where you are?"

"We're near the border," she noted and watched him for quite a while before reaching for her novel. When she did he felt relieved, though he was careful not to show it, and he had almost succeeded in putting her out of his mind when she said, without even looking up, obviously only pretending to be reading, "I wonder why you asked me to come with you." He sighed in frustration. "You know men don't stare at my legs and that I don't understand what you write, so I'm not much to show off. Yet you practically begged me to come along. You would have insisted."

'She deserves better than she's getting,' he thought, but could think of nothing to say. Success is always incomplete; defeat at least offers a confirmation; but most lives move in the middle ground, that vast shifting area where events are rarely comprehended by reference to some standard, rather by feel. Perhaps she was too young to understand that there are times when the last thing a man wants is to be known.

He felt old. He wanted to bathe, to sleep, not to hurt her. She wasn't really reading, he knew that. As he stared at her, at her calm, hurt, slightly bored face, terror rose up in him as he felt his knowledge of her recede like an undertow, until in desperation and fear he saw some total stranger sitting across from him, a young woman, pleasant but not notable, with nylons and cosmetics, smoking a cigarette and reading a pulp thriller. Why, he wondered, was he in this train? What, precisely, did he mean to do? Exile had been granted him in stages; he had, in a sense, started with exile; but inclusion had been thrust upon him without time to prepare a new face ... if it was inclusion. He was wary as a patrol in hostile territory, no act was above suspicion. Keep your guard up. If you must write, write to kill.

This memory came to him: One winter, when his son was very young, he had taken him out on a sled, pulling him down the lane beyond the little house where they had lived then, between fields and woods in deep snow. There were no cars, no people, both of them utterly mute, his baby bundled up in warm clothes, with a scarf wound around his face so only his eyes could be seen, those little, huge eyes, just looking, looking. How long ago was that? He could see it now, feel it now, as if— They'd been able to live there such a short time. But those eyes, those little, huge eyes ... There'd be deer in the back yard and the little child, climbing up on a stool, would watch them from the window with complete attention while he protected him from falling.

"I'd like to hear about the novel," he said suddenly, surprising himself. He hadn't known he was going to say that.

She studied him, then said, "Okay. It's not really very good, though."

"That's okay," he whispered, trying to put conciliation into his voice.

She sat up straight, put her head back to stretch her neck, breathed deeply. "Let's have some more wine, okay?" When their glasses were full, she began. "It's kind of silly, really. There's this art professor who used to be a secret agent, and they want him to do one more mission, but he refuses, so they force him. It's kind of clever, actually, how they do that ... "

He'd met her in a café, not far from the train station, where he'd been watching her and her girl friends giggling and poking fun at each other. There were three in all, all young, possibly students, but more likely working women, he thought, and he couldn't help but attach himself to their banter and merriment. Whenever he entered a café or restaurant he tried to sit at the edge facing in, not from some fear of leaving his back exposed, but so that he could scan the whole scene, an explorer looking down on new territory, an astronaut looking down on new worlds. They were seated some distance from him, he felt secure, but suddenly, as if on signal they turned to him and waved, then, giggling and exhorting each other, they waved him over. Naturally he was embarrassed, but decided instantly he would hate himself if he refused, and, with a few drinks inside him, he was feeling a bit brave; so, astonishing himself, he rose and approached.

Sitting, he glanced furtively to see if anyone appeared to be remarking upon a man his age sitting down with three girls, considered an apology for having eavesdropped, and settled for a self-conscious introduction.

They asked him what he did, and, when he replied that he worked as a translator, their faces all went blank, as though they didn't know what that was. He was about to explain when one of them said tentatively, "I think Sylvia wins." Considering it, the others agreed, and then she explained. "She guessed teacher. We guessed shopkeeper and office worker. You don't work in an office, do you?"

Later they strolled about town, always one on each of his arms, while one of them waited her turn, irrepressibly merry, cracking jokes and asking him question after question about life and age.

FROM

Exhalations

of the

Intellect

THAT THE FIRE WITHIN US MAY SINGE THE
HOPE OF HEAVEN IS A FACT TOO EASILY MISLAID.
THUS HAVE WE NO CHOICE BUT TO INHALE
IN SMOKY DOUBT THE FIERY EXHALATIONS
OF OUR INTELLECT.

Doing
the Right Thing

Microbiology is my field. In the early seventies I was a pioneer in recombinant DNA research, though only a post-doctoral fellow. My ex-husband used to be a political scientist. My grandfather was a socialist who had been active in trade union activities before going into business for himself.

Not long before he died I visited him at the nursing home. Always he insisted on watching me leave, so I wheeled him to the door and kissed him on top of his head. Something came over him; slowly a large grin overtook his face—an unusual occurrence those months since my grandmother had died. They had been married sixty-two years; think about that: sixty-two years.

"What's funny? What?" I asked, smiling.

As always, he didn't respond immediately. "I remember," he said slowly, still smiling, his hands gesturing, "when I kissed the top of your head. Now you kiss mine. Oh yes, I remember."

It seemed his eyes watered, and I felt tears in mine as he looked at me, a whole history in his loving gaze, ages and ages of doings, ideas, successes and failures, whole philosophies and systems tested, discarded, reworked. The world he was born into, a distant land, an abandoned language; another age, a wholly different time upon the earth, yet prepared to give birth, through struggle, discovery, heroism, and bestiality of every sort to the banal trivia we call everyday life. "That was a long time ago, grandpa," I whispered.

He nodded, smiling even more broadly. "A long time. A long time." The way he said it, it wasn't a long time. To him, I knew, it was the day before yesterday. Even to me it seemed recent; I could almost remember with my skin how he would kiss me, his hands gripping my shoulders, and then how he would wag a finger at me, half joking, half serious, admonishing me to study hard. "Study hard," he would say. "Some day you'll be a leader!" A leader. I remember how he would say that, the magical meaning of that word, and my mother would always scold him, "Pa, she's only eight years old. Pa, she's only ten years old. Pa, she's only in ninth grade, she's got time."

"So," he said finally, with a hint of a sigh, "you have things to do, and I have things to do … "

"Goodbye, grandpa." I kissed him again, called over an attendant, and left, turning at the door to wave. He waved back, but it wasn't really waving, it was a different kind of gesture, like a blessing, both happy and sad.

Fifteen years ago Philip Janowitz, the faculty member in whose laboratory I was working, suggested to me a very elegant and very exciting experiment that would become my project. Shorn of its technicalities it was really quite simple. Our lab was studying— "looking at" was how we liked to express it—the functioning of animal cells; that is, we were looking at the processes by which genes, the complex molecular formations that somehow contain in their chemical structure the information for a certain trait, caused a cell to "express" that trait. You could say we were trying to find the answer—really, trying to discover pieces of the answer—to a question such as, "How does a person come to have a certain protein, hemoglobin for example?" Or, perhaps more importantly, "How does a person come to have cancer?"

You can see the significance of the research.

But, truth to tell, we didn't talk much about significance. We didn't even think that much about it. Even today, after all that's happened, I'm not sure why. Maybe it seems too pretentious. I suspect, though, it has more to do with the fact that science has a way of functioning on a technical level. We talk about our research, about the details of our science, and of course we converse in the jargon of our trade. There isn't any easy or clear or even necessary method for jumping to a different perspective (some would say higher level).

The main work of the lab was to see if a bacterial virus gene would "express"—exhibit its trait—in an animal cell, but my particular experiment was to test the opposite: to see if an animal virus would express in bacteria. In addition to what we might learn about cell functioning, we would discover a relatively easy and efficient way to culture an animal virus. Obviously it's easier to grow and harvest a monkey virus in a dish full of bacteria than in a lab full of monkeys.

I was deeply troubled by the experiment, so troubled that I wasn't sure I wanted to perform it. You see, in the process of studying cell function we were developing techniques as an aid to lab efficiency, as almost a by-product of our research, of altering the genetic structure of viruses and plant and animal cells. The alterations we were capable of effecting were quite elementary compared with the complexity of most organisms; nonetheless our work was the beginning of developing the capability to intervene in and manipulate genetic structures and processes. Even we ourselves referred to the whole business as genetic engineering. And if that term had an exciting ring to some, to others among us it was disquieting, even frightening.

Even if you didn't let yourself get carried away with nightmare visions of *Brave New World*-type scenarios, with test-tube mass production of half-witted human slaves, you had to wonder about the implications of scientists learning how to alter life-forms and create new ones. What purposes would this capability serve: good ones only? How would this capability be controlled, regulated, directed?

And how would we know whether what seemed useful and desirable would turn out to be harmful, perhaps catastrophically so?

It seemed to me that no scientist with a social conscience, that no scientist who gave any thought to the possible applications of her work, could fail to at least pause in thought over what might happen when this Pandora's box was opened.

"Okay, then," said Michael, holding the forkful in mid-air, "let's damn well pause."

"I'm pausing, I'm pausing. But what should I do?"

"Tell him to go screw himself, how's that?"

I chewed slowly, not tasting anything. "Aside from the fact that not even biologists have developed that capability, I fail to see how it would improve the situation."

Michael was unmoved. "You know what I mean," he said, his mouth full.

"You mean, not do the experiment, right?"

"Right and damn right."

We ate in silence. I could feel his eyes on me as I studied my food. "You know it's not so simple."

"Never is," he replied quickly, then added, "it really is, though, isn't it? I mean if you can't do the experiment, then you can't do the experiment."

"But I'm not sure," I began.

He cut me off. "Not sure of what? You told me yourself you couldn't do it, otherwise what are we talking about? I mean what do I—?"

"I didn't say I couldn't do the experiment, I—"

He threw his fork down. "What? Who said it then? I could have sworn I was eating dinner with you."

"Shut up, Michael. I said it, but if I was so sure I wasn't going to do it, I wouldn't have asked you about it, would I?"

He shook his head. "I don't see where you've got any choice."

"There's always a choice."

"Between right and wrong? Where's the choice?"

"Oh Michael, spare me," I snapped. "You always do that. Maybe it's not that simple. First of all, I'm not sure I'm right. I mean, aren't I being just a little grand about the importance of my work?"

"Come on, Joanie, you'll have to do better than that."

"Maybe we can do it differently. Redesign it."

Michael paused. "Can you do that?"

"I don't know," I whispered. We ate in silence. I was eating for something to do, my appetite was gone. "Even if it could," I said quietly, "it's not for me— I mean, he's the teacher, I'm the student."

"That doesn't make him God, you know."

I nodded energetically. "It might as well. I mean, what did we go through so I could study with him." It wasn't a question.

I remember when I told my grandfather I was going to major in biology. I was sixteen. "Biology," he repeated. "Biology." He was thinking, but looking right at me.

"Biology," I repeated, nodding, fixed by his gaze.

"Biology. So, what will you do with this biology? Become a doctor?"

"Uh-uh—"

"What, uh-uh? You have some objection?"

"No, grandpa, I just haven't decided yet."

"Pa, what's your hurry?" shouted my mother from the kitchen, "she's only sixteen, she's barely half-way through high school."

Immediately my grandmother said, "He's only asking. There's harm in that?"

"I haven't decided yet, grandpa, I just know I want to study biology."

He made a gesture with his lips to show he was impressed, looking at me sideways. One thing about him, he was never in a hurry to speak. You couldn't rush him. "You'll go to a fine university," he began, "and study with the best. Study hard," he added suddenly, "and"—I could have finished the sentence—"one day you'll be a leader."

"Pa," shouted my mother, "again with the leader?"

I smiled uncomfortably. I didn't really mind him saying that, but it bothered me when my mother objected. Grandpa was still looking at me.

"What?" I asked, unable to wait any longer.

He smiled, nodded, never taking his eyes off me. "Biology," he said finally, slowly. "The science of life. You will study life." The way he said it, there wasn't a grander pursuit under the sun. I wasn't sure I had thought of it that way. He made it seem grand. "You will study life," he repeated just as slowly.

That night, in bed, I heard him again, over and over. To him it was somehow implicit in the decision that there was a moral purpose. I think that business about the leader really meant that I would be some kind of force for good in the world . . . in some as yet unspecified way. Because I always associated my grandfather with a kind of moral activism. Not for any reason you could pin down. A saint he wasn't. But I had grown up with his stories about his former days, when he had fought for a better world, and I had built into me the notion that what he expected of me—and what I expected of myself—was to improve the world.

"That's fine for when you're sixteen, Joan, but you're not a teenager anymore. Yes," he added quickly and with emphasis, "of course we have to maintain an awareness of the potential good or harm that could come from our work," and then continued in his normal voice, "but we've got to do it within a context of a mature professionalism. No, I'm serious," he said in response to my look.

"Context of a mature professionalism? Give me a break, Dick."

"You don't agree?"

"Agree with what? It's double-talk." Then I added more frankly, "It's bullshit."

Dick looked sincerely offended. "Maybe the bullshit is in elevating a post-doc experiment to the level of a major intervention in the natural order and a revolutionary breakthrough in biology."

I almost surprised myself at the readiness with which I nodded agreement. "You could be right. If I'm blowing this all out of proportion, I need you to tell me that."

Dick looked at me and said gently, "You're blowing this all out of proportion."

Michael and I had finished by arguing. It was ridiculous; I knew I was just frustrated, and that made him frustrated. There really wasn't anything he could do for me. He realized that himself: He came into my study a little later and said quietly, "Look, what does a political scientist know about biology? You need to talk to your colleagues. Someone you can trust."

That of course is what I should have done in the first place instead of picking a fight with my husband. I'm not sure why I hadn't done that. Part of the reason is that the colleague I had always most trusted, and whose opinion I would still greatly respect on a moral question in science, was Jeff Hardwick. But there was a problem: for most of our years in grad school we had gone together. We had broken up in my last year after I'd met Michael, who was also a grad student, and, though he wasn't the cause of our breaking up, there were some messy triangulations for a while. I think it took some courage for Michael to make that suggestion, because he'd have known I'd call Jeff.

Except that I didn't call Jeff, and I worried that the main reason was that I knew what he would tell me. Instead I asked Dick Davidson, on the grounds that, as a co-worker in the lab, he was in a better position to evaluate the project. Of course it would also avoid any possibility of some unpleasantness. I respected Dick; he was a good scientist. I also knew, though, that we weren't the same—he had a very different background, outlook. I told myself that that was a plus—it would lend another perspective—but it's possible I chose him because I knew he'd tell me to go ahead. I have to live with that.

"I really think you're blowing this out of proportion," Dick repeated.

"Somehow I suspected you'd say that."

"Is that a compliment?"

I was embarrassed. "I'm sorry. Can we strike that comment?"

We talked for quite a while and in the end he convinced me, I convinced myself, I let myself be convinced that it was okay to do the experiment. Perhaps the clincher was his pointing out to me that it wasn't overly logical (his choice of words) to select a post-doc primarily for the purpose of working under a certain researcher, and then refuse the project he suggested. Philip Janowitz was one of the most highly regarded microbiologists in the country. His lab was doing pioneering research. He had a shot at a Nobel, and he had accepted me to work with him. Not everyone got to work under Janowitz.

Dick also pointed out that, "not seeking to offend your vanity," the contribution I would be making to recombinant DNA research would be quite modest indeed. I smiled and thanked him.

"Are we done?"

I nodded. "I think we're done."

"Good. Now can you help me with something?"

"Of course. If I can. What's up?"

"We're having a problem with the lambda phage … "

So I consented to do the experiment. At least I would proceed with the problem (at that time it wasn't clear how to successfully insert an SV 40-lambda phage hybrid into a bacterium) on the grounds that, even if successful, we would still be a long way from manipulating human genetics. My very strong desire to work on cell function and to work under Janowitz—a desire that seemed to me (then and now) reasonable and justifiable—eventually controlled the decision.

Later I went walking alone so I could talk to my grandfather. What do you say, grandpa, am I making the right decision? I'm studying hard, with the best; someday I could be a leader. Is this what you meant? I'm a pioneer in rDNA research, my mentor may get a Nobel Prize, the potential for my own career is pretty exciting. Is all this what you meant?

It took the next six months to work out a procedure for getting the hybrid into the bacterium, but by June we were pretty sure we had it. Not bad for my first year after grad school. Now all we needed was the hybrid. That was the project Dick Davidson had been working on, and it had proceeded slowly.

A few weeks later I went to Long Island for a three-week course in cell culture techniques. I'd been conflicted over it because there was a reasonably good chance Jeff would be there.

"Are you worried for me or you?" asked Michael.

I shrugged. "Both, I guess."

He turned away from me, thinking, then turned back shrugging with his eyes and shoulders. "My science doesn't provide ready answers for this sort of question. What about yours?"

"Mine doesn't either."

He really didn't seem worried—maybe he should have been—so I went. So did Jeff.

I was understandably edgy, not only because Jeff was there—a turn of events that made both of us just as uncomfortable as I was afraid it would—but also because this was really my first foray among my colleagues outside the lab since having made the decision to do the experiment. I had to confess I wasn't so secure in my position that I was anxious to have it reviewed, especially by a group such as this. In a very curious fashion it turned out that my anxiety was justifiable, but for an entirely different reason.

The course was taught by some very able people, including some of the big names in the field, and among the students were several at least who were brilliant and were likely to do some exciting work in their careers—including Jeff—but, characteristically, the course functioned entirely on a technical level. There was no attempt to pull back, try to scan what we were doing, discuss its possible implications, maybe even its applications. Instead it was all details, and naturally our language was so thick with jargon, an outsider couldn't have understood ten percent of what was said.

And here I was, bursting with the desire—the need—to look at the issues. That's my background, that's who I am. But in that whole group—and there were lots of people there—there was only one person I knew who would sympathize with my concerns: Jeff Hardwick.

You must understand, I'm not suggesting the others were not concerned scientists, were not moral people. It's just that—as I've said—science operates on a technical level most of the time. Few if any among us—including myself—are comfortable on any other level. True, there are many who disparage any attempts at "philosophizing"—a reaction deeply imbedded, I'm afraid, in our training; but even many of these would be willing to confront larger issues when presented with the desirability of doing so.

Paradoxically, at the same time that I was yearning for someone to talk to about "significance," I was dreading it. Aside from my insecurity, this nightmare fantasy kept recurring of Jeff and me locked in a shouting match, surrounded by our non-plussed colleagues who thought we were arguing over political differences.

Two weeks into the course there was a session on lab safety. Most of us were there, including Jeff. It was led by John Dederick, who was a very very good scientist. If I hadn't gone to work with Janowitz, I might have applied to work with Dederick—which is what Jeff had done.

As expected, the session was occupied with hazards to lab workers, with numerous suggestions for safety procedures. We came out pretty well—Janowitz's lab, I mean. When he had changed over the lab to work on SV 40—that's the virus we were using to try to insert genes into cells—a number of procedures had been instituted, and a fair amount of hardware installed (such as laminar flow hoods, negative-pressure rooms), to increase personal safety. At the time we probably had one of the safer labs going. But, remembering my student days, when we did everything right out on the bench—mouth pipetting and all—it didn't surprise me that a lot of jaws were hanging out, listening to Dederick recount the hazards to which people in that room were routinely exposing themselves.

All right, that was good; consciousness was being raised on an important issue; but I was squirming in my seat. Wasn't this all beside the point? No, not beside the point, but not the main point. Here we were, talking about lab hazards, as though the safety issue ended at the lab exit. What about hazards outside the lab: the impact of our work on society at large? In my mind I heard myself speak the words 'society at large' and felt embarrassed smiles, awkward glances, and tired sighs. Convinced of the futility of raising my concern, and of the inappropriateness of doing so in this session, I resolved to say nothing (afterwards, over coffee, perhaps, I could present it gradually to a few people) ... but then raised my hand.

It will never be known who was more astonished by what followed, my colleagues or I. To introduce the issue of genetic engineering, I began by describing our work and, in particular, my experiment. That's as far as I got. It's no exaggeration to say that Dederick was dumbfounded, which heartened me tremendously, because I believed he was seeing the same implications I was, and was equally concerned. (Perhaps, unknowingly, I was affected by the fact that Jeff worked under Dederick, which in some non-logical way implied a common "political" outlook.) It soon became apparent, however, how utterly wrong I was.

Of course everyone was well aware of the fact that SV 40 virus had been shown to cause cancer in lab mice. The lab had been beefed up precisely to counter the risk of anyone ingesting the virus and possibly getting cancer, but that wasn't Dederick's concern. He was focussed on the fact that, when I ran my experiment, I would be injecting a known carcinogen into a bacterium that was capable of colonizing the human intestine.

"But, as I've explained, we've pretty well covered the ingestion hazard."

"For which I'm pleased," said Dederick without any show of pleasure. "But just bear with me a moment." He paused for emphasis. "Suppose—just suppose—that by injecting your SV 40 you induce carcinogenicity in your E. coli. And further suppose that despite your estimable safety barriers a little of this carcinogen escapes from your lab—in any of a dozen ways you or I could imagine. And further suppose that this carcinogen survives just long enough to find a human host. Would I be totally out of line to fear a possible cancer epidemic?"

Even if I could remember my thoughts and feelings at that moment, I am not a good enough journalist to describe them. In a way it was almost comical how I'd been totally and unexpectedly turned around, but neither I nor anyone else in that room was chuckling.

Dederick... You could see him mentally reeling in front of us; and I was reeling with him. My project had been almost an afterthought to the main work of the lab, which was to see if a bacterial virus would express in an animal cell. I'd originally been working on an assay procedure for the virus, but dropped it in my excitement to test an idea that had occurred to Janowitz in the middle of a lecture ... which was, of course, to see if an animal virus would express in a bacterium. The symmetry of the proposal was so attractive, none of us considered the fact that bacterial cells are fundamentally different from animal cells in the following crucial way: they can survive and propagate outside the lab.

I heard myself defending the experiment, citing the extensive physical and procedural safety features we had instituted; but Dederick was unmoved. He spun out one scenario after another showing how, one, the bacterium could escape the lab, and, two, how it could create a public health hazard of catastrophic proportions.

Against each scenario I posited one or more defenses that would serve to greatly reduce the perceived risk, even if I had to agree that any complete elimination of risk was probably impossible. For example, what if we used a mutated form of the bacterium, one that was incapable of surviving outside the lab? Dederick replied very calmly—was it my imagination that there was a trace of hauteur in his manner?—approximately as follows: "Ms. Barrett, you have nobly defended an experimental procedure that I dare say excites all of us for its scientific promise. However, I think that upon careful reflection you will be moved to concur that, whereas the risks I have posited can be reduced—perhaps substantially reduced—by means such as you suggest, they cannot be reduced to zero. And I suggest to you that, in this case, given our present level of ignorance, any risk greater than zero is an unacceptable one to impose on society."

The discussion continued—a discussion in which about three dozen scientists sat in stunned and embarrassed silence while two debated—even though the question (the one that hadn't even been asked) had been resolved. I have no clear memory of anything said at this time. I do remember my attempt to leave the room while meeting as few eyes as possible—one pair in particular (but he had left, I believe out of consideration for me).

The next three hours I spent in my room, ostensibly listening to some German opera. In the dinner line Dederick suddenly appeared, having asked the person behind me if it would be permissible to cut in. "Jeff Hardwick, who sometimes fills a useful office regarding such matters, informs me that I may have advanced my position this afternoon with too much force. If that's the case, then I believe apologies are in order."

"Not at all," I replied diplomatically, trying to smile, "I value your insights."

"I have it on Jeff's authority that you are a dedicated and earnest investigator. Considering that you work with Phil Janowitz, it would be foolish to doubt it."

Jeff wasn't there. In fact, from furtive glances I couldn't discover him anywhere in the cafeteria. I found myself wishing he would join us. He had evidently developed a close relationship with a man who, despite his stilted manner and the apparent adversarial relationship of our positions, I very much wanted to talk to further. Apart from anything else, I yearned to have him know that, far from being adversaries, we were really in complete agreement.

There were eight of us at table, and, though Dederick had communicated his wish to converse with me alone, there was an unavoidable tendency for the others to listen in on us, which, of course, did little to ease my tension. I told him how I myself had raised the same concerns as he regarding a potential risk to society.

"Ah, so you were, in fact, aware of the problem of external viability."

"No, I wasn't actually. No, my concerns had a different basis."

"Indeed," he said, raising his eyebrows disconcertingly. "What basis, pray?"

Gulping, I forged ahead, but, as I expected, I couldn't arouse his concern over the implications of genetic engineering (and of course I never used that phrase, but always 'recombinant techniques'). How I wished Jeff would show up!

He didn't—or chose not to—deny my concerns, as he might have, as others I could name would have; rather he suggested (with unexpected delicacy) that they were negligible.

"I hope it won't seem paradoxical to you," I inserted quickly, "if I tell you that I agree with you. That's why I consented to do the project." His style of speech was infecting mine; I hoped he hadn't noticed. "No," I continued, "it's the longer-range implications I'm concerned about." Even as he nodded seriously in appreciation of my concern, it was obvious (to me at least) that the range was so long he couldn't see it. When we got up to return our trays I noticed that Jeff was somehow sitting a few tables behind me.

Not one person spoke to me that evening about my position. How could they? I kept telling myself, they don't know what my position is. Of all the ludicrous ...

When it was dark I went out for a long walk. There was a week of this course left and I wanted to make sure I knew what I wanted to get out of it. Whether or not I succeeded in working anything out I don't recall: I have no recollection of anything during that walk except that I covered the same ground several times and was faintly ill from dinner.

Five minutes after I returned to my room there was a knock at the door. "Hi," said Jeff.

"Hi."

"How are you?"

"Okay."

He nodded, at what I'm not sure. "I, um, I thought I'd stop by. I thought maybe ... to see if you might want to talk."

"I think I might," I replied too loudly, with a forced laugh. He nodded. "Cup of coffee maybe?"

"If you want," I shrugged.

"I don't care, really. I mean, just a place where we can talk."

"Why don't you just come in. I mean is that all right?"

"Yeah, sure," he said easily. "The simple solutions are usually the best, right?"

"Right," I agreed with false energy. "Anyway, it's private here."

"Even the walls have ears, huh?" he teased.

I shrugged. "I don't know. It's foolish. I can't help feeling everybody's looking at me."

Jeff was suddenly serious, as he shut the door. "They are." I made a pained face. "Wouldn't you look at someone who was about to make history?"

"Oh come on."

He just looked at me, nodding. My hands fell to my sides and I turned away.

"But, Joanie, haven't you thought of the engineering implications? I mean you're cloning DNA—"

I turned back quickly. "But that's just it, Jeff!" I almost shouted, "I've spent the whole year worrying about it! And then to come here and … It's crazy. It's ludicrous." Jeff was always a good listener; I told him the whole story from the beginning; then I answered the question; then I asked him the question. He agreed and I nodded.

"There goes my project."

"There's another one."

"Where?"

"Janowitz'll find one."

"If he doesn't ask me to leave."

"Don't over-react."

I nodded to myself, then to him. "Thanks."

"You're welcome."

"Why didn't you join us at dinner?" I asked suddenly.

He shrugged. "I wasn't invited."

"I wish you would have. It would have made it easier. Thanks for talking to him." Silence again. "He's not an easy guy to talk to. How do you do it?"

"You mean just cause he talks like a … ?" he laughed. "You get past it."

I shook my head. "Past it, my foot. Before I knew it, I was talking the same way."

Jeff laughed knowingly.

"Thanks for talking to him."

We sat in silence for a while. "It's funny how it turned out. Strange. Isn't it?"

He smiled. "You know what they say." I smiled and we said it together: "The path of the righteous is not very wide!" Our laughter lingered a bit, then drifted again into silence.

When Jeff broke it, his voice was a little tense. "Things seem to be going well for you. I'm— I just wanted to say … that I'm happy for you. I really am." I reached over and squeezed his hand. "How are things going?"

"Fine. Good. You mean with Michael? Good. I mean we're not the perfect couple, but—" He looked up at me suddenly and we almost shouted together: "Life is less than perfection!"

After the laughter and the silence I asked how things were going with him. "Okay," he answered breezily. "No complaints."

"Are you going with anyone?"

"No."

"Any prospects?" I suggested with a nervous giggle.

"Maybe. One or two."

"Lots of women in Cambridge."

"Don't worry, I can take care of myself."

I bit my tongue and re-tuned the radio.

Finally Jeff half-smiled at me. "Sorry."

There wasn't much sleep that night. Each time I turned off the radio the silence was so disturbing I turned it on again. Finally at about three AM I fell asleep over a novel, and then the alarm went off at six forty-five. I wrestled with my conscience valiantly, then surrendered on the premise that my career would survive missing the morning session. It was too early in the day to face anyone.

During lunch I contrived to meet Dederick and informed him abruptly that of course I had decided to cancel my project. If he was surprised or pleased he didn't show it.

"Could I be allowed to proffer a suggestion?" He offered to speak to Janowitz before I did. He said he would outline the concerns for him and let him know that it was upon his recommendation that I 'proposed' to cancel the experiment. Considerably relieved, I thanked him more than once, frankly surprised at the degree of tact in his suggestion.

"Ms. Barrett, I believe you are doing the noble thing." (I couldn't help noticing that he seemed to like the word 'noble,' and had to quickly suppress a giggle.) "I am cognizant of the disturbance to your line of investigation caused by the cancellation of the experiment. Perhaps you can find relief in the knowledge that you are responsive to the larger concerns."

I thanked him again, realizing that Jeff must have gotten to him before me.

Events took another unpredictable turn: Janowitz declined to cancel the experiment. According to Dederick he had two objections: First, he thought the biohazards issue was blown way out of proportion, and, second, since there was as yet no way to create the viral hybrid we needed, the whole issue was moot.

Michael met me at the airport with one question on his mind, which he managed (with visible effort) to postpone until after we had said hello. "You're not going to do it, are you?"

"No, Michael," I replied evenly through clenched teeth, "I am not going to do it."

In retrospect it seemed clear that it was because of Michael's attitude that I had gotten it into my head, without really considering it, that Janowitz would be pissed at my refusal to do the experiment. As it turned out, however, he chose to believe that I was simply requesting an alternative project—"a development not unknown in the annals of post-doctoral work." I couldn't help asking if he was upset by my decision, that is, request. "I do have other students, Ms. Barrett," he replied tersely. It hurt that he called me Ms. Barrett, but if that was the extent of his show of anger (it was), I could stand it. (Another twist: the experiment was never performed. He was to abandon it later, after conferring with other colleagues.)

That evening I blew up at Michael. While we were making dinner I told him what had happened with Janowitz; then he disappeared suddenly and returned with a bottle of wine.

"What's that for?"

"I think we should celebrate," he said gaily.

I threw the lettuce down in the sink, breaking a glass. "For Christ sake, Michael, what the hell is there to celebrate!"

"Doing the right thing?" he suggested simply.

I stormed out of the kitchen. "The right thing! The right thing!"

He followed me into the living room, still holding the wine, a calm quizzical smile on his face. "Don't you think you did the right thing?"

"Ooh!" I hollered in frustration. "Don't you understand? One more stunt like today and my days as a biologist are over!"

I fairly leaped out into the hall, slamming the door behind me. Michael immediately opened it, no doubt with the damn wine still in his hand, and called after me in a calm voice, "I wouldn't call what you did this afternoon a stunt."

I hit the elevator button so hard I hurt my hand, but then strode into the stairwell, my eyes almost blinded with tears.

Grandpa, I kept thinking as I paced the campus, I studied hard; I studied with the best; but it doesn't look like I'll be any kind of leader.

When I returned, Michael was in the study. He would have heard me come in, but still it was startling when I heard his voice behind me in the bedroom. "What are you doing, Joanie?" he asked too evenly.

I was packing. "I'm going to see my grandfather. I'm taking the car."

"When ... when will you be back?"

"I don't know," I almost shouted; then a bit more quietly: "I haven't thought that far ahead."

After a pause he said, almost to himself, "It's a long drive."

"I can't make it any shorter," I snapped.

"I was going to offer to go with you," he replied, and I could hear his anger.

All I said was, "Thanks, I can handle it."

"Suit yourself," he muttered and left the room. As I was going out the door he asked very quietly, his eyes smoldering, "Care to leave a number where you can be reached?"

"My mother's," I mumbled, unable to look at him, and left.

I had in fact intended to stay over at my mother's, but when I got to L.A. I couldn't face it for some reason, so I checked into a motel that was way too expensive, feeling guilty and generally miserable.

By the time I got to the nursing home, having slept poorly and gotten up late, it was almost lunchtime. I found him playing pinochle with some of his cronies. "Grandpa, hello," I called across the room, and immediately felt foolish when half the men looked up expectantly. When he saw me, his face was blank momentarily, so unexpected was my appearance, but then a great big grin filled his face, his whole body even, as he flopped his cards down and put his hands up. "Hello, grandpa," I repeated at his side, beaming.

We talked for a long time. He talked slower than ever and thought even more deeply before he spoke. There was nothing wrong with his mind; if anything it was even sharper; his age was slowing his rhythm. At one point I asked, "Grandpa, do you remember when

I was sixteen and I told you I wanted to be a biologist? When I first told you, I mean." He appeared to be carefully scanning the past. "Remember, you and grandma were visiting—"

He nodded as if to say he didn't need any hints. "Do I remember? Of course I remember. I should forget something like that?"

Maybe it was—I don't know what it was—my chest began to heave. I almost sobbed. "Grandpa," I almost whispered, "you were proud of me."

He looked at me almost blankly, then perhaps questioning; then his head almost began to shake with emotion. "I was proud of you," he intoned forcefully. "Could a man be prouder? My grand-daughter—my grand-daughter—a biologist, a scientist!" I began to sob. "I was proud of you then. I'm proud of you now. And I've been proud of you every day in between." Unable to contain myself any longer, I burst into tears. It's a measure of him that he made no attempt to stop my crying. He simply sat there a while and, as the wave subsided, handed me a handkerchief. We both laughed.

Later, when saying goodbye, I went to kiss him on his cheek, but then for some reason kissed him on top of his head. I'll never forget the look on his face when I did that, and then his eyes, watered over, looking at me as I stood before him and as I had stood before him a little girl.

I always want to remember him that way, saying so much in a simple gesture with his hands. And how he chose to say goodbye—who knew if there would be another one? "So. You have things to do, and I have things to do … " As it turned out, that was our last real goodbye: shortly afterward he suffered a stroke and things were never the same. Then his health really slipped fast …

For most of the drive back I was pretty weepy. I kept thinking I needed to say the following to Michael: "I may have advanced my position with too much force. If that's the case, then I believe apologies are in order."

THE GODDAMN
STUFF OF LIFE

Y ou told me—a complaint almost—how promising the suitcases looked, finally closed with difficulty, still on the bed in case you remembered something else. A clean rupture, a fresh context, not merely to be transported but transubstantiated, a new beginning. Three weeks outside of your lives, "let's get the hell out of here," your husband had said, "we can't think straight anymore." Nothing but distractions, his life, your life, it had become impossible to focus amid all the clutter, to remain calm.

You'd been fighting more than usual, especially about the possibility of you joining Biosys, which your husband called selling out for big bucks, a.k.a. prostitution. The usual pattern, though: Intellectual disagreements became emotional arguments became marital strife became real hurt, made real wounds. You believe now that your husband realized more than you how close the two of you were to the edge, how close all that tearing was to a final tearing. It just hadn't occurred to you, you told me, you assume that you love your husband because you used to, and because you're supposed to and you want to, and because the last time you looked you did, but you haven't looked in a long time, and suddenly you're afraid to look again.

So it had been your husband's idea to leave everything and go to Europe. You sighed, nodding. Yes, you needed it too, you could see that. You had tons of ideas in your head, but the lab always slows down in summer and— Yes, he was right, just simply right for once. You nodded again. "No argument there."

He made the arrangements and then there they were, the suitcases on the bed. The apartment seemed different, like it wasn't yours anymore, like maybe you'd never see it again, the trip loomed like a wave, that sensation you couldn't quite label was fear. Your husband appeared leaning against the doorjamb balancing a bottle of wine between two fingers. "Let's celebrate."

"We'll probably drink ourselves silly on the plane."

"Let's start drinking ourselves silly right now."

You were trying to feel gay. Your husband had been very solicitous recently, trying visibly to push the idea that a page was being turned, trying to be more patient, less sardonic. You could see the effort he was making, not that it was so difficult, but that it was so apparent, and you were trying to meet him halfway.

"I have a better idea," he said, hustling the valises off the bed.

"Do we have time?" you asked almost nervously, but then you too wanted to celebrate.

Even that you told me, though we've barely just met, that before making love with your husband you asked, "Do we have time?" And how afterwards you drank wine together. That you had wanted to, wanted it to be good for both of you, and that it had been. All that you told me. Of course a man knows that a wife makes love with her husband, or at least has sex with him; it cannot surprise him to learn this, it cannot cause him pain, though he may be jealous.

*　*　*

You told me that in Paris you walked everywhere arm in arm, afraid, perhaps, of having separate experiences. Your husband's aggressive campaign to repair the marriage eventually caught you too, so it was husband and wife both who threw themselves into it, wanting it to succeed, going everywhere arm in arm.

This was Paris, not a place but an incarnation of romance. Its monuments, its intersections, boulevards were not merely exciting in their fame and beauty; they were physicalizations of the sigh of love, the exhalation of sentiment. Paris was an urban garden in which two new beings would rediscover each other.

It was childish, it was like being teenagers again. You both giggled like teenagers. You embraced on the Tour Eiffel, you meandered along the Seine, fingers entwined, you laughed as the jam dripped on your husband's shirt from the crepe you bought him in the Jardin du Luxembourg. He "pointed out" that the *baguette* is a phallus and that's why the French, men and women both, are so hung up on their bread. You chided him for another of his cockamamie theories; he wagged a warning finger at you, and then you both laughed at the puns, and then he cradled your face in his hands and kissed you full on the lips.

Because the hotel had to be part of the Paris experience, your husband had splurged on a room on St. Germain, with a tall French window opening on a terrace overlooking the boulevard. In the evening before dinner, after having showered, both of you fresh, worn out by the day's walking, you would stand on the balcony, arms around each other's waist, and watch the cafés begin their evening trade. Then, too tired to stand any longer, you would return to the room, to the bed that commanded the room. Your husband would close the satin curtains and I will not complete this sentence. You won't admit it, but I know that you're shy in discussing matters of the flesh. I don't wish to embarrass you, or to— Do you know what it feels like to know that another man is where you dream of being? Do women feel that way also? I don't dislike your husband; I have a high regard for his taste. Try to understand if there is an irresistible tendency to treat him perhaps more severely than he deserves in this...

What is this, a memoir, confession? I think it's a work of fiction, its plot device, the armature upon which its art is constructed that most ancient, enduring, trivial, and arousing of themes, what the French call *le ménage à trois*. Forgive me if in writing this, worse, in letting you see it, I feel so weak. It's not me doing this, it's the poet in me, that asshole, incurably callow. Have you ever detested yourself? That's also very French, you know, providing it's done with a certain panache. Don't worry, I'm not falling into any depths of despair. I don't care what the French say, despair is cowardice.

So it was a wonderful week the pair of you had in Paris. Your husband insisted on reading a novel in French, trying to resurrect his dormant school-days expertise, dictionary at hand; while you mocked him as you sailed through some easy read in which all the women are irresistibly attractive and control powerful men by sleeping with them, while all the men achieve power and wealth by never erring in knowing whom to kill and whom to buy. To this point neither of you spoke about your ... what we Americans of our generation insist on calling a relationship. You knew that you felt better. Your sleep was still troubled occasionally, by dreams, by awakenings, but your laughing was becoming more sincere. You were certain your husband's face had changed, due to the relaxation of certain muscles. Each conceded instantly to the other's wish—what to visit, where to eat—and never seemed short of things to say.

There was that tale of his about when he had last been in Paris, during an undergraduate summer, and, arriving in the early evening by train—"Where was I coming from?"—was unable to find a bed at a hostel. "It was hot, I remember, and I was all sweaty from my trip. And here I was, marching around with my backpack, being turned away by hostels. They were near here, too, just a few blocks, I wish I could remember where. Actually, no, that's wrong, I don't know, somehow I ended up way the hell out somewhere, I have this sense it was in the northeast part of the city, a long metro ride, not near the student quarter at all. Anyway, I know I'm walking down this street, kind of a working class neighborhood, not bad, but, you know, not touristy at all, and by this time I'm in a panic. Three or four places have turned me down, maybe I called some others—I can picture myself using the telephone—my French was decent then, not good, but I could make myself understood—it's getting late, I'm sticky, I smell, I'm bushed, and I'm in the middle of nowhere ... Oh God, I think I remember. As I'm telling you this story I'm trying to figure out why I have this sense that I already knew my way around. I was returning to Paris. That explains the train."

"Michael, your story's falling apart."

"No, no, okay, see, the plane left from Paris, this was the end of the summer. I had been in Paris near the beginning of the trip for maybe a week, so I knew my way around, but, see, now I was returning to catch my plane. I was coming from Amsterdam, oh God, that's a whole story in itself, I got stranded at the French-Belgian border, well, before that I'd gotten lost in the middle of Holland, and some policemen had gotten me a hitch—incredible, that's another story, they actually pulled over a trucker and told him to give me a ride, you believe that?—and then I got stuck in Belgium and I had no Belgian money—this is all one day, I was hitching from Amsterdam to Paris. It's a long story, but I end up camping with some French kids, and the next day they put me on a train for Paris. Okay, I'm back in Paris. Oh, wait a minute."

"Now what?"

"I have to tell you about my button."

"Michael!"

"I have to tell you about my button or the story won't make any sense. I had a button on my jacket, I wore it all the time, that said 'End the war in Vietnam.' And it was amazing, I had some real adventures because of that button. I mean in London some guards let me into a wing of a museum that was closed to the public, and when I asked them why they were doing this—I wasn't used to being treated well by people in uniform—they said, 'because of your button.' There are lots of stories I could tell about that button. Those Dutch cops, they told the driver I was an American against the war. I made out the words 'American' and 'Vietnam.'

"Another one was at the Belgian border where I got stranded. Evening is falling and I'm facing this long road—it's perfectly flat, I found out later some major World War One battles were fought there—but I don't really feel scared. By now I'm a man of the road, you see. I've hitched around Europe, slept in fields. More like another adventure to hang on my belt, but I'm starving, I hadn't been able to eat all through Belgium, and I notice a bar, so I go in and order a ham sandwich and a beer. There's maybe six guys at the bar. As I'm reaching for my money the guy behind the bar points to my button and asks, 'What's that say?' Actually he said, '*Que veut dire ça?*' I'll never forget it, I can picture him saying it so clearly.

"I tell him what it says and he just looks at me and says, '*Oui?*' '*Oui,*' I reply. The bar is quiet, everybody's listening, looking at me. Then the guy closest to me points to the button and says, '*Que veut dire ça?*' As if he doesn't know. So I translate it again. '*Vous êtes Américain?*' asks the guy next to him. '*Oui,*' I reply. 'Yes, I'm American.' Then the guy next to him asks, '*Que veut dire ça?*' pointing to my button again, and so I tell them again. And it goes down the line like this, each one of them wants to hear it personally.

"You'd think I would have told them I wasn't alone, that many Americans, at least young ones, opposed the war. But I'm tongue-tied, all I can say is '*oui.*' '*Oui.*' So I drink my beer—the whole bar is quiet—and I leave with the sandwich."

"Didn't anybody try to talk to you?"

"Only '*que veut dire ça.*' But the bartender wouldn't take my money."

You smiled. "Michael, that's a wonderful story."

"Yeah, but it's the wrong one. I'm supposed to be telling you about my brush with oblivion in Paris. Well, I leave the bar, I hike down this road, maybe five miles, and end up in a campground where I stay up half the night with some crazy Frenchmen who squeeze me into their tent because it's raining cats and dogs. And the next day we spend some time together, they put me on a train for Paris and I arrive around six o'clock, seven o'clock, and then I go through what I told you about.

"So—you with me?—I'm walking down this street, hot and sweaty, and all of a sudden I'm in a panic. I can't find an open hostel, where am I going to spend the night? The idea of finding a cheap hotel, that never occurs to me. I was stupid, okay? I'd just spent the whole summer going from hostel to hostel, and it just never dawned on me that I could go to a hotel. So what am I going to do, it's starting to get late? How hard would it be to get out of the city, find a field somewhere? Impossible, too late already, and how the hell would I know where to go? I know I can't sleep in a park. I can't just stay up all night, I'm beat, I stink, I've got this forty pound pack on my back. I'm really in a panic.

"As I'm walking I see a police station and without a thought march in and announce that I want to be taken to jail! You have to picture this. I'm obviously an American kid spending his summer touring around and I cry out in despair, 'take me to jail!' Now if this was a movie the desk sergeant might say something like, 'But, *monsieur*, what crime have you committed?' But instead he looks me up and down, absolutely straight face, and asks, 'You are American?' '*Oui*,' I reply. '*Passeport, s'il vous plaît*.' I give him my passport, he looks it over half-heartedly, looks at me, looks at it, looks at me, you know the routine. Never says a word, never cracks a smile. Suddenly he hands it back to me and says something quickly to the beat cop who's standing there watching this little farce. He takes me outside and gives me directions to a nearby hostel that will take me in. I hoist my pack and follow his finger. I'd give anything to see the expressions on those two cops' faces when he returned inside the station.

"I walk a few blocks—it's dark now—and I find the hostel. I'm not nuts about it at all, I'm wondering where the police sent me, I know this place isn't on my list, but I've got no choice, so I go in. The office is closed, I go looking for the guy in charge and find him in the middle of a large room where maybe twenty people are eating. The guy's maybe twenty-five and looks okay, but I don't like the looks of the others. Pretty rugged. But—no choice—I ask the guy for a bed. He looks me over and says, 'Sorry, we are full. *Complet*.'

"Panic again. Desperation, fear. 'Look,' I say, 'you have to give me a bed.' I'm practically shouting, crying, and then I blurt out, 'the police sent me here.' Now, nothing really changed dramatically, but suddenly it was a lot quieter in there, and I noticed that a really mean-looking dude—looked like a biker—had his fork stopped halfway to his mouth. The guy looks me over again and says, 'Please, come with me.' I follow him up a flight of stairs, he opens a door, turns on the light, and I see several vacant beds, and, when I turn to him, his face is one big grin.

"But I'm not laughing. I'm pissed. 'What the fuck's going on?' I demand."

"That's what you said? In French?"

"Well, he got the tone of voice. You know what he says to me then? He says, 'We are socialists here. We must be very careful.' He laughed. He said when he first saw me he thought I might be an *agent provocateur*, sent by the police, because of my button. But when I announced that the police had sent me he figured I must be okay because not even an *agent provocateur* could be either that stupid or that smart.

"So he tells me to leave my pack on one of the beds and takes me back downstairs where I find out that all those cut-throats and thieves are college kids. That shaggy biker turns out to be a physics major from Berkeley, and I get adopted by a very bourgeois art professor and his wife who take me out for some decent food, and he tells me something about how his whole trip is being paid for because he arranged to take slides for the art department!"

How you laughed! "Dear Michael," you sighed sweetly.

*　　*　　*

You told me that's how your week in Paris went, a little decameron; but after a week, you both felt like seeing more of France, and so you left that hotel on the Boulevard St. Germain. It was a mistake; you should have stayed there.

Like the most memorable cataclysms, it started inadvertently. You rented a car and drove down to the *château* country, and were looking across the water at Amboise, perhaps just this once, fatally, not touching— Let's put this in the present tense for immediacy. The two of you are looking at Amboise, where Leonardo da Vinci lived out the last years of his life. You're both quiet for a moment. You're saying to yourself that, despite its undeniable grandeur and some delicacy of design, it's essentially a work of pomposity and arrogance. Your husband starts to laugh, you look at him inquiringly, tell me, I'd like to laugh too. He turns to you, all good humor, saying, "Leonardo just lived here, you'll be able to buy the place."

It's such a bolt from the blue that first you're dazed. "I don't get it. What?" He's already biting his lip, reaching for your hand, which you snatch out of his grasp.

"I was only kidding, Joanie," he says lightly, but actually pleading, praying that he hasn't done what he knows he's done.

You turn and stride away; when he stops you with his arms around you and puts his cheek against yours he feels your tears. "Joanie," he whispers, wheeling you around almost violently, "I didn't mean anything, God, it was just a thoughtless remark, stupid … " Your tears won't stop, your husband is desperate now, terrified. He pulls you to him, squeezes you. "I love you, Joanie," he cries, "I'm just an ass, I love you, I love you."

His distress is so profound, you're almost frightened into forgiving him, and soon you're comforting him more than he's comforting you. For dinner he insists, all gaiety now, on taking you to a breathlessly elegant but horribly expensive restaurant, where you dine in a splendid garden by candlelight. Between forkfuls he kisses your hand, and with each caress you grow more depressed. You try to hide it, for his sake, but he knows it, he's consumed by it, telling jokes, anecdotes furiously, finding ways to flatter you, but you find yourself only becoming sullen. The effort of trying to appear gay … Before he pays the bill you insist on seeing it and it almost makes you burst into tears again.

That night is the first time you do not make love. You never told me this, I imagine it. I imagine your husband doesn't even try.

The next morning over breakfast—in defiance of your explicit resolve—you say quietly, "Michael, we have to talk."

Immediately he's pleading, apologizing. "Believe me, Joanie, I hate what I said, I don't know why it … I'm just tense, we're both tense, we're still carrying all this baggage. I feel that way, don't you? I mean it's only been a week!"

"Michael … "

"Please, Joanie. I'd give anything to take that back. I don't know who said it, it wasn't me. We've been having such a good time … "

"Did you sleep well last night?" It's a cruel remark, you regret saying it.

He turns away, almost smiles, but when he looks back, shaking his head slowly, his eyes are teared over. "No, Joanie, I didn't sleep well," he whispers.

Suddenly unable to look at him you look down at your lap and discover that you're clutching the tablecloth. It's such a predictable bit of dramatic business, real forties Hollywood, but that doesn't occur to you. Taking a few breaths, you look at him and say, "Michael, what we're both feeling is not going to go away by itself."

"Haven't you been having a good time?" he interrupts.

"Of course. But—"

"Then no buts. Let's just … We got thrown off course. Let's—"

"Michael, I didn't sleep well either last night. We had a good week—"

"We had a wonderful week."

"A wonderful week—"

"We came together, we found each other again."

"Michael, you're interrupting me."

"I'm sorry. I'm sorry, go ahead. What do you want to say?"

"Just what I said before. We have to talk."

Then the two of you sit in silence, sipping from coffee cups that are already empty.

*   *   *

You told me that neither of you even suggested looking at any more *châteaux.* There'd been talk earlier of going to Brittany, the attraction there its ancient mystic aura, but that too fell away with unspoken consent. Your husband proposed that you head straight for the Riviera. Obviously, the romance to be recaptured there … But that being a very long drive, and not being positive it wouldn't prove more hot, crowded, and expensive than romantic, you proposed an alternative, and so you traveled to the magical medieval land still called Périgord by its inhabitants. And so you met me, in the land of the troubadours, of castles and knights.

In the car, hours of silence, deepened by talk. In essence you asked your husband one question: If you accepted the proposal, would he be able to live with that? In essence he replied that he didn't know. In essence he asked one question back: Were you going to accept it? In essence you replied that you didn't know. It took hours and hours to say that.

You arrived late afternoon, found a hotel, showered, dressed, went out for dinner, and returned at sunset to sit in the garden and say little, nursing coffees. I noticed you from my window, obviously fate because usually I'm about at that hour, waltzing the town at day's end, my hours at the window come earlier, while I'm working. Why did I come over, I don't know, to chat up some fellow Americans? I've long since stopped thinking of myself as an American. (How could a British subject, a hopeless Francophile, who marries a South African and later has a ludicrously painful love affair with a Czech be simply an American?) To get some news of the old country, then? Because I was lonely, because at the first glance I was already drawn to you? Because you were obviously a couple that could use someone to come over and take your minds off whatever it was they were focused on?

Had I been my usual self I might have bowed smartly and introduced myself as Zelentino Gavansky, a Sicilian of noble Hungarian blood. Why are strangers so afraid to meet each other? Sometimes it seems easier to jump off a cliff than step up and say hello to someone you'd like to meet. I'm sure I said something brilliant like, "Beautiful garden, isn't it. The French, you know." But I'd like you to remember that I bowed smartly and introduced myself as Zelentino Gavansky.

Though weighed down by the somber air hovering about the two of you—the way you sometimes feel on one of those terribly hot muggy days—I rose to something of my usual humor when you asked me what I was doing in Sarlat. "It sounds like you've been here quite a while," you said.

"Five weeks, actually."

"Now that's a vacation," declared your husband.

"Well, it's not exactly a holiday."

"Really," you said, "what brings you to Sarlat of all places?"

"I'll tell you what. I'll give you several alternatives and you pick the one you like best. I asked the travel agent for a place on the beach and this is where she sent me. I was here many years ago with my wife and I've returned, condemned to retrace our missteps. I was hitchhiking and got stranded here. I'm working for a Japanese food cartel, trying to corner the market on the rare Perigordian black truffle. I have a thing about castles. I'm a linguist studying regional French dialects. I'm a lover studying regional French women. I'm a wine enthusiast seeking out obscure labels. I'm on a pilgrimage to the holy shrine of Rocamadour. I didn't realize I was in whatever you said, I thought this was Italy." I can't remember what your husband did then, but you smiled.

"There's an English quality to your speech. I can't quite ... "

"I live in England. Have been for—what is it?—about twelve years now."

"Really."

Try to understand if I have an irresistible tendency to treat myself perhaps a bit better than I deserve in this ... What is this, a missal, a travelogue? I think it's an epitaph on the tomb where our—that word again—relationship lies buried, for you will never read this and we will never see each other again. Forgive me if I steep myself momentarily in the sad beauty of that tragic thought—I told you I was a hopeless Francophile.

When I learned you had a car, I instantly invited you to accompany me—in your car—on a sightseeing tour the very next day. Work be damned.

*   *   *

You told me that if it hadn't been for us coincidentally bumping into each other on the street some nights later—fate again, if you ask me—things might have turned out differently. The next day wasn't too bad. It was obvious something was on between you, but you kept it under wraps well enough while we were together. Anyway, I was having a good time because I didn't get to roam about the countryside that often.

But then apparently things fell apart. There must have been some private talk because I had thought we were going to dine at this wonderful restaurant I know at the *château* Montfort, but then it seemed we were going to drive straight back to our hotel where two of us were going to eat separately while one of us could go to bloody hell. The next day a note from you was delivered containing an apology. It arrived while I was sitting at my window overlooking the garden, which was where I was spending my days working.

Work had been going reasonably well. I'm not one of those inspiration writers, feverishly penning in a flash of brilliance, then groping at the edge of despair for the next one. For me it's more a matter of settling myself into a routine, a comfortable setting, a well-defined goal. I've never been short on things to say. (In the brief time we were together, did you ever know me to be at a loss for words?) I moved the writing table to the window and that's where I spent my days.

For me to have that window looking onto the garden ... Not merely that the garden was beautiful, but to look upon it through that window from my room! How shall I explain it? I don't know if I can. I used to spy on the guests who would dine there, note the change in light, the shifting shadows as the day moved. Utterly French that garden. Who else (except the Japanese, but that is a different sensibility, perhaps more profound, but less lovely) could impose so on Nature, concoct something so obviously man-made, yet liberate something that seems so artlessly casual, exquisite. What was that garden but some wire chairs and tables, a paving of white gravel, some shrubs and potted plants?

You probably don't realize that I used to take my breakfast—what the French call breakfast—in the garden. I stopped after that day we went sightseeing, I'm not sure why, to spare us all some embarrassment maybe. Actually I know why, but I don't want to say. I used to sit there eating up the garden, the guests, the maids already hard at work, washing walls, floors, that's how I prepared myself for my day of writing. After that day I stayed in my room and spied on you, you and your husband. I can't believe neither of you noticed me, calmly sitting at the window sipping coffee, watching you, watching you.

You two hardly spoke, it made me sad, it hurt me. Even more so on the third day—it was the third day, wasn't it?—when you appeared alone. Later you told me that you and your husband—all right, I'll refer to him by name—that you and Michael were too angry and upset to travel together, it had become impossible to even think of going on to the Riviera. Your holiday was stalled, you were prisoners in the hotel.

The two of you became experts on the streets in the vicinity because now one, now the other would storm out of the room, no longer able to restrain his or her voice—you say you can't believe the whole place wasn't listening, but I tell you truthfully I myself heard nothing (though I could feel it, I'll swear I could feel it)—and then whomever it was would return to blurt out something, to sit in sullen silence, or—failing always—to try to resolve matters. Then you appeared in the garden alone, and I knew the situation had deteriorated further. I was staring at you brazenly—you tell me you never realized it, but that's impossible, you're lying. You ate the *croissant,* drank your coffee, never looking round, and then you looked up, perhaps you were looking for your husband, but instead you found me, and I did something cruel then, though I decline to apologize. You were looking round, you say for no reason, a mindless movement, you saw me, and after some embarrassment (because from my position, settled at my table at the window, cup in hand, you knew that I'd been watching you) you waved hello, tried to smile, and I... continued staring at you, not greeting you at all, just staring.

You looked at me so long I became frightened, I became the weaker one, the victim. I wanted to look away, but I— Suddenly you stood up and left, just like that you vanished from my window, my garden, and actual panic came over me—don't ask me what I was thinking, I have no idea—what should I do, run after her? It was childish, I couldn't sit still, my writing hand began to tremble, the only thing I knew for sure was that I couldn't open my notebook and continue my story. The vision of the blank page, that every writer must obliterate each time he sits down to write, was simply too strong for me then. For some time I continued to stare at my garden, but you were gone. (This is pretty maudlin, isn't it? The hell with it, I retract nothing, I shall have the courage to be as silly as the French.)

I asked myself, what would I be doing now, were I in your position? Since, as it happens, I was able to answer that from personal experience, I turned suddenly for the door and launched myself into the morning bustle of the town, taking one street after another with the explicit goal of finding you, but lacking any idea what I might say if we met. I realize you're just learning of this now. You thought— Yes, I searched the town for you.

I never did learn where you were. I felt foolish and, frankly, ashamed of myself. Another man's wife. And that aside, what was I up to? Besides, who's to say it was all your husband's fault, people might have said that about Katherine and me. So I went shopping for my lunch as I usually did, cheese here, fruit there, a *baguette,* and returned to my room, where I sat at the window eating absent-mindedly. Want to hear something else melodramatic? After lunch I stared at my notebook, afraid to open it. That's not me, I don't do that, I work like a water wheel: the water flows, the wheel turns. I'm going to jump ahead to the evening because this is supposed to be about you, not me. All right, I'll say that at the earliest possible hour for dinner—when the heat of the day has not quite conceded to evening's breeze—I returned to the prowl, seeking at one restaurant after another. Where the hell were you?

It was my habit, as the French say, to stroll in the evening after supper. Still no sight of you; and then it's dark and I'm still walking. (This is more about me than you, isn't it? I'll try to do better. But, on further reflection, isn't everything I choose to write about me really about you?) Suddenly I think I see you ahead of me in one of those alleys that were streets in medieval times. I run, you turn the corner, I run faster and call out, but you must not have heard me because as I turn the corner you're still walking.

"Joan?" I call again, "Joan, is that you?"

You let me catch up—I'm walking now—watching me without saying anything. Evening stroll? I ask; something like that, you reply; we smile out of courtesy.

*   *   *

We walked the narrow streets of the old town, all the time my hands trembling, whatever I do to stop it only making it worse until I think I might lose control of them entirely. I couldn't tell if you'd been crying, I'll assume you had been, but by now your voice was unwavering.

I asked what kind of work you did. "I'm a scientist," you said, "a biologist." There was something almost aggressive, defensive in your reply.

"Wow. What does it mean to be a scientist? What do you do actually?" When you told me I was staggered. "We're both doing the same thing, aren't we?"

You turned to peer at me. "We are? A novelist and a scientist?"

"That's just the outer form. I'm interested in the nature of life, the process of living. Isn't that what art is, really, a meditation on life? And doesn't that also describe what you do, your experiments?"

I think you were embarrassed. "I'm not sure that, uh … Meditating on life is not a phrase that exactly comes to mind when I describe my work."

"Maybe it should."

"You sound like Michael." That hurt, but there was nothing I could think of to say. I wasn't about to— We walked on in silence. "Maybe I should be more tolerant of that point of view. You know, we had a journalist in the lab. She spent several months with me and we got to be friends. I'll never forget her face the first time we extracted DNA. You draw it onto a twirling glass rod, and when you get enough it becomes visible. It is pretty amazing, don't get me wrong, but Linda's eyes were bugging out of her head. 'Holy Jesus!' she said. I'll never forget it, she was practically whispering. 'Holy Jesus, you're holding the goddamn stuff of life in your hands!'"

"Maybe she was right."

You mused. "We don't use the term 'stuff of life.' We prefer to say 'deoxyribonucleic acid.'"

"I wonder which one is more accurate."

"'DNA' is more accurate, but let's not talk about that, okay?"

We continued in silence again—which made neither of us uncomfortable, did it? When we'd passed a stretch marred by the smell of someone's urine, you made a face. "Takes away some of the magic, doesn't it?" you remarked.

"Men have been pissing against these walls since the Middle Ages. Think about that."

"It doesn't make the smell any better."

"No, but it's that smell that transforms some vague notion of history into a concrete experience of it."

"Urination as an historical act?"

"As a jarring reminder that this is not a museum."

Silent walking again and suddenly you laughed quietly, privately. "I'm sorry," you said, "that's impolite."

"I enjoy simply being with you."

You ignored that. "I know you know Michael and I are not getting along. You'd have to be blind and deaf to miss it."

"I'm neither blind nor deaf," I replied quietly.

"Would you like to know why?"

"Only if you want to tell me. I just want—"

"It ties in with your— I'm sorry, what were you going to say?"

"Uh, nothing."

"It ties in with your urination theory of history."

"Hmm," I said, "I didn't realize that was a whole theory."

"Michael thinks I'm about to piss on science." You kept talking, but silently, to yourself, then became audible again. "I'm sorry, I feel like, for you to understand I'd have to give you an entire lecture."

"Try me," I said with gentle arrogance.

You sighed. "On the face of it it couldn't be simpler. I've been approached to commercialize some of my work. To join a company to market products—one in particular, a very important medicinal—created with techniques I've developed. I'm consider-

ing the proposal seriously. Michael can't stand it." Silence again—
I think you were still talking, but to yourself only—then an abrupt
"that's it."

I have to admit I didn't like what I was feeling. For reasons that
I presume need not be articulated at this point, I wanted to take your
side … but that part about commercialization … For me commercialization is prostitution, pure and simple. "What did you mean," I
began tentatively, "when you said 'products'?"

You sighed again, a sigh of obvious impatience.

"I'm sorry, I—"

"No, no, it's just … that's what I mean. You don't know where
all this is coming from. You can't know."

"I could know if you told me." Yes, my hurt broke through
there. "I'd like to … You seem very alone, very … If you want … I'm
here." I shrugged, afraid to look at you. "I'm here."

"There are many practical applications of recombinant DNA
research. In medicine, agriculture … Lots of very exciting, beneficial
possibilities. There are not so nice ones too. Military applications,
germ warfare. That's part of the problem. But there are other issues."
You looked to see if my eyes had glazed over; I nodded you on. "The
concept is not exactly without precedent, you know. It's been going
on for years in other fields."

"What concept?"

"The inter-penetration of research and industry. There's nothing
new in that. But Michael can't stand it. He says the whole vocabulary
he finds repugnant."

"Vocabulary?"

"Industry. Business. Marketing, product development. Not to
mention words like shareholder and profit. Maybe you find it repugnant too."

I tried to abstain, but you waited for my response. "Not necessarily," I lied.

"Do you have a philosophical objection to money?" you asked
bluntly.

I chuckled. "That's not an issue I've had to confront."

"What if you wrote a best-seller? Sold a book to Hollywood?"

"Perish the thought," I blurted out foolishly. Trying to cover up I added, "That's hardly likely."

"I think Michael can't stand the idea of having money. I won't deny there are connotations that bother me."

I gestured noncommittally.

"But it's more than that. It's the business connection. All these guys in suits, Michael won't even meet them."

I almost said this out loud: "I don't blame him." What the hell was going on here? Was this the woman I— "Can I ask you a question? Why do you want to do this?" I couldn't help it, I gulped, at least I think I did.

"I don't know if I want to do it." You were defensive.

"You're considering it. You're attracted to the idea."

You stared at me suddenly, then nodded, sighed again. "Is that wrong, or bad, or something? I mean—"

"No, no, I'm— Hey, don't mind me, I'm just—"

"It's okay, you don't have to— It's my fault, this thing has got me wired."

"It's a big decision." We walked on in silence, nodded to an old woman who passed us, tried to make a joke of holding our noses as we encountered another concrete experience of history.

"Can I help it if it's exciting? That my work has potential to do good things? Don't give me that crap about science being pure. Was Pasteur a whore because he took his germ theory and tried to cure disease with it? If money's the hang-up we can give the damn money away. He knows I'm not hung up on money. But it's very exciting. It's incredibly exciting, if you only knew! The possibilities... Okay, in a perfect world we could do it with only the purest of motives. But because there are men in business suits and men in uniform, does that mean all motives are base, or that good things can't happen?"

We walked on in silence again. Since it was dark, it didn't matter perhaps that I'd kept us meandering through the same narrow streets. "Now I understand what you meant before. When you said my urination theory of history."

"Science is a living process. Maybe to outsiders it's something abstract and sanitized, but to us it's ... it's our life. There are conflicts, there are rewards, pressures. You go to work, you come home, you think about your job. We're people."

"I understand now."

"Michael thinks it's wrong to make a profit. Maybe it is wrong, but I didn't design the system. The point is, you can't suppress the quest for knowledge. What he can't stand is that the quest for knowledge and the quest for profits are overlapping here."

"And you can." A surprising burst of bravery on my part.

Again you sighed, loudly.

After a long pause I asked, "Can I tell you something else about history as a living thing? Look at this street. Go ahead."

Obeying, you looked, not knowing of course what you were supposed to be looking at.

"Perhaps, like me, you love the quaintness, the cozy intimacy, the textures of the stone, walls and streets, each doorway a new discovery perhaps. It's beautiful, even with the piss it's beautiful, wonderful—magic, really. Am I right? But what was it really like? And in particular, what was it like for the creative ones, the artists, the philosophers? Leonardo may have died at Amboise, but he was born in a town like this."

You said nothing, simply waited for me to continue.

"That's the most amazing of all, that from these dwellings, these narrow streets, sprang great poets, artists and architects with grand visions. To them these streets must have seemed indeed narrow. Narrow-minded. Thus the art created out of this life"—I gestured like an actor—"was both an extension of it and, inevitably, a defiance, a plea, an alternative." I fell silent.

"You sound like you're quoting."

"I was."

"Who?"

"Me. Can I tell you a story?"

"Do you think we could find a café first? I've been walking a long time." You smiled then in a way that started my arms trembling again.

I led us to one well away from the hotel. We ordered espresso and then, as you sat there taking in the ambience of the square, the townspeople, the young couples, I sat there watching you. Watching you.

May I say, madam scientist, without offending your dignity in any way, that as I sat there watching you, both of us—though you were too busy talking to yourself, arguing with yourself or with your husband, to notice—both of us bound up in this unspeakably Gallic evening town square café loveliness, I found you—to borrow a phrase from my adopted countrymen—frightfully attractive. At that moment I believe I might have been capable of any villainy. Or foolishness. How then did I manage to sustain, not only my dignity, but yours? Though we talked half the night, I know so little about you.

And all this despite the fact—the crazy, unforeseen, confusing fact—that I was having as hard a time with this exciting proposal of yours as your husband was. I'm old enough to realize that much of you was a creation of my own fantasy, but was there nothing there to fit the part, were you utterly wrong for it? Sitting there watching you, I couldn't accept that, and I won't now. We're all crazy; in that context my loving you makes perfect sense.

"May I tell you my story now?"

For a moment you didn't hear me, then you bolted suddenly and stared at me. I smiled gently and you took a deep breath. "Yes, please. I'd like to hear it."

"When I left the States I had no intention of going back. Within days of my graduation I was on a plane for London. When the guy asked me my purpose in the U.K. I said to get as far away from the U.S. as possible. His face jerked up at me for a moment. 'And how long do you intend to stay?' 'As long as I can.' Slowly he removed his glasses as he raised his head to look at me again. 'Might one inquire why?' 'Because of the war,' I said, looking straight at him. 'I see,' he replied, looking down again.

"I learned only later, when I had to look for work, that he had given me a special entry permit, very unusual, that allowed me to be hired without a work permit. I was subletting a room from a family of white South African refugees. Quite a story, theirs—midnight escape and so on. In my arrogance I compared my flight to theirs. I signed my letters back home 'expatriate American writer.'

"They had a daughter and, to compress this tale so you won't be completely bored—"

"No no, please—"

"In any case we were married six months later and moved into digs of our own. A year later there was a baby. I had crazy odd jobs. The best of them was hanging lights in a theatre. I hauled trash—I don't even remember all of them. But I was writing constantly, every spare moment, bursting with things to say. I think I wrote six plays in a year—I was into theatre then—and not a bit of it worth a damn. Useless, the whole lot. And there I was, hopefully making submissions ... One of my plays was a life of Michelangelo, lovely rejection letter. My problems began innocently enough, as they say. Actually, let me take that back, what was so innocent about it? Well, wait a minute, I have to back up, I have to tell you where that Michelangelo play came from. Are you bored?"

"No, no, I'm enjoying this, go ahead."

"Let's have some more coffee, or would you like something else to drink, ever try Pernod?"

You smiled indulgently. "I'm okay, really."

I summoned the waiter and ordered two Pernods. "It's the French national drink, you have to try it. You'll hate it, don't worry, you have to be French to like it." As you looked at me, those pieces of smile in the turn of your lips, the reflection in your eyes, I stared at you.

"Shall we get back to your story?"

"What story? Oh, my story, it's all true, I swear it, well it's substantially accurate, okay, it's fiction, isn't that the essence of living?" Does it matter that I'm inventing this now, can't I at least be debonair in my imagination? So let's pretend that you laughed appreciatively, our eyes embracing, as the waiter set down our drinks.

"A few years earlier I had been to Rome and seen the Sistine ceiling. Have you ever seen it?"

You shook your head.

"It's arguably one of the single greatest achievements of the human race. If you haven't seen it—"

"I've seen pictures of it."

"Then you know it in its trivialized form. To stand in the Sistine Chapel is something else. The urination theory again. To stand there in a real room and try to look at the ceiling, your neck killing you— I'm getting ahead of myself. I thought it would be like Saint Peter's, some grand cathedral, but you walk down this endless corridor, around the bend, up stairs, down stairs, through a small door, and there it is. A chapel after all, shockingly small after what your anticipation has spawned. And of course it's jammed with tourists. But you look up at the ceiling and shivers run through your body. It transcends all rendering of it.

"I'd known it since I was a kid, from pictures, but to actually be there... If you could take yourself back in time, you could see him working up on a scaffold, four years crawling on his back. The pope barely glanced at it, noted that the entire ceiling had been duly covered, and instructed his bursar to pay off the artisan. It's such a crazy idea, putting all that on the ceiling, where you can hardly look at it. I'm standing there fighting with my neck. Stop hurting, let me look at this thing!

"You know the famous panel, the creation of Adam, where their hands are outstretched towards each other, God's and Adam's? The gesture... I mean what can you say about it? Except that for me, standing there with my whole life coming down on me, the war, the civil rights struggle, the vast slums of the cities, the riots, the demonstrations, the impossibility of reaching the conscience of the nation, yet trying anyway, all this was very real to me, I was consumed by it, everything I learned and did in college was interpreted in terms of it, and then to be there, looking up at that... that gesture... But you can't look, you can't really look, because it's literally overpowering, and on top of that your neck is killing you, so you've got this ridiculous juxtaposition of the sublime and the ridiculous.

"I spent hours there, trying to merge myself with the ceiling, I'm down here, it's up there—it's all very symbolic, I'm twenty-one, very romantic—and as the guards begin ushering people out, this fantastic idea comes to me. Hanging back—it's hard to believe I did this, but I swear I'm not making this up—somehow they overlooked me and suddenly I'm absolutely all alone—all alone—in the Sistine Chapel. I swear this really happened. I lay down on the floor right under the creation of Adam, and for a few blessed minutes I have it all to myself, without my neck reminding me how corporeal I am."

"It must have been wonderful."

"Wonderful, yes. Good choice of words. It didn't last long. When the guards found me they were furious. Now where was I going with all this?"

"I don't know."

"Oh yeah. Okay, back to London, and a certain ill-fated encounter with an extraordinarily beautiful young Czech woman. She came to live with some friends of my wife's parents, and we were all having dinner together. This was, what, '69, '70, I'm terrible with dates. She had left Czechoslovakia in '68 after the Prague Spring, the Soviet invasion, the backlash—you know about this?"

"Of course."

"She'd come to London, like I had, and she wanted to go back to see her people—family, friends—and collect her things. The problem was, she wasn't sure that if she returned they'd let her out again. I think also, while part of her wanted to stay out of there, another part wanted to go home. I know what that feels like. I found her— I was helplessly attracted to her. I'm sure, objectively, she was very attractive, maybe beautiful, but heightened in my imagination by the drama of her circumstances, the longing in her face, the gestures of her body made me ache for her."

"Ache for her? Do men really ache for women?"

"You're mocking me."

"No, no, I'm seriously asking."

"That's the best way to describe how she made me feel. I could say more on that subject, but I won't."

"Please say more."

"All right. No, in deference to your husband, I'll return to my story."

You turned away suddenly, didn't you? You did, don't deny it.

"The next few months were hell, sheer hell. I couldn't get her out of my mind, it only got worse. It was like a medieval temptation. I contrived to meet her, by which time she was godlike in my eyes. I assure you I was totally in her thrall. Witchcraft. She, of course, was distant, which only fanned the flames. She tried to escape me, but I pursued her relentlessly. Each meeting she would tell me sadly must be our last, but I would make her see me again.

"We didn't meet that many times. But each time was a Greek drama. She was so over-wrought. I wanted more than anything to soothe her, and sometimes she'd let me. Not sex. There was that too, but I wanted to give her everything. Everything.

"The pain was so exquisite, it was ridiculous. There was obviously no way to hide what was boiling inside me. I told my wife. I didn't want to lie to her, I didn't want anything to be cheapened. How do you think she responded? Anger, jealousy, acquiescence? Would you believe amusement?"

"I hope you're not really asking me."

"I'm telling you she was amused. At first I assumed she was pretending, but it soon enough became clear she wasn't."

"Let me guess. She was seeing someone herself."

"Oh, that's the least of it. She was seeing two people in fact, but the clincher for me was that she really didn't care. I mean she had this notion— No, that's wrong, it wasn't an idea. She behaved as though there was nothing terribly profound in love. Like our being married meant we were together a lot, but our feelings for each other needn't be any deeper than our feelings for others. So she was happy to live with me, but she could be just as happy with someone else. And there was certainly nothing to suggest that our being married precluded her behaving with others as she behaved with me. So— are you ready for this—she actually encouraged me! She asked me if the sex was good!

"At first I was enormously relieved. I was free to ... to pursue my fate, free to be enslaved by this alluring refugee. We saw each other a few more times, I forget. We never spent that much time together, it's just that the time we were together was so intense. But I remember the last time. I remember the last time.

"Well I'll spare you the gory details. When a man is in love with a woman, so passionately in love that he racks his brain to think of more ways to open himself up, to take everything that he has and make it hers, to take all her pain and torment and fear and swallow it eagerly so her portion should be less, when a man feels all that and all he hopes is that she love him back and his greatest fear is that she doesn't—you see what a state I was in? I was young, so young, an artist on the run, a self-proclaimed refugee—when a man feels all that for a woman, what is the cruelest, most devastating thing she can do to him? Don't answer, I'll tell you. She can allow him, that's right, allow him to make love to her.

"She was inconsolable. Not hysterically, quietly. I was utterly helpless. And the worst part was, she did love me, she wouldn't have lied about that. I was a mess. She never even said goodbye. I just called one day and they told me she'd gone back. I don't know what happened to her."

How long did we sit in unnerving silence before you inquired almost inaudibly, "And your wife?"

"She tried to cheer me up. You believe that? But I was... I was in pieces. Lost in a storm at sea. Really frightened because I knew I'd lost my bearings. I told her I had to go away. She said it was all right, not to worry, she'd be okay. I told her I'd send her money, but I never did.

"I wandered around Europe, odd jobs, peeling potatoes, washing dishes, until I ended up in Israel picking grapefruits. Stayed there all through the winter, with this kerosene heater that fumed all the time. Never wrote a word. After six months I was coming out of it. I gave notice and flew to Rome.

"Of course I went back to the ceiling. There it was, the same gesture. And the power of it—it's a physical thing, it was actually painful. Excitement, recognition, a sense of having lived through hell. I actually sobbed out loud. A couple turned to look at me. I moved away. And then the ridiculous: What a pain in the neck that ceiling is!

"So I'm standing there holding the back of my neck and I see this kid—are you ready for this?—holding a mirror in his hand and looking down in the mirror! I mean is that brilliant or what!

"'Say, kid, I'll buy that mirror off you.' 'It's my mom's,' he says. She says I can use it when they're done. So I wait and wait and wait, maybe a half hour, and the kid brings it over, and says they're leaving but I can just have it.

"So there I am, looking down at the Sistine Ceiling, laughing like a drunk. How can I explain it? If you ever see it you'll know what I mean. That gesture: the languor, the majesty ... "

Somewhere in there I drifted off into a confused silence, while you waited, a little embarrassed, for me to continue. "Is that the end of the story?" you muttered gently.

I nodded.

"Do you mind if I ask if you went back to your wife?"

"There was nothing there. Well, no, I shouldn't say that. It wasn't for me, let's put it that way. We stayed friends. We see each other all the time, when I come for Julie—my daughter. Sometimes she cooks and we eat supper together. She's a terrible cook, all the English are. But my daughter's really something."

MAKE A WISH, JOAN

ere's how it started. I was in my office, standing at the only window, a tall narrow one overlooking the Pomodoro sculpture, frustrated with a grant application. At first I thought it was okay, the sculpture, a little pretentious maybe, or just silly, something architects put in courtyards of buildings like the Waldron Center for Microbiological Research. Then I guess I just stopped noticing it, no more than you notice any particular tree or foundation shrub.

It was a NIH grant, a big one. On the other hand I was pretty sure we'd get it; I knew who'd be reviewing the application, so I knew how to slant it—so why was I sweating it? I felt fed up with the whole process, but who knows, it could have been just fatigue. People don't become scientists for the easy hours, I can tell you that.

The phone rang. Is that how all big events begin, with a phone ringing? That's probably how World War Three will start. Probably a wrong number ...

*   *   *

The phone rang. By how violently she startled Joan realized how deeply she had sunk into reverie. Crossing to the phone, her heart stupidly beating loudly, she noticed how dark the office had become. It was Philip Janowitz, her former mentor. It had been his idea for her thesis project that had triggered the initial recombinant DNA controversy and the consequent "instatement"—imposition, many said—of bio-safety guidelines by the NIH. Those guidelines were expected to be substantially relaxed for most types of rDNA activity fairly soon.

"Joan, what are you doing for dinner?"

"Nothing. I mean I'm just going home."

"Good. Don't, I'll pick you up. Seven okay?"

"It sounds urgent. What's up?"

"Not really. Well, I do want to consult you on a problem. Mostly just to catch up, see if I can steal an idea."

"Tell you what. You finish my grant application, you can take anything you find."

"Don't I know the feeling. Seven, then?"

"Yeah, well, let me call Michael, I'm sure it's okay."

Janowitz had bought a new BMW again. Not that Joan disliked her Honda Civic, but she was weary of Michael's "statements." Would a more comfortable car have been a crime against humanity? "Jesus, Joanie, it's not a statement, it's the way I want to live! All right, it's a statement!"

After Janowitz had rung off, she had stood there with the phone in her hand before dialing.

"Michael, is it all right if I have dinner with Phil Janowitz today?"

"Janowitz? You're not really asking me, are you?"

"I'm asking if you had any plans for supper."

"I don't have any plans for supper." She sighed, didn't say what she almost said, thought of something else and didn't say that. "Recruitment time again?"

"Don't worry, Michael, I have no intention of losing my virginity tonight."

At a silent stoplight Janowitz noted that she seemed unusually tense.

She tried to laugh. "Unusually tense?"

"You're always a little tense. Tense, intense. Don't you know that about yourself? Did you get the grant written?"

She turned to him. "Time is so precious, you know? And to lose an entire afternoon … "

"How are things at home?" he asked gingerly.

"It's green. Let's see, how should I put it?"

"You don't have to. We've known each other a long time."

"It has been a long time, hasn't it?"

"Yes, but I hope you're not counting!" They both laughed the same false laugh.

He suggested a restaurant Michael would not have gotten near. Looking around from her chair, scanning the menu, she admitted it was pretty pretentious.

"Is this all right?"

"Fine. Sorry, I was wandering."

Janowitz leaned forward a little, studying his wine. "When did we last see each other, two months ago, three? You seem more tense. How are things, Joan? Home, work."

"Work's fine. You know, not perfect, but … "

"Of course not, never is. And this grant you're writing."

"I hate it. I don't know what it is about this one."

He swirled his wine. "And Michael?"

"That obvious, huh?"

He gestured noncommittally. "Are you two … have you thought of seeing someone?"

"Michael would never do that." Then she added, "I'm not sure I would either." Suddenly she smiled. "How's your divorce coming?"

Janowitz sat back raising his glass. "Obviously I'm in no position to be giving advice." They both laughed.

After ordering, Joan asked how life was at Biosys.

Janowitz replied intensely, "Good, Joan, very good."

"But you have a problem."

"Problem? No, what do you mean?"

"You said you wanted to consult on a problem."

"Oh, that. Yes, I do. It's in our interferon project. We're going to be moving more people into it— What's so funny?"

"I'm sorry."

"No, come on, what'd I say?"

"This wouldn't have something to do with the Genentech announcement that—"

"That they fermented leukocytic interferon. That's funny? Believe me, no one's laughing at Biosys."

"I wouldn't think so."

"The thing is, we believe we may have a handle on a more efficient process."

"And efficiency is yield and yield is money."

For the first time Janowitz looked stung. "No one's pretending otherwise. But efficiency is also elegance and elegance is good science." He wiped his mouth. "I make no apology for the fact that Biosys is a business whose primary purpose is to make as much money as possible. I think that's about as forthright a statement as—"

"Oh, Phil, you don't have to—"

"No, no, let's let it all hang out. But here's the thing, Joan: The only way we make money— Wait a minute, wait a minute, let's back up. I know money isn't your thing, how'd you get me on that? Let's see if I can't excite your competitive spirit."

"For what?"

"Just … bear with me, Joan."

She smiled. "Okay, I'll bear."

"Good." He leaned into her. "The interferon race is worldwide now. There are groups working all over Europe, Japan, even Israel. Breakthroughs are starting to be made."

"Like Genentech's."

"Yes. But there's one nut no one's been able to crack."

"Glycosylation."

"Of course. But—Joan—we think we may be able to crack it. I don't have to tell you what that would mean in terms of medical applications. Smaller, less frequent doses, possible increased anti-tumor and anti-viral activity—"

"You're right, you don't have to tell me."

"Right. But there's a group at Sloan Kettering working along the same lines, injecting mRNA in X. laevis oocytes, and we think they may be ahead of us."

"I begin to see where this is going."

"Do you? Joan, if you could produce a true glycoprotein interferon with rDNA, you could get a Nobel."

She threw herself back. "Wait a minute, how do I get the Nobel? You're the one—"

"X. laevis, Joan. We think that may be the key. You know more about X. laevis than anyone."

Janowitz stared at her to reinforce his words. Joan stared back to gain time.

*　　*　　*

He had tried to recruit her before. The last time he had tried to contract with her to do some research, and she had been tempted—it was like a blank check without the grant application rigmarole—but it had been too much for Michael.

"No way, Joanie. Whether you do the work in your lab or their lab, what difference does it make?"

"You make it sound like prostitution."

"It is, goddamn it. You're selling science for money. If that's not prostitution, what the hell is?"

"That reminds me of the little girl who asked her mother what a prostitute was. The mother says it's a person who gets paid for giving people love, and the little girl says, 'When I grow up, I want to be a prostitute.'"

They were sitting in the courtyard of the Waldron Center facing the sculpture. After working late they had been on their way to dinner when she had told him that Janowitz had approached her again, and that this time it was so attractive she was seriously considering his offer.

"Cute, Joanie, real cute. Doesn't it mean anything to you that— Look, I'm a political scientist. I'm taught that institutional structures have significance. This is a university. You're a professor here. That is a fundamentally different kind of institution than a private corporation, which has different goals and purposes."

"Which you despise."

"A lot of which I despise, and so do you, but not all, so let's skip the debating bit, okay? The point is, you have to convince me that it's okay for the important distinctions to be blurred, if not obliterated entirely."

"Michael, how many times have we had this conversation?" She sighed, stood up, went nowhere. "The thing I haven't figured out is why all my decisions have to meet with your approval."

"Only the major ones. Don't exaggerate."

"But I want to know what gives you veto power over me. A political science question."

"Then I'll give you a political science answer. Because we're married."

She started to walk away, then came back. "You're good, Michael, you're very good, but you see it all falls apart. All this bullshit about institutional integrity. The point is—"

Michael rose, bristling. "I'll tell you what the point is."

"The point is," she shouted, then, suddenly looking around, lowered her voice. "The point is that you want everything to be pure. Well, it just isn't like that. Maybe for you it is. But not for me. Not for me, Michael." Tears started welling up.

He replied in such an even voice, with such seeming disregard for what she'd said, that she began to tremble. "The point is, Joanie, that you don't want to see the larger significance of what you do."

"Larger significance!" she shouted, no longer able to care who might be within earshot. "You dare throw that up at me!" She turned away and stomped around the sculpture, in her rage idiotically ending up before him again.

He was somewhat conciliatory. "I didn't mean that the way you took it." She allowed him to put a hand on her shoulder and gradually the heaving in her chest settled somewhat, then started up again.

"I have to go back to the lab," she blurted out, turning away.

Michael tried to keep his hand on her shoulder. "What about some supper?"

"I'm not hungry," she mumbled, pulling free.

"It won't go away, you know," he called after her. She bolted around to face him, trying and failing to speak. "Come on, let's go get a hamburger." Her jaw trembling, arms crossed as though holding herself, she could only stare at the ground. "What do you say? I'm starving."

With an effort, she raised her eyes to meet his. "For you, everything is categorical. Everything has to adhere to— I think your only goal in life is to be politically correct."

Michael tried to smile. "Come on, let's go eat."

"You know what it is, Michael? You want everything to conform to your abstract categories. This is—"

"Oh, that's bullshit, Joanie, and you know it."

Now it was she who wore the false smile, amazed herself at the violence of her rage. "Me, I look at a set of facts. I'm excited by the work, it harms no one, it could be very beneficial, why not do it? But you, you say no, you can't do it. Why? Because there's a profit motive behind it, therefore it's evil and detestable. No matter what it is. It's infantile, Michael. It's infantile."

He controlled himself with difficulty. "Where shall we eat?" He approached her to put a hand on her shoulder again, but she pulled away.

"Go to hell, Michael," she shouted and ran inside the building, where she accomplished nothing, but stood at the window watching the sculpture become vague and inscrutable until evening overtook it entirely.

*   *   *

Janowitz rose energetically as she came into his office. "Thanks for coming, Joan. How are you?"

"Fine," she answered blankly, looking around. She chuckled to herself. "You have space."

"Wonderful, isn't it?"

He immediately took her to the labs, introducing everyone they encountered. After each meeting he would tell her where the person had worked, with whom, on what. The strength of the staff was very impressive, and the physical plant was a match. Every piece of equipment she could have wanted was there; and the latest models. Laminar flow hoods, isolators, everything. "You think this is something," crowed Janowitz, "wait till I show you P3 upstairs."

Before doing that, however, he showed her two rooms: the office that could be hers and the lab that could be hers. It was impossible not to be excited. "We've got fifteen people on the interferon project. We're prepared to double that if you come aboard. All you have to do is tell us what you need. Staff, equipment, whatever. We're going all out, Joan."

She drove home in a daze. They had over two hundred employees, by year-end they planned to have forty-five Ph.D's. Eighty thousand square feet of space, every lab fully outfitted with the latest and the best. A Science Advisory Board with the likes of Roger Solomon and Sidney Heilmot. Herself to be in charge of a very difficult project. Instead of going home, she detoured to Tina's apartment.

"Hi, what's up, you and Michael have a fight?"

"Not yet," she said striding into the living room. "What have you got to drink?"

"I don't know, orange juice?"

"No, I mean to drink, as in booze."

"Jeez, Joan, what's up?"

She filled her in. "It's your decision too. You know if I go, you go. I mean, if you want to."

"It sounds incredible."

"Yeah," said Joan, leaning back into the sofa and looking through her glass. "I just have to decide which means more to me, my career or my marriage."

There was a very long silence before Tina responded. "Sure he wouldn't go along?"

Joan shrugged. They finished their drinks in silence.

With a lurch she jumped to her feet and paced the room. "I can't sit still. You should have seen it, Tina. Let's go to a discotheque or something."

Tina was shocked. "Joanie, I have work to do. It's Monday night."

"Okay, a bar."

Tina followed her around the room, shaking her head. "You should've seen it. I'm going back on Friday."

"Really?"

Joan nodded. "God, look at me. When was the last time I was this excited?"

"Really. God, Joan, a discotheque?"

She was expected at five, but arrived at four, then, feeling silly, remained in the car, where, not to waste time, she pulled out a journal to catch up on some reading. When she did go inside she found Janowitz as energetic as before.

"I'm so glad you came, Joan. Can I get you something to drink—glass of wine?"

"No thanks. I don't want to get ahead of everybody else."

"No fear of that!" he bellowed. "They started an hour ago! You know, I don't know if I've ever seen you dressed like that. High heels," he marveled.

"Oh God. You said cocktail party..."

"Don't worry about it." He settled across from her in a plush chair. "The money people tend to dress."

"The money people?"

"They're the ones not wearing plaid ties and corduroy." He laughed, making a show of crossing his arms to hide what he was wearing.

"The money people?" she asked again.

"We're the idea people, they're the money people. It's not really fair, they have ideas too—"

"And you're not exactly oblivious to money."

Janowitz suddenly lurched forward. "I don't apologize for what we do here. This is a business and I'm not ashamed of that. If I'm compromised in any way—as a scientist, as a person—then you'd do me a favor by telling me."

Without realizing it she was squirming in her seat, unable to look at him. "I don't think that's for me to say, Phil," she mumbled.

"You mean you think I am." He was still leaning forward.

She tried to look at him, but couldn't. "No, it's just what I said. Oh God, if you had any idea how many times I've been over that."

He paused before speaking. "You ... or you and Michael?" he asked gingerly.

She smiled meaninglessly, looking one way and another. "Bingo."

"I'm sorry. I needed to ask—"

"No, you're right. I'm a big girl, I should be able to make my own decisions."

"Do you think he could live with it? I assume you don't agree, or you wouldn't be here."

"If only it were that simple."

He leaned even farther forward. "Hey, it's okay. That's who you are. People like you are the conscience of the profession. It's okay, we need that."

"Thanks, Phil."

"Joan, look at me. You know we practice open science. We publish in the standard literature, we do the conferences. Okay, there are limits. Granted. But what about campus research? You keep some things under wraps until you publish."

"I know that, Phil," she pleaded. "You don't have to—"

"Is it the money?"

She breathed deeply, expelled loudly, turning to him. "Phil, let me ask you something."

"Anything, Joan. Really."

She had to struggle to speak. "—I mean, do you ever wonder if money is directing your thoughts? Wait a minute, start again." She looked around, as though the correct words might be lurking behind the Tizio lamp. "Science is messy. Mistakes lead to discoveries. Crazy ideas become insights. There are always loose ends. You know how it is, there are never enough hours in the day to chase down everything that looks interesting."

"I hear you, I hear you."

"Sure, your lab was always a case in point." She paused to focus her idea. "But I never felt that where we went—you know, what got followed up, what didn't, it was all because it seemed inherently useful or important or ... or just exciting. But now, there's another factor, like will it lead to a new product." She made a pained face. "Know what I mean?"

"Of course. You're asking if profit is a consideration here, and it is. No question about it. This is a business." He shrugged his shoulders to show how unapologetic he was, and leaned forward again. "But Joan, if we do set aside anything, it doesn't mean our work is compromised. The sheer amount of science that goes on here is incredible. Just look at what we've published."

She was nodding vigorously. "I know, Phil, I'm not—"

"No, it's fine, I want you to. Like I said, Joan, let it all hang out, so we can get past it."

"I feel like I'm setting myself up ... "

He stopped her with a raised hand and smiled. "You remember when you came back from Dederick's workshop and told me you couldn't do your project?"

She made a face. "You were pissed."

He agreed. "But it was an important thing that you did. Gutsy, too, by the way. And I've never regretted the self-appraisal we all went through as a result of that action."

"Never regretted?" she teased.

He chuckled, nodding. "I'm lying. But this is not a lie: I can live with your conscience. I don't know if you can, but I can. Consciences are a pain in the ass. They make simple things complicated. But I truly believe—scout's honor—that science is better for it."

"What about business?" she asked gingerly.

"Let's be candid. Biosys is not trying to recruit your conscience, it's trying to recruit your expertise. But this firm is big enough and strong enough for both."

"Sure?"

"We've got all types here. Some guys have dollar signs in their eyes. Others just like what they're doing. Lab rats, just like on campus. You'll see for yourself. Why don't we go over—" He glanced at this watch. "Yeah, let's go over to the party. See for yourself. Okay?"

"Okay."

They both smiled and stood up.

*   *   *

She took one look at the room where the party was and knew she couldn't accept the offer. He saw it immediately on her face. "Everybody either loves this room or hates it," he said with a casual gesture.

Joan kept looking it over. "Michael would kill me," she muttered.

"How's this for an idea: Don't make Michael's decision. Make yours."

"I'm not sure I'm not, Phil. It's so pretentious. Don't you find it pretentious? Jesus, marble walls."

Janowitz wasn't giving up. "Come on, Joan, it's not real marble."

"That's what pretence means."

His smile was forced now. "For Chrissake, Joan, what do you want? So it looks like marble. You're not going to judge us by our architect, are you?"

It was a room large enough for fifty people, with a marble floor, devoid of all decoration except one large sculptural piece that seemed to Joan the kind of meaningless thing that got put in rooms like this. The tables on which the food and drink were opulently spread were of avant garde severity.

"If you want to know the truth, I can't stand it myself," continued Janowitz, staring at her. "It's just a room, Joan."

She exhaled loudly. "I wish it were."

He forced another smile. "Shall we forget it? There's people here waiting to meet you, but if you want, I mean, hey ... I'll tell them you didn't like our architect."

Joan flashed in anger. "No, Phil, it's not just your architect. I agree with Michael in this case. This much pretence is a statement, and I don't agree with that statement."

"What's the statement, Joan?" asked Janowitz tightly.

"It's flaunting wealth. And I don't like that."

"And you think I do."

"I didn't say that."

"No. But I'll tell you what. For the sake of argument I'll grant your point. Yes, Joan, this is a company. It's not an educational institution. Its essential purpose is to make as much money as possible, not to do science. But: In the process of pursuing the former, it excels at the latter." He let the point sink in. "By any measure you care to use, this company"—he emphasized the word—"rivals any research lab you can name. Will you deny that?"

"No, Phil, I won't deny it, but if this company is so wonderful, why don't you give up your professorship?"

"Why should I?"

"You're saying this company is as good as any school, what do we need schools for?"

"Because I defend this company, don't think I denigrate schools. Both are essential. That's my point. I don't want you to leave the university." Again he paused to let his point sink in. "So everything won't be just the way you'd like it. In some ways it's pretentious. Okay. But that's not what it feels like to work here. You'll work in your lab, not here. You don't like this room, don't come here. Is this the end of the line, or do I introduce you to some people?"

Joan took a deep breath and smiled weakly. "Lead on, Macduff."

He led her to a smiling man in his mid-thirties wearing an expensive dark gray business suit with a paisley yellow tie and matching pocket silk. "Joan Barrett, I'd like you to meet Rich Iselin, our Chief Executive Officer."

"Joan, thanks for coming, did Phil tell you he gets a bonus for getting you here? Just kidding, really, I'm glad you came. If nothing else, I hope you'll see that, despite what you may have heard, we don't have horns." He continued before she had a chance to speak. "By the way, we don't do this every Friday. I mean we do get together, but it's usually on a keg of beer. People seem to like it, sort of relaxes things." She must have looked at his tie knot because he laughed as his hand went to it. "Yes, I've been known to loosen my tie on occasion. Phil, do I lie? Come on, help me out here." He chuckled disarmingly again.

Phil also chuckled. "Don't worry, she knows about you. I told her there's two types here, idea people and money people, and the money people dress."

"Anthropology 101: everyone dresses according to expectation. We all wear the uniforms of our professions." He laughed easily and

Joan was unable to locate any phoniness in it. She noted that she was feeling surprisingly comfortable, even as Iselin gradually became serious. "There's a certain amount of crossover between types—I've been known to brag that before I got my MBA I got a BS in biochemistry—but the concept does set out the essential feature of this enterprise, which is the marriage of two activities, scientific research on one hand and product development and marketing on the other."

Janowitz was already interrupting him with a raised hand and a smile. "Don't worry, Rich, Joan is well informed on that topic."

Iselin became even more serious. "You know, there's nothing new in that. The journalists invariably write that by commercializing biological research we're breaking new ground, but it's bullshit. What the hell do the drugs do?"

"The drugs?" asked Joan.

"Sorry, the drug companies. We are doing something new, but that's not it. What's new is that we've forged a direct link between product development and basic research. No thanks to us, really. You're the one who made it possible."

"Me?" asked Joan, uncomfortable now.

"Not you personally, I mean scientists. Or rather it's in the nature of rDNA research itself, that there's almost no distance between the techniques of basic research and the technology of product development. That's why business and science are so close together here, and that's what's new. That's why they're here."

"Excuse me, who's here?"

"The drugs. Most of our joint venture work has been with Lilly, but lately Merck has been taking a closer look at us. Most of the suits here are Merck people. That's why it's wine and brie instead of beer and pretzels, didn't Phil tell you? Phil, come on. Has Joan met Pete yet?"

"Not yet."

"Peter Drucker is president of the company," he explained.

Joan looked confused. "I thought you … "

Iselin smiled. "I'm CEO, Pete's president. I'm supposed to be the deal-maker, but Pete's in charge of day-to-day operations. Incidentally, before getting his MBA he went to med school. I want to make sure he meets you this afternoon."

"Hey, there's Roger," said Janowitz, pointing to Roger Solomon, who had just walked in.

"Oh, good, he told me he'd try to stop by," said Iselin. "Him you know, of course," he said to Joan.

Janowitz waved to him and he came over swiftly. "Joan, good to see you. May I say I'm looking forward to working with you."

"Not yet," chuckled Phil, "she hasn't said yes yet."

Only faintly embarrassed, Solomon looked at Janowitz and then at Joan again. "But surely you'll say yes, and the sooner the better, because until you do we'll be sucking wind from Sloan Kettering. Besides, I'd like to consult you on one or two items myself."

Joan was aghast. Roger Solomon was technically a colleague, but they'd had little contact despite being at all the same conferences. He was a Nobel laureate and was always surrounded by younger scientists or in company with his peers—like Phil. Moreover, Joan had always felt uncertain about his regard for her, because of her role in the whole rDNA self-assessment business. They'd had clear disagreements. And he was hoping she'd join the firm so he could consult her?

"There's Pete," said Iselin. "Let me get him over here. Pete," he called, waving at him, and they all waited till he came. "Pete Drucker," said Iselin as he approached, "meet Joan Barrett."

"Joan," he said warmly, taking her hand.

"Excuse me," said Iselin, "but I need to play host. Joan, it was good to meet you. And—what can I say?—I hope you'll join us."

"Thank you," she said.

"Are there any questions I can answer for you?" offered Drucker.

"I don't think so."

"Well, then, is it fair to ask how we're doing?"

She noticed that all three men were waiting for her to reply. Before she could, Roger said, "As far as I'm concerned you can have whatever you want. Just tell us what it is."

"Make a wish, Joan," urged Janowitz.

She smiled. "Okay. I wish I didn't have to write so damn many grants."

"Done," said Drucker immediately, utterly serious. "That's easy.

Currently self-funded research accounts for forty percent of all R and
D expenditures. We see that number going up as our products come
on line."

Janowitz smiled at her. "See what I mean?" he asked with just a
touch of smugness.

*   *   *

She knew that Michael was waiting for her with dinner, but she
drove to Tina's apartment. When there was no answer to the buzzer,
she ran back to the car to drive home, but went instead to the lab.

Marty was just leaving. "Marty. God, you're still here? Is Tina
here?"

"She left over an hour ago. Is everything all right? You look a
little … "

"What?"

"Out of breath maybe. Everything okay?"

"Fine, fine. Do you know where she might be? She's not at her
place."

"Gee, I don't know, I didn't see her leave."

Joan looked at her watch yet again. "What are you doing here
so late anyway? It's Friday."

Marty smiled. "I was just finishing something up."

"Marty, you work too hard. I need to talk to you about that.
Have you got a date or something?"

"Yeah," he lied.

"You're lying. Marty, we're going to have to do something with
you."

"Hey, what can I say? I'm a grunt."

Joan shook her head. "You're a good person, Marty. And a good
scientist. But you work too hard."

Marty left and Joan let herself into her office. The desk was piled
high with journals and papers, the easy chair had a stack of books on it;
she smiled, thinking of Janowitz's spacious office, and sat at the desk,
reaching for the drawer where she kept the picture of her grandfather.
"Hi, grandpa," she began as she always did when starting to "talk" to
him. He had died soon after she completed her Ph.D. "My grand-
daughter is studying the science of life," he liked to say. "She will get

her doctorate." She would imagine his look as he watched her, in doctoral robe, step forward to receive her diploma, and it usually brought tears to her eyes. "Help me, grandpa," she whispered, then fell silent. Suddenly she looked at her watch and jumped.

Michael was in the living room reading. "So good of you to come."

"I'm sorry, Michael, okay?"

"It might be okay if you sounded the least bit sorry."

"I'm sorry," she repeated in a conciliatory voice. "What's for dinner, it smells great."

"It's ruined."

"Come on, Michael," she said quietly.

"What do you mean, come on Michael? It's after eight. I've been sitting here over two hours."

"I said seven," she pleaded.

"You said seven at the latest. You didn't even call."

"I'm sorry," she murmured, truly sorry. "I don't know why I didn't think of it. I wasn't thinking."

"I'll bet you weren't."

"What does that mean?"

In reply he made some non-specific gesture and appeared to return to his reading. Joan stood there, not sure what to do, not sure what she was feeling. Finally she ventured quietly, "Can we eat?"

At first he seemed impassive; then his hands began to tremble and he clenched them, not looking at her. When he did look at her she could see the anger in his face, though his voice sounded almost neutral. "So Joanie," he said finally, "are you going to bestow your sweet favor on them?"

At first she was just confused. Her mouth opened to speak, but no words appeared, and then she was stomping down the stairs, the picture of his distorted smile pasted before her.

There was no feeling, no thinking, just the car driving itself back to Tina's. This time she answered the buzzer and Joan ran up the stairs and paced around the living room.

"God, Joan, you look wired. Did you have a big fight?"

"No, actually, we didn't fight at all. Michael just asked me ... well, he likes to use this sexual imagery. I just left." Tina offered to put her arms around her, but she pulled away. "No, I'm fine. Really. Where were you before? I rang over and over."

"I must have been in the shower. Sorry."

"No, really, it's okay. Really. I'm not going to let him ruin this, I'm not."

Later, after she had had a good cry and Tina had cancelled her date, she told her about it. "The thing is, they want an answer on Monday. I don't know if I can decide that quickly. It's the end of my marriage. Maybe it's the end of my marriage anyway."

"What are you going to do about your trip?" asked Tina gingerly. At Michael's insistence, Joan had agreed to go to Europe for a few weeks with a view to improving their relationship.

She shrugged.

After a silence Tina said, "I mean if you go, what's the point of giving them an answer Monday? You could tell them when you get back." When Joan didn't respond, she added, "What do you think?"

"Oh God, Tina … In some ways it's just fantastic. I mean the equipment, the facilities … "

"And the people?"

"That too. Roger Solomon, Sidney Heilmot, Phil Janowitz? I mean come on. Believe me, Tina, it'd blow your mind."

"But is it what you want to do?"

"What do you mean? That's what I'm trying to figure out."

"I mean do you want to do applied work?"

"Do you?"

Tina thought carefully before answering. "I don't think so. I mean, look at it this way: Take away everything you just said. Now do you want to do applied work?"

Joan also thought carefully. "Even that's attractive. It's still interesting science. Wouldn't you like to develop a drug that could prevent infection in chemotherapy patients?"

"I guess."

"You guess?"

"Well obviously I'm not against it. But … I don't know, I mean if I wanted to make drugs, I'd work for a drug company. I guess I've always seen myself doing pure research. You know, science."

"Me too. Me too. But that's just it, we can do both. There's no necessary conflict here."

"Sure?"

"Tell me."

"I don't know. This is new to me too, Joan."

"Come on, it's not new to either of us. Everybody but us has either formed a company or joined one."

"A slight exaggeration."

"Make a list of the rDNA people and show me how many are not affiliated."

Tina hesitated before asking, "How about Jeff Hardwick?"

Joan threw a hard look at her, then turned away in thought. Finally she replied. "I need to talk to Jeff."

"Is he affiliated?"

"I would doubt that very much."

They both thought in silence for a long time. Tina spoke first. "It's bound to take up a lot of time. That could hurt your work."

Joan shook her head. "All the top people are affiliated and they're all publishing like crazy."

Again they thought in silence, and again it was Tina who spoke first. "Okay, let's assume all those considerations can be taken care of. That leaves two fundamental issues, as I see it."

"Only two. Praises be."

"Wait. First is commercialization. The whole patent issue is part of that. And the structure of the profession, the free exchange of information, we haven't dealt with any of that. And the integrity of institutions."

Joan smiled weakly. "That's all the first issue?"

She nodded. "The other one is your marriage."

*   *   *

Tina woke Joan at midnight to tell her Michael was on the phone. She sat up wordlessly and rubbed her eyes.

"Take it in the bedroom," said Tina gently.

She sat in the living room, where Joan had been sleeping. Very soon, it seemed, the phone was slammed down and Joan appeared in silhouette in the doorway.

"I'm sorry he woke you. Let's go back to sleep."

She went to the couch and the two of them sat there in the semi-darkness. Later Joan said, "I can't get it out of my mind."

"What did he say?" asked Tina gently.

"No, the interferon project. As I see it there are four basic problems: glycosylation, purification—because we have to get rid of all the toxins—stability of course, and then yield. They keep focusing on glycosylation, but actually there are four problems."

"Joan, would you like to talk?"

"Stability is going to be a bear."

"Joan?"

"It's funny, I can't get it out of my head. I'm excited."

"Are you going home?"

Joan looked at her almost uncomprehendingly, then shook her head.

"Can you go back to sleep?"

When she didn't answer, Tina put her arms around her. Joan sobbed only once, more like a sudden outburst of air, but there was fear in it, like a prisoner escaping.

* * *

A week later Joan and Michael flew to Paris, Joan having agreed with Phil Janowitz that she would let him have her answer immediately upon her return. But no later: Biogen had just announced that they were nine months from producing enough leukocyte interferon from E. coli to begin clinical trials. In addition, NIH was expected to issue revised rDNA bio-safety guidelines very soon that would allow most E. coli experiments to be done at lower containment levels, and thus more quickly.

The trip began with lofty hope, continued with a kind of desperate good will, but aborted in disaster. The last days were a nightmare. Michael had told her he needed her and she had announced that they needed some time apart. On the flight back they sat in different rows.

She told Janowitz she needed a few more days, practically hanging up on him before he had had a chance to fully express his anger, then called Jeff Hardwick and hopped a plane to Boston, leaving a note for Michael.

Jeff met her at the gate and drove her to his apartment in Cambridge, where, within an hour, the issue had been decided. He had affiliated with a small, specialized biotech firm more than a year ago.

"Well, that wasn't too hard," he pronounced. "I still haven't learned to cook. Do you still like Chinese? I vote for take-out."

That evening he said, "You look tired, Joan."

She told him everything. Later she slept well for the first time in a while; he lay awake half the night. In the morning, over coffee, he announced that he was calling in sick for the day.

"My plane leaves at eleven."

"I'll get you another ticket. Call Tina."

"Jeff."

"Don't … say anything. Just call Tina."

"What should I tell her?"

"That the consultation's taking longer than you expected." He smiled. "Call Janowitz too. Put him out of his misery." Later, in the car, she admitted she hadn't called him.

"Why not?"

"I don't know. Where are we going?"

"Penobscot Bay."

"That's a long way, isn't it?"

Jeff didn't reply.

During dinner on the wharf she said, "You planned this, didn't you?"

He didn't reply immediately, didn't smile. "Not really. I just decided to do what I wanted for a change, instead of what I thought was, quote, correct. If I'd asked, would you have agreed?"

"Probably not. I'm not sure I can go through with this, Jeff."

He stopped her. "Don't say anything, okay? Just … "

As he was pulling into a motel she asked with a twinkle in her eye if he had secretly packed. "No, I didn't secretly pack. I'll get a room and then I know a place where we can sit on the rocks and watch the sun set."

"Ahuh. Come here often, do you?"

Later, before a brilliant sky and a quiet sea, they touched each other for the first time. Joan trembled.

"I'm nervous too," admitted Jeff quietly. "I don't know where this is going. Right now I don't want to know." He added, "They say you never get over your first love. Last night, when you were telling me about that guy you met in France, I was so afraid you were going to tell me you slept with him."

The next morning, lying side by side in bed, he begged her not to feel guilty. She gestured noncommittally. "I have to face my husband."

"You don't have to tell him we slept together."

"He'll know whether I tell him or not. That's not the point. You said last night you didn't want to think. I didn't want to think either. I'm exhausted from thinking. But at some point we have to think, don't we?"

"Not now. Let's not spoil this."

"Help me."

In reply he embraced her again.

At the departure gate he said, "I love you, Joan. I don't know how—my head's too full to think—but there has to be a way for us to be together. I'm not asking if that's what you want."

"Thank you," she mumbled.

He shook his head. "Don't thank me. It's for myself I'm not asking." Later he added, "I'll call you. I could come out next weekend."

"No," she whispered. "Don't. I'm not … "

"Then what?"

She looked down and finally shrugged.

*   *   *

That evening I was sitting in my car in front of the Biosys building, "talking" to my grandfather, trying to convince him of the correctness of my decision. All the issues were now moot, I explained, simply because so many people had acted without me. It's a whole industry now, grandpa, I explained. They say interferon will be worth five to ten billion dollars a year within ten years. What I do or don't do doesn't matter anymore. You can't be a leader if you're way behind. Patents, biohazard, professional integrity, social control, all the issues to be decided in practice, not in theory. Time will tell whether, on balance, we're all better or worse off.

I'd been there more than an hour when suddenly floodlights came on and a voice on a bullhorn commanded me to step out of the car slowly and keep both hands in full view. Of course I jumped in my seat, but then I don't remember feeling scared.

I was spread, frisked, and questioned, my license checked, the car searched. I made no protest and volunteered nothing. A guard came out of the building and said he'd never seen me before. Only when they asked me to get into the police car did I realize I could be in trouble. I told them that if they called Dr. Philip Janowitz, he could explain everything, and I gave them his number. At first it looked like they weren't going to do it, but then they did. One of them left to call and came back saying, "He's coming down to ID her."

I asked if, while we were waiting, they could point their riot guns at somebody else and promised not to try to make a run for it. I also asked if I could sit down and almost fell to a sitting position.

Phil came roaring in about fifteen minutes later—fifteen minutes of which I recall absolutely nothing—and jumped out of his car. "Joan, for God's sake, what the hell … ?"

"Is that Joan Barrett?" asked one of the cops.

"Yes, officer," he replied with obvious restraint, "that is Doctor Joan Barrett."

Unblinking the cop said, "She says she works here. The guard says he's never seen her before."

Phil did a double take and immediately tried to cover up in a way that almost made me burst out laughing. "I am executive vice president here. I can assure you that Dr. Barrett is one of our most important people."

After they'd left Phil was a lot easier on me than he had a right to be. "I've recruited a fair number of people," he said with a dry smile, "but never quite like this."

FROM

Against

Us,

Tyranny

ZOLA, A FICTION

In 1898 the celebrated and despised French writer, Emile Zola, having published a series of articles on the explosive Dreyfus Affair in an influential Paris daily, then, after that paper has been constrained by the volume of critical letters and terminated subscriptions to cancel the remaining articles, having published two more in pamphlet form at his own expense, writes yet another, the most inflammatory to date, hoping to arouse the conscience of his nation. He calls it simply, "Letter to [the President]," but the new publisher prefers the title "*J'accuse*" ("I accuse ... ") and that is how it appears. It is this act above all that unleashes the fury of those whose aims, customs, and loyalties seek, not merely the destruction of the Jew Dreyfus, but the suppression of those who, for whatever presumed venal or traitorous reasons, support a "revision" of his case.

While Dreyfus is incarcerated in solitary confinement on Devil's Island, formerly a leper colony, for a crime he has not committed, Zola is tried for defamation of the army. This for a single charge made in *"J'accuse,"* that the Court-Martial's acquittal of the guilty man, Esterhazy, after its condemnation of the innocent man, Dreyfus, was done "on orders." The trial is a national sensation, ceaselessly argued in print and on street corners, from pulpits and lecterns. Angry demonstrations occur throughout the nation, sometimes violent, these latter perhaps instigated by *agents provocateurs*, with cries of 'Down with Zola! Down with Jews! Death to traitors!' and occasionally singing of *La Marseillaise*, the national anthem. In Paris a large crowd marches from one business to another, bearing names like Salomon, Schill, Dreyfus and Company, and Bernheim's, smashing windows and jostling passersby while police watch. Every day Zola receives piles of hate mail, even from public officials, such as this from the mayor of a provincial town: "You speak to us on behalf of humanity, truth and justice. But we are not deceived as to your real self. Whether he is called Iscariot, Dreyfus or Zola, every Judas is a traitor. The injuries you have hurled at the Army cannot lower the flag. This flag, which has carried the glory of France to the four corners of the earth, laughs at those worms who crawl on their bellies." Even in the Chamber of Deputies, angry debates, harangues, and denunciations break out, even physical blows requiring settlement by duel, with only the socialists calling upon the government to explain its actions.

After the first day of the trial, Zola, by arrangement, meets with his lawyer at night in his elegant if somewhat spare and dimly lit wood-paneled office, to discuss the day's events and what steps may be taken.

"If we are to be prevented from calling our witnesses, we must assume the worst regarding the judge's willingness to allow us to present our case," says Labori. He is tall, said to be handsome and affable, with a blond goatee. Zola has none of these attributes.

"We must p-p-persist in our efforts to establish the t-t-truth," replies Zola. He is much older than Labori, almost sixty, considerably over-weight. Ten years earlier he had managed to lose a lot of weight, a result of his pleasure in taking a young mistress, but the stresses of his self-imposed regimen of work and his fondness for eating soon reversed that accomplishment.

"*Cher* Zola, are you sure you won't take a glass of port?"

"Thank you, no, *Cher Maître*, I couldn't p-p-possibly, but I beg you to please yourself."

"With your indulgence then," sighs the lawyer, reaching below the top drawer of his desk for the buzzer, and for a single moment only each man feels nearly exhausted, though the trial—a trial in every sense—has only begun.

"*Cher* Labori, allow me to c-c-congratulate you on the way you maintain your comp-p-posure in the face of the most outrageous provo-c-c-cations. I shall not soon forget how, when the judge refused your reasonable request to introduce pertinent information, you said, 'Will you p-p-permit me then, *Monsieur le Président*, to ask in our common interest what p-p-practical means you see by which we may ascertain the t-t-truth?'"

"While I," responded the lawyer, smiling gaily, "shall not soon forget his reply, that that was not his concern. Nor the fine stir you, *mon cher* Zola, aroused when you rose in your own defense. 'I demand to be allowed the same rights accorded thieves and murderers. I have the right to prove my good faith, my integrity, and my honor.'"

"That, I assure you, *mon cher* Labori, was nothing beside your elo-q-q-quence when you said, 'The debate has now gone far beyond the issue of the condemned man on Devil's Island. It is justice, freedom, and law that are now at stake.'"

"You are kind, *mon cher* Zola, though, in point of fact, I have not yet said that. I will not say that until day ten of the trial. In any case, what is that beside your rousing utterance, 'Truth is on the march and nothing will stop it!'"

"Though of course I did not sp-p-peak it. It appeared in my first article in *Le Figaro* several months ago. But, *mon cher Maître* Labori, what is that to us?"

A discreet knock at the door—the arrival of the glass of port—brings to an end this spirited exchange of compliments. Later, their *tête-à-tête* concluded, the lawyer asks what arrangements his client has made for the return journey home.

Zola looks confused. "But of course I shall simply find a carriage."

Labori smiles gently. "No, *cher monsieur*, you shall not. I cannot allow you to be on the street, especially at this hour. Who knows what elements may be lurking in the shadows, perhaps even across the street. Not to mention some of Guerin's hooligans."

Zola rises to his full short height. "I can assure you, *cher monsieur* Labori, that his antics do not concern me. As history shall be my judge, so shall it also be my p-p-protector."

The lawyer is indulgent now. "*Monsieur* Zola, if you will not be afraid, then I insist on being afraid in your place. No, it is settled. I shall have a carriage summoned," and again the lawyer reaches below his desk drawer.

"Perhaps," mutters Zola, as if to himself, "I shall take that glass of port now. It may help me sleep … "

Later, Fernand Labori stands at his heavily curtained window, facing the street. He sees, beneath the dim gas lamps, made dimmer by the mid-winter night fog, the carriage pull safely away, and, when it is beyond his sight, imagines he can hear its unique clop-clopping on the cobblestones as the horse turns the corner and breaks into a trot.

*   *   *

"We must caution you again," yells the judge, trying to be heard over the commotion in the courtroom, while at the same time pounding his gavel, "you ask questions that violate the decree which we have rendered!"

"*Monsieur le Président*, I—"

"You shall not put questions that violate the decree of this court!"

"I insist upon the right—"

"No, you shall not!"

"—of a lawyer to put questions—"

"No, no, no," bellows the judge, leaning into the court, "you may not question this witness—"

"I may not question a witness?" splutters Labori, pretending to be incredulous.

"You shall not ask questions that violate our decree!"

"*Monsieur le Président*, I shall ask all the questions—"

"You shall not ask questions—"

"—I think useful to my needs—"

"—that violate our decree!"

"—whatever your opinion of them may be."

"You shall not, you shall not!" and the judge pounds on his gavel for an entire minute until the gallery is sufficiently subdued to allow the trial to continue.

Zola sits in silence, shaking, watching this, trying to believe that this is the Palais de Justice, that these are his countrymen. His clothes are still soaked; though the room is stiflingly over-heated, he worries about catching catarrh and falling prey to the ague or worse. On top of that, his cheek is starting to throb where the glass shard struck him. "Hatred," he had written a third of a century earlier, "hatred is the militant scorn of those who are angered by stupidity and mediocrity ... Hatred brings about justice, hatred makes greatness ... I am glad to isolate myself, and in my isolation to hate that which wounds what is just and true." He sees himself rising majestically, striding with measured commanding steps to the dock, slowly turning to face, not the judge, not the jury, but the ranting gallery, and in a voice sonorous and meditative declaiming grandly, "Hatred is the militant sc-c-c-c ... the militant sc-c-c-c ... "

He had awakened that morning at his habitual hour, though, as usual, he had slept poorly. Alexandrine, his wife, had also, as usual, not slept well, complaining of the foul weather and a headache attributable to a faulty damper in the chimney. You may wonder if, in their first waking moment, each suddenly remembered what they had managed to forget while asleep—hail to the canny resourcefulness of the soul—that the trial was not over. Had, in fact, scarcely begun. And in those next waking moments, did their memories flash a reprise of the first three days, the circus atmosphere, the refusal of the judge to allow witnesses to be called or, if called, questioned? The derision, the abuse, the jostling by the crowds, which the *gendarmerie* seemed unable to contain? Did Zola wonder, this man who had placed his faith in justice only one rung below the judgement of history, did he wonder whether that faith had been too highly placed?

He arises from bed slowly, in silence, expecting to feel exhausted and depressed, but discovers to his surprise that his energies are already being marshaled for the day's trial and in his eye is the glint of proud determination. For Alexandrine, however, it is not the same. On her face, in her prostration, he reads plainly what he had feared discovering in himself. "Never mind," he says. "Rest."

"Just give me a few minutes," she complains, protests.

"It's all right. Rest."

By the time he is ready to leave, the carriage is out front in the sleety February rain, having been brought by Fasquelle, his publisher and faithful friend. They proceed by the same route as previously, it not occurring to them to do otherwise. As they are approaching the embankment of the Seine, Zola's window is smashed by a cobblestone appearing without warning, and a band of men suddenly rushes the carriage and forces the horse towards the river. The driver jumps for safety, but, hitting the cobblestones at a poor angle, is later found to have broken one of his legs. Zola sits, suspended in time and place, unaware as yet that he has been struck by flying glass and is bleeding. He feels nothing and sees little, though he will claim to remember an intense alertness. His sole specific memory will be that of the face of one of the assailants seen in pieces through the hole and shards remaining of the window, a face profoundly unconscious of itself, contorted, whether by purpose or rage will not be known, but made nonetheless into a mask, a repulsive version of itself. Though in five minutes Zola would be unable to identify the man in a group, he will later confide to Fasquelle that he will carry the vision of that face to his grave. "Such intensity, Eugene," he will say after they are safely in the custody of the gendarmes who intervene just in time to keep the carriage out of the frigid river. It's all he can think of to say.

Fasquelle replies, "Your face, Emile, you're bleeding."

The gendarmes say nothing, only stare through the pouring rain as if they are not sure whether in their charge they have humans as commonly understood. The assailants have managed to escape. When Fasquelle, recovering some measure of composure, demands of the sergeant that some effort be made to apprehend them, two gendarmes are dispatched at a walk in a direction known to be oblique to the one taken. Then, after a conference, it is determined that the police shall escort Zola to the Palais in a carriage they happen to have parked two blocks away.

There are large crowds outside the Palais de Justice huddled beneath umbrellas, with here and there groups shouting slogans, and the gendarme, concerned for his horse, insists that Zola and Fasquelle disembark at a distance and proceed on their own through the mob to the massive staired entrance to the court. As is characteristic of mobs, most people are preoccupied by hysteria and few aware of their surroundings, so the two men, miraculously, are able to move through the mass, with only here and there someone recognizing Zola soon enough before he has moved out of reach to spit at him or claw at the dried blood on his face. He himself moves trance-like forward, unafraid, not from courage, but the strange dreamlike state that has overtaken him.

Only as he approaches the top of the stairway does Labori spot him and immediately rush to his aid, though he needs none. "*Mon cher* Zola, *Dieu alors*, are you all right?"

Zola tries to speak. "What f-f-f ... What f-f-folly t-t-t ... "

"What's that? What folly?"

Zola nods. "P-p-p. P-p-prevent his-history ... "

"Prevent history?" presses Labori, concern across his face. "Is that it, prevent history?"

Zola nods desperately.

"Ah!" Labori understands. "What folly to think one can prevent history from being written!"

Zola nods again, sighing with relief, his eyes opening and closing.

"Indeed, *mon cher* Zola," whispers Labori, leaning closer to him and touching his arm. "Indeed." Then he turns to face a knot of young officers, resplendent in brocade, sword, and spurs, who stand disdainfully a short distance away under cover, snickering. "What folly," he calls loudly, "to think one can prevent history from being written. It will be written, and those responsible will be duly named and recorded, no matter how small their role." The soldiers either do not hear or pretend the same. They only continue to snicker. Labori turns back to Zola. "From your 'Lettre à la France,' yes? Did I get it right?" Zola nods yet again and takes one of the lawyer's hands long enough to squeeze it.

After having testified at the court-martial of Dreyfus on behalf of the prosecution, Lieutenant-Colonel Picquart, becoming head of the *Deuxième Bureau*, Military Intelligence, discovers that the flow of French military documents to the German Embassy has not been stanched by the dispatch of Dreyfus to Devil's Island. In the course of lengthy investigations, he not only realizes that Dreyfus is innocent, that he has been convicted on the basis of forged documents, but that Major Esterhazy, the son of a general, is the traitor. Naturally he informs his superiors, unaware that they not only know this, but commissioned the forgeries, and is forthwith relieved of his position, transferred to the colonial war in Tunisia, and replaced by the man who executed the forgeries.

In court the general who headed the subsequent investigation of Esterhazy prior to his acquittal by the court-martial, testifies that, during that investigation, he had searched Picquart's apartment (illegally), but not Esterhazy's. He is questioned on this by an associate of Labori. "How did it happen to occur to you to search the premises of a witness, but not those of the accused?"

Labori and Zola, as if on signal, turn to each other and smile. The former admires his colleague for his ability to capture the sublime humor of the situation without so much as a twinkle in his eye, the latter, who rarely finds anything funny, for his deft circumvention of the judge's obstacles, thereby reading into the record for all to see the true condition of the honor of the Army of the Republic. Nonetheless, both men will have to leave the courtroom by a side exit.

*　　*　　*

The trial will last nine more days (the jury, after deliberating thirty-five minutes, will vote seven to five to convict; the judge, after deliberating five, will hand down the maximum sentence), nine more days during which the imprecations and the threats will not cease. Rocks will take out most of the glass in the Zola apartment windows, until

Madame Zola, unable to contain herself one evening as her husband returns from a meeting with Labori (hastily called by hand-delivered message to avoid police interception), weighs into him before he has even had time to hang up his overcoat. Why must he do this? she cries. And for a Jew. They themselves do not even like Jews. At the last words her voice twists off with a hysterical plaintive accusatory whine.

Zola hangs up his coat, comes forward into the room offering to embrace her tenderly, if formally (his warm embraces have long gone to Jeanne and the children), and, being rebuffed, asks quietly if a cup of hot chocolate might be prepared. Alexandrine leaves without look or word; Zola's eye moves, as if instinctively, to the windows, where he is fairly certain at least one more pane has been replaced with cardboard. He sighs once, twice, and goes to his study, where he stands in the doorway surveying his writing table and bookcases until Alexandrine recalls him to the sitting room, where he finds a steaming cup of hot chocolate but no wife.

Zola in his garden. Zola, emerging from his precious roses at his country house, hearing distinctly the distant if muffled cries of children chasing each other through the village to the river, sighs without realizing it, sighs inwardly without making a sound. If he were thinking at this moment, he would think, 'I am not an unhappy man,' but, though he assumes he is thinking, in fact he is looking towards the lawn chairs, where Alexandrine is leading Paul Alexis, who has just arrived before the others. He waves, and the other, the younger man, the self-appointed acolyte, waves back, and, even at this distance, Zola believes he can see the unrestrained smile of long friendship and common origins, whereas in actuality he cannot.

Zola in his garden. Alexis, as usual, all schemes and intentions, is asking advice and entreating favors; Zola, as usual, is advising and, yes, consenting with an impatience inexplicably devoid of anger. He is thinking, 'If only Paul would simply work harder—what kind of man of letters hardly applies himself to letters?' Alexis is thinking, 'Why doesn't he ask about my wife or the children? Does he manage to forget I have a family?' At last he is done and inquires about his friend's novel. With a quiet smile expressing the satisfactions of self-discipline, Zola informs him that it is complete. Alexis congratulates him, while he, inhaling deeply, enjoys the aromas of a late summer afternoon, and, scanning the landscape, discovers a certain familiar tension. Yes, another novel has been finished. The long days, the months of a taxing regime, punctuated with insomnia, are over. Will he be able to start again? Has he exhausted, not merely his flesh, but his well of ideas, his passion to express the depths of an outrage he claims he has still not fully plumbed? No, not the passion, nor the ideas, but the will to submit to them again. Though wonderful, it is a cruel enslavement. Only a man who has written as much as he has—a mountain of pages—could know how wonderful, how cruel.

Zola, in his garden, acknowledges, if wordlessly, the second great concept: After struggle there is love. For him they do not go together; they are not inter-connected or inseparable; there is one and there is the other, and for many years the first alone has been satisfactory. But the last years, with Jeanne and then the children … he has realized he erred in not asking Alexandrine for a divorce. Theirs has always been a loveless, passionless, fretful marriage. He is a married man with a family, but the sad marriage is here, while the happy family is over the hill in a house he rents every summer, one house in particular for its location. He feels a yearning and begs Paul to excuse him for a few moments before the others arrive. Walking with quickening step up the slope to the house, he senses that he is yet capable of great zeal, and though clearly he has earned a respite from the labors of his beloved profession, there is this disturbing business concerning a certain army captain about which he is hearing more and more.

He has installed a fine copper telescope on the balcony of his study and his wife well knows on what it is trained. While she still possesses the energy to make his life intolerable should he attempt to visit more than occasionally, she at least suffers him to gaze at length, if he must, from a respectable distance. He puts his eye to the glass and, only then, seeing both children, does he acknowledge the disappointment he would have felt had he discovered no one. His pleasure is such that it doesn't disturb him to have happened upon them in the act of pulling each other's hair and apparently shrieking in anger and pain. To his joy, Jeanne appears to pull them apart, turning quickly from one to the other, and then giving each a smart slap on the cheek before leaving, no doubt to return to her *toile*. Even as he shakes his head he is uttering little sounds of satisfaction, but suddenly the children have run off and there is nothing to be seen but grass and, where there was fullness, there is now yearning.

The situation, he declares yet one more time, is intolerable and cannot be endured. He must speak to his wife, to insist finally that he cannot forever keep himself at a distance from his children (to include his mistress would only provoke her to another shrill outburst) merely to satisfy her notions of propriety. He will go to his family—yes, his family, by what other name are they reasonably to be called?—as often and for as long as he pleases. (A smile now replaces the frown as he imagines this.) He would go to them with gifts. He would go every day after lunch and nothing could prevent him from going, neither foul weather nor intolerable heat, nor even a physical ailment, and every day he would find some excuse to bring gifts. There would be little ones to fall from his pockets, as if by mistake, or sweets hidden in some knick-knack for Jeanne, a miniature Chinese chest of drawers or an enormous incense burner studded with fake jewels. They would each throw their arms around his neck and then, still laughing, have English tea in the garden under the plane trees or play *boules* or croquet... or set off on bicycles for the woods... or row out to the little island in the Seine and have a picnic...

Zola in his garden realizes that he will never stop fighting injustice, ignorance, and stupidity. Repeatedly he has imagined himself saying to the crowds passing on the grand boulevards of Paris, 'Though you may wish to ignore me, yet will I command your attention. And though I may not have your approbation, I will obtain your respect.' "Paul," he shouts from the balcony. "Paul! I have a f-f-favor to ask!"

Alexis, startled, jumps to his feet as though commanded to attention and, shielding his eyes, squints towards the balcony to ask what Emile wants.

"F-f-find out everything you c-c-can about this man Dreyfus!"

Alexis doesn't reply.

"Is this too much to ask?" shouts Zola.

"Of course not. It's only—"

"Then stop this p-p-prevari-c-c-cation! If there has been an in-n-njustice, we must seek to rectif-f-fy it, no matter what the p-p-personal risk! Oh, some will try to drag my name through the mud—w-w-what of it! Yes, unfortunate that he is a J-j-jew. But shall we allow re-p-p-pugnance to restrain us when the nation's honor is at stake?"

In his thoughts he continues, 'To feel the constant irresistible need to cry aloud what one thinks, especially when one is all alone in thinking it! Especially then! This has always been my passion, Paul.' For a moment he is at the bow of a great ship heading out to sea, then he is seated at a table surrounded by friends, all men of letters, among them Flaubert, de Maupassant. They do not all agree with his "naturalism" or share his passion for the noble cause, but they respect him as a writer and as a man.

'You remember, my friends, when *Germinal* appeared, I was denounced in some quarters as a revolutionary. But *Germinal* is not a work of revolution, it is a work of pity. Those poor miners, I only wanted to raise a cry for pity and justice. For their plight has filled my eyes with tears.'

Flaubert, of course, says nothing, but de Maupassant, who scanned the book and felt little, says quietly, 'Bravo, Emile, bravo.'

Paul Alexis, hearing Zola shout from the balcony, thinks, 'After all, Emile has always cared more about strangers than about his friends.'

From the day of the assault on his carriage, Zola never travels without personal bodyguards: two close friends, Bruneau, with whom he collaborates on several successful operas, and Desmoulin, an artist, the latter armed with a pistol. The police ask to be informed daily of *Monsieur* Zola's movements to and from court and provide an escort to prevent any further surprise attacks.

Arriving the first morning so protected, Zola and his friends are amused to see a fistfight erupt among those negotiating for places in line to get into the courtroom. The crowd is larger than ever and they are reliably informed that more is being paid to see Zola in court than his works at the Opéra-Comique.

At the trial, Labori and his associates fight on. Although several generals testify that secret documents were used at Dreyfus' court-martial, they are unable to get the judge to order that they be produced. Again witnesses are excused before cross-examination, or allowed to refuse to answer questions, or else questions themselves are disallowed. An exhausted Labori clashes repeatedly with the judge. When an exasperated associate asks how it is that one cannot speak of justice in a courtroom, the judge replies, "There is something above that: the honor and safety of the country."

For the final day of the trial, Madame Zola sits at her husband's side in the service of propriety and Labori's feeling that it might help sway the jury, and is surprised to find herself moved to hear her husband, in a calm clear voice, without a stutter somehow, declare to the jury, "My person is nothing. I have sacrificed it, satisfied to have placed in your hands, not only the honor of the army, but the threatened honor of the entire nation. I do not defend myself. I leave to history the judgement of my act." As he sits amidst the jeering and catcalls from the gallery, she takes his hand to caress it and is shocked to find it cold and trembling.

By the time Labori rises for his summation, the shouting and stamping is such that he can barely be heard. Several times he pauses so the judge can command order, but the judge makes no such attempt and the lawyer presses on to the grim finish. When the jury's verdict is read after its brief deliberation, pandemonium erupts; Alexandrine, bursting into tears, throws her arms around her husband. Zola, shaken himself, murmurs in a voice suddenly hoarse, "These people are cannibals."

Five minutes later he is given the maximum sentence of one year's imprisonment, and the court is adjourned. Alexandrine, almost unable to walk, is helped out the main entrance by one of the lawyers, where they are met by hysterical crowds, some singing *La Marseillaise*. Zola, Labori, and his bodyguards meanwhile leave by a side exit, where barely twenty people stand near the waiting carriages, strangely silent. For the first time there are no taunts, just silent staring, not even with hatred, just ... staring. A single voice calls out, "*Vive* Zola!" It sounds small in the narrow street and it goes unacknowledged. Thousands of police patrol bridges, main boulevards and squares, and government buildings, hundreds more are held in reserve. A thousand mounted soldiers are distributed throughout the city and cuirassiers patrol certain areas. While victory celebrations are held in numerous halls and clubs and salons, the Zolas sit glumly with their friends until unable to remain awake. Returning to their flat at midnight, they find their street cleared of all pedestrians and vehicles and police stationed along its entire length at intervals of five feet.

*   *   *

Several weeks later the decision of the court is overturned by the Court of Appeals on a procedural technicality. Labori advises his client not to extract any comfort from this and, indeed, Zola promptly receives another summons, this time to the Assize Court in Versailles, outside Paris. By the time the trial starts, Esterhazy, the actual guilty person, has been arrested, though he will soon be released (and will flee to England and grant interviews detailing his crime, while the man who forged the documents used to convict Dreyfus will commit suicide after confessing). At the same time, Picquart, who first reported Esterhazy's crime, is also arrested for revealing classified documents. (He will serve more than a year in a military prison before being released and later rehabilitated, eventually rising to the rank of general, following the resignations of the generals who imprisoned him.) Zola protests Picquart's arrest in another open letter, this one to the prime minister. He accuses the prime minister of poisoning the nation with lies, of having compromised himself and lost his political honor, of being the assassin who has killed an ideal, for which he will be punished. "These are times," he writes, "when souls cry out in anguish." The article appears on Saturday; Monday morning he is en route to his new trial for defamation, looking distractedly out the window of the carriage. His friend and bodyguard, Desmoulin, sits silently beside him.

The trial proceeds as poorly as Labori feared, and Zola, even though he was warned to expect no better than the worst, finds himself helplessly dejected. Apparently he has done precisely that, despite all evidence to the contrary, despite his own admonitions to himself not to entertain false hopes. Perhaps it is a defect of his nature—or a positive quality—that ultimately he cannot entirely abandon all hope. On this day he hates himself for the stupid naïveté that has rendered him weak before his adversaries. Removed to a private conference room during a requested recess by Labori, he feels so depressed he almost cannot appreciate the significance of his lawyer's advice to abandon the trial and flee the country.

"*Mon cher ami*, it is useless to continue the trial, the result is certain. From prison you will not be able to write or speak freely, either for yourself, for Captain Dreyfus, for no one. Only from exile can you carry on your work."

"But, *mon cher* Labori, are you asking me to leave France?"

"Yes, yes, and at once! We have no time—"

"But … " Zola appears to be thinking as he turns away to face out the window, but he is not and he turns back. "But how can I just leave?"

Labori tries to remain patient. "You must choose, prison or exile. They have given you no other choice."

Zola remains unfocused. "*Mon Dieu*, do you realize what you are suggesting? I've been out of France only once in my life."

Labori sighs loudly with frustration, sadness, anger, then has an idea. He tells Zola that, if he allows himself to be imprisoned after such courtroom farces, he will have granted victory to his adversaries. Only by continuing to speak out on behalf of truth and justice can the true honor of the nation be upheld. "I know it is a terrible sacrifice," he concludes sadly, "but, faced with such a choice, is there really a choice?"

For reasons amenable only to speculation, the local prefect of police actually aids their escape by fetching their carriage and permitting them to slip out quietly. Unbeknownst to them, large unruly crowds on the main road are being forcibly restrained by police, for they are already in the woods of the Bois de Boulogne, driving slowly, speaking little. Labori is still pressing Zola to consent to flee. He has only to nod and others will make the arrangements. Finally Zola nods and only then does Labori fully realize the impact of his counsel.

That evening Zola is in a first class compartment on the boat-train to London, though he knows not a word of English. With him are Alexandrine and Desmoulin. It was impossible to see Jeanne or the children. He has nothing with him—Alexandrine could bring nothing but his nightshirt wrapped in a newspaper, for the flat is under continual police surveillance. At the final whistle everyone embraces and then he is alone, still too stunned to sense anything clearly. At the first tentative jolt of the train, terror like a bolt of lightning strikes him. Can you imagine such a moment? He turns down the lamp, sits back in the near darkness, and hears at a remove the clanking of the wheels.

Some time later he discovers himself talking to himself. "All my life," he is saying, "I have fought with my pen against injustice. Who else has combined such a passionate desire for social amelioration with such a profound disdain for politics and politicians? Madame Dreyfus several times tried to see me in the days preceding my first trial when my articles defending her husband had appeared, no doubt to express her gratitude, but always I positively refused, yes, refused to see her in order to preserve my perfect independence, to maintain complete freedom of action. Once she even appeared at Labori's office when I was there—clearly she'd found out somehow—and I had to be quite firm in my refusal, almost rude, no, plainly it was rude, but also necessary."

He is exhausted, more exhausted than he has felt at any time since before the first trial, in fact since his long depression of years ago when sales of his novels were in decline. He pulls out his watch, notes that it is past midnight, and immediately forgets what time it is. He doesn't feel like sleeping and hasn't read the newspaper that's been in his lap for three hours. 'Not only are the guilty ones free,' he thinks, 'but they are toasted as national heroes. Heroes! And I am in flight. How grotesque.' The train is slowing for a station, he notices, and suddenly he finds himself famished. As the vendors approach the train, he beckons one to his window and buys an entire chicken, a baguette, a bottle of water, a half liter of wine, and two bars of chocolate. 'How grotesque, like one of my own novels,' he thinks as he eats greedily.

For a time he is modestly comforted, for eating has always been one of his great pleasures. He reminisces about a time when he had first been on his own in Paris, a young provincial without prospects, truly starving, working for ruinous wages as a clerk for a publisher. How one day, walking briskly through the quarter to keep warm and forget his hunger, he is stopped dead in his tracks by the intoxicating aroma of a patisserie. A plump young girl is setting out a tray of freshly baked temptations, whose smell torments him, not only because he is so hungry, not only because they seem so delicious, but because he has enough money in his pocket to buy one, money he requires for the barest necessities. Reduced almost to tears of frustration, he succumbs, and with the first bite is subjected to a flavor so wonderful that tears actually do fill his eyes.

Alas, pleasure only triggers the desire for more pleasure so that all too soon he is tormented by the desire to squander his precious coins on more of this heaven-sent delicacy. His problem—or salvation—is that he cannot identify the filling his palate finds so intoxicating. Only years and years later, on a rare excursion with Jeanne, when he happens to buy a pastry with the same filling, does he learn that the magic word is marzipan. How she laughs at him! And how many times since has he brought marzipan pastries for the children and they, insouciant little devils, merely curtsy and say 'merci, papa' and run off chewing in lighthearted gaiety.

The train slows again. Zola thinks about buying more chocolate and re-opens his window in anticipation, but, when he realizes from the station sign that he is at the port, terror races through him again, although, by the time he is off French soil standing at the railing of the ferry watching the twinkling lights of Calais withdraw into the clear moonless night, it has become a continual dull aching in his stomach. You may surmise that tears fill his eyes—he himself will later employ that exact expression, not 'I cried,' but 'tears filled my eyes'—even as his attention shifts from the grand metaphor suggested by these physical circumstances to the banality of worrying how, with his utter ignorance of English, he will manage to find food and lodging when he arrives in London in the morning. That and his great fatigue and the seasickness that overtakes him within minutes of the boat reaching the open waters of the Channel sustains him mentally until his arrival at Dover and transfer to the last train, when he thinks of these words from his open Letter to the Youth of France, "We are marching towards humanity, towards truth, towards justice!" and ridicules himself with the parody, 'We are running from humanity, from truth, from justice.'

Could it be, he wonders, half delirious by now with sleeplessness and nausea, that he is wrong about his most fundamental and cherished assumption? He sees again Labori's associate rising to his aid in court to ask the judge in exasperation how it is that one cannot speak of justice in a courtroom, and hears the judge reply, "There is something above that: the honor and safety of the country." This pronouncement that rendered him speechless with stupefaction, was it possible, could it be that the judge was right? He has always found it self-evident that the precise value of justice, insofar as it needs any practical justification, is in its support of honor and safety, but now he frets that maybe he has been utterly wrong all his life, and particularly in his shrill defense of that Jew, by assuming that the claims of the state must give way to individual rights and legitimate claims made in the name of justice and truth. Is it truly indisputable, as he has always maintained, that the injunctions of a universal morality are superior to the social order? What if the social fabric will be severely torn—are the rights of an individual to be upheld even at such cost?

Finally, a mere hour before the train arrives in Victoria Station, he drifts into a sickening troubled sleep, which makes his malaise only worse as he is forced back to wakefulness by a porter knocking increasingly loudly at the door. He forces himself up, attempts to smooth his clothes, and, forgetting his nightshirt, walks with dignity into the morning downpour to hail a cab. Opening the door to seat himself, he tells the driver, "*L'Hôtel Grosvenor, s'il vous plaît*" (which Labori's assistant had recommended), but the driver grabs the door and says, "You don't need me for that, governor, she's right there, she is," and he points to it. Zola is too distraught to understand, so a little tussle develops over the door as the driver, trying to hold it shut, keeps pointing to the hotel. Finally, with a shrug and a philosophical comment—"It's your shilling"—he lets the foreigner inside and drives him the hundred or so yards to his destination.

Humiliated, realizing he has no English money, Zola gestures for the driver to wait and goes to the counter inside the hotel where he holds out a French bill to the night clerk while pointing outside. Eventually the man understands and takes care of it. "Now then," he says politely, betraying nothing of his discomfiture at the foreigner's appearance, "I expect you'd like a room."

Zola only stares at him.

"Yes, well then. I say, your luggage— Perhaps you've left it at the station?"

Zola stares at him.

"I will need a deposit," says the clerk, hesitantly pushing a registration form across the counter.

Zola is silent, unblinking. He signs it 'Monsieur Pascal,' the title character of his most recent novel.

"I'm afraid I will need that deposit, sir, strict rules and all that. Uh, deposit, money?" He holds up the bill Zola has given him and points towards the pocket it came from.

Uncomprehending, Zola reluctantly hands over another bill, which the clerk takes gingerly as though it might be contaminated before turning over the key to the hotel's least desirable room, the one at the back of the top floor reserved for suspicious and possibly indigent travelers.

SAINT CAMUS

The curious events which form the subject of this fantasy are pretended to have been thought between January 17 and February 8, 1947 at a hotel in Briançon. According to general opinion, they were not usual, but a bit out of the ordinary. At first sight the hotel is, in fact, an ordinary "Grand Hotel" and nothing more than a vacation resort in a remote location in the French Alps. The hotel itself, it must be admitted, is reasonably attractive. Of seeming tranquil aspect, one sees at once that it is like so many other resort hotels in every latitude, its rooms commodious, its views expected to please. Yet at the time it was different, in these ways: Beneath falling snow it had neither electricity nor hot water; save for a single occupant it was completely devoid of guests; and this guest, used to his native north African coastline, found the Alpine scenery boring and oppressive, when all is said a neutral place. On arrival, after an exhausting sixteen-hour trip, he would note in his journal, "The evening which flows over these cold mountains ends by freezing my heart."

As soon as he arrives, Camus wishes he could leave; but he knows he cannot, his tubercular condition requires a rest cure and this site has been selected by his physician. Yet the entire hotel is empty, save for him. He can imagine it full, what it would be like, the absent and frenetic air with which one would do everything, for in a resort the population naturally seeks pleasure and soon acquires the habits of pleasure, performing the same acts, whether it be sport, drinking, or making love, without an intimation of something else. How difficult, then, to be sick in such a place. Not so much 'difficult,' a better word might be 'uncomfortable.' The sick naturally need calm, to rely on something, but here every activity requires good health; a consumptive would find himself very much alone.

One should not exaggerate. What must be emphasized is the banal aspect of resort life. If its habits suggest a life that is not very passionate, at least it is not disordered, and its population seems frank, amiable, and active. But, to repeat, during the brief period under consideration, Camus is the sole resident and one can readily admit that nothing could have prepared him for the grave events which one proposes to describe here.

*   *   *

The main lobby is empty, the capacious dining room empty, the long hallways empty, all dimly lit by gaslight. Here and there at long intervals members of a skeleton staff, apparently bent on their tasks, but without urgency. First shock, then amusement, then fear and anger, finally a grim amusement with the amusement again quickly slipping away. He locks the door carefully and sits on the edge of the bed, lips pursed, staring at the floor.

There is a discrete knock; he is politely summoned to dinner. Slowly he changes his shirt, puts on a tie, his tweed jacket, and goes into the hallway, long and empty. Ushered to a table among dozens, he sits tight-lipped gazing at the unlit chandeliers, the shadows, the empty chairs. Where hunger should be he feels panic; abruptly he snaps for the sommelier, orders an excellent bottle, gulps the first glass. Jean Tarrou, the hero of *The Plague*, the novel he has delivered to the printer only weeks earlier, sits across from him, explaining that he can never resist the chance to share a good bottle with a friend. "How did you do it?" asks Camus hoarsely. "Struggle?" He shrugs. "Seeing how life is, struggle is the only natural response." Camus shakes his head. "Indifference is also natural." "I don't have enough courage for that," replies Tarrou with a sad smile. Camus becomes silent, shaking his head. "In ten years," he says suddenly, "they will award me the Nobel Prize. The official citation will claim that with clear-sighted earnestness I illuminate the problems of the human conscience in our times." Tarrou waits. "Tomorrow I will again take up work on *The Rebel*, which is to provide the philosophical basis for your behavior. Barely a week later I will be fighting the desire to abandon the project." Tarrou drinks. "It needs a simpler heart, a greater intelligence."

"Would you like me to summon Rieux? He's in the lobby."

Camus gestures energetically. "You see, for the doctor it is simple: Health is good, sickness and death are bad."

"But they always win."

"Wait. Suppose you were pressed to choose where the alternatives were not pure."

"As in real life? But you confronted that during the Occupation—"

"No, a more difficult choice. Eventually I acknowledged that fascism must be defeated militarily, even if that meant— But here both sides … "

Tarrou smiles. "Have you forgotten what you have me tell Rieux? I claim that we cannot make a gesture in this world without risking getting someone killed. Because killing or allowing killing is in the logic of peoples' lives."

Camus nods. "Everyone carries the plague in him."

"Exactly. The microbe is natural. The rest—health, integrity, purity—is an effect of will."

A long silence falls between them. "When I wrote that," whispers Camus finally, "I didn't know what was coming."

Back in his room he writes, "A hotel without guests is absurd."

*   *   *

He awakens slowly, luxuriously, amazed, once he reaches conscious-ness, that he has actually slept through the entire night, not waking once, and no disturbing dreams. Smiling, he thinks perhaps this sojourn will work after all, is suddenly imbued with energy, envisions filling many pages. The room is warm. Avoiding the window he calls for breakfast, which normally he would never eat. He must gain weight, the doctor insists on that point, but now he wants to eat, to have an appetite and indulge it. He feels almost rested, ready to work.

Bouillie, they bring him, porridge. He laughs, eats it all, after instructing that the coffee be made stronger from now on, and no milk, not even in the morning. The chambermaid curtseys and leaves with her tip. "And now," he instructs himself, "I must organize my time." He resolves to focus on his current task, to explicate the forms of pure revolt. He manages to read and take notes for a few hours. You will see correctly in this his explicit commitment to the resolu-tion of a certain moral dilemma. It motivated his entire life, from his first maturity to his untimely death. "The first attack of tuberculosis came when I was seventeen," he explains. "As the doctor described the disease, I became horrified. This soon acquired and merged with terror, not at death per se, but at how death transforms life. My ill-ness distanced me, became a form of exile.

"I first married a drug-addict. We all knew her, she was beauti-ful and provocative and wild—one of my friends remarked correctly that Simone could have driven any one of us to suicide. Of course the marriage didn't last. I learned that she had been prostituting her-self to a doctor for drugs. We were traveling with a friend of mine at the time, canoeing through central Europe. My strength failed and they continued without me. Everyone assumed they slept together, perhaps they did. Even if Yves insisted on separate rooms, she could have gone to him in a transparent nightgown. Simone would do that, she was that unhappy."

Camus finds himself at the window. The snow has stopped falling, but the sky is still gray. Such grayness afflicts him. To rescue his optimistic resolve, he pulls himself away, orders another coffee. The doctor prescribed long walks. "You must go out. No hiding." Camus smiles privately. "But I am always hiding."

Sartre and de Beauvoir ask him if he will be at the Café Flore in the evening as usual.

"As you see, I am here." He adds, "I have been exiled."

"Too bad," replies Sartre. "Can you get drunk here? There's no one to talk to, no one to dance with. Won't you miss women?"

Camus nods seriously. "Not merely exile, but prison."

Sartre's eyes sparkle. "Not merely prison, but an *oubliette*."

De Beauvoir muses that the one consolation of the *oubliette* is that, though confined to a hole in the ground, you can always see the sky.

"Through an iron grate," mutters Camus.

"My dear," replies Sartre with a chuckle, "that is no consolation, but the most exquisite torture." He moves around the room slowly, as if to note its details. De Beauvoir waits by the door. He tries the bed, reads off the titles of the books Camus has brought, even tastes the coffee.

Camus raises a hand to cover his eyes, he whispers, "Our friendship still has a few years left. Don't abandon me."

"No matter what you are doing, you could be engrossed in the most animated argument, the moment a woman comes into view, you will break off." De Beauvoir is speaking. "As though it is your responsibility as a man to appraise her, girl or woman, it makes no difference."

"I can tolerate occasional conceit," says Sartre behind his back, "but your unending rhetoric about honesty and goodness when we are rivals in seduction is too much."

"Regarding conceit," replies Camus coolly, "by all accounts yours will far exceed mine. As to the other charge, I will admit— I have often admonished myself about this. But I will never be able to stop, because—"

"What I can't stand the most is that you get more women than I do."

"I thought you were my close friend. All the good times we have together."

"After work," says de Beauvoir, "you relax in a café, drink, stare at girls, wait for some friends to show up. Francine is left at home with the twins."

Sartre says, "You always take delight in being the center of attention. Raconteur, dance show-off."

"When you break with me in the most brutal fashion, in the pages of your journal, I will be crushed," says Camus.

"Yet you judge yourself more harshly than I shall."

"But you do it publicly." Camus turns slowly to look at him with a pained expression. Wearily he raises himself to his feet, walks to the door, goes out into the hallway. It is dimly lit, more dark and shadow than light, completely empty. A void. Slowly he starts down its length, noting the number on each door as though it might have some meaning, as though looking at the door might cause it to open. How does he know there aren't people behind these doors? He gazes down the long hallway; in the half-light he can't make out how it ends. A few doors ahead, he sees one is open. He peers in. A woman who looks old and tired turns from her dusting to face him. He stares at her. She waits. A gentle hand touches his arm. He turns, certain it was his mother. His breathing returns to normal.

Returning to his room he is elated to find Maria waiting by the window with her big Spanish smile that withholds nothing. "Maria!" he cries, rushing to embrace her, "what are you doing here? We aren't to see each other again until June."

They had first met four years ago, backstage after one of her performances, but it was more than a year before they became lovers, when she had the lead in one of his plays. It has been said she appealed to his dark side, his Spanish blood. "With her I could shout and sob, even weep, and talk about death." At the time, Camus was forcibly separated from his wife by the war; after the Liberation, when Francine could rejoin him, he and Maria broke off. That was a little over two years ago. But in five months they will run into each other on the street and be unable to continue alone. He is showering her with kisses, clutching her. She too gives herself to this passion.

"Let's walk!" he exclaims. "With you I could go out."

He tells her his life is a failure. It hurts him when she laughs. "*The Plague* will be a best-seller," she cries, "you will be a celebrity and have all the praise and women you want."

"But that's because they won't understand it. They'll think it's about the war and the Occupation."

She pokes him in the ribs. "You will have many opportunities to be consoled."

Camus giggles reflexively, but remains somber.

"I know," says Maria, "it's about life itself, the challenge of life as it is, the necessity of revolt—"

He turns on her, grabbing her arm. "You understand," he shouts, "but they won't. They won't ever understand me, or know me. And when *The Rebel* is published, which is the same book in a different form, I will be vilified. Sartre himself will train his guns on me, our friendship publicly broken. Don't you see, I will never recover from that blow."

"I see that," she snaps, "but I also see that your stature and influence will continue to grow."

"While I disintegrate," he mutters. "Writer's block, claustrophobia, I drive Francine into mental illness—"

"Later, later. First you will play the celebrity, as you earlier played the Resistance hero—"

"That's not fair! I never exaggerated my wartime—"

"You let others do it for you. You enjoyed playing Bogart."

"Maria, that's just not so." He is truly offended.

"All right, never mind, I admit you were never a *farceur* like the others, but you must admit you enjoy attention, not least the attention of beautiful women."

Camus suddenly looks down, unable to suppress a smile. Then he looks around at the alien landscape, wondering how people can find it inspiring.

"You look tired," she says. "You should eat a big lunch and then take a nap."

"Will you be there when I wake up?"

"I'll always be there, you know that."

Camus enters the dining room and seats himself in the same chair. Soon a waiter brings soup and bread. Camus quips that he doesn't remember ordering; the waiter, embarrassed, informs him that, as he is the only guest, the menu is fixed. He surveys the dining room again. With the filtered daylight, it seems less oppressive. He believes again he will be able to work here, that he can reflect on his calling. He tries the soup and finds it good. "After all," he muses, "the monastic life should be good for me."

*   *   *

Suddenly he is awakened by the chambermaid summoning him to dinner. Bleary-eyed, he stares at his watch, momentarily unable to comprehend the time, then rolls back, closing his eyes, waiting to see if a headache will come. Eventually he arises, washes and dresses, and goes downstairs. As he enters the dining room, he is surprised to see Doctor Rieux, the narrator and, with Tarrou, the other hero of *The Plague*, sitting immobile at his table. The doctor rises to greet him formally. "I would not have imposed my company," he apologizes, "except at Tarrou's urging."

They sit and Camus orders wine. Neither speaks much during the meal. There are long silences in which neither feels uncomfortable. The large dining room, as usual half-lit, empty and soundless but for these two, seems surprisingly without menace. Camus asks if the doctor would like to know something about him.

Rieux's entire response is to smile at him.

He speaks for a long time; here is his discourse, nearly reconstituted:

> In August, 1942 I was exiled to a depressing old fortified farm where my wife's family used to vacation, called Le Panelier. I had had a severe attack on my left lung and the Vichy government granted me a pass. Francine traveled there with me, but soon returned to Algiers to try to find jobs for both of us. I was repelled by the place, the pine-covered hills, usually misted over, it had a sad quality. I tried to settle into my exile. Twice a month I had to go to St-Étienne, a depressing little industrial city, for lung treatments. Then in November the Allies landed in North Africa and the Ger-

mans occupied Vichy France, and my wife and I were cut off. We wouldn't be reunited until after the Liberation.

Occasionally I went to Lyons, an ordeal by train in those days. That's where I first met René Leynaud. I knew he was in the active resistance, though only later did I discover he was regional second in command for the organization Combat. We became instant friends. He was a poet, though unpublished. I had just published *The Stranger* and *The Myth of Sisyphus* and thus already enjoyed a certain stature. We exchanged some writings as a token of friendship.

René had served in the regular army, but in the onslaught was among those who had fallen back to Dunkirk and escaped across the channel. He soon returned under cover to join the Resistance. He never spoke about what he was doing unless it was necessary. For example, once he told me to be very careful what I said to a certain person because he was suspected of being an informer. But typically we spoke of mutual friends, soccer, swimming, books. We were both passionate about soccer.

When I came to Lyons, he would put me up in his tiny room. It was so small, he himself would have to go elsewhere to find a bed. He would slip out just before curfew. But until then we would smoke and drink ersatz coffee and talk quietly but passionately. The little room was crowded with books of poetry, I recall feeling reassured by them, sensing the heavy silence of Occupation nights settling around us outside.

He told me he had stopped writing. He said he would return to that, afterwards. I remember how he emphasized that word, 'afterwards.' He fell silent then, smoking and drinking pensively, and in that pause I saw how differently his world was constituted than mine. The notion that there could be an afterwards... It implied a concrete struggle between good and evil and especially a confidence that good would prevail. Whereas I felt crushed by the war. How can I explain? For me the war was not an exception to normal life, but a horrifying excrescence of it. Others—René, those like you, doctor—might believe it could be defeated with a sufficient will and effort and then there could be a general return to normal life. In this view the Germans were the enemy and victory was to be achieved by killing enough of them to force a surrender. Even those who acknowledged that the true enemy was fascism could reconcile themselves to killing, if not fascism, then fascists, or, if not fascists, then those who wore its uniform. Therefore their struggle was just, if not pure. Whereas I felt in my bones that war itself was the enemy. How then could violence, which, in enlarging itself from local flarings to global incendiarism had clearly presented itself as the prevailing feature of human interaction, how could violence employ itself to end itself? Do you see? Not that I was a pacifist, I myself would eventually support the Resistance. Rather I believed that the true enemy would survive the ending of the war. Judge for yourself whether I was right.

But René, René was not afflicted with my disease. My act was to write. Recall how I justify your chronicle of the plague, as a lucid decision to not be one of those who keeps silent, to bear witness for the victims, to leave a record of injustice and violence, and to say simply what one learns from such events, that there is, in humanity, more to admire than despise.

René carried on to the end. He was caught only weeks before the Allies landed, on the very spot—Place Belle-cour—where we had strolled, he and I, more than once, making eyes at women. It could even have been there we decided we would work together, afterwards. He tried to escape, but they shot him in the legs. By that time I was in Paris, working on Combat's newspaper, so I heard when he was captured. Not long after, he was executed when the Germans prepared to withdraw from Lyons...

After the war, a volume of his poetry was published. I was honored to contribute a preface.

We would also meet in St-Étienne, where I had to go every other week for treatments. How I hated that industrial city. I told him, if hell existed, it would be like those interminable gray streets. I called it "the hopeless city." If he could, he would meet me there for a few hours and we would walk around from one depressing café to another, each deserted, filled with flies.

Once, sitting alone in some godforsaken little place whose name I probably never even knew, I confessed how my illness pressed down on me, paralyzing me with a sense of futility. The war was so utterly beyond my control, the only way I could conceive of opposing it was to write. And what a struggle that was. (I would labor on *The Plague* for six years and then I only gave it to the printer because I could no longer stand to look at it.)

If writing was so difficult, what could I hope to accomplish in the Resistance? Anyway, I continued ruefully, it would be extremely difficult to undertake any resistance activity in the hopeless city, a city ready-made for fascism. And, even if it were, I myself would be useless, since I could not feel anything but the most unreasonable of torpors. René at first said nothing in direct response, then only that I was exaggerating. His silence didn't strike me at the time, we would often remain comfortably silent together.

I sometimes wish he had corrected me. As second in command of the region, he knew full well that he had a network operating precisely in St-Étienne. He also knew the Resistance was active in the hills around Le Panelier, in Le Panelier itself. Recalling the things I said, I am ashamed. Aside from sounding ridiculous, I must have hurt my friend. But René said nothing. Had he tried to recruit me, would I have responded? I was recruited later, but to clandestine newspaper work, not the active Resistance.

On our way back to the station we passed a dead cat in the gutter and, such was my mood at the time, I fell into uncontrollable fits of laughter. René looked at me and then he too started roaring, until we were hanging on each other, barely able to stand up. As we were finally catching our breath I shouted, "You see, nothing can succeed here!" and we doubled over again, holding our stomachs.

Finishing, Camus was gently tapping his foot against a leg of the table. After a silence, Doctor Rieux raised himself a bit and asked if he had an idea of the path it was necessary to take to arrive at peace.

"Yes, sympathy."

A waiter arrives to take away the dishes. Both men watch him pile them on his arm and carry them off.

"In sum," continues Camus with simplicity, "what interests me is to know how one becomes a saint."

The doctor raises his eyebrows, but says nothing for a while, then asks if he should bring Tarrou, who is in the lobby.

Camus shakes his head. "I'm going out," he says wearily.

"Shall I join you? It's dark."

"Isn't it always?"

As he passes through the lobby, Tarrou calls out behind him, "Be careful, Camus, it's dark out."

Indeed, the dark seems complete, once beyond the dim lights of the hotel. There are no stars, no moon; the sky is completely overcast. He listens to the crunching sound of his steps on the packed snow of the road, walking slowly. Since the war he has been lionized as a Resistance hero. It began when it became known that the anonymous editor of the underground newspaper *Combat* was the author of *The Stranger*. For reasons that must be obvious, he is extremely embarrassed by this and points out that others did and risked far more. The new government awarded him the Resistance Medal with Rosette six months ago, but he has refused to wear it. "What I did was very little," he wrote, "and it has not yet been given to friends who were killed at my side." Yet others, friends of his, who did much less, were magnifying or inventing their own actions. He looks around at where the trees are, trying to make them out in the dark, to smell them. Perhaps he can do it, at least a little. He tries to feel their presence, to find in them something comforting and beautiful as so many others do.

Suddenly he turns back and marches through the lobby and across the dining room to the entrance to the kitchen. For a moment he hesitates, then pushes the doors and enters. He stands just inside, staring, as the startled workers, suddenly immobile, stare back. They all remain like that for what seems a long time, until Camus mumbles, "Excuse me. I wanted to see…" He turns and exits and practically runs to his room, where he slams the door, locks it, and sits panting at the table he has made his desk. "Jean!" he cries, "what am I to do?"

"What you can," replies Tarrou gently. "You find all places indifferent, even those you love."

"This place is alien to me. How can I work here?" Camus stares at his table for a long time. Calm now, he says, "What you said was true. I find all landscapes indifferent, even, perhaps especially, the ones I love. Is it because they can't return your love?" Then he adds, "I'm failing, Jean. I can't write because I can't live. Both are immobilized by evil indifference."

"Is it really indifference," asks Tarrou, "or is it a love so large and fragile that every movement causes something of it to break?"

Camus looks up and stares at his character. After a long time he gets up and goes to the window. "Is that why I chase women all the time? Only in the arms of a woman do I lose my indifference. But it only lasts as long as the encounter." He turns from the window. "This is a place where people go when they are happy and healthy, but I am sick and miserable." He returns to his desk and picks up his journal. "What should I do?"

"You cannot leave."

"I don't mean that." They stare at each other.

Tarrou nods. "Can you show me a way to choose when there is no choice?" He watches him sadly.

"I am a French Algerian, a '*pied noir*,' but an unusual one in that I believe Algeria should be for all Algerians. Unusual, but certainly not alone. And prepared to work for complete equality and integration. But that, of course, presents a dilemma, because I cannot condone the terrorist methods of either— I detest it. The paras will torture and the FLN will throw bombs. With every fiber of my being, I—" Tears appear in his eyes. "Children, Jean. Boys and girls, tortured, blown up. How could I... "

After a silence Tarrou asks, "Is there perhaps a second reason?"

Camus turns and stares at him, finally lowering his eyes. He nods slightly. "Each side will want Algeria for itself. Justice is with the Arabs, but I am French. Am I to support the expulsion of my own people? My friends, my family? My mother is there, my brother."

Tarrou nods, though it is not clear to Camus what that means. "Do you remember how Rieux responds to Rambert's attempts to escape the city?"

Camus waits.

"As something fine and proud. Because his motive is to escape servitude. For him, escape is a form of confrontation, silence a variety of speech."

"He also sees his efforts as vain and contradictory."

Tarrou shrugs. "No less honorable for that."

"I can't conceive any escape. Silence is precisely what no one will accept. But I refuse to speak if, in speaking, terrorism is promoted." His eyes are narrow and his fists clenched. "For my refusal, they will accuse me of indifference, of doing nothing. Let the record speak: My constant preoccupation, my frequent interventions, yes, privately, in my own way. I never withdraw from the crisis, it tears me apart. My distress grows as the war does, more and more, until I can barely function, until— Until my death." He turns to the wall, raises one of his clenched fists as though to strike, then lets it fall. His back to Tarrou, he shakes his head, lowers it. "Jean," he whispers, "perhaps I lack courage."

"No," replies Tarrou in a clear voice, "you lack grace."

Camus turns. Tarrou smiles, slightly.

"I have to remind you of what's in your own novel. Do you remember when the boy dies after a terrible ordeal and Rieux, grief-stricken, rushes out, past Father Paneloux? The priest says that such a death is revolting because it passes our measure, but perhaps we should love what we cannot understand. You remember? Rieux is filled with passion and declares that he will refuse to the death to love a creation in which children are tortured." Tarrou leans toward him, his eyes inquiring. "You must remember: you wrote it."

"I remember," says Camus.

"What comes next?"

Camus sighs deeply. "Father Paneloux says he has just understood what is called grace."

"And?"

"Rieux says he knows he doesn't have it."

Tarrou takes another step closer. "Why did you write that, Camus?"

"Because it's true."

"That you lack grace?"

"That Rieux does."

*   *   *

The next morning Camus is awakened by the chambermaid bringing breakfast. "It's so late," she explains, stammering, "they sent me."

"What time is it?" he asks, still half-asleep, rubbing his forehead.

"Late," she explains. "May I come in?"

He makes no reply. She enters, places the tray on his writing table.

"Close the door," he mumbles.

Flustered, as though caught at something, she hurries to shut it, then hesitantly opens the curtains, looking at him for permission. "Look," she says, "the sky is clear. Look how blue."

Camus has his fingers in his eye-sockets, motionless. He can feel her watching him, not knowing what to do. She is young.

"Perhaps I could bring you something," she suggests.

After a while he opens his eyes, finds her staring at him, smiles wanly. "It will pass," he assures her gently. He shakes his head, still smiling. "Would you hand me my journal, please. The notebook, no, that one." She holds it out to him. He looks into her questioning face. "And my pen?"

He sits upright, opens the notebook in his lap and writes, "If a terrorist throws a grenade in the market where my mother shops and kills her, I would be responsible if, to defend justice, I defended terrorism. I love justice, but I also love my mother." He crosses out the last sentence and writes, "I believe in justice, but I shall defend my mother above justice."

He turns to look at the chambermaid. "Would you like to hear what I have written?"

She makes no reply, only stares at him. "In nine years," he explains gently, "I will make a speech in Algiers, my native city, calling for a truce. My desperate hope will be that, by negotiation, Algeria can be made into some sort of federation. Like Switzerland, perhaps," he adds, thinking that might help her, then pauses. "But there will be no truce. I will be under tremendous pressure to come out for Arab nationalism, but I know a single word from me will be taken as support of the armed struggle." He shakes his head. "How could you possibly understand? I have just chosen." He turns away and begins to tremble.

He feels her hand on his shoulder, tentatively, just her fingertips. He turns to her, his eyes filled with tears. "Have you heard of the Nobel Prize? Yes? I will win it, the second youngest writer ever. But even in Stockholm they won't let me be. There will be an ugly confrontation with an Arab student. I tell him that if I must choose between my mother and his struggle, I choose my mother." Gently, easily, he takes her hand. She takes a step closer, her face filled with sympathy. He kisses her, first on the forehead, then on the lips.

Later he tells her that this will get worse.

"What will?" She is staring at him again.

"This." He sighs. "It will reach the point where I won't be able to use the Metro because I have become claustrophobic. More than once I will begin to suffocate on the street and require oxygen treatment. Work—all work—will have become so arduous, I will accomplish next to nothing. My physical condition never improves, is always a torment. Francine never recovers from the breakdown I cause, but gets only worse. I become so terrified someone will approach me on the street, my secretary has to walk me home."

The chambermaid reaches out a hand to caress his cheek. "Poor Camus," she whispers innocently. She could be his mother.

He looks at her with a grief that is almost hostile. "I spend my last year with a young woman I pick up in a café, a girl perhaps no older than you. I read the first pages of my new novel to her. She comes with me on trips. She's very beautiful, I make love to her whenever I can. She has no connection to anything in my life."

The chambermaid withdraws her hand, asks, looking down, mumbling, how he will die. Camus turns away, gets out of bed, puts a cigarette in his mouth but doesn't light it. "Auto crash," he replies in a clear voice. "Forty-six years old."

She begins to weep. Camus goes out into the hallway. Slowly he walks its entire length, having forgotten the unlit cigarette in his mouth. "This hallway could be the road," he thinks, "each door a tree lining the road. It will be perfectly straight and flat like this, only the light will be different, broad daylight, not murky."

He will be at his country home, recently bought with Nobel Prize money. He will have sent his young companion away so his family may come for Christmas. The twins are then fourteen. Francine is teaching at a private school in Paris. She will be especially concerned: he seems more morbid than usual. He will confess he feels strange, is afraid he may be losing his sanity. He tells her where he wants to be buried and the kind of funeral he wishes. There will be a long silence, painful for both of them, when they just look at each other.

After New Year's Day the family will return to Paris by train, while Camus arranges to drive back with long-time close friends, Michel and Janine Gallimard, their daughter Anne, and their dog. The men will sit in front, the women and dog in back. Without warning the car will swerve, smash into a tree and then a second one forty feet farther on. Camus will die instantly of a broken neck; Michel will die later in a hospital; the women and dog survive without serious injury.

The cause of the crash is never clearly established. It occurs in mid-afternoon on a long straight stretch of highway thirty feet wide, with little traffic. The driver will be well rested and will not have consumed much alcohol. The road surface is slightly damp, but experts rule out skidding. The best assessment is a blowout or broken axle; witnesses guess the speed at about ninety miles per hour. Despite the facts, no one even suggests it is not an accident; only Camus will know the truth.

Although he doesn't know exactly when he decides to kill himself, he feels his determination rising as the car gets closer and closer to Paris. They are on the second day of the drive, having spent the night in a fine *auberge* and celebrated Anne's eighteenth birthday with a festive dinner. Michel talks about death—like Camus, he is tubercular; he and Janine and Anne make sick jokes about corpses and wills. At a certain moment Camus will simply reach over and pull on the steering wheel; that's all that's required.

He asks himself how he can risk killing his friends. He thinks about *Les Justes*, his play in which a terrorist is unable to throw a bomb at the grand duke's carriage because unexpectedly two children are in it. Then somehow all thinking and feeling stops, replaced with a simple certainty that his life is over. It's as though a wall suddenly appears right in front of the car. Nothing else can penetrate his consciousness. He pulls the wheel and dies.

*   *   *

In reply to an attack on his political position, Camus would write, "My role is not to transform the world, nor man... But it is, perhaps, to serve in my way the several values without which a world, even transformed, is not worth living... "

A short story of his, considered self-referential, ends with an artist alone before a canvas on which is written a single word, but it is not clear whether the word is 'solidaire' or 'solitaire,' 'solidarity' or 'solitude.' *The Plague* ends describing a man who was solitary.

As mentioned, Camus would fly to Algiers in 1956 to deliver a speech. He will have long sought for a way to intervene in the growing crisis (the armed struggle for independence having begun a year earlier) and when he is invited by long-time friends to deliver a speech to launch a movement for a civil truce that seeks to bring together the French and Moslems, he agrees.

By the time he arrives at the airport, he has already received threatening letters, warning him not to speak. His friends, concerned he may be abducted, urge him not to go to the hotel, but he insists.

Preparations are feverish, numerous meetings held. To prevent disturbances, admission will be by "invitation" only; cards are printed by a trustworthy printer. At one meeting Camus remarks, "We cannot approve the crimes of either side." A Moslem boy—he looks about fifteen—rises to say that Arab attacks are justified by the struggle for liberation; Camus severely rebukes him: ends do not justify means. He can feel the looks exchanged, but ignores them.

Hours later at another meeting a Moslem nationalist makes some frank statements, warning that, if no agreement is reached to grant Algeria independence, terrorism would be extended. From the back of the room, Camus snaps, "Then I wonder what I am doing here," and walks out. Later, to his friends, he is pessimistic about their mission, fearing the war will become even more atrocious. They encourage him, at the same time thinking he is naive.

A dinner for the planners is held at an Arab restaurant. Everyone stares at them: the French no longer come here. Camus is proud. This is how it should be, he feels, French and Moslem eating couscous together. At the same time he can't avoid noticing the obvious political tension as arguments flare up during dinner. And that the Moslems are plainly pro-FLN, the clandestine organization leading the armed struggle through terrorism. When does he realize—or admit—that the Moslems at his table, at least one of whom he has known for over twenty years, are actually leaders of the FLN? Shortly after the meal he will be discretely contacted by a man he recalls from elementary school, now an undercover intelligence officer, who assures him he is being duped by his Moslem former friends, who are FLN members and anti-French; but Camus does not want to believe him.

The day before the event the mayor withdraws his offer of the use of City Hall; the location is quickly changed to a large building owned by Moslem organizations, located on the edge of the Basse Kasbah, an Arab section. Across the square begins a working class European district. During a planning session at the new site, one of Camus' friends is called to the phone; it is an old friend, now head of the special police intelligence force.

"How did you know I was here?" he asks.

"I know everything," snaps the officer, and suggests an immediate meeting at a nearby café.

The friend brings a second; the officer appears to be alone. He removes a handful of forged invitations from his pocket, tosses them onto the table. "The ultras will stop at nothing to sabotage your meeting," he warns. He assures them it will be rough, not just heckling. "You will have to arrange your own security. I wish I could be of assistance, but alas…" There is a gesture of his hands.

The two return to the meeting and inform the others; when Camus arrives they tell him everything. At first he makes no apparent response, only the habitual seriousness of his face becoming more disturbed. He tells them he has heard from a certain French official, well placed, whom he knows personally, that his life could be in danger from the ultras; he asks if the meeting should be cancelled.

The Moslems advise against it and promise that the security of the building can be guaranteed.

Camus looks at them closely. "How?" he asks.

"We have many friends," replies one. "I will personally assume responsibility for the security of the meeting."

Camus stares at him; neither man's face changes. The man says he has heard rumors that Camus might be kidnapped and suggests finding him a safe place until the meeting. Camus declines, saying he will not hide. He does, however, turn to his friends and request bodyguards, two or three from his old neighborhood, personally known to him.

They meet again the next afternoon before the meeting. Camus is troubled; he has heard reports of a mass counter-demonstration by the ultras and wonders if the meeting should be cancelled. One of the Moslems confirms the report, but suggests that canceling the meeting will discourage those trying to bring together the two sides and hand victory to the ultras. Camus agrees; he will speak. He says, "These hot-headed Algérois better realize I'm one too, and I can be as hot-headed as they." He is told the FLN has publicized a communiqué disavowing the civil truce initiative; he stares at them again, but their faces tell him nothing. He will never even suspect the extent of the FLN's intrigues surrounding the meeting.

Afterwards, the man he is looking at now will write a book in which Camus will be described as "both tense and determined, resolved but anxious, precise in his judgements but uncertain as to solutions—and still very far from the realities of the moment." How could such a person be expected to realize that the other Moslem facing him created the truce initiative knowing it would fail, so that the French would come to realize that violence was the only available means to achieve justice?

Well before the meeting is to begin, the main hall and adjoining rooms are jammed with people, perhaps two thousand or more, part Moslem, part French, all standing. Hearing the first cry from the square of "Camus to the wall!" Camus asks the one in charge of security to show him the arrangements. He takes him outside and watches him, utterly without expression, as Camus gazes in astonishment at the countless thousands of Moslems who have literally filled the vast square. Every one of them is standing facing the thousand or more ultras, men, women, children, the aged, an entire population, hands at their sides, absolutely quiet. The only sounds come from the ultras, contained across the square behind a thin cordon of police. Camus begins to tremble; the man puts a hand on his shoulder and Camus turns to him, blinking away tears.

Trying unsuccessfully to smile, he quips, "You did say you have many friends." Then he asks, "Are your friends armed?"

The reply is, "I don't know, but if they are, they have orders to use their arms only in an emergency."

They return inside and climb the stairway to the hall, Camus now realizing it is lined on both sides with young guards. The meeting begins. Various community representatives address the crowd and then Camus is called to the podium. He rises firmly from his chair on the platform, places the pages of his speech on the podium, and begins to speak immediately. He sees his country before him, feels his chance to speak without compromise, no sense of exile, aware of his stature, of the possibility at hand. Nothing of his weakness or his doubts matters now; he is respected, a leading intellectual of his time. A man without lungs, he wants his voice to be clear and strong; he coughs a few times, sips water.

He sees the audience attentive, undistracted, as he is himself. Then there is an interruption of applause for a well-known Moslem nationalist who has just arrived and is ascending the platform. Camus knows him and has written with sympathy about his movement; he goes to him and they embrace emotionally while the audience continues its applause. Camus seats him in his own chair and returns to the podium. He takes a few deep breaths, smiling at the audience, and continues to read his speech.

He repeats the proposal he has already published in his magazine column, for a civil truce to spare innocent lives. Suddenly, it seems, there is an upsurge of shouts from the square: "Camus to the wall! Camus to the gallows!" Even, "Camus to the stake!" His face turns white, he struggles to maintain his composure, glancing, barely aware he is doing it, at the large windows facing the square, though they are above the crowds. He grips the podium, his voice seeming more tight. Suddenly a rock comes through a window, then another, falling into the audience with splinters of glass. There are cries and everybody tries to see if someone has been hurt. Camus can see several young Moslem men moving through the crowd, but doesn't see any evidence of serious injury. He turns to the others on the platform; one of them signals. He finds his place, clears his throat, surveys the audience grimly, drawing its attention, and continues. He doesn't like the way he hears himself, resolves to rise up to the place he has sometimes been accused of being: above the crowd.

Someone is taking his arm. Distracted, he hears him say that the police may not be able to hold against the ultras; it would mean open confrontation with FLN militants. It is as though another Camus is hearing it; he doesn't even know who is telling him this. Reflexively he begins reading more quickly, too quickly to be clearly understood, no longer looking up, clenching the pages.

When at last he reaches the end, he simply stops, straightens up, scans the audience as though for the first time. He is ashen, bathed in sweat. The applause seems loud and long; he allows it to take him into its midst. It's as though he was standing on a terrace overlooking his city, the terrace of the house he had lived in thirty years earlier with friends that they had dubbed 'the house before the world.' He feels the crowd's force, its innocence, that in this he can be part of it, and feels strong, strong at last, hopeful if only for a passing moment.

Toward
the Annihilation
of Distance

Prologue

from *Cold Mountain Poems*

---

in winter is the structure revealed
the true shape of trees
the precise flow of the bare earth
snow has a meaning beyond the gentle
and still words we lay upon it
and the battering wind has its own
beautiful clarity
Cold Mountain where I live
naked trees
the call of the small bird
annihilates all distance
snow world, tree world
the rock exposed
our house is old, but we are cozy in it

I

AUTUMN
MORNING
CHILD
TREE

Whthat he would remember, for some reason, would be the crunching of the shale as the car skidded to a halt in the middle of the dirt road. His father seemed to jump out of the car, leap over the old tumbledown stone wall along the roadside, and run onto the field where the people were. They had just started out for the city, far away, to buy him a new winter coat when his father must have seen what was happening out of the corner of his eye. When he slammed on the brakes, the child almost hit his head on the dashboard.

He thought maybe they had hit something; you always had to watch out for animals; when his father started running, he saw the people. His father was running towards them, but then he stopped suddenly and came back a little and shouted at him to stay in the car. The child thought he was angry. He was a little scared because the car was right in the middle of the road and he knew he was never supposed to stay in the middle of the road.

He saw his father crash right into the man who was standing up and make him fall down and then jump on the man who was fighting with the woman. Then the man who had fallen down got up and grabbed his father and pulled him and then they were hitting him. The child wasn't aware of feeling any emotion, it just seemed like everybody was very big. They were hitting his father really hard, but he kept breaking loose and turning and hitting them. The woman got up and ran away, but then she came back with a big stick and when she swung it at one of the men, the child could see him kind of arch his back and grab where she hit him, and then he turned, but the woman stepped back and swung again. The man put up his arm and that's where the branch hit him, and it seemed like he must have screamed, but the child wouldn't remember hearing him or hearing anything, it was all happening in silence. Then he saw the other man try to hit his father, but it missed him and his father hit him really hard in the side and the man fell down.

Then he heard the first sound. He heard his father panting for breath, leaning over and grabbing his side. He was standing by the woman and he told the men to get the hell out of here. Then it became silent again, even though the men turned to yell things as they were walking away, while his father kept breathing like it was hard to breathe, bent over with his hands on his knees.

When you couldn't see the men anymore, he turned to the woman. The child could see they were talking. Then he saw his father look around until he found her coat and he helped her put it on; that's when he noticed that her shirt was ripped. Suddenly he saw his father turn to look at him, almost like he had just remembered he was there, and come back to the car, bringing the stranger with him.

His father opened the back door for her to get in, then got in front and turned to him to say it was all right. That's when his jaw started to tremble and his father reached out to caress him. "It's all right," he repeated, "it's over."

It seemed to take a long time to turn the car around and then they drove very slowly back to the house. He was looking for the men, but his father was just facing straight ahead, not saying anything, just driving very slowly for some reason, so it seemed like the car was hardly moving. When they pulled into the driveway the car made the sound it always made, that special one he recognized as the sound of coming home, and his mother appeared on the porch to ask what they forgot. He pushed his door open and ran to her, and she laughed, asking what was the matter. Then she realized something was wrong; although he had his face buried in her stomach, he could tell.

He stayed that way for a long time. When he heard the car doors open, his mother's arms tightened and she tried to undo his grip, but he held on harder, and so she waited until his father came up the porch steps and he knew exactly what her face looked like when she asked in a whisper what had happened. It frightened him that she was as scared as he was, and that's when he started to cry.

"It's all right," said his father, pulling him from his mother to himself, "mommy needs to help the woman."

His mother took the stranger into the bathroom and his father lowered himself into his recliner chair and closed his eyes. Then he opened them suddenly and turned to where the child was, on the couch. "Why don't you get Giant? I think Sesame Street is still on. It's still morning." Then he closed his eyes again and the child went upstairs to get his teddy bear.

Later his mother came out of the bathroom and his father asked her for an ice pack. When she brought it, she saw his foot. "Oh my God, it's swelling up!"

"It's no big deal. It's stupid. I turned my ankle getting over the stone wall." He shook his head.

"Don't you think we should have that looked at?"

"I think it'll be okay. I just turned it. How's she doing?"

"She's got some bruises. Not too bad."

"But how's she doing?"

The child saw his mother shrug her shoulders. "How should she be doing? It's hard to know."

"Probably too early. She probably doesn't even know herself."

"Oh, I'm sure she doesn't."

The child saw his father turn to look at him and then he lowered his voice. "I think I got there before anything really happened. I think her shirt was ripped, but I'm pretty sure…"

His mother nodded. "Yeah, no, that part's okay. It's just, you know."

"Of course," said his father. Then his mother reached an arm out towards him and asked how he was. "I don't know yet."

There was silence then, except for Sesame Street, and the child told his mother, "Daddy beat up those men and made them run away."

He was surprised to see her look of fear. "Oh my God," she exclaimed, "I didn't even think! What happened? There was more than one?"

"It's all right," said his father, trying to smile, "daddy beat them up and made them run away."

"It's no joke," she said, "you could have been really—"

"How do you know I wasn't?" he asked, smiling now.

"What do you mean?" Suddenly she shouted. "Are you going to tell me what happened?"

"Yes, but can't it wait a bit? Right now I'd just like to rest, okay? I'm sure the little one could use some more hugging. And... you might see how she's doing."

"She's washing up," she said, turning towards the child with hand outstretched. "Shall we go see if the sun's going to come out today?"

He looked away from the TV, out the window, considered, then shook his head. "Grey day," he sang.

"Let's go look. Come on." She took his hand and he took Giant Sevrit's and they went to the window. "I think you might be right," she said, "but you know what? See how the trees are? The colors are best when the sun isn't shining right on them."

"How come?"

"The sun makes everything whiter, so there's less color. See how bright that orange is?"

"That's a maple. Maples turn orange, oaks turn red."

"Would you like to go out? With me, I mean."

The child shook his head slightly.

"It's awful pretty out there. It's okay, you don't have to. You want to watch a little more TV?"

When the stranger came out of the bathroom she had on make-up and asked if his mother could give her a lift to someplace. His father, startled by the door opening, made a funny face, and asked if she was sure she wanted to do that.

"You're welcome to stay," added his mother. "No need to leave so soon. Wouldn't you like a cup of tea or something?"

"There's pancakes," added the child. "They're yummy with syrup. It's real syrup, we made it ourselves, from trees."

She took the tea in silence, and for a while the child was distracted by Sesame Street, buried in it wide-eyed with his legs straight out in front of him on the couch, absent-mindedly clutching his teddy bear, and only dimly aware of his parents whispering and his mother going back and forth to the kitchen, where the stranger sat by herself.

*   *   *

His father limped to the kitchen, followed by his mother. "Mind if we join you?" he asked, and they both went in. The child quietly climbed off the couch and tiptoed to the other entrance, where he silently stood and watched. Nobody noticed him.

"You don't have something stronger, do you?" replied the stranger. She hadn't drunk any of the tea, but she was holding the cup with both hands. She looked like she had been staring into space and they had surprised her.

His mother and father apologized at the same time and she looked at him, but he didn't seem to notice. "Mind if we join you?" he repeated.

The stranger shrugged and said, "It's your house, ain't it? How's your leg?" she added, watching him seat himself carefully.

"Stupid," he replied. "I mean I feel stupid hurting myself. It would have been more... exciting if, you know... "

"Never mind," said the child's mother, "it was exciting enough."

The stranger looked at them like she didn't understand. She looked bored.

"Actually, my leg is what we ... need to talk to you about. Well, partly."

She waited.

"My wife thinks I should get it looked at. You know, emergency room. The swelling seems to be getting worse."

"Yeah," she said, "I know what you mean."

His father started to smile, like he thought she was making a joke, then looked confused. "Anyway, the thing is, it's not just my leg, I've got several bruises and he's—the doctor's—going to notice them... and, you know, he's going to ask questions. I can tell him I fell off the wood pile, but I don't know if he'll buy it."

"I can't go to no police," she insisted. She had figured out what he meant right away, realized the boy.

His father gulped. "Mind if I ask why?"

The stranger made a face and looked away. He waited for her to say something, but she didn't. The child's mother looked at him again in that way, and this time he looked back.

"The thing is," he began.

"You got to do what you got to do," she interrupted. Then she shrugged.

They all sat in silence. Then his father asked, "Have you ... thought ... about what you want to do?"

"Thinking about that usually gets me in trouble," she said, and everybody knew for sure she was making a joke. While he laughed, his father told his mother without saying anything that she should say something. She cleared her throat.

"Fortunately, nothing like this has ever happened to me," she began.

"You're lucky," said the stranger, turning to look at her.

"So, you know," she continued. The child found something funny in the way she was talking. She was always stopping and starting again. The stranger looked funny, too; she looked like she knew all along what they wanted. The child wondered what was so funny. He tried to figure it out, but couldn't. Maybe, he thought, she's getting ready to cry.

"We know people who've been mugged," continued his mother, "and of course that's not the same as this, but—"

"The point is," his father interrupted, "these things have emotional consequences, and, you know, you need to look at this thing. To confront it."

"We're concerned. Rape is serious."

"I didn't get raped," snapped the stranger. She looked a little angry all of a sudden.

"You might have," snapped his father, and he suddenly looked a little angry, too.

"I told you," said the stranger, "I ain't going to no police. If you need to go to the hospital, you should just go, and don't worry about me."

The child's father and mother looked at each other and took breaths and then his father asked quietly, "Do you mind telling us why?"

"Suppose I just say I don't want to."

"I can understand that," he replied quickly, "but the thing is, that's how you feel now. Tomorrow, when the anger sets in, you'll want something done, but the longer you wait—"

"Let me tell you something," interrupted the stranger calmly, "the anger's already set in. You might say the anger set in a while ago." She breathed loudly. "I appreciate your help, they could have really … and I appreciate what you're trying to do, and I appreciate your hospitality, but— Excuse me for just saying it, but what you don't know is a lot and I think, since it's me they were after, it's me who gets to decide."

"Oh, of course," jumped in his mother, "we'd never go to the police without your permission."

"Then nobody's going." She was calm, stubborn.

"The doctor'll go," insisted his father. "Or might. I can't control that."

"Like I keep saying … "

"I know. But we think you should go."

"I pretty much figured that out."

"And right away," he added, "before the trail gets cold."

"Well, what I think," said the stranger, starting to get up, "thank you very much, really, but I need to be going."

Again, the child's father and mother looked at each other and shrugged. "Okay," said his father, "we'll take you where you want to go and then go to the hospital. But I really wish you'd think about it." He started to get up.

"Sit," said his mother, "I'll get him ready." She nodded towards the television in the living room and saw the child. "Hey, pooh, what's up? I thought you were watching television."

His father still seemed not to notice. "You know," he said, lowering his voice and leaning towards the stranger, "they could try to hurt someone else."

"Yeah," she replied, raising her voice for the first time, "they could. Maybe they will. Maybe they have."

There was silence and then he asked suddenly, "Wait a minute. Are you saying you know them?"

She waited a while and said, "Yeah. I know them." She watched him.

After a while he said, "Shit," and whistled. "What do you think?" he asked the child's mother, turning.

She shook her head. "It's her decision."

"Yeah, but what about other people?"

She shrugged again and gave him another look.

"Listen," he began, turning back to the stranger, "why don't you stay here? Wait a minute. Let me go to the hospital, let's see what happens. I'm not taking you back, what if they try it again? Stay here for a day, two days, give yourself a chance to... sort things out."

She thought it over, then said, "I don't want to hear about no cops."

"That's out of my hands, if the doctor goes to the cops, he goes to the cops."

"From you."

He put his hands up. "Suit yourself." He turned to the child's mother and shrugged. She shrugged back.

Two weeks later the child tapped on the door of his father's study. The music stopped and he could hear him coming to the door. He opened it and, without a word, the child entered and sat at the desk.

"Yes?" he asked with a big grin.

"Dad?"

"What, son?" he replied, still grinning.

"What are you doing?"

"I'm playing, what do you think I'm doing?" He added, "I'm practicing. My hands are still a little stiff."

"You keep playing the same thing over and over."

"Don't you do that? Don't you build things with your blocks over and over?"

"Sometimes you yell at yourself."

He smiled. "Sometimes it doesn't come out like I want it to. But you're right, I shouldn't yell."

"But how come you play the same thing over and over?"

"I'm trying to tell the truth about this music. It's hard."

"What do you mean?"

"Well, it's hard to say in words. You have to listen to the music."

"So play," the child commanded.

Smiling, his father took up the instrument again. When he finished, he looked over at his son who was studying him.

"You look funny." His father nodded, making a silly smile. "Your eyes," he continued. "I want to play the cello."

"It's not easy," he warned.

"How come?"

His father tried to think of how to say it, but couldn't. "Because it's hard," he said finally, shrugging. "My teacher used to say it's not possible to play Bach. Bach is the name of the person who wrote this music." The child saw his father start to remember things; it was almost like he was watching television, that way people look.

"Tell me," complained the child.

"Well ... I studied this music very hard with my teacher. I remember so clearly, we would work together on each bar, each note. My teacher would say, 'The music is impossible. The technical problems are immense. And the intensity ... Yet it must be played. How are we to play music that cannot be played? Our task is to fail in the most beautiful possible way.' And then he would add, 'It is the work of a lifetime.'" He smiled. "Can you understand that at all?"

The child shrugged.

"I hope I never forget that, the words, the way he spoke ... And how he would take up the bow to demonstrate his point, looking it over before putting it to the string."

"Dad," interrupted the child.

His father turned to him suddenly, smiling again. "What, son?"

"How come you never play for anybody?"

He laughed. "Who should I play for?"

"I don't know. You never play for mommy."

"I play for everybody. But I guess I'm kind of shy." He smiled a special kind of smile then. "I'll tell you a little story." His father knew he loved stories. The child sort of shook himself as if to get ready, and his eyes immediately became larger. "There was a cellist who was famous all over the world for his playing of this music. But he wasn't just a musician. He was also someone who believed very deeply in everybody getting along and being friends. He had left his country because the government there was very bad, and he said he wouldn't go back so long as that bad government was there. And so he spent many years of his life without being able to see his own country. Well, when I was younger—"

"How old?" interrupted the child.

"I forget. Older than you. I saw a program about him on television ... and I remember the interviewer asking him, 'If you could say anything you wanted to the world, what would you say?' Casals was an old man then, he lived to be very old. What do you think he said?"

"You say."

"He said, 'I would tell everyone to stop fighting. Love each other ... And then I would play them a little Bach.'" Saying that, he seemed to choke, and he coughed on purpose. The child wasn't sure he understood the story. His father was watching him think, waiting for the question to form.

"Dad?"

He made that smile again. "What, son?"

"How can something be happy and sad both?"

His father's eyes became wide. "Did I say that? What made you ask that?"

"Well," said the child slowly, "the man said everybody should love each other and that's happy ... but then he played that music and I think that music is sad."

His father nodded slightly, and the child noticed his chest go in and out. "Go to the window," he suggested, "and tell me what you see."

"Leaves," declared the child simply, without moving from the chair. "Colored leaves."

"Go ahead," urged his father gently.

Going to the window, he said, "Mommy says colors have feelings."

"Mommy says colors can make you feel things," he corrected. "How do those colors make you feel?"

"I like the red ones best."

"I get excited when the trees turn colors. Every autumn they turn colors and each time is like the first time because it's so special, and I get excited because it's so beautiful. Don't you think it's beautiful?"

"Mommy says it's real hard to draw."

"It's hard to draw something that beautiful and special. But we keep trying."

"How come?"

"Because it makes us want to try. Doesn't it make you feel good inside?"

"Makes me feel yummy."

"Yummy," repeated his father, like he was tasting it. "Yeah. Well, that's the happy part. The sad part is that it doesn't last very long. Soon the leaves will fall off the trees and turn brown."

"I know. Mommy told me."

"Well, doesn't that make you feel a little sad?"

"How come?"

"Because there won't be any more colors. No more leaves."

The child thought about it, but he didn't feel sad. For no reason, his father leaned over and kissed him on top of his head.

One morning his father raced outside, screaming for everyone to come out, shouting, "Geese! Geese!" The child was the first one out and then came his mother and the stranger. First he watched his father, because he was so excited, but his father shouted for him to look up in the sky. "There they go," he screamed, pointing. "Damn, look at them! Do you see?" He grabbed the child, kneeled down and pointed up. "See? It's the geese, flying south for the winter."

"I see them!" shouted the child at last.

"See the formation, how they make a V? Watch how the one in front changes places. Did you see that?"

"Yeah!" whispered the child excitedly.

"Do you see?" shouted the man, turning to the child's mother.

"I see, I see," she said impatiently.

"Listen to them!" continued his father. "Honking the whole time. God, I love that! It's amazing, isn't it?" he asked the stranger with more calm.

She nodded. "I've heard about geese going south in winter, but I never seen it."

The child's father turned back to him. "And they fly right over our house. Look, there they go, right into the clouds. Wow." He stayed with his arm on his shoulder, watching where the geese had been. "I think I can still hear them, can you?"

"I think so," said the child, but he wasn't sure.

"Right through the clouds." His father kept watching the sky, as though he might still see them, and so he did, too. Then the sky became silent and his father became sad. He looked around. "That's it. They're far away already. And they won't be back till the winter's over." He looked at the child's mother and shrugged. "They're gone," he concluded, shrugging.

*   *   *

One morning the child knocked on the stranger's door and went in while she was paging through a magazine. "Want to see my fossil?"

She shrugged. "Sure." He came forward the rest of the way and placed the rock on the bed in front of her. She picked it up and looked it over. It was about the size of her hand and on one side you could clearly see the imprints of two shells. "Pretty cool. Where'd you get it?"

"Found it," he answered proudly.

"Where?"

"In front of my mommy's studio."

For the first time she looked impressed. "You mean right around the house?"

"Sure. It's easy. Want to see?"

"See what?"

"Where they are. Then you could find one and you could keep it."

She thought briefly and replied, "What the hell. It ain't like I'm so busy."

"Come on," urged the child, already at the door.

"Well I'll be goddamned," she muttered a little later as she turned over a fossil. Her eyes suddenly got very big. Her mouth opened, too.

The child was watching her. "I told you," he whispered triumphantly.

She looked up at him and grinned. "Fucking amazing," she muttered. "Fucking amazing. You know what this means?" she asked loudly. "These are sea shells. This place used to be the bottom of some ocean."

"And now," continued the child gleefully, doubled over with pleasure, "it's the top of a mountain."

"Wait a minute," she snapped. "Is this a trick? Did you put this here?" She seemed angry.

The child, his smile instantly gone, shook his head forcefully.

"Did your mother or father? I bet they did, to keep you busy. It's a trick, right?" The child just stared at her and then his eyes got watery. She took his hands and spoke more quietly. "I thought maybe we were playing a game where you try to trick somebody and you tricked me. But it's not a game, huh? These fossils are really here?"

Very seriously, the child nodded, his teary eyes looking up at her.

"Well, then," she said, nodding, "that's pretty amazing, isn't it?" She leaned towards him a little. "Should we see if we can find another one?"

"Okay," replied the child hopefully.

Later he showed her how to feed the chickens and look for eggs while avoiding the rooster, and after that he took her to the pigs. "People think pigs are dirty, but they're not dirty," he instructed. "They're smart."

"What're their names?" she asked.

"Well, they don't have names. My daddy says it's better not to."

"How come?"

"Because, silly, we're going to eat them. Food is not pets."

When she asked him if he wanted to walk down the road, he shook his head, his expression changing immediately. "Don't you want to show me the trees? Everybody's always talking about trees around here. No? How come?"

The child turned away and kept watching the pigs. They were lying in the straw and one of them lazily stretched out his neck and got some corn into his mouth. "He's funny," said the child. Then nobody said anything for a while.

"How about if we just go a little way?"

Eventually he agreed to go as far as the end of the barn, no farther.

On the way back he said they had to go to the woodpile. He said every time he came inside he was supposed to bring a piece of firewood. That way it wouldn't seem like such a big chore. When she grabbed several pieces, he warned her not to take too many. "If you take too many, you might hurt yourself," he explained.

After adding the firewood to the pile in the kitchen, he asked her if she wanted to see a magic trick, but she said she needed to speak to his parents first. She stuck her head inside the pottery and knocked on the open door. The child's mother and father both looked up and the stranger cleared her throat.

"I was wondering if maybe you could use some help."

They looked at each other. "What did you have in mind?" asked the child's mother.

"I don't know," she replied, shrugging. Her voice was like the child's, when he had said the pig was funny. "Why don't you let me sweep the floor. At least I can do that much." The child's mother and father looked at each other again. "Hey," she said, "it was just an idea. I don't care, I can just stay in bed and count lint balls."

"No, no," interrupted the child's mother. "There's plenty to do. Believe me."

"What'd you have in mind?" asked his father.

"I don't know," she replied, shrugging. "The two of you are in here all the time. I figured there must be something I can do."

A little later the child begged her, "Now can I show you my magic trick?"

"Later," she replied gently. "I'm working."

*　　*　　*

For Sunday brunch, always a special meal, the child's mother asked him if they should have pancakes with homemade maple syrup.

"Yeah!" he replied, drawing out the word excitedly.

He helped her make the batter, mixing in the dry ingredients and then—his favorite part—breaking open the eggs and stirring them in. He had gotten the eggs himself, though he had made her come with him.

"A feast, a feast," cried his father, entering with an armload of firewood. Nodding towards the upstairs, he asked under his breath if there was any sign of the stranger. His mother shook her head. "Hey, little one," he exclaimed, turning to the child, "you the chef here? Don't let them burn."

The child was standing on a chair by the stove, spatula in hand. He had been watching the looks between them, but turned back quickly to the griddle and inspected each pancake. "Almost ready," he said seriously.

They started without her and she came down in the middle of the meal.

"Morning," said his mother.

"Morning," she replied and helped herself to pancakes and coffee.

The child watched her pour on a lot of syrup. His parents had just warned him not to take too much, because it was precious. "It took ten gallons of sap to make that one jar of syrup," his father had reminded him.

"I know," he had replied. "I helped, remember?" He looked at them, but they were both looking at their plates.

"It's gorgeous out there," announced his father. "We've got to take a walk or something. Hey," he added, turning to the child, "what do you say we try to find some good apple trees? There should be some real good ones by now." The child shrugged and his father turned to his mother. "What do you say?"

"I could go," she replied.

"I know you could go. I'm asking you if you'd like to go."

"It's kind of cool out there, isn't it?"

"It's autumn," he snapped, then added, "It's breezy, but it's nice. Just wear a jacket. What do you say, team? How about a little enthusiasm here?"

"I said I'd go," his mother complained. "What do you want?"

"Enthusiasm," he shouted.

She shouted back. "I'm enthused, I'm enthused."

The child turned back to his pancakes.

"What do you say, little one? A ripe apple off the tree is pretty special."

The child shrugged without looking up.

After breakfast, while his father did the dishes, he went up to his room to play. There was a knock on his door and his mother came in.

"I came to see what you're doing. Wow, what's that?"

"Something," he replied with quiet pride. He was always building. "It's not done yet."

"Can I watch?"

He didn't answer. She just sat on the bed and he went back to building. After a while she asked him if he wanted to come pick apples. He didn't reply. "Hmm?" she asked again. He shook his head. "How come? It'll be lots of fun. Last year you were too little. And it's so pretty outside." After getting no response, she asked again, "No?" Finally he shook his head again. "How come?" she repeated. "Your blocks will all be here when you get back."

"Because," he shouted, "I don't want to."

"It's okay, you don't have to. I just asked you how come." When he didn't reply, she said quietly, "Daddy and I have noticed that you haven't been going outside much these days and we were just wondering if maybe something was bothering you."

After a while the child asked, "Like what?"

"I don't know, we thought maybe you were a little scared. It's okay to be scared, you know. Daddy was scared."

"Are you scared?"

"Not anymore. I was scared when you and daddy came back. But those men are far away and they'll never come back. And they wouldn't hurt you, anyway."

"How come?"

She started to talk a few times, but kept stopping. Finally she said, "Because you don't have anything they want."

"Are they robbers?"

"They're like robbers."

"They hurt daddy." It was a question.

Again she tried to find words. "Anyway, you'll never see them again."

"How come?"

"Because they won't come back."

"How come?"

"Because daddy stopped them. He scared them. Wouldn't you be scared if you were them?"

The child thought for a while, rubbing a block, then shrugged.

"You don't have anything to be afraid of. Daddy and I would never let anyone hurt you." The child kept rubbing the block. "So, shall we put your sneakers on?" The child shook his head and she watched him. "What would you like to do?" she asked gently.

"I would like … " he began slowly, thinking, "a story!"

"You want to stay in the house?" She sighed. "Okay, which book?"

"No, a made-up story."

After he arranged all his animals, she began. "One day Benjamin Butterfly was sitting on the front steps of the porch, wondering what to do."

He nodded happily: that was how every made-up story began.

"He heard his friend, Robert Redwing, calling him from the top of a tree on the other side of the field."

"He was in the top of the tree."

"The very top of the tree, because that's where the redwing blackbird always perches. Right on the top."

"But his nest is in the bottom."

His mother smiled. "Where is his nest?"

"In the bottom."

"That's right. Right on the ground. And he makes his nest early in the spring, before the farmer comes. So sometimes, when Farmer Campbell comes to plow the field, he runs over the nest. So the baby redwing starts on the ground, but when it learns to fly, it—"

"Why was Robert Redwing calling?"

She smiled again. "Because he wanted to visit his very good friend, Benjamin Butterfly." The child was looking straight ahead, not at his mother, waiting for the next sentence. "So Benji Butterfly walked down from the house and the redwing perched on his shoulder and they went down the road together."

She paused and the child impatiently asked, still gazing ahead, "Then what?"

"What do you think happened?"

"They met Ronquist Cheddar."

"And what was he doing?"

"Getting in trouble!"

"Just like always." She shook her head like always, pretending to be angry, and the child made a great big grin because it was so funny.

"Go!" he cried, and she continued the story to where the two boys find a huge tree, so tall the redwing can't reach the top, and they decide to climb The Biggest Tree in the World.

"And they climb and they climb and they climb and they climb, until they can see the whole world."

"How high?"

"Very very high. So high that all the other trees on Cold Mountain look tiny. And Benjamin Butterfly can see his house, but he doesn't recognize it at first because it looks so tiny."

"Is he scared?"

"No, because Robert Redwing is with him."

The child thinks about that. "Does he like it up there?"

"Yes, he does, because he can see the whole world and everything looks very beautiful. The trees are all bright colors. But after a while he and Ronquist start to get hungry, so they decide to climb down. And they climb and they climb and they climb, and by the time they get to the bottom it's starting to get dark. When Benjamin Butterfly finally gets home, his mother is standing on the porch, looking for him. And when she sees him she cries, 'Benjamin Butterfly, where have you been?'" As she speaks these words, each one separately, the child forms them with his lips as though he is silently saying them too. And as his mouth moves, there is a sweet smile on his face.

11

WINTER
AFTERNOON
MAN
HOUSE

It was months after the attempted rape before the stranger would talk about it. Even then, when she would talk with the man's wife about what had happened, it apparently never occurred to her to thank him for fighting off her attackers. Not that he desired thanks; but then, in the face of her continuing silence, he began to think maybe he did. One afternoon in the pottery, while outside the winter winds surged around them like a rising sea, the man's wife asked him if that changed anything.

"You know, I've had this fantasy that one day something like this would happen. I always wondered what I would do."

"Were you afraid?"

He thought it over. "I'm not sure. I don't think so. Only because I don't think I felt anything. I was just acting. I was doing things ... I finally realized I was going to have to hit as hard as I could ... and when I did that ... and he screamed and went down ... "

"What?" she finally urged.

"I don't know. It was strange. I don't know what I felt. I don't know what I feel now."

"You can't feel bad for them."

"Why not?"

"You know what I mean."

He had his back to her, taking pottery off the shelf and packing it for shipment. He continued working intently.

"You used to think about this?"

He shrugged, not turning. "I shouldn't have said anything, huh?"

She stopped the potter's wheel, where she was finishing a large vase. "I just didn't know, that's all." She asked for how long.

"What difference does it make?" he replied impatiently.

"I just feel bad that, you know ... "

"Why should you feel bad? You didn't make the world."

He still had his back to her. He knew what she would do. When he felt her hand on his back, he waited before gently shrugging it off. "Your hands were swollen," she murmured, then there was silence again.

"What?" he asked suddenly.

"I didn't say anything."

"Yes you did."

She chuckled quietly, then asked him what he thought about the stranger.

He said he didn't know what to think. She was a mystery. "She doesn't say anything," he concluded, still working. "Honestly?" he added, "I guess I regret asking her to stay. I mean I know she has things to work out, but she never helps out—"

"She does a little."

"A very little. She never offers to wash a dish, peel a potato ... "

"Did you ever ask?"

"Why should I have to ask?"

"She did offer to work."

"I don't get it, is this a woman thing? Okay, she helped out in here a few times. Then back to her room." He interrupted himself, calmed his voice. "This is not a hotel. We just can't afford to carry her indefinitely. But more important, if she has things to work out, she has to work them out. You have to do something, you can't just sit in your room all day."

"She was almost raped."

"What, I don't know that? Suddenly you're defending her? You know damn well she's getting on your nerves as much as mine. Admit it."

"I admit it. Now can I say something?" She stared at him and he smiled and then she smiled.

"Talk," he commanded gaily.

"Shut up," she replied with equal gaiety, "I'll talk when I'm ready. Are you going to let me speak?"

"I will let you speak. My lips are sealed. I am bound to silence. I will never again—"

"I can't talk," she declared. He drew a finger across his lips to indicate they were sealed and made a face at her. She made a face back, baring her teeth. After a pause, she told him what had happened when she had taken a load of laundry upstairs.

She said the stranger had come out of her room and approached her with one of their art books in hand, opened to a particular page, and, before she could say a word, held it up and asked her if she could explain it. It was a sculpture by Modigliani, a stone head of a woman.

"She just walked up with a picture and said, 'explain this?' Did you know she was going through our books?"

"I had no idea."

"Wow, what did you say? What did she say?"

His wife told him the stranger had apparently picked up the book out of boredom and had simply started leafing through it. Something about it attracted her, particularly the portraits of women, so she kept the book in her room. What was strange, she said, was that she had never looked at art in her life and didn't know a thing about it. As she kept going back to the same portraits, she came to feel that she was getting to know them. "She thought it was amazing that you could make a painting in such a way as to show someone's personality."

"Wow, that's great."

"Wait. What she wanted me to explain… " Most of the portraits, the stranger had said, were of particular people, but some of them, mainly the sculptures, weren't. "The one in particular she showed me, she said it wasn't any one woman, it was all women, or just 'woman.' She wanted me to explain what made that one different and how an artist could make something that could stand for everybody."

"Wow," he repeated, shaking his head and smiling appreciatively, "what did you say?"

She had told her it was partly the quality of sculpture, something about the physical characteristics of stone and our emotional perception of it. It was also the way he had treated the subject: By distorting the features, he made it less specific and more suggestive. Finally, there were the eyes, Modigliani's eyes …

"I guess we should let her stay, huh."

"It was pretty neat. She said it had different moods, too. Sometimes she thought it was in pain, other times it seemed peaceful. She wanted to know whether I thought she was making it up or whether it was really there."

They agreed he should talk to her. Actually she suggested it and then convinced him. He found her, as expected, in bed. Snow, the outdoors, nature evidently held no attraction for her. He tried to convince himself she was hibernating, a strategy for survival, but it didn't work.

"Hi, mommy," the child called from his room.

"It's daddy."

"Hi, daddy."

"Mind if I come in?" he asked the stranger through the open door. She gestured him in with a neutral look, then said, "You're going to ask me to leave."

He startled. "Why do you say that?"

"You telling me I'm wrong?"

"Yes. I am." He was instantly annoyed. "But I wouldn't mind knowing your plans—"

"Plans," she interrupted. "I've heard of that." She chuckled.

He suppressed his annoyance, forcing a vague smile. His wife had made the same assumption, that he would ask her to leave, because he'd said he regretted having urged her to stay. "I wasn't intending to just boot her out," he had snapped, "but what do we know about her? She says she knows the men who attacked her, but refuses to go to the cops ... or let me go. For all we know, she's involved with them in some way." So as not to stare at her, he pretended to look around the room, actually observing little. Meanwhile, she stared at him; he realized it, turning back to her. She looked— She shouldn't have looked the way she did, he felt certain, but more ... expectant, if not troubled. Suddenly he turned to shut the door and sat on the edge of the bed. "Why do you think I came to ask you to leave?" he asked, looking right at her.

She shrugged. "Seems about that time, don't it?"

"Why?"

Again she shrugged. He waited, determined, for her to say something, but she didn't, she just stared at him and then shrugged yet again. He looked down at last and smiled privately, shaking his head ever so slightly, then looked at her again as though, in that way, he might at last discover who she was. "Do you know how long you've been here?" he asked almost conversationally.

"A long time," she replied, smiling.

He gestured noncommittally. "Months, anyway. Does it seem so long?"

"You mean, am I bored out of my mind? Let's just say, to each his own."

"Amen to that," he replied generously with a nod, then added, "I'm sorry you can't find anything worthwhile here."

"It ain't that." He looked at her. "Don't forget, you got a lot going here. I'm alone."

"I guess," he began tentatively, "we were hoping you'd feel less alone." He rubbed a nonexistent piece of dust from the corner of his eye.

She was sitting on the bed cross-legged, resting her chin on her joined hands. "Don't feel hurt or nothing." Her eyes drifted down. It was the first time she had looked away.

"Nor you," he replied at last. "Look, for us, this place is a refuge, a safe-house. We just ... Obviously you don't owe us anything."

"Hey, don't think I don't appreciate what you done." He looked up suddenly. "Sure, I appreciate it. You let me stay in this nice room, you feed me ... " He couldn't help chuckling as he turned away. "What? Come on, what?"

He rubbed his eyebrow, covering his face, then smiled at the floor and shook his head.

"Hello?"

He turned to her, almost whispering, "It's all right, you don't owe me anything."

She just stared at him with that same waiting-to-be-told expression.

He went to the dresser for something to do and so he could turn his back on her and picked up the art book she had propped there, open to the stone head. "I hear you've become a Modigliani fan."

She didn't answer right away. "Yeah, I was talking to your wife about it." There was another silence; this one pleased him. "She knows a lot about art," she added at last, like dropping words into a bucket of silence, hoping to fill it up.

He waited to let her know that bucket is not so easily filled. "She's an artist." In his mind, the way he said it was not so much a statement about his wife as a question about the stranger. Then, scolding himself for his harshness, he turned and gentled his voice. "I'm a Modigliani fan, too." He picked up the book and brought it to the bed, opening the cover on his lap. "Did you notice where this book came from?" She shook her head. "London. Charing Cross Road." He showed her the little green sticker underneath the front flap. "Ever been to Europe?"

She shook her head, then chuckled suddenly. "The farthest I ever been is here," she explained.

There was a knock at the door and a little voice shouted, "Dad. Come here."

"What is it, little one?" he asked.

"See what I made."

"In a minute. I'm busy right now."

"Now," whined the child.

"I'm busy right now. I'll be there in a minute." There was silence and then he heard the child return to his room. He smiled at the stranger and she smiled back.

"He's a great kid," she offered.

"We like him," he replied with a great smile. Then the silence opened up again and he nodded into it.

"I think you were getting ready to tell me a story," she suggested.

He tried to see if she was mocking him, but couldn't be sure. "Want to hear it?"

"It ain't like I'm so busy."

"I didn't ask you if you were busy, I asked if you wanted to hear it. I'll make you a deal. I'll tell you mine if you tell me yours."

"I don't have any stories." He could see she wasn't bantering, she was serious.

"Everyone has a story."

"How do you know?" she challenged. "You know everyone?"

He shook his head, challenging her back. "I don't know anyone."

He had more to say, and he was certain she did too, but neither of them said anything. Later, she said, "I guess you been to London."

He thought for a while, then decided to risk it. "Lived there. We both did. Right after we got married." She waited, drawing her knees up to her chest. "It was during the Vietnam War. This whole country seemed like an ugly place and we just wanted to get away. I had been to England before, and liked it, so we went there." If she was responding to this in any way, he couldn't detect it. "I had a connection with a family there and we rented a room in their flat. They call apartments flats. We stayed with them for a year. They were refugees from South Africa. I felt like an expatriate from the U.S." He stopped there to study her, to try to know if any of this mattered to her in the slightest.

"Draft dodger?" she finally responded.

He felt relieved. "I had publicly pledged to refuse the draft. As it turned out, I had a medical deferment. I would have refused. Leaving the country was a statement. I hated this place. It seemed evil. I couldn't forgive people for being indifferent. I was too young to understand how indifference, even when it's evil, can be simply indifference."

"Dad!" called the child from the next room.

"Soon, little one," he shouted back. "Another minute." He smiled at the stranger and she smiled back. "Well, Modigliani." He sighed. "I used to take these long walks through the city, and sometimes I would end up on Charing Cross where the bookstores are, and I'd poke around. I really don't know what it was about this book, Modigliani was one of the very few artists my father didn't appreciate—my father was an artist—and so I had learned to dismiss him. But, anyway, I bought it and brought it back, and here it is, and when we got here, after we'd been here a while, I picked it up for some reason, and something … opened inside me. I don't know how else to say it. … And these pictures became very important to me." He was looking at the floor but finally he turned to her and shrugged, praying without realizing it for something extraordinary to happen.

*   *   *

One afternoon he stole a few moments from the work that seemed interminable to stare out the window. The intense cold, drying the air, made it clear, making every detail more apparent. Sunlight would add brilliance, dappling the scene, but many days were like this: a uniformly gray cloudless sky draping an even light over everything. He was staring at nothing in particular, at the world. The branches were still, nothing moved. There could be winds strong enough to rattle the roof, but not now. Now, everything was still.

There were rabbit tracks, but no rabbits to be seen. He knew an unseen world was out there. He was in his house, looking out on the world. He felt a kind of calm fill him, a kind of satisfaction. Reflexively, he moved his hand around the window frame. When the wind rose again, cold air would stream in, though now, with the calm frigid air, there was only a trickle. He sensed how his security was provisional. Like the time they had awakened one morning to find the water line frozen and he had had to wade through hip deep snow to the barn with a blowtorch. The house must struggle against the cold; its warmth was won, not given. The trees grew without him, but he must cut them, split them, haul them, stack them. Before dark he would have to go out again to bring in more firewood and in the morning the stoves would be cold and it would start again.

He didn't mind; he accepted that, seeing it metaphorically; but he saw how fragile the relationships were. If his strength should fail? And after he was dead? It took organization, knowledge, skill. Staring out the window, his hand on the frame where the warmth met the cold, it suddenly seemed very fragile. There were always people, it seemed, to assail it, while others took it for granted. Was it just him getting older, confronting mortality, that made it seem so fragile?

He would spend part of the afternoon in the back woods, weeding out undesirable trees for firewood. He would take the child with him, pulling him in a little sledge he had knocked together, since the snow was fairly deep, the child and his toy trucks, and while he sawed down small trees, the child would play nearby in the snow. They both loved the feeling of trekking to the back of the property, far from any road, the house out of sight, but comfortably there, the small fields they would cross, and then the woods of tall maple, oak, beech, with poplars at its edge, encroaching on the fields, and everywhere deep snow. Once the child was settled, he would select his first tree, set the blade, and watch it work its way through the trunk. He would work without resting, without fatigue, as would the child with his trucks, the two of them never exchanging a word, until he would realize he was tired and sweaty; then they would load up the sledge and he would pull the beaming child home, both of them glad to be back, as glad to be indoors again as they had been glad to be out.

Once, four men appeared, actually one man and three teenagers, who looked about seventeen, though it was hard to tell with their faces blackened. They were not hunters. They wore camouflage suits instead of reflective orange vests; and instead of shotguns they had rifles. They came up on him suddenly from three sides, the older one in the middle, the others on the flanks, one of them passing near the child, who stopped playing with his trucks to stare. He looked them over quickly, then focused on the leader, waiting for him to say something.

He didn't say anything; just stared with a kind of smile on his face. That could have been a grimace from being out of breath at having just come up the hill in deep snow; his combat boots were lashed to snowshoes, but still it would have been hard going. He just stood there with his hands on his hips and that look on his face. The man stared back, not sure what he was doing. He didn't feel any fear, though clearly they were trying to frighten him, especially the young ones who moved in around the leader and adopted similar poses. Their faces implied a kind of inchoate dare to do or say something and face an unspecified retaliation. His only response, though he was unaware of it, was to shift his weight forward and slide the bow saw in front of him to grip it with both hands.

The leader spoke first. From that ambiguous grimace he produced an ambiguous chuckle and the words, "We thought you might be an animal."

The boys found that amusing, but their faces returned to supercilious smirks as the man turned to stare at each of them. To the leader he said, "You're trespassing on my land."

"It's not posted," he replied dryly.

"It will be, this time tomorrow. Don't ever come back here."

One of the youths took a step forward and the man immediately turned to confront him. The two stood there, unmoving, staring at each other until the leader made some kind of gesture and the boy's weight settled. The man turned slowly back to him and said, "It's illegal to hunt with a rifle."

"It's illegal to hunt deer with a rifle," snapped one of the youths and they all sniggered.

"That your boy?" asked the leader. "Cute little kid, with those trucks."

Unconsciously his hands tightened on the bow saw. He noticed that the leader had a long knife strapped to his thigh. He realized they all did. He knew that normally his son would have approached at a remark like that, taking it as an invitation to talk about his trucks, being talkative and not shy at all. For the first time the man felt something clearly. Trying to master his voice, he almost whispered the words, "Get out of here." When they didn't immediately respond, he almost said more, but refrained, not sure he could control himself.

After a final look at the child and a final stare, the leader turned and started back down the hill, followed by the others. From a few paces away, without turning he shouted, "Good luck!" The youths laughed. The man watched until they were completely out of sight, still standing there with his weight on the front of his feet and his hands gripping the bow saw.

Only then did he turn to look at his son. He was sitting where he had been, holding a truck in his lap, watching his father. The man tried to smile, went over and kissed him on his cheek. "Well," he declared with false gusto, "shall we get back to work?" He returned to the tree he had been sawing, but after a few minutes noticed the child had still not moved. He stopped abruptly and jerked completely around, sweeping the woods with his gaze, his eyes unconsciously narrowing as that feeling returned. When he raised a hand to his face he noticed it was trembling. He held it out and observed it: truly, it was trembling. He lowered it quickly and turned to his son. "Shall we go home? I'm getting chilly, what about you?"

He knew he must say something, but didn't know what to say, not wanting to lie. Only when they were most of the way back did the child ask, "Daddy, who were those men?"

It startled him, though he had been expecting it. "I don't know," he replied without stopping. "Just some hunters."

"How come they didn't look like hunters?"

He tried to think how to reply, but each alternative quickly led to questions he didn't yet know how to answer. Finally he said, "I don't know, son, but they'll never be back here again, so it doesn't matter. When we get home, are you going to play with your blocks?"

"But how come they had black paint on their faces?"

The man sighed forcefully, lost a step, but quickly continued, then stopped again and turned to face his son. "Because," he said, trying not to sound angry, "they were being very silly. They were playing a silly game."

The child immediately asked, "What game?"

"I don't know what they call it," he snapped, trying to end the conversation, "it was just a very silly game, and they were very silly people, dressed up to look ridiculous, and we'll never see them again, so can we just drop it?" Before the child could speak, he turned and continued back to the house, trying to will to a stop the trembling of his hands.

*   *   *

One Sunday before the incident in the back woods, they had awakened late to find a renewed world: Heavy snow had fallen through the night and now everything was made smooth again. When the plow came, the child ran to the window. Since they were at the end of the line, it turned around in their driveway, suddenly an enormous machine dwarfing their pick-up, with huge wings, flapping massively when not pushing snow. The drivers waved and the child waved back and his father could see his eyes. After brunch, while the child pretended he was driving a snowplow, the man went out to shovel; afterwards he pulled him on his sled.

Beyond where the plow had stopped, a four-wheel drive had cut neat tracks into the deep snow on the road, just wide enough for the sled. The child climbed on with wordless excitement and they set off alone into an untouched white world. Before them the road rose several feet, shortening the view, so there were no sweeping vistas. The world was intimate, a silent, a white birth world. The trees, empty of all clutter, took only the snow to their undefended arms.

The man felt so … lucky, so inexplicably lucky, to be there with his son, for them to be able to see it, to be part of it. He took a deep breath and exhaled forcefully. The cold air felt good inside, felt like, for that time, he could be inseparable from this world. A slight smile came to his face. His son was absolutely quiet, completely still, but for the slow turning of his head, his arms at rest in his lap, his face seriously observant.

Recorded history had it that the first European landowner in the area had been a Dutch shoemaker named Vrooman who had tramped out from the city, several days' away, to buy six hundred acres of prime valley land from the Iroquois. This valley lay below him, about five miles down the winding hilly roads that connected the valley farmers and villagers with the hill people. The Iroquois finally concluded that, by "buy," the impulsive white man meant "barter;" but he could not comprehend how anyone could propose to barter for land, which could no more be possessed than the sky or the wind. Finally, as much to humor him as to be rid of his poor manners and childish eagerness, he took the quill and scratched a mark where the man pointed; then, after he had left, shook his head in wonder that someone could imagine he could possess the earth.

"So move!" the child barked suddenly. Over the rise, the man pulled the sled between two fields, uncultivated meadows in the warm seasons, speckled in spring with tiny sweet wild strawberries and thicketed in summer with large sweet blackberries. But now they were snowed over, wind swept. Fields of the cold time, keeping huddled rabbits. The loudest sound was the call of the chickadee.

"I want to see a rabbit," announced the child.

"They're keeping warm under the snow."

"Where?"

"I don't know where."

"I wish we could see," sighed the child.

"You can see the birds. Do you hear the chickadee?" The child listened intently and at the next call the man pointed.

"How come they don't go away like the other birds? Don't they get cold?"

"I don't know. They don't seem to."

"They're so little."

"Maybe they're watching over us."

"What do you mean?"

"What do I say when you go to sleep?"

The child smiled. "And all the birds watch after you in your dreams," he recited.

"Maybe that's what they're doing: watching after us in our dreams."

The child considered it. "I think they're just too little to go far away," he countered soberly.

The man laughed. "Maybe you're right."

On the way home from the back woods after the incident, with the questions, the man knew he must speak, but couldn't figure out what to say without frightening the child. He decided to give himself some time, but couldn't bear to leave him, and he wasn't sure the child would let him, so he proposed an early bath. He convinced himself that just being together would be enough; it wasn't.

As usual, he sat on the floor by the tub, half reading a book, when he looked up to see the child absent-mindedly pushing one of his boats and realized what was different: the child was silent. He closed the book and watched him.

Finally the child said, "Dad?"

"What, son?" he replied quietly. This was how it always began when he was pondering something. Invariably it was the beginning of a long dialogue punctuated with an endless succession of questions. Normally he would have smiled, but not this time.

"What's 'trepspass'?"

The man couldn't suppress a heavy sigh. "'Trespass,'" he corrected. "It means being on someone's land without permission." He knew he couldn't stop there; he struggled for what to say, finally just asking, "Did those men frighten you?" The child said nothing, just stared ahead, and then his jaw started to tremble. The man snatched him from the water and clutched him against his chest with uncontrolled ferocity, squeezing his little body. When he felt the child's arms go round him and hold him tightly, it was all he could do to keep his entire body from trembling.

* * *

Only with all his will power could he bring himself to say anything to his wife. When he did, he was staring out the pottery window instead of working, trying to get up the courage to tell her. "Something happened out back," he muttered at last. He suppressed his emotion so thoroughly, she didn't pick up any signals and so just continued to work. This immediately made him angry, though he knew what had happened. "There were some men back there," he added, but still she didn't get it. He wondered if it was she or he, and fell silent.

"Yeah?" she replied, turning toward him. "Hunters?" Clearly she still felt no distress and he knew it was because he had expressed none for her to feel. He might be telling her he had met one of the neighbors. Then, for some reason she felt something. In a voice suffused with concern, she asked, "They came back?"

"Not the same ones," he replied tautly, annoyed without justification.

"Oh God." All at once, fear was all over her voice. He had thought to make it easier, but instead had made it worse. "What happened? Tell me!"

He nodded, knowing he must raise up words through his throat. "Nothing happened." He paused, till he could pull up more words.

"Tell me!" she shouted again, but it was a shouted whisper so no one else would hear.

"I am! I'm trying to!" he shouted back, annoyed. "Calm down, I said nothing happened. I'll tell you." Then he added more moderately, "Why do you think I brought it up?"

"I can't believe you didn't say anything."

Instead of saying he was trying to figure out how to spare her, he said, "I'm telling you now."

He told her everything, but suddenly it seemed there was little to tell. He admitted they had frightened the child and him too; he was trying to figure out what he needed to do. She asked him how he was so sure they were skinheads.

"They had insignias on their sleeves."

She asked what they said; he snapped at her that he couldn't remember, what difference did it make, something stupid. In fact, he couldn't remember if they wore any identification at all. They both took several breaths, a tacit apology for having snapped at each other, then began speculating.

They fell silent. He kept asking himself, were they really in danger from a gang of thugs? If so, what should he do? In fleeting fantasies he was doing horrible things to them, but, along with fear and rage, he felt frustrated and depressed. He actually felt sick in his stomach.

Startled, he heard her asking him if he was okay. He shrugged and inquired the same of her, and she also shrugged and again they fell silent.

He turned to stare out the window again. The sky was milky blue with wisps of white. The intense blue-green of the spruces was accentuated by the snow weighting their branches and, here and there, tufts of dried grass and mounds of rock punctuated the heavy snow cover. He found it unspeakably beautiful and this deepened his gloom. "If this keeps up," he mumbled, "life will pull out to a better location."

"What do you mean?" she asked finally.

He didn't turn from the window. "The human predicament is not mortality," he complained impatiently. "It's stupidity."

She came to stand beside him and gingerly touched his shoulder with her hand.

He continued. "Why isn't it obvious how stupid we are? Why do we feel so clever? That has to be some defect in the design." He knew she was letting him talk. "And so the human response has to be shame. At times like this, I'm ashamed to be human." She put her arm around him. "Just look at the trees," he continued. "They're saying something grand about how it is to be alive."

"I love you," she said.

"I love you, too," he replied. "Don't worry, we'll figure something out. It's just … why?"

"I know," she whispered, then added, "but we still have the birds."

"Yes, yes, the birds," he sighed. That thought perked him up. "The birds, the trees … " He turned to her. "It's just like it says."

"What do you mean?"

He quoted, "'Yet do the birds, sky-flecked and touched by the rain, sing for us from their towers, as though even people might pick up a note or two.' Right?"

"Right." She nodded confidently, smiling.

"And we still have this house."

"Do you know what I like about this house?"

"What do you like about this house?"

"I like that it's built right on bedrock." She nodded for emphasis.

He looked at her. People—kind of marginal people—would stop by to see her. She had this quality, everybody liked her. She seemed easy to know; that was wrong, a deception of affect. She was as hard to know as anyone really worth knowing. But they would come by, hang around, tell her their troubles.

"What?" she asked.

"Nothing."

"You're staring at me. You must be talking to yourself."

He shrugged, thought of telling her how much he loved her, but just nodded. "I like this house, too," he added, to be saying something.

"Where's the little one?"

"He's okay. Watching television. The problem isn't so much right now, it's from now on."

"I know," she said sadly.

They came together and embraced. He felt cozy. Unspeakably cozy.

"So," he barked in mock severity, "what do you say, shall we get some work done around here?"

"Yes, sir!" she shouted back, then added in a normal voice, "Don't you think somebody needs to talk to you know who again?"

He nodded, with the beginning of a smile. "Who should that somebody be?"

"I nominate you," she announced, smiling.

He sighed deeply. "Later. I need to think." Then he added, "Everything is different now."

III

SPRING

EVENING

STRANGER

BIRD

What impressed her most about the family, having lived with them for months, was how damned solid they each were, even the kid, as though they actually believed it was possible to live a decent life. When they got pissed off, they just ... let it out, and then it was over and they went on. That's what amazed her the most, even more than the way they seemed so self-sufficient, living in the middle of nowhere on top of a hill. To her, life seemed, at best, beyond control, usually one thing after another she couldn't win, each one shaking her a little more. She couldn't even imagine feeling good, let alone experience it. So, when the man came to her room one evening, where, as usual, she was staring into space, to tell her about the skinheads, instead of feeling rage or fear, as he obviously did, she felt victimized by the inevitable and simply offered to leave.

He shook his head. "I didn't come here to ask you to leave. I came here to find out if you know anything about this. I guess you do," he added, and simply waited.

She could have found it in her heart to hate him for the way he came at her so directly, but she had learned that being straightforward was his way of being gentle. When he had fought off the two jerks who had come after her, she had convinced herself that would be the last of it and so he had no need to know anything. Also, he wanted to go to the cops and she knew what kind of trouble that would make. But now ... now he had to know.

She had gotten involved with a guy who turned out to be wacko. She said every guy she'd gotten involved with turned out to be wacko, but this one was really wacko, that's why she had finally run away. He was one of those white supremacist fanatics who was preparing for war against the government and all 'mongrel races.' "His idea of fun is to dress up like a commando and go out in the woods with knives and guns strapped all over him."

"So that was him?" He was referring to the man who had come upon him in the back woods through the deep snow, when he'd been out cutting firewood. The child had been with him. She nodded. "And the others?"

"Kids he recruits off the streets. They're his warriors." She said it with contempt, then added, "If they weren't so scary, it would be ridiculous. He finds them crazy and makes them crazier."

She watched him think. "Have they ever done anything? Actually hurt anyone, I mean."

She snorted. "Besides me, you mean?"

He asked her who the two men were who had tried to rape her.

She dismissed them with a gesture. "Lunkheads. They hang around. Forget them, real losers." But, so far as she knew, the 'warriors' had never actually done anything. "They could, though," she warned. "He's crazy enough to try something."

He thought some more. "Such as?" She shrugged. He asked her why they hadn't done anything when they had had the chance. "Four guys, armed to the teeth, they came up on me from three sides."

"He likes to scare people."

"So he's not really dangerous. He's just for show." He was asking.

She shook her head. "I told you, he's crazy. Who knows?" She said there was an easy answer: she would just leave. She said she'd stayed way too long, anyway. "It's time to get on with my life ... whatever the hell that means."

He replied he'd hoped she'd get on with her life right where she was. "Life goes on, even here."

That was the kind of crack he could make. His weird sense of humor. You didn't know whether to laugh, or be pissed, or take it seriously. "My life has a way of not going on anywhere." She snorted again.

"Maybe you could do something about that," he suggested.

Involuntarily she waved away the idea, then repeated her offer to leave, not certain herself if she was totally serious. What she had said was, "I should leave." It wasn't exactly an offer, nor, she realized, did it state an actual intention. Perhaps if she knew where she would go, what she would do ...

He asked her where she would go, what she would do. She shrugged, then added, "I've got one or two friends who'd put me up for a while. Once I get a job, I'll be okay. I can waitress." She snorted in embarrassment again, for a reason she pretended she didn't know.

He raised a hand like a traffic cop to stop her, saying obviously she was always free to leave, but there was no way he was kicking her out because some asshole had showed up in the back woods. "If you're in danger, you're in danger. Leaving here won't fix that. And if I'm in danger ... If I'm in danger, I guess I have to deal with that." She noticed he didn't say 'we.'

She never actually said she would stay, she just stopped talking about leaving and he started talking about coming to a better under-standing about what the expectations were. "Maybe you could get into the flow a little more," was how he put it. She knew he was telling her to haul her butt out of bed and do some work around the place. She mentioned she had asked for something to do before and he replied that it hadn't lasted very long and she found herself getting angry, though she knew he was right.

He settled it in his typical direct way: There was no point argu-ing about the past, but, if she was going to stay, he wanted to do a better job of letting her know his expectations. He said they just couldn't afford to keep feeding her indefinitely, but if she would at least do some day-care, he and his wife could get more work done. "Also," he added, "I've got to say it might do you some good to get out of your room a bit more."

As for the safety issue, what was decided was that they would all go on as before, except no one would go any distance from the house alone, except the man, who would continue cutting firewood out back ("without firewood, we freeze," he stated). He agreed to carry a whistle, in case something happened. Also, grudgingly, he installed locks on the doors and windows. ("I feel like a prisoner in my own house," he complained.) Finally, he told the sheriff's office about the incident. They said there wasn't much they could do with no information and no crime being attempted, but they would look into it.

One evening at dinner the man announced gaily that spring was coming, which she first took as a joke, since there was still deep snow on the fields and, between the damp cold and the winds of mud season, going outside generally meant feeling more chilled than ever. But he was serious, as he explained that, with the days getting longer and the daytime temperatures getting above freezing, sap would start to rise in the trees. "And when the sap rises, the buds swell; and when the buds swell, the leaves and flowers come out and you can smell spring in the air," he continued with an enthusiasm she found a bit much, but also, in spite of herself, infectious.

"But . . . what makes the sap rise?" asked the child. It was a question that had just occurred to her.

"Magic!" shouted the man, putting up his hands as though he had just performed a trick.

"Don't tell him that," criticized the woman. "What's he supposed to think?"

"Okay, we'll look it up in a book and find out how the trick is done. But even after we know, we'll still be amazed. And if that isn't magic, what is?"

"You don't think it can be explained?" she persisted.

"Of course it can be explained," snapped the man, as the stranger tuned out. This was the kind of argument they could have. Weird folks, she thought. Nice, but weird. She noticed the child was listening intently. What's he supposed to make of this? she wondered. In the end it was agreed they would start collecting sap to make maple syrup ... and find out what makes sap rise in the spring.

But the next day the weather was miserable, so they went out the day after. They all bundled up and trudged across the back fields to the woods—all but the child, who was perched in a sledge like a little king, beaming gaily as he hugged a stack of buckets between his legs. When they had selected a healthy-looking maple, they each took a turn with an old auger bit; then the man produced a tap from his pocket and the child banged it in, hung a bucket, and everyone waited expectantly. Within seconds a clear liquid began dripping.

"There it is!" shouted the child.

"Magic!" proclaimed the man, and he made a face at the woman, who made a face back.

In truth, thought the stranger, there was something magical about it. "How do we know it's not water?" she asked.

"Taste it."

She did and then they all did. "Sap," she concluded. Though she had never tasted sap before, it had a slight sweet flavor.

"Sap!" shouted the child.

"Sap," agreed the woman.

"Magic!" exclaimed the man.

The child turned to him and warned, "It's not magic, daddy, it's sap."

The stranger turned back to the tree to watch the liquid roll off the tap into the bucket. Truly, she felt to her gradually increasing amazement, there was something wonderful about this whole experience. A secret had been discovered: While she had been shivering and cursing at the mud, the earth was silently waking up. Looking at the dripping sap, she suddenly felt the entire woods as something living. For her whole life she could have walked through it or around it and never have ... felt part of it. Now here she was, inside looking out, for the first time. And this was the same woods where the "warriors" had practiced their commando techniques. That seemed a bad memory now. "I don't think they're coming back," the man had said. "If they are, where are they?" She watched the family, intent on selecting the next tree. Even the child, who could hardly be coaxed out of the house, seemed to have set aside any fears for the occasion.

The next day the buckets were full and then the work began. "It takes more than two full buckets to make one jar of syrup," warned the man. "That's a lot of boiling." They wrestled the buckets back to the house without spilling too much and started a fire. "There's no trick to it, you just boil it down." He noted that the Iroquois had made syrup when they had lived here centuries ago.

"Right here?" suggested the child.

"Hmm, more likely down in the valley." The child looked disappointed. "But nearby," he added. "Who knows, maybe they were here." The child looked happier.

* * *

"Why don't we go outside and see what your father's doing?" True to her word, she was spending several hours a day taking care of the child. Surprisingly, for someone who never wanted children and didn't expect any (at least so she told herself), she didn't mind. He was pretty cute and, for his age, amazingly smart. She couldn't believe some of the things he came out with. But, ever since the skinheads, he had grown fearful. He had grown fearful after the first incident, when he had watched his father fight the two men who had assaulted her; but that had gradually worn off and everything had seemed fine … until the skinheads showed up. Since then, he wouldn't go outside without a lot of coaxing and generally didn't like to be alone. He had used to play for hours by himself; now someone had to be with him. And, she knew, he was having nightmares, which was new. She felt bad for the kid; in fact, every time she thought about it, her stomach knotted up and she saw herself doing violence to the man she thought of as Shithead. "What do you say we go outside," she repeated. "It's a nice day and we haven't been out … "

The child just shook his head.

"You sure you don't want to see what your father's doing? Maybe we could help him." She tried everything she could think of; finally she found it: "I bet there's some neat birds out there we could see."

"No there aren't."

"You mean you've seen every single bird?"

The child thought. "Well," he said tentatively, "there's nests ... "

They went out to see a kingbird's nest that was under the roof overhanging the pottery. She'd never even heard of a kingbird before; he informed her it ate bugs in the air and was the only bird with a white band along the end of its tail. They went for a stepladder and quickly set it up under the nest, the child pulling her away.

"You can't stay," he explained, "it scares the mother. You can only look for a second." In fact, a bird had flown from the nest at their approach and was flying about nearby as though in distress. So they took turns running up the ladder to see the small eggs in the nest, and the child found it great fun, bent over with excitement. "I can't wait till they hatch!"

Across the road in front of the house was a field used for hay by a farmer who lived down the road, and the child explained it was a perfect place for redwing blackbirds to make their nests. That was news to the stranger, who wasn't certain she'd ever heard of redwing blackbirds and had more or less assumed all birds made their nests in trees. "I wonder why they build them on the ground." Then: "How do you know all this?"

"My mommy and daddy tell me stuff," he replied with a mixture of humility and smugness.

They wandered around the field for a while, bent over, but it soon became clear to her that the odds of finding a nest that way were pretty slim. She suggested they sit on the front steps and wait for a bird to show up. The child thought that was a great idea. He sat with his hands on his knees, plainly expecting one to show up any second and point out its nest. Eventually there was a call in the distance. "Hear that?" he whispered dramatically. "That's a redwing." But the bird never showed and the child was disappointed.

They were about to give up when a bird suddenly appeared in the air and dropped down into the grassy stubble of the field. "There's one!" shouted the stranger, jumping up. "Keep your eye on the spot." They hurried out to the vicinity where the bird had landed and started searching, but couldn't find anything. The child dramatically put a finger to his mouth and stepped around carefully, then whispered, "Be careful you don't step on any eggs." It was no use; either the bird was hiding, she had imagined it, or it had somehow flown away without her noticing, but they could find neither bird nor nest.

"I don't get it," she whispered, "where could it be?"

The garden was nearby. The man had a wheelbarrow he was filling with rocks he pulled out of the ground. "Hi, daddy," shouted the child.

"Hi, little one!"

"We're coming to help you!" the child announced.

"Well, he is, anyway," laughed the stranger. The man nodded to her in thanks, presumably for coaxing the child outside.

"How come there's so many rocks?" asked the child, approaching.

"That's what I want to know," complained the man without stopping. "Around here they say, every spring you get a good crop of rocks."

"How come?"

"The freezing and thawing brings them up. Watch out now, don't get in the way."

"I guess we could give you a hand," offered the stranger reluctantly. She noticed he was sweating, though it was cool out, and looked tired.

"Nah," he said at first, and then, "Well, if you really want to." He explained the job: "There's nothing to it. You pick up rocks and put them in the wheelbarrow. When it's full I take it over there and dump it." The child went at it with gusto, picking up each stone as though it were a collector's item and carefully depositing it in the wheelbarrow. Mentally groaning, the stranger followed. To her surprise, once she got going she didn't mind it that much, although the job seemed endless—the fifty by fifty square of earth suddenly seemed all rock. There was something almost pleasurable about the idea: working the land. The child pointed to a few birds darting about in the air around them. "Swallows," he said nonchalantly. "They eat bugs, too." She watched them briefly, then returned to the rocks, gripped by some feeling that she was part of something and that it was satisfying, even—somehow—exciting.

*   *   *

One evening they got caught in a spring snowstorm. They had gone to the city to shop and then to a restaurant, and had gotten caught unawares by the sudden storm. Unusually, the stranger had gone with them. For her, it was weird to be back in the city; it seemed a lifetime since she had run away. Strange also to be leaving it for her farmhouse retreat.

When they left the city it was snowing, but, as they climbed, the storm intensified and driving became extremely difficult, with poor visibility and slippery roads. The man fell silent, hunched over the wheel, the woman also staring into the headlight beam. The stranger, in the back seat with the child, who had fallen asleep soon after starting out, instinctively put a hand on him.

"It's getting worse," the man muttered into the silence. "The more we climb, the worse it gets."

"I don't believe this," said the woman. Then they were silent again.

The wind gusts were sending billows of snow across the road, blocking all visibility for seconds that seemed minutes. The section of road they were on was a series of rises and falls and turns; with the swirling snow, the stranger was sure he had to be driving from memory as much as anything else. Several times she thought she felt them lose traction on a turn.

"Why did you go this way?" asked the woman in a voice she probably thought was neutral.

"Because," snapped the man, "I'm not sure we could have made it up the big hill."

Gingerly she suggested that maybe they should stop; the man didn't respond for a long time, then muttered that the storm was not going to stop and the roads would only get worse. The woman turned to ask the stranger if the child was still asleep, though that was obvious. She nodded. It occurred to her that they hadn't passed a single car.

At one point, coming out of a snow cloud, the car almost lost the road, which turned unexpectedly. The man jerked the wheel and the car went into a skid, just missing a large ditch. When it was again under control, he cursed, sighed, and leaned farther over the wheel.

Eventually they reached the beginning of the last hill, where their dirt road branched off. The man let the car roll to a stop and looked up the road. "I don't know if we can make this," he said.

After a while the woman asked what they should do.

"Try," he said simply, and he backed up the car to get a head start. He managed to get up some speed, but as soon as the car hit the hill it started fishtailing and quickly lost speed. When he tried to back down for another try, it went into a skid and slowly slid off the road into the ditch, coming to a stop at a fairly steep angle.

"End of the line," was all he said. He seemed curiously unruffled.

"Now what?" asked the woman.

"Two choices," he snapped, "we call a taxi or we walk. Shall we get the hell out of here? Wake up the little one."

The child cried at being awakened, but gradually calmed down as the woman told him about the adventure they were having.

"How about if we all get out of the car before it flips over," growled the man. The child asked what was wrong with daddy, and the woman said, nothing, he had just had a hard drive, and she urged him out of the car. The man climbed out last. "Leave the packages," he ordered.

They started up the hill, but, as the snow was thick and slippery, it was hard going. The child started to cry. "Carry me," he whined.

"I can't carry you," shouted the man. "It's too slippery. You'll have to walk."

"I can't," he complained and continued crying loudly.

The woman tried to comfort him, but he wouldn't let her. "Here," grumbled the man, "take my hand. Okay, don't take my hand."

"Maybe if we all held hands," the stranger suggested hesitantly. She was having trouble herself. The woman said it wasn't a bad idea and they all linked up.

"See," panted the woman to the child between breaths, "this isn't so bad."

At last they made it to the top and paused there to catch their breath. "I'm cold," complained the child. It was another mile to the house.

The man snatched him up without a word and, clutching him to his chest, set out. A little later he whispered gently, "Put your arms around my neck. We'll be home soon," and turned to make sure the others were with him. Occasionally he turned to curse at them, to keep them moving.

By the time they reached the house they were all exhausted. "Here we are," whispered the man, "you can stop now." The child had been whimpering. "I'll have you in your bed in no time, you'll be all cozy." The stranger and the woman, who had been holding hands to support each other, turned and nodded for some reason, panting for breath. No one noticed anything was wrong until they went inside and realized it was as cold inside the house as out. When the light was turned on, they saw the broken glass.

For a moment, everyone was stunned, wordless. Then the stranger said, "both windows," pointing out that both living room windows were broken.

The woman went into the kitchen and turned on the light. "Oh my God," she screamed. "These, too!"

"What the hell," muttered the man, incredulous, letting the child slip to the floor. The child started screaming. "Look upstairs," said the man in a suddenly flat, controlled voice.

The stranger ran upstairs and came down right away, saying, "Every one."

The child screamed louder and the man tightly shut his eyes and grimaced fiercely as though battling to master himself. "Turn the lights off," he shouted suddenly as he lurched to slap them off himself. "Away from the windows!"

"I'm scared!" bawled the child and the woman pulled him to her and held him tightly.

"Think!" commanded the man to himself.

"Where can we go?" asked the woman.

"Nowhere," he screamed with finality. "This is our home." They looked at each other. The stranger offered to fire up the stove. "Right. You start a fire, I'll bring in more wood."

"You're not going out there," ordered the woman.

"We were all just out there. If they wanted to do something … "

"Then why'd you say to keep away from the windows?"

"I don't know. Just to be safe. I don't know."

"Daddy, don't go," pleaded the child, sobbing.

The man sighed. "See what you did?" He knelt down and took the child by the arms. "Now, you need to be very grown up and try to help, okay?" As he left he said, "See what you can find to cover the windows, I don't know, cardboard, towels … Do the kitchen windows, we can all sleep there, it'll warm up pretty quickly."

Eventually the windows had been covered and blankets hung in the two entries from the living room and, though the wind gusted through the gaps in the makeshift covers, the kitchen was reasonably warm. The broken glass had been cleared away and mattresses brought down. The woman was sitting on one of them with the child, singing to him softly, trying to calm him. He was still whimpering. The man and the stranger were in the living room. She noticed the couch was covered with snow.

"I wish there was something I could say," she began.

"What do you mean?" He looked at her almost angrily.

"I feel … so shitty."

"Why, did you do this?" She searched his face. "You didn't do this," he explained, "this is not your fault."

"I feel like … in a way … "

"This is not your fault," he almost shouted. "You didn't do this. They did."

She asked if they should call the sheriff. He slapped his forehead and went to the phone. While he talked, she started covering the living room windows. She had no thoughts, just one clear sustained feeling. "They'll be up in the morning," he reported. "No point trying to get up here now. I'm sure those assholes are long gone. They did this before the storm. They might even have watched us leave." She imagined them spying on her and thought that sounded just about right.

She lay awake for a long time, the hatred never loosening its grip on her stomach. She realized the man and woman were also awake, though no one spoke, except once, very late.

"What should we do?" asked the woman. Her voice was clear, even calm.

"I don't know yet," replied the man in the same flattened voice he had used earlier.

The child stirred and the woman kissed him. "Mommy," he whispered, not really awake. She kept kissing him till he was fast asleep. The stranger felt sobs growing in her stomach; she had to clamp her teeth to stay silent.

In the morning the man returned from the barn to report that all the animals had been killed.

*　　*　　*

The sheriff's men admitted there was little they could do, with no clues or anyone who might have witnessed the vandalism. With the information the stranger had given them, they would coordinate with other law enforcement agencies; if he was under surveillance, there might be enough evidence to bring him in for questioning. That was when the stranger thought seriously for the first time about swearing out a complaint over the attack on her. But that had been many months earlier and she didn't know how they would take it, so she decided to think about it before saying anything.

Days passed, a week; the sheriff's office had nothing to report. They advised taking reasonable precautions and to call them immediately if anyone suspicious showed up. The man took the pick-up and returned with a shotgun.

Taking the child with him, he had left the woman and stranger with instructions to stay inside and keep the doors locked. Normally the kid might have come running up breathless with news about what daddy got, but this time he followed the man and watched silently as he displayed the purchase.

The woman stared at it, aghast. He let her react. Finally she asked if he'd like to explain that.

"It seems self-explanatory," he replied evenly, but with an edge.

There was a long silence, finally broken by the child. "Daddy says it's to keep woodchucks from eating the whole garden." He said it quietly, almost like a question, as though he knew it wasn't the whole story. The woman ordered him to go upstairs and play, though she would know he was too frightened to be alone; he didn't budge.

She strode away, then turned back, accusing in a shaking voice, "You might have consulted me."

He stared hard at her. "I will protect my family," he muttered through clenched teeth. He said it slowly, almost in a whisper, like a prayer.

"Protect?" she shouted. "That's protection?" Turning suddenly, she yelled at the child, "Didn't I tell you to go upstairs?"

"I want to stay here," he pouted. "With you."

"Listen," started the stranger, "I think maybe I ... "

"Good idea," said the man wearily, mistaking what she had been about to suggest, "why don't you take him upstairs."

The child made a fierce face as though daring anyone to try to move him, clearly on the edge of tears. Everyone stopped to look at him, breathing heavily.

That evening, while the man was involved in what had become the lengthy process of putting the child to bed, the stranger quietly asked the woman if she could speak with her. "This is not working, is it?" was how she began. She was certain the woman was pretending not to know what she meant. "Did it always take this long to put him to sleep?" she asked with a tilt of her head. "You know it didn't."

The woman was watching her.

"Can you swear you and him haven't talked about asking me to leave?" Without waiting for a reply, she added, "I got to believe this is going to stop when I go."

"No, it won't," replied the woman with an odd quietness. The stranger looked at her quizzically. "Once you get scared like this ... "

The stranger touched her arm. "No. You'll see. I've been there myself. Hell, I'm there now. Life goes on, you know?" She snorted, adding, "such as it is." They were silent for a while, not looking at each other, then she added, "Count on it, when I leave, they leave. You won't hear from them again."

The woman hesitated, then asked, "How can you be so sure? Do you mind if I ask what your ... relationship is?"

She smiled. "Let's just say there is one. Was one. I don't like it, I'm not proud of it, but what happened happened. Believe me, I hate that shithead like you do. Especially after sending— You know."

"But, where would you go?"

Somehow it almost surprised her. She paused, then smiled. "Don't worry, I'll find a place. I got a friend will put me up. For a while, anyway," she added with a chuckle.

They were sitting in her room, cross-legged on opposite ends of the bed. She watched the woman sweep the room quickly. It was exactly the way she had found it, except for the book of Modigliani reproductions she had adopted, which was on the dresser, open to the stone sculpture of a woman's head she liked. At least at first she had liked it, then it had captivated her, she found it exciting, then it became confusing, and finally it had begun to depress her. "You know," she spoke into the silence, "don't you think art is ... I don't know, kind of like a mean trick?"

The woman startled. "What do you mean?" she asked, almost hurt.

"Well, you know, first it seems ... it's like an invitation to something. You know, like that sculpture, when I first saw it I thought, 'wow.' I kept coming back to it and finding things in it, you know? Well, you know, we talked about it. But, after a while it started to ... change."

"What do you mean?" asked the woman, cocking her head in a certain way.

She searched for words. "I think ... whether the artist means it or not ... a line is created, a boundary line. That you can't cross. Like the art is something you can get into, it invites you in. But, when you try, like to study it more and more, you get to a point and then

... you're kept out. You know what I mean?" she asked sheepishly. "Does that ever happen to you?"

"Wow," replied the woman, thinking, "you know, I'm not sure."

"There's a distance. No matter how hard you try, you can't cross it. No? I guess it's just me." She snorted.

"No, no, I just— I'll have to think about that." She fell silent and so did the stranger.

"You know," she said finally, quietly, "you folks have been more than nice to me, putting up with me this long— No, really. But ... " She paused a long time before continuing. "Don't take this wrong, okay? But what you got here ain't for me."

"I'm not sure I know what you mean," the woman replied quietly.

"Don't matter. The main thing is, I been here long enough. Even without this shit ... But look, the windows are all boarded up, you can't ... "

The woman said her husband just wanted to wait a while before repairing them.

"Yeah," interrupted the stranger, "he said it was better that way because then you could walk around the house without worrying about being seen from outside."

"Well, he just doesn't want to repair them if they're going to get broken again."

"Come on, we both know what's going on. I mean ... Your kid won't even go into a room by himself anymore. Not even the bathroom. He's sleeping in your bed ... And now the gun ... I don't like guns," she added passionately.

"I don't like guns either."

"I mean, that's— You know, from now on, it's not just ... "

"I know," the woman whispered, barely audibly.

"I really thought about going to the cops, you know. I really did. But ... it wouldn't help."

"Sure?"

She shook her head no, meaning yes, making a face to suggest it was hopeless. "Cops. I mean ... you had much to do with them?" She shook her head again.

The woman smiled suddenly. "I'm going to have to think about what you said about art."

"Really off the wall, huh?"

"No, no." She looked like she was trying to say something, but then fell silent.

The stranger snorted.

"Do you mind if I— Before you came here, were you … living with him? I know I shouldn't ask, but … I'd hate to think I was sending you back there."

"Forget it! Me go back there?" Their eyes met for one brief moment. "Don't worry, I ain't going back there. To that wacko?"

"I'd hate to think … Why do we do things like that?"

"Who?"

"Women. Why do we go back?"

"Beats me. You won't catch me going back."

There was another silence and then the woman smiled again. The stranger watched her. "Oh, I was just remembering something about that child of mine. He came in the pottery once and made a little pendant that said, 'I love my mommy.' He spelled 'my' m-i." She smiled to herself. "Then he made a second one that said, 'I love myself.' I asked him why he made that and he said, 'You can't love someone if you don't love yourself.' I have no idea where that came from. Must have been TV." She was shaking her head in admiration.

Love yourself, thought the stranger. Interesting concept. "Don't worry," she said, "I won't go back. I got a girlfriend I can go to."

"Any family?"

She shook her head. "Don't worry about it."

"If it doesn't work out, come back, okay?"

The stranger nodded. "Thanks." She nodded again and they looked at each other. "Would it be okay if I kind of stayed a little longer?"

The woman clearly reacted in surprise, then tried to cover up. "Oh. Sure."

"Just till I work out my next move."

The woman nodded like she really meant it.

A few days later, while the family was down in the valley buying food, the stranger quickly packed the few things she had accumulated and hurried down the muddy road. Though it was spring, the evening air was cooler than she had expected, and she was shivering. She had torn that page out of the Modigliani book to take with her, the one with a stone head of a woman. She left no note, telling herself she'd write when she got settled.

IV

SUMMER
NIGHT
WOMAN
ROCK

As spring grew into summer and as the heat and humidity mounted to the brilliant and stifling days of high summer, some of her child's fear gradually fell away. Paradoxically, he became more willing to play outside again—perhaps the attractions of the mountain in summer were too much to resist—but remained fearful inside the house, still unable to enter a room alone or play by himself.

He was still sleeping in his parents' bed. Even after witnessing his father fight off the two attackers who had assaulted the stranger, he hadn't had to do that; and after the encounter with the skinheads, he had only been temporarily unable to sleep by himself. But the attack on the house was too much for him. She watched him sleep. It appeared the pure sleep of childhood, like any other, like it had used to be, like a mother's hope of what a child's sleep should be, his face calm, almost smiling, with no trace of what had to be assuaged in order to fall asleep, in order to get through each day now. She looked across the bed to her husband, who was doing the same thing, and they exchanged looks that told how much they loved this child and how unspeakably precious he was to them and how soothing it was to watch him sleep.

When they were in bed around him, somehow an argument emerged again, another hissing whispered argument about the shotgun the man had bought after it had become clear the sheriff's department couldn't protect them. "What are you going to do," she complained, as much to the darkness as to him, "shoot somebody?"

"You didn't see them," he snapped back. "Armed to the teeth. I don't know what they might do. You heard what she said: they're crazy. And from what I saw, she's right." The skinheads had only been seen once, with their putative leader, a self-styled white supremacist. It had been during a winter afternoon in the back woods, where he had been out cutting firewood, their child nearby playing in the snow with his trucks, when they had suddenly appeared around him dressed like commandos, weapons, black face paint and all.

"What did you see?" she challenged.

He caught his breath, lowered his voice. "They're dressed for combat. They've got real weapons. Now maybe they just like to dress up and play war games, but I saw them and I looked into their eyes, and I'm not going to just wait and see what they do without any way to defend my family." He added, "You didn't see their faces. It's not just the sneer, it's feeling that they don't really see you."

Of course she had heard that before, she knew that; why did she need to keep asking? "But that was months ago, last winter, you said yourself if they wanted to do something—"

"They did do something!"

"Okay, they vandalized the house—"

"And killed all the animals—"

"But that was last spring."

"—And scared the shit out of you and the little one and me too. And the stranger. She was damn scared. She said they're crazy." Again he lowered his voice. "You think that was the end, but what if it's only the beginning?" He stared at her, hard.

Suddenly she became really scared; scared like she had been the evening they had skidded off the road in a snowstorm, tramped the last mile home, and felt the broken glass crunching underfoot in the living room. They assumed it was the same people, because of the stranger. To punish them for sheltering her. "But ... " Her voice was very different now. "Would you shoot someone?"

He was silent a long time, then turned toward her in the dark. "I don't know," he whispered slowly. "I hope I never find out. All I know is, I can't go to sleep anymore feeling like we're completely at their mercy. I have to be able to protect my family." The way he spoke, she thought, emphasizing almost every word, it was as if he were before some judge defending himself.

Another night in bed he explained that they were pretty safe during the night, upstairs, because there was only one way up and he could put a lock on the door to the stairway.

"You're going to lock us in each night?"

"We lock the outside doors. This is just another one."

"We didn't used to lock any doors," she complained.

"That's over," he replied bitterly, then added that he would also have to board up the window in their bedroom. She was incredulous. He explained that someone could easily get on the pottery roof and so to the window.

"My God, what do you think they'll do?"

"I don't know what they'll do," he shouted, unable to whisper. Somehow the child slept through it. "That's the whole stinking point," he whispered, hissing. "They're lunatics."

"Okay, okay." She tried to calm him down, reaching over the child to find his hand in the dark, tears filling her eyes. "I don't believe this."

"I don't believe it either," he snapped.

After the vandalism he had refused to let the windows be re-glassed, arguing that there was no point if they were going to be smashed again; but after the stranger left—after they had returned from town with groceries to find her mysteriously gone, without warning, without a note—she had said she couldn't go on this way. He asked her bitterly whether she was sure she had a choice. How could she be sure they hadn't been back? "What do you mean?" she asked, her face suddenly fearful again.

He tried to be gentle, but she felt it hard, almost cruel. "How do you know they don't watch us? How do you know she left on her own? It's odd, isn't it? No note or anything, after she asked you if she could stay?"

She thought about that for days, convinced that her not leaving a note meant she had left on her own. Eventually she persuaded her husband that that was at least likely, so he relented about some of the windows and their home looked more like their home again, even if it couldn't feel like it.

He didn't respond to it like she did. Her fear made her fatalistic; he called it passive, she called it accepting: what would happen would happen; they would confront it and go on. His fear made his mind spin, laying awake at night brooding about protecting his family and, he admitted, retaliating. That frightened her. In her fantasies they just went away; in his they came back and he defeated them. Her reaction allowed her to remain calm, inexplicably calm, he marveled, almost complaining; his made him edgy, irascible. One night he told her she was stronger than he: she could be pushed this hard and not be unbalanced, while he was still reeling. She replied that he was stronger, because she couldn't keep dwelling on it, it scared her too much, but he could. "You're more diplomatic than I am, too," he murmured. She could feel him smiling in the dark, calmer for the moment, and their hands met in mid-air over the child.

But he boarded up the bedroom window and put a lock on the stairway door. And started using the shotgun. Woodchucks had already taken the first crop of lettuce. "They know when you're about to pick and come in the night before," he joked, but added that they had to decide whether the garden was for them or the woodchucks. Besides, it was free meat; no additives, either. One brilliantly bright afternoon he spotted one and said he was going to shoot it. Said it in a way that invited her to respond.

"Do you have to?"

He shrugged meaningfully. "Is the garden for them or us?"

"Don't expect me to clean it."

"I wouldn't dream of it," he replied, smiling, "the thought never ... But you will, right?" he added on his way upstairs for the gun.

"No!" she shouted after him, laughing.

"You're so good to me!" he shouted back, laughing.

When the gun went off she jumped straight up, ruining the pot she was making, ran upstairs into the child's bedroom and asked him if he was crazy.

"What do you mean?" He really didn't know.

"From his bedroom?" she accused.

"What difference does it make where I shoot it from?"

She shook her head, then turned to the child who was right there, not missing a gesture. She shook her head again and left the room, returning immediately. "What did you tell him?"

The man took a breath. "I told him that killing a woodchuck so we could have food is not a sin. And that there's nothing wrong with hunting if you hunt for food." She thought it over briefly, nodded ever so slightly, and left the room again. "Wait a minute," he shouted after her; she returned and waited for him to speak. "There's something else," he added quietly, seriously. "That woodchuck just died a better death than my father did." She waited, knowing he would continue. "One instant he was there, and the next he wasn't. No pain, no indignity, no deteriorating ... " He shook his head, his voice starting to choke up, finally just whispering, "I'd like to die like that."

She went to the window and looked out. There it was on the barn road between the house and garden. She waited for some reaction, but there wasn't any; it was just a dead animal on the road, no big deal.

He went out to dress it, making the child stay behind, but returned later to say he couldn't do it. He explained that the trick is to quickly get the carcass from animal to meat. He had taken pigs to the slaughterhouse and watched. Before you know it, the pig has been scalded, split and gutted, and then it's just meat on a hook. But he couldn't bring himself to handle the carcass, to flay it, open it. He reasoned if he could get the head off ... He used the hatchet but closed his eyes and missed and then it was worse.

"What did you do with it?" she asked, almost amused. How many chickens had she feathered and gutted? True, he had slaughtered them, she knew she couldn't do that.

He made a face. "It's still there."

The child, seeing it was okay, seeing it was funny now, laughed.

*　　*　　*

She worried about the stranger. It was months; still, no letter, no call. Occasionally she was brave enough to wonder whether she had, in fact, been forced to leave under duress. She had never seen this former lover, this white supremacist, this self-styled warrior and leader of men, so naturally he was magnified. Or maybe not: maybe she imagined him as he really was, devoted to intimidation, which he would call commanding respect, and seriously playing out fantasies of race war and assassination against a cowardly government in the grip of mongrel scum.

She had never asked her husband how the animals had been killed, whether it had been done neatly or ... He had never complained about letting him clean up the whole mess himself. Nor did he ever joke about it, which is what made her think it must have been bad. He had had to dig a grave, which itself was a job with all that rock, haul out the carcasses, layer them with bags of lime ...

She felt certain the stranger would return to him. The way she'd talked ... And, if she did, what was the difference between voluntary and involuntary? How could returning to an abusive situation be considered truly voluntary? Would that mean they had failed her in some way? Maybe they should go after her.

It was so strange how she had appeared from nowhere. While her husband and child were getting ready to go to the city to shop for a winter coat, a woman was running away from two pursuers. While they were getting in the car, she was fighting them off. As they drove slowly down the dirt road, admiring the fall foliage, the men were trying to rape her. How had she made it all the way out here before being caught? And why here, in particular, halfway to nowhere? She had never volunteered any information and made it clear she didn't want to be asked. They had never even learned whether she was headed somewhere or just wandering.

"Are you awake?" she whispered, suddenly getting the feeling that, like her, he was unable to sleep.

He woke up. "What's going on?" he mumbled sleepily.

"I can't sleep."

He turned on his side to face her. "What's up? What time is it?"

"Late."

He turned heavily to look at the clock. "Jesus," he complained. "What's the story here?"

"I can't sleep."

"So I've heard. What's the story?"

She hesitated, then asked if he thought they should go after her.

He was silent for a long time. "What would that mean?" he replied finally. "How would we find her? And, if we did, what would we do? Huh?"

"I don't know." He was always so systematic.

"I mean, if you're just expressing a feeling, I share it. But if you mean it literally … Which is it?"

"I said I don't know," she snapped.

They both fell silent, then he asked, his voice still husky from sleep, "'Do you want me to get you something?' he asked, hoping she'd say no."

She chuckled.

"By and large she was kind of a pain in the ass, wasn't she? Never helping out, just sitting on her bed, staring into space, but always showing up for meals … I know, eventually things got better, but … "

"She was good with the little one," she offered generously, wanting to defend her for some reason.

"I didn't say she wasn't, did I?" He added, "I think we did the three duties."

"What are you talking about?"

His voice was awake now. "One, do no harm. Two, try to make things better. Three, do number two without screwing up number one."

"Where'd you get that?"

"I've been thinking, too," he replied merrily. He was proud of his little homily.

"Who knows why she left," she wondered out loud.

"I know something," replied the child in a clear voice.

"What are you doing awake?" exclaimed the woman, and the child giggled with pleasure. "How long have you been awake?"

"I don't know," he sang.

"Hey, little one," asked her husband, "did we wake you up?"

"Yes," he replied, not at all annoyed, and added, "and I know something."

"What do you know?" he asked indulgently. The child proceeded to reveal an incident that made their jaws drop. One night, when the stranger was baby-sitting, they had been watching television side by side on the couch and she had put her arm around him. Gradually, she had pulled him closer, and he had let her because it hadn't bothered him; but when she tried to pull him on her lap, he pulled away. In a too calm voice, the woman asked what happened then. Nothing, he replied. The parents repeated the question as many different ways as they could think of, until the child lost patience; they looked at each other and nodded. But they had to ask: did she try it again? The child shook his head impatiently. Did she say anything?

"No!" he snapped.

"So nothing happened?"

He thought carefully and then replied, "I think she cried."

Again, they exchanged looks. After he was back asleep, they satisfied themselves it had been just as he had said; then they both lay in silence.

"Are you asleep yet?" she whispered later.

"Didn't you ask me that already?"

"Shut up," she whispered pleasantly, "you'll wake him."

"What is it now?"

"I was just thinking ... Don't you think it's amazing how little we know about her? I mean, she was living with us."

"For a long time, too," he agreed. "She must have been very ... unhappy. To stay that bottled up. But you know what? I actually feel a little hurt. By her leaving. Rejected, almost."

"Really? You're the one who was always annoyed by her."

"I know, but that's not it. It's like we offered her something, you know, and she basically turned us down."

"That's kind of what I mean. I mean, what do we really know about her? Practically nothing. She was a complete stranger."

"That's for sure," he agreed, nodding in the dark.

"She never really ... fit in. Or tried. She didn't want to ... participate ... "

"And yet I think we just learned she wanted something that was here. The whole thing just ... bothers me."

"You know what I keep thinking about? The way she went through those art books. She spent days just paging through them. And then that fascination with the Modigliani head. She took it with her!"

"Yeah, ripped the page right out of the book."

"Oh, I don't care that much." She shrugged.

"And left the book open to the page. It's almost as if she wanted us to know."

"Maybe she did."

"You mean that was her note?"

"Maybe."

"Then what did it say?"

"I think I know what it said."

"I'm listening."

She paused before replying. "Do you remember the sculpture? I mean, she really picked a good one." She was looking toward the stranger's room when she said that, as though she might be in there, studying it. "She said it expressed opposite feelings, sometimes joy, sometimes sorrow, sometimes peace, sometimes agony. And also, she said sometimes she felt left out."

"What do you mean, left out?"

"I told you about that conversation."

"Oh. Yeah." He remembered.

"Don't you think that was kind of ... interesting?"

"More like depressing. She felt rejected by a work of art?"

"In a way. I guess."

Several nights later, out of the blue, he said, "The issue is not control, it's purpose."

"What? What are you talking about?"

"Her. I think the issue is not control, it's purpose."

"What issue? What are you talking about?"

"Depression. Don't you think?"

She nodded, but said, "Don't forget, she was raped."

"Almost raped. But I don't think that was the main thing. Actually, I think she's still in shock over that."

"I think you might be right. That explains a lot, actually."

"But the depression … You could say people are depressed because they feel they've lost control over their lives."

"I think they do feel they've lost control."

"I agree. But what I'm saying is, that's not really it. What they've really lost is not control, it's purpose."

She shook her head vigorously. "How can you say that? What control did she have over her life?"

"Very little. But so do we. What do we control, really? We can't even control who wanders onto our property. Some idiot decides he doesn't like us and … "

"Yeah, but, come on, we have more control than she does."

"Sure, but so do lots of people who are depressed. It doesn't seem to matter how much money you have, how successful you are … But something is lost and that's purpose. You know, why work, why strive, why even try to have a good time?"

She thought about it. "You think people get depressed because they don't have anything to believe in?"

He gestured to indicate that was partly what he meant. "We're taught that nothing exists except what you see. And everything you see is reducible to something mechanical. So when we look for meaning, for an essence, a context, for something larger, something spiritual … we can't find it. Why? Because we denied it at the outset. Everything is just a machine."

"You think she was having a spiritual crisis?" she asked dismissively. "I think she was just depressed about her life."

"I'm talking about her life," he countered impatiently. "What the hell do you think I'm talking about?"

"Yeah, but, don't you think she had more pressing problems than the meaning of life?"

"What could be more pressing than that?" She made another dismissive gesture. "What do you think she was doing with those art books? And—" he lowered his voice suddenly, "what do you think she was doing with our child?"

She nodded hesitantly.

"What's really sad is that I think she was right on the edge. She was gripped by that picture, she saw something in it, but it flickered, it wasn't steady for her, maybe because she doubted herself, and in the end maybe she lost her nerve, she turned away from it. She said it rejected her; think about that, she made it into a person."

"I think she meant the artist rejected her."

"Okay, but, obviously the picture didn't reject her, she rejected it, she turned away."

She nodded in the dark, wishing the stranger had left a note.

*   *   *

One night they were awakened suddenly by the crash of thunder directly overhead. The child startled violently and yelped, but she hugged him and said it was just a thunderstorm. It was evidently passing right over them, because the lightning was almost continuous and the thunder followed quickly. Her husband was too tired to get up, but she and the child went to his bedroom window to watch. Many of the windows in the house were boarded up, but the window in the child's bedroom was still open because it couldn't be reached from outside.

The sky repeatedly lit up as though celestial lights were being thrown on all at once, but not so much to light up the sky as to make it glow. This was followed immediately by the rolling crack and roar of thunder. Several times the child startled violently, then turned to her and made a funny face as if to show he wasn't really scared.

They watched the rain pounding the surface of the pond, making the water dance in the wonderfully eerie and fleeting light. The downpour was so hard, the sound it made was a continuous loud whoosh, and the pond's surface looked like standing cones of uprising water. The child watched in silence, or perhaps he wasn't really watching, then asked where the birds were. She replied that they were probably in the trees where they usually were, and the ducks were probably in the grass. Don't they get wet? he wanted to know. She explained about the feather oils that ducks—and maybe all birds—had, adding that the rain didn't hurt the birds. There was more silence and then he asked if they were scared. No, she replied, she didn't think they were scared.

"But what," he persisted, "what if the lightning hits them?"

"Well," she pondered, "I suppose lightning could hit a tree, but maybe they could fly off before it fell down." As she said that, it seemed incorrect to her, and then she guessed that when lightning strikes a tree, any animal on it would probably be electrocuted.

"But what if they couldn't fly off?"

She took a breath. "Well ... then they might get hurt. But, you know, it's very rare for a tree to get hit by lightning."

"How come?"

It went on from there, questions without limit, until the storm subsided as it passed and she was able to get him back to bed, but at least the fear point seemed to have been crossed. Getting back in bed, the child woke up his father to say, "Daddy, I saw lightning."

Every night the child played interminably in his bath. The water would be cold by the time he would agree to come out. Surrounded by his boats, some of them made by himself by banging oversized nails through a few pieces of scrap lumber, he would power them two at a time through the water by hand while supplying continuous sound effects. Meanwhile, either she or her husband would be seated on the floor nearby, reading a book. One midsummer night, she realized it had become silent and looked up to find him staring at something in the water.

It was a dead fly. Without thinking, she scooped it up and dropped it in the toilet bowl, then returned to her book. But she noticed that he remained silent, unmoving. Finally he said, "Mommy."

She looked up.

"Is that fly dead?" he asked.

She nodded, watching him. He remained poised, still, plainly thinking. After a long silence, he asked, "Does everything die?"

She watched him closely. "Yes. Everything dies."

He continued as before, his face a complete blank, his eyes open but unseeing, his lips very slightly pursed. Finally he asked, "Will you die?"

She was looking right at him. "Yes," she replied gently, "I will." She let that sink in, then added, "But not for a very very long time. Not until you're all grown up. And daddy, too. So you don't have to worry about that at all. Okay?"

He thought a little longer, looked up at her for the first time, and, with the slightest of smiles, said simply, "Okay."

That changed something big within him. Almost from the following day, his fear of being alone, of being outside the house, seemed to fall away. He became excited by the garden and danced up and down the rows, joyously harvesting green beans and raspberries directly to his mouth, and only later to the bucket in his hand. It was a brilliant midsummer afternoon, stiflingly hot when the air was still, but with the merest of cooling breezes every so often, gently rustling the leaves of the poplars, maples, and fruit trees that bordered the field. Nearby were flowering meadows and, in the wet spots, wild irises. "Mommy!" he shouted.

"What!"

"Look what I have!" And he proudly held up the pot containing a half-inch of berries across its bottom. But how he moved among the tall canes, oblivious of the thorns, his entire being focused on his bounty, which he plucked with great care and urgency, one berry at a time.

That night they ate raspberry pie, the best in the whole world.

He even went so far as to ask if he could go 'asploring.' So one bright summer day, a child's vision, with a big blue sky and white fluffy clouds, the two of them set out to the calls of the blue jays and the redwings. Not, she decided less than consciously, to the back woods where the skinheads had suddenly appeared, but up the road a short distance to a large stand of pines. The child talked a blue streak about birds and trees, pointing out that a robin never perches on the top of a tree, whereas the redwing never perches anywhere else; but, when they entered the grove, he became silent. According to his face, he fully expected something magical to happen, perhaps a rabbit popping up and calling him by name.

There was a formation of rock that made a kind of ledge and they sat on top of it, on a bed of pine needles, looking around at everything that surrounded them, the grove of evergreens, dappled sunlight, the forest floor of pine needles and moss and moss-covered rocks, the jays and woodpeckers and nuthatches darting through the trees. The child had his legs folded underneath him, with his hands on his knees. Once or twice she could see him take a deep breath, but he said nothing. She reached over and caressed his shoulder; he appeared not to notice. "Mom," he said finally, quietly, almost hesitantly. "How come we can't see God?"

She thought for a while and replied, "I think you're seeing God right now."

"No, I'm not. I don't see God."

"I bet you do. Isn't it beautiful here?"

"Yeah."

"And special?"

"Yeah."

"Well—in a way—that's God."

The child thought it over. "But how come we can't see God?"

"Because God is not a person. It's more like a feeling."

"I know. But what do you mean?"

"Hmm," she said, taking a deep breath, "it's not so easy to explain."

"Try," he urged.

She smiled. "Well … God is … Wow," she mumbled to herself, "how do you answer this one?" The child watched her, waiting. In the end, all she could do was repeat herself, that God was what made things beautiful and special.

The child continued in silence, frowning, and then complained, "I want to see God."

She took him back to the house to show him a postcard of a Modigliani sculpture, the same one that had so affected the stranger. "This is an example of what an artist creates when they want to see God, but don't. Look at it and tell me what you see."

"I know this," he announced. "She had a picture of this in her room."

"That's right, she did." She was only mildly surprised that he would recognize it. "Tell me about it."

"Well," he said very slowly, studying the picture with complete attention and earnestness, finally stating, "it's silly."

She wasn't prepared for that. "Silly?"

"The nose!" He laughed.

She explained how an artist uses abstraction to go beyond how things look to how things make you feel, and how Modigliani had been struck by the power of the abstractions used in African masks, and how Africans had used masks to represent and evoke the forces of nature.

"What's a force of nature?"

"Like thunder and lightning. Or the sun. Or even just the energy that brings life and makes things grow."

The child studied the postcard some more and then asked tentatively, "Is this God?"

"No, honey, I told you, God is not a person. But, in a way, this is about God. This is about how a person can be special just like the woods are special."

That night, after the child had been put to bed, she sat on the porch, listening to the summer sounds and watching the sky.

*　　*　　*

What she would remember, for some reason, would be the sound of the shell being pumped into the chamber. It was late one night, one hot summer night, very late, with no air moving because the window was boarded up, when she was roused part-way out of slumber by her husband's stirring. She just assumed he was going to the bathroom, but then she heard that sound and her eyes suddenly opened wide. He heard her and turned immediately—she must have started to say something—and made a gesture, she wouldn't remember what it was exactly, but it was a gesture that stopped her cold, and he commanded in a whisper for her to keep the child quiet.

He went to the top of the stairs and took up a position aiming the shotgun at the locked door at the bottom. He did it without hesitation, as if he had practiced it, and she realized he must have practiced it. He had been able to imagine this; she hadn't, couldn't.

She listened for whatever it was, but heard nothing. There were no sounds other than the usual night summer sounds, the shrill whir of cicadas, the creaks and rustlings the house seemed to produce. She watched him. He was unmoving: concentrated, focused, entirely attentive. Ready. She looked at him and saw he was ready and it was this, she felt, more than the sound she finally heard of what seemed to be a man moving downstairs, that caused her gut to contract suddenly and send a streak of fear right up her throat to her jaw and eyes. She saw him blink slowly and move slightly to shift his weight.

Suddenly she remembered her sleeping child next to her and in that instant she too became focused and attentive. Her eyes fully adjusted to the dark now, she looked at him and what she saw was his hand, one of his hands, the little fingers, still pudgy, still baby fingers, half curved in perfect relaxation, just that, and at that moment, as an unmitigated anger was born and grew to fill her entire being, she understood what her husband must have been feeling. The child's face was absolutely peaceful and still, but she fought off an almost irresistible trembling of her whole body.

She watched her husband. He would move a little, every now and then, to try to relieve tension, but the gun never moved off its target. She could hear them now, or imagined she could, imagined there was more than one, moving slowly from the front door they had somehow opened, across the living room. To where? What did they want, what would they do? It was as if he read her mind. "They won't come up," he whispered. He didn't move at all, didn't even turn towards her. It amazed her that his voice seemed calm. It couldn't have been calm. She realized he was that focused.

"How do you know?" she whispered back. It seemed to her her own voice was suffused with trembling.

The silence seemed long before he answered. "They must have heard me pump the shell." And then, after another long pause: "I'll have to go down."

Her eyes widened involuntarily when she realized what he meant. He had whispered it so quietly, so calmly, she had to replay it in her mind to be certain she had heard him correctly.

In her imagination she reacted violently, crying out, leaping from the bed, but all she did was whisper one word: "No."

She heard him breathe, or felt him. "I have no choice. They'll just keep coming."

"They'll keep coming whether you go down or not," she replied, her gaze riveted on him as though the slightest move would tell her what he would do. Perhaps he was waiting for the same information himself, because now his body remained absolutely motionless.

She knew, when he did that, he was deep in thought, or in reverie, often in pain or frightened. Once she had found him like that, sitting on their front steps, seemingly staring at the trees at the far end of the field across the road, and, when she had managed to coax him to speak, he announced, in that same superficially calm voice, that he had estimated the time required to do the jobs that were essential if they were to be prepared for winter and there wasn't enough time. "What have I done?" he asked rhetorically. "There's no way we can make it here." They had bought an old wreck of a place on top of a hill, a charming but broken-down old farmhouse on some exhausted acres, miles from any community, much farther from the city, to make a life for themselves and their child. They had made it.

Suddenly, slowly, he began to get up.

"No!" she cried. It was a whisper, but a shriek.

Carefully he rose to his feet. He still had the shotgun pointed at the door below. She watched as though she knew there was nothing she could do, though at that moment she knew nothing. "Stay here," he whispered, his eyes never leaving the door.

"No," she answered, not sure what she meant. Her eyes were wide again and that pain again shot through her.

"Stay here," he repeated in that falsely calm voice, and carefully shifted his weight down to the first step so as not to make the stair creak.

EPILOGUE

His father, an artist who couldn't play any instrument but who had taught himself a great deal about music, had, like his teacher, taught him to revere Bach, perhaps above all other composers, and art generally as the greatest human achievement. He too had made him feel that Bach was impossible to play, because he discovered that, no matter how much he practiced and how well he played, his father would never be satisfied. When he was done, his father might suggest they put on a record to hear how the masters played it, and he would feel defeated. Yet he knew his father was proud of him, and could inspire him to love music with the greatest intensity, and to work at it with all his will. Occasionally, while he was playing, his father would shout, "That's it! That's it!" when he played a phrase especially well, standing right near him, hunched over, fists clenched, like someone else might have coached a boxing match.

He had once played the first movement of the fifth Suite for him, played it with a secret effort reserved for the most important occasions, and with immeasurable relief noted that at the end there wasn't a single word of criticism. On the contrary, his father seemed excited by his playing and he began to talk about it dramatically. "Du-u-u-m-m-m!" he shouted, drawing out the first sustained note of the piece, adding a gesture of his hand to show how it went on, then dropped his voice for the ascending scale, "duhd-uhd-uh duhd-uh duhd-uh," and the four-note descending figure, "duhd-uhd-uhd-uh." Here he paused, as though preparing for the chord that starts on the lower strings and tears off them wrenchingly to the upper note— "duhd-uh!"—and he raised his hand to emphasize the crescendo in his voice and the elongation of the phrase. "It's humanity's cry," he proclaimed intensely, "an elemental plea, and also an affirmation. All in those few notes." He said it was Bach's most painful work and could be compared only perhaps to Michelangelo's final pietà, where limbs are hacked off and the sustaining figure of Nicodemus eliminated entirely.

"Just take the first note," he continued. "Loud, strong, with the full pressure of the bow, strained to the limit." He wasn't even talking to his son anymore, he was addressing humanity. "The artist has to struggle against his own body, maintaining constant intensity of sound as the bow moves away from its point of force, but also surrender to it, so that the tone begins to crack and transform from a kind of fearful optimism to a plaintive wail. Don't you see," he cried, turning suddenly to his son, "it's not just a cello anymore, not just music, not just an artist ... And then, " he continued in a hush, "a moment of silence. Imagine: silence. Where has it gone?" he asked, raising his voice, "this one-note introduction? Then a string of equal notes, first ascending as though trying to regain the confident height where the piece began, then descending ... Then the chord. Again, out of the depths, the two lower strings, the artist pulling sound from the strings even if the tone becomes scratchy ... and then the upper note, alone. Son," he concluded, "nowhere else—nowhere—has a composer more quickly and firmly placed us face to face with the profoundest depths of our nature."

About David Vigoda

I grew up in New Jersey and received a BA degree from the University of Chicago in 1968. My father was a cartoonist ("Archie"), my mother a bookkeeper. In Chicago I was active in the civil rights and anti-Vietnam War movements. I guess my claim to fame is having marched with Martin Luther King Jr., I think in 1966, as part of a campaign to desegregate Chicago. The marches met with tremendous hostility and violence. We didn't desegregate Chicago.

After graduating I began to think of writing as my vocation. I got married and (a week later) we flew to London with one-way tickets. I wrote and studied writing every day while Liz went to art school. I wrote plays, my passion was theatre. Fiction was years away.

A year later, money low, we moved to Israel and worked on a *kibbutz* for a year. Then I made an even bigger mistake, I decided to get a Ph.D. in playwriting and to get it at the University of Utah. 'Nuff said.

Cold Mountain was next, the hills west of Albany, New York. Arguably that was a mistake too, but, if so, it was the best mistake I ever made.

Where do you go from there? To one of the biggest banks in the country to become a vice president and trust officer. Isn't life interesting?

I appreciate hearing from readers about their responses. Interesting conversations have developed that way and I've had the privilege of meeting people I never would have met otherwise.

So, if you feel like contacting me, please do. I can't guarantee to answer every message, but I do try. You can reach me by email at <vigoda@whyitsgreat.com>

I'm available to teach workshops, address audiences, appear on radio, and give readings. Also, I write a *free* email newsletter, "Why It's Great," about great writing from authors ancient and modern, 'popular' and 'literary.' For more information, please visit the Collioure Books web site: www.whyitsgreat.com

About Collioure Books

Our goal is to advance peace and goodwill among people and respect for the natural world.

We maintain an active (and inter-active) web site at

www.whyitsgreat.com

devoted to the appreciation of great writing. Whether you love to read great fiction or are involved in writing or editing, the site is full of information, insights, and tips to increase your understanding and appreciation of what makes great writing great.

At the heart of our web site is David Vigoda's *free* email newsletter, "Why It's Great." In each issue he takes a piece of great writing—from anywhere, from Homer's *Iliad* to Raymond Chandler's *The Big Sleep*—and discusses *why it's great.*

There's also lots of information about us, our books, and about David Vigoda, as well as links to important sites. And of course a facility for ordering books.

Collioure Books is a small publishing company in a book industry dominated by a few huge companies. 80% of all book sales are made by a handful of publishing conglomerates, more than 80% of books are sold by a few bookstore chains, and two wholesalers distribute more than 80% of all books to bookstores and libraries. The chain bookstores generally order only from national wholesalers and the two giant wholesalers exclude most small publishing companies. For various reasons, small publishers also have limited access to review media, especially the ones that most influence book distribution and sales.

There's nothing necessarily wrong with this situation except that it leaves out thousands and thousands of interesting, important books that readers want to buy. We know this because they're buying them from thousands of mainly small independent publishers.

How do independent publishers survive to bring important books to interested readers? The most important way is with the support of those readers. We operate on a non-profit basis and depend on your willingness to spread the word. If you have enjoyed, appreciated, benefited from this book, here are ways you can help:

- Buy another copy as a gift. (Use the order form in this book or visit our web site.)

- Tell people about us. Tell them about our web site and the "Why It's Great" newsletter. We can even send you a supply of our picture postcards.

- If you or someone you know would be interested in writing a review, please contact us. Material for reviewers and journalists is on our web site.

- 50% discounts are available to not for profit organizations on quantity purchases for the purpose of supporting their work. If you are connected with one, you could let them know about this opportunity. More information is on our web site.

- We seek reciprocal marketing arrangements with compatible publishers. Inquiries welcome.

- Have a compatible web site? Please contact us about possibly linking.

However you decide to support our efforts, thank you!

ORDER FORM
Annihilating Distance

Collioure Books
21 Aviation Road
Albany, NY 12205

colliourebooks@whyitsgreat.com
(800) 720-1170
www.whyitsgreat.com

Price per copy: $15.95 [1]
Number of copies: _____

Books	$_____ . ____
Shipping [2]	_____5. 00__
Sales tax [3]	_____ . ____
TOTAL	$_____ . ____

[1] $8.00 per book donations are available to **NOT FOR PROFIT ORGANIZATIONS** on quantity purchases for the purpose of supporting their work. Inquiries welcome.

[2] There is a flat shipping charge of $5.00 regardless of the number of books ordered.

[3] New York State residents, please add 8.0% sales tax ($1.28 per copy). **PAYMENT IN FULL MUST ACCOMPANY ALL ORDERS.** For credit card or international orders, please visit our web site or contact us.

NAME: _____

ADDRESS (NO PO BOXES): _____

_____

DAYTIME PHONE NUMBER: (____) _____

EMAIL ADDRESS: _____

SHIPPING TIME: We *normally ship within 3–4 days*, often 1–2 days, in any case within a week, unless we have posted a notice on our web site indicating otherwise.

RETURNS POLICY: You may return the book *at any time* if you are not satisfied and your full purchase price, less shipping, will be refunded, no questions asked. Please return it in resalable condition.